THE HEMLOCK SWITCH

ENIGMA SERIES IX

TIERNEY JAMES

4

Publishing Coordinator – Sharon Kizziah-Holmes
Cover Design by Sweet 'N Spicy Designs

Owasso, OK

ISBN – 978-1-965460-26-9 (Paperback)
ISBN - 978-1-965460-27-6 (eBook)

DEDICATION

This book is dedicated to all those alphabet agencies in Washington DC who continue to protect us from unknown enemies of our country. Although we may never know who you are,
THANK YOU!

ACKNOWLEDGMENTS

Wizards of Publishing: Much love to my editors Kate Richards and Nan Sipe. You continue to teach and encourage me on each new adventure with the Enigma Team.

Sweet and Spicey Designs: Jayce DeLorenzo never disappoints with her cover designs. She is creative and an excellent listener to what I need.

Paperback Press Publishing Coordinator Sharon Kizziah-Holmes is my major hand holder as she prepares my manuscript for publication. Anytime I get anxious about a problem with a book she rushes in like a knight in shining armor.

Lipstick and Danger Street Team: Thank you for always giving me your support and encouragement. What would I do without you?

PROLOGUE

Tiny purple lights edged the baseboards along icy floor tiles that were kept at a constant temperature of 1.667 degrees Celsius or 35 degrees Fahrenheit. The owner stood staring down the long corridor without so much as a shiver or twitch. Everyone present, except Andre Lavelle Vion, wore warm clothing beneath white lab coats. He'd slipped one on over his expensive suit then shifted pale-blue eyes both beautiful and terrifying to those who worked for him.

When he took a step forward, the others behind him released the breath they'd been holding. It was wise not to distract the man when he became deep in thought. He glanced at the assistant to hurry him ahead to reach the door at the end of the corridor.

Once there, one of the lab coat personnel entered a code and did a retinal scan, followed by two others who repeated the gesture to make sure no breach was in progress. The pressurized door *swooshed* and opened at a snail's pace. The air inside hovered around forty degrees to make it more comfortable to work. Each worker wore a bright-yellow hazmat suit, lined with a thin layer of fabric created by NASA to prevent possible distractions connected with a cold environment.

The stainless-steel-walled room contained twenty tables surrounded by purple lights beneath the surface of the tables. Atop each lay a person who appeared unconscious. The owner toured the room and moved calmly around each table without asking questions as to each occupant's condition. None of the scientists spoke or made eye contact with him. It might be misconstrued as an act of confrontation. Not everyone understood his methods.

He stopped at one table where a young woman lay covered by a thick sheet. She was blonde with Nordic facial features; thin lips, non-prominent cheekbones, light-colored skin, and her tall frame took the length of the table.

Suddenly, she gasped, and her bright-blue eyes fluttered open to gaze about in confusion. He smiled down at her and reached under the sheet to take her hand then lifted it higher to gaze on her naked body. "Don't be afraid, my dear. You are among friends." He laid his free hand against her cheek and stroked it gently. "Someone get her a warm blanket. Now."

Within seconds, he was laying a blanket retrieved from a warming drawer over her body. He tucked it around her like a loving father, followed by sliding his hand down her long locks of hair. The others knew where this was headed.

"Sir?" His assistant stepped forward, touched the screen of his tablet, and scanned through the information quickly before informing the boss of what he wanted to hear. "She is perhaps twenty-three. Found wandering alone after getting separated from her friends on the Laugavegur Trail in Iceland."

"And her blood type?"

"Like the others, O negative."

"Any abnormalities in the DNA?"

"No potential red flags, except for one. A history search of her family indicated her mother died of breast cancer, as did her grandmother and two aunts. Although she doesn't appear to have the BRCA1 or BRCA2 gene, breast cancer can't be ruled out in the future. It does appear she has been sexually active and maybe miscarried or aborted a fetus not so long ago."

He gazed down into the wide blue eyes of the young woman. "Interesting."

"What are your orders, sir?" His assistant kept his full attention on his boss as if he might throw him a treat for being efficient.

"When she is fully awake, bring her to my cabin. Along with clothes and whatever she might need for the night."

"And in the morning?"

He turned and pointed to one of the scientists. "Be prepared to draw blood."

"How much?"

"All of it." He smiled down at the woman who appeared confused and frightened.

"All of it?" the scientist stuttered. The owner cut a gaze to him and arched an eyebrow. "Of course. We'll be waiting for your call when you're done. Anything else?"

"That will depend on a number of things and expectations." He spoke softly, lifting the young woman's hand to his lips.

After a full day of touring the Bio Terminal of Life, going over expenses and progress of the research, he remembered the girl who must be at the cabin by now. What Andre didn't expect was the surprise waiting for him. He didn't care for surprises.

"What do you mean there's no trace of the girl?" He turned toward the assistant.

Andre Lavelle Vion's voice contained an eerie calm, similar to the moments before a tornado hit. Only his eyes hinted at disappointment, a signal there would be a price to pay for whoever made a miscalculation. The bright-blue iris most often turned either navy or, on occasion, had appeared grayish opaque. Bad things resulted when this occurred. The bearer of bad news, rather than take the blame themselves, usually suggested an alternative solution or threw an innocent under the bus for immediate retribution. This was definitely a time to point the finger at security.

The personal assistant's stomach turned as it always did in the presence of this man. With the help of several anxiety drugs and antidepressants, he'd been able to fulfill his duties flawlessly without a hint of stress. There had been whispers he was no different than Andre Vion. Nothing could be further from the truth. The only thing keeping him under the man's thumb was the ridiculous amount of money he was paid and the possibility of selling what he knew to the highest bidder, when the time came.

"Explain." Andre Vion raised his chin and stared down his

narrow nose.

"After security delivered her…"

"There are cameras in and around my residence."

"A power surge took them offline for approximately twenty minutes."

"Why?"

"I believe it was—"

"You believe?"

"We were notified of a storm near the power substation, and lightning struck outside the perimeter causing a chain reaction. It was quickly repaired, since it didn't take a direct hit. The woman was still mildly sedated and clothed for a—quiet evening, so security did not enter the residence."

"How long until someone checked on her?"

"Several hours. When I checked the security logs, they hadn't been updated in that section of the compound, I went myself to—"

Andre held up a finger for silence then tapped his chin one time before walking toward the security control center. His neck turned then tilted his ear down at the assistant's anxious steps. When he burst into the control center, two computer techs jumped to their feet.

"You appear surprised I'm here. Why were you unaware of my presence just now?"

"Uh. Uh." The younger of the two techs choked then swallowed hard and stole a quick glance at his partner.

"Where are the guards who were supposed to be on duty?"

"S-searching for the girl," the tech continued with a stutter.

"Release the dogs." Andre's eyelids became hooded as he continued to make eye contact.

"I'll alert the guards." The second tech notified the guards of the danger.

"Very well." Andre waited until a text message was sent. "Thank you, gentlemen. Take a break. I'm sure you need one with all this going on. I believe the cafeteria has prepared a late supper for those still working."

They nodded obediently and left.

Andre stared at the screen when the images of two guards appeared. "Release the dogs."

The assistant stepped up next to Andre. "Sir, they are not in the controlled perimeter. They can't outrun the dogs. And if the girl…"

Andre turned his icy eyes toward the assistant. "Release. The. Dogs."

The assistant reached down with a trembling hand to touch the button on the console to allow the dogs to escape their compound. His fingers hovered over the button as he licked his lips and a drip of sweat formed at his hairline. As he started to withdraw his hand, Andre laid his gently on top then shoved it down on the button. The screen displaying the area where the dogs were kept brightened. They raced out into the woods.

"I need to step away for a minute, sir."

Andre waved him off.

The assistant rushed to the restroom, barely reaching a trash can inside the door to empty his stomach. His hands were clammy and his head pounded. After washing his face and rinsing out his mouth, he squared his shoulders and returned to the corridor. Andre exited the computer room. In passing, he gave more instructions void of emotion.

"Get the handlers to call in their dogs. Have security retrieve the two guards. They've had a terrible accident." He strode away and disappeared into another corridor.

CHAPTER 1

"Hey, buddy, you old dog, I heard you were getting hitched this morning. I hope it's to my favorite little Grass Valley commando." President Buck Austin gave one of his deep laughs.

"Yes, sir!" Captain Hunter said, proudly glancing at Tessa standing next to him in her pearl-pink dress. "And she is beautiful, Mr. President."

Another big laugh came from the other end of the phone. "Well, all I can say is it's about damn time." There was a pause and a loud yelp. "Ouch. Careful with that. I'm not a pincushion," the president growled.

"Mr. President is something wrong?" asked Chase.

"Nah. Time to check me out head to toe to make sure I don't put the country at risk with a weird kind of medical condition. Drawing enough blood to please a vampire. I hate needles." He stopped to fume at a person in his presence. "Get away from me. Show him out, Agent Andrews," the president instructed his Secret Service Agent. "I want this other guy to do it. Dr. Kelley trained him." Chase could imagine him waving at people to take up new positions. "I'd better go, Captain. Congratulations, and tell Tess I want to give her a big ole kiss the next time I see her."

"Yes, Mr. President, I certainly will. And thank you."

~ ~ ~ ~

When Chase suggested a cabin to spend their first few nights together as husband and wife, Tessa anticipated rustic logs, antique furnishings, quaint knickknacks, and the smell of honeysuckle in the air. Maybe they would be miles from nowhere and would have to cook their own food. She didn't really care what it turned out to be as long as she could spend the time with Captain Chase Hunter, the man she'd loved secretly for way too long. This would be a new beginning for both of them.

Their relationship over the last few years, actually since the day they'd met, had been akin to an 8.5 magnitude earthquake. Everything always seemed like it crashed and burned around them, setting up roadblocks to discover how they felt about one another or how to fight the attraction. As a result, both of them went in different directions or turned to others for love and comfort. For Chase, it was his job, the military, and Enigma. Tessa, on the other hand, turned to a notorious scoundrel named Roman Darya Petrov. Those days were behind her now. She hoped.

She and Chase had reconnected at a small airport in Montana. The world around them disappeared so suddenly, it resembled a dream, or maybe the nightmare had just ended. The battle-wearied captain was still recovering from injuries sustained in Syria, yet he scooped her up in his arms as if his life depended on it. Maybe both their lives depended on it at that point.

They hadn't much more than returned to Sacramento when Director Benjamin Clark met them at a private airport with a physical therapist, both wearing expressions that could melt steel. He first addressed his comments to Tessa, knowing she'd make the right decision.

"The euphoric, kumbaya expressions on your faces are probably going to give me a cavity. It's sickening," he growled. "Captain Hunter needs to finish up his physical therapy and make sure none of those stitches have come unglued—if you know what I mean." His damning glare caused Tessa to fidget with embarrassment. "Whatever you two are planning, it can wait."

"No, it can't." The captain cocked his head as his jaw tighten and released.

Tessa placed her hand on Chase's back and pressed lightly, drawing his attention to her. He grinned, making butterflies flutter in her stomach, when she thought of what might lie ahead for them. Even though he'd suffered horribly in Syria and sustained life-threatening injuries, he was still one hell of a man, both physically and mentally. The last few hours had gone a long way to reassure her of that as they flew home.

"Chase, what's a few more days? I'm not going anywhere. I'd rather know you're okay."

"Excuse me, Ben," he quipped then pulled Tessa off to the side. "Fine. Pack a few things, and I'll make a reservation for us some place private. I'll be back within the week. At some point, I still want a real wedding, with family and friends."

Tessa took his hands in hers. There was a time the captain didn't like being touched, especially by holding hands. Now he couldn't resist. "We can wait until later if you still want it. I just want…" She felt her eyes flutter nervously and a heated blush crept up her neck into her cheeks.

Chase touched her face and smiled. "Me, too."

The director stepped forward and cleared his throat. "You know I can hear you, right? I'll perform the ceremony. Now, get in the damn car with the physical therapist. Tessa, Dr. Wu is waiting for you inside the terminal. He'll be taking you home."

"Great," she moaned. "Guess I'm getting a therapy session of my own."

Chase opened the car door and frowned. "Well, don't let him talk you out of marrying me. You know we've never been on the best of terms. He might place a subliminal suggestion in your head to poison me."

"I'll be careful." She stood on tiptoe and kissed his mouth quickly. "I love you," she whispered.

Now, here she was, a newlywed as of three hours ago, staring at a beautiful lodge standing among the redwoods. Chase slipped inside to register while she strolled to the overlook, showcasing a lazy river so clear, she was sure she spotted trout. The gurgle of water tunneling between boulders and a distant roar of a waterfall raised goose bumps on her bare arms until she hugged them against the chill.

Her children were on spring break with their father. It was his turn according to the divorce decree. They were headed to Squaw Valley for some end-of-season skiing. The kids loved the sport, and her ex did as well. He'd rented a condo, and there would be plenty of board games, movies, and eating out, which they didn't get to do much with her.

There were lots of hugs and kisses during departure, and her ex had suggested maybe she'd want to tag along. Robert knew nothing about her relationship with Chase, that she worked for Enigma, or how close she'd come to death protecting the fragile security of the country. In spite of having their differences, she cared for him and wanted the children to never fear the breakup had been their fault. There had been times she felt Robert might be hinting they try again. The trust between them had been severely broken and, for Tessa, there was no going back. Her life, the real life she lived, must remain a secret as long as possible to make sure he didn't try and take the children from her.

"You look deep in thought," came a masculine voice. "Any regrets?" Chase circled her waist and pulled her to his chest.

"Just one."

"What's that?"

"I let you go with the director. It was a long couple of days." She smiled up at him and realized the world stopped each time she gazed into those dark Cherokee eyes. "I thought he was going to cry this morning when he married us. Who knew he was a softy?"

"Better not let him hear you say that. But, yeah, I was surprised, too. He claimed it was allergies." He took her hand and led her back toward the Cadillac Escalade they'd rented. "I passed all their benchmarks for recovery and, although they said I should expect occasional discomfort in my leg when it rains, I was good to go. Ben's reply was, 'Humph, we'll see about that. Don't overdo it.'" He chuckled as he opened the passenger-side door.

Tessa ran her hand down his chest and could have sworn he flinched. He'd taken several bullets there and almost died not that long ago. "I promise I'll be gentle."

He held her gaze as his mouth formed a firm straight line. "I make no such promises." The deep voice and suggestion stirred up another round of goose bumps.

Pulling her into his arms, Chase kissed her with passion and hunger, until a person strolling by yelled, "Get a room, Romeo." They broke apart and saw a couple of teenagers who pretended to kiss their arms and blew kisses to them. Both laughed as they proceeded to get in the car.

"Our cabin isn't ready. The manager gave us a few vouchers for lunch in town. Suggested we drive through the grounds and take in the sights. Besides, I didn't have two days to get everything together. I need to pick up a few things." Chase turned the car around and headed out of the area known as Hidden Waters Resort. He smiled over at her. "Guess I was in a hurry to see you. By the way, you look beautiful today."

"And just like that, you melt my heart."

They drove the three miles to town to spend the rest of the afternoon, stopping at a few overlooks to take pictures. Life was about to get crazy again.

~ ~ ~ ~

Andre Lavelle Vion adjusted the binoculars, lowered them in surprise then lifted them to his eyes again. Captain Chase Hunter, the proverbial thorn in his side for all these years. What was he doing here? Did he discover he was back in the US? Many times, the man got close to exposing him and the various enterprises that turned him into a wealthy man.

The last few years, the turmoil of the world had occupied the soldier's time. Keeping tabs on Chase Hunter had turned into an annoying routine. At one point, he'd sent a contract killer to do his bidding, but failed to take down the captain. Now here he was with a woman. Fortunately, the man sent to do the job died of a sepsis infection before any information could be extracted, thanks to the little security measures injected into his arm.

He readjusted the binoculars as she turned her head his way, causing him to suck in his breath.

"My sweet Abigail," he moaned. "You are reincarnated. And what mischief has Captain Hunter forced you into, my love?" He stared as the captain forced a kiss to her lips. What madness was this? This was too tempting. He'd finally finish the man who had taunted him for years over a dead sister he could never prove was murdered. "Abigail, we will soon be together once more. You can be assured of that. I will finally rid the world of Captain Chase Hunter, once and for all."

CHAPTER 2

President Buck Austin clicked off after talking to Captain Hunter. He turned to the young man applying a cotton swab to his arm and could smell alcohol. Next came the cool sting of it. "Who was the lamebrain who couldn't find a vein?" he asked, gazing up into the face of an airman with a five-o'clock shadow. He had served with his personal physician, Mary Pat Kelley, at Walter Reed Hospital. Now he was dressed in leather and it had been a while since he'd had a haircut.

"A trainee, most likely, considering what a mess he made of your arm. I think he was nervous, sir. He'll do better next time. But, in the meantime, have Dr. Kelley check this out. It appears he cut you a little."

"Won't be a next time. You'll do just fine."

The airman applied a bandage then stood back. "You're all done, sir. I'll take the sample to the lab as instructed and you should have results by this evening or no later than tomorrow morning, Mr. President." He took a step back as the president rolled down his sleeve. "I'm leaving today, Mr. President. I won't be able to come next time. I came today because Dr. Kelley wanted me to watch the guy you booted out." He grinned.

"Yeah, you're a little underdressed for the White House. Forgot you were jumping out of the frying pan into the fire today."

"I apologize, sir. I wasn't expecting to drop by. Dr. Kelley didn't give me much warning. She got tied up at Walter Reed."

"Just a note of warning—dressing like that will make Director Benjamin Clark spit nickels and give you a pretty hard time. He's military through and through."

"Yes, sir. I've been warned by Vernon Kemp. Thank you. I am what I am." Standing six foot five at attention created the appearance of a much taller man and towered over most people in the room. When he stood at attention, like now, he appeared even taller.

"Maybe you'll decide you miss all the geo-politics. If you do, let me know. I'm sure we can find a place for you. You received high marks at NORAD, being one of those computer wizards. Then you come here and get a degree as a physician's assistant."

"Thank you, sir. Dr. Kelley was amazing to work with, and you, of course. I'll do my best to not disappoint you in the future."

The president rubbed a finger around the bandage. "Itches."

"To be expected. I'll be going. I don't want to miss my plane. I want to speak to Dr. Kelley's new intern before I leave, too."

"Good luck. I probably scared him. I should try and be a little more patient. Thanks for taking the time, Lazarus. Good luck at Enigma."

He saluted then smiled as he took his leave.

The president thought the bandage was overkill but had already rolled down his sleeve. Tonight, he'd rip it off.

~ ~ ~ ~

Chase couldn't shake an uneasy feeling. Dr. Wu, the Enigma psychiatrist, had helped him work through a great deal of baggage from his experience in Syria. His resolve remained strong through it all. The determination to heal was a top priority so he could kick his drug habit. Finally, he learned to forgive himself for things outside his control. All he'd ever known was being a soldier who served his country. For many years, his heart and mind grew so calloused, the act of eliminating the enemy became as easy as breathing. Chase's conscience evaporated and suffered from a lack of empathy that became a way to scare the hell out of the enemy. Then Tessa Scott happened.

She wasn't supposed to be home, but there she was, the perfect picture of the girl next door. When Tessa opened the door, the smell of chocolate chip cookies wafted from inside. Words failed him until she hurled one of her snarky comments at him as fast as a pitcher for the St. Louis Cardinals, snapping him back to reality. The woman had changed the insensitive brute he'd become over the years almost in the blink of an eye. He didn't believe in love at first sight, or love at all, for that matter. But when his chest began to hurt as she invited him into her home, the soldier knew he'd crossed some invisible line he was going to regret. Within the next thirty minutes, they were running for their lives to escape Libyan terrorists through the California countryside. Nothing was ever the same again. As dire as the situation was at their first meeting, he could now remember it fondly, although he doubted Tessa would feel the same.

Having committed to never settling down with just one woman, now here he was, married to the woman who had been both a curse and a godsend to his troubled soul. The truth was, he couldn't get her to say those vows fast enough. He'd lost her several times over the past few years, and the last time convinced him to stop being an idiot and marry the woman. Life was a gamble no matter how you looked at it, so why not tackle it with the one person he could trust? Having his best friend as a partner, for however long he had to be on this earth, felt like a win.

He watched her leave the boutique with two shopping bags and marveled once more how lucky he was they'd crossed paths. No doubt he'd be dead by now if they hadn't. In spite of his zero faith in mankind, she had brought light into that dark world. Yet even now, he scanned the rooftops of buildings, watched those who walked alone and moved slowly.

"You know those mirrored sunglasses make you look like a badass?" Tessa smiled up at him.

"I don't like being out in the open." He let his attention turn to her and felt the familiar rapid heartbeat he once believed to be a medical problem. Now he welcomed it, knowing it meant he was capable of experiencing something other than anger and revenge. "I am a badass, and you love it."

"I most certainly do." She paused as he opened the door for her then took her bags. "Chase?"

Now she had his complete attention. The tone in her voice meant she was overthinking a problem or was in trouble. "What?"

"I-I…"

The stutter she often had when she was nervous used to be a tipoff of an incoming lie or a screwup. Hopefully the problem wasn't that she'd married him. "Tessa?"

"Nothing. Let's go."

He'd revisit this moment once they drove back to the resort. They had been in town too long, and he'd gotten a text two hours earlier that their cabin was ready. With sunset approaching and a bank of clouds rolling in, he figured the ache in his leg hinted at rain. The doctors warned he might predict the weather for the rest of his life. At least, now, he had a life. A few months ago, he'd doubted this kind of happiness was possible.

The scenic drive back to the Hidden Waters Resort meandered alongside a mountain stream. Several times, Tessa asked him to stop. She wanted to listen to the ripple of rapids crashing against smooth boulders. They stood with arms wrapped around each other taking in the solitude, deep in their own thoughts.

"This place reminds me of the Smokey Mountains." Tessa sighed and tossed a rock into the churning water.

"Me, too. The Oconaluftee River runs through Cherokee, the Qualla Rez, where my grandfather still lives."

"I would very much like to meet him." She gazed up at him longingly. "Please."

He nodded and kissed her shortly. "He is the one man I respect more than anyone. I owe him so much." A low rumble of thunder forced them back to the car. As he started the engine, he reached over and took her hand. "Tessa, we talked about leaving Enigma and going back to our roots. If that is really what you want, I'll start looking for property right away."

She squeezed his hand. "I want that more than anything. I'm not sure how Robert will react to me taking the children to another state."

"Let me worry about him. He'll agree." He spoke in his commanding voice he often used with the Enigma team.

"You can't kill him," she reminded him as she patted his hand. He started to open his mouth when she grasped his hand. "Or have anyone else do it for you. He is not to be harmed in any way, shape, or form."

"I'm capable of negotiations without violence."

She smiled sweetly, giving him fair warning. "Me, too."

"Sometimes you're scary." He laughed but admitted to himself the woman could be devious even when she used her honey and Southern drawl on him. "I promise to be diplomatic. Now, let's get back to the resort. Looks like rain, and I don't want to be on the road during a downpour."

Although focused on the road, he was keenly aware Tessa was quieter than usual. What was she hiding from him? Ever since they had arrived, she had been a little off. He had picked her up that morning after being released from "physical therapy jail," as he called it. She waited at her apartment in Sacramento with Director Benjamin Clark. He hadn't seen her since they had arrived back from Montana. Leaving her in the director's capable hands was not the plan, but waiting MPs insisted he follow them. Dr. Wu was also there, the one person who had saved both of them mentally over the last few years. The doctor became quite attached to Tessa, like everyone else on the team, and thought it best he be their witness to the rushed wedding. The other team members would not be happy they weren't invited, but he wanted to marry the woman before she changed her mind.

"Okay, you two. Remember I still have to get the final okay from the papers from Darya Petrov's attorney saying Tessa is free to marry you. This is just a formality. We may be doing this all again—"

"Ben, just marry us." Tessa took Chase's hand and gazed up at him like he was some kind of superhero. "I'll marry him again and again if I need to. It's okay if the paperwork hasn't been finalized."

A new feeling of completeness washed over him like a warm blanket when she spoke the traditional vows. It took all of ten minutes.

"You may kiss"—Chase pulled her into his arms and they kissed like there was no tomorrow until the director cleared his throat—"the bride," he managed to say then cleared his throat for a second time. When they separated, both laughed and hugged the director who smiled in spite of trying to push them away. "Go. Before I change my mind."

Tessa threw herself back into the director's arms and hugged his neck, followed by a kiss on the cheek. He held her tightly and planted a kiss her on the temple. Whether the man ever admitted it, he had great affection for her.

Next, she tackled Dr. Wu who stood stoic and glum. At first, he barely moved but then slowly lifted his arms to embrace her. In spite of having issues with the doctor, Chase was grateful he'd saved Tessa from herself through the trauma she'd suffered because of him and, of course, the Tribesman.

While he held her, Dr. Wu's cold dark eyes met Chase's, sending him a signal to tread lightly. In defiance, Chase lifted his chin and glared back. He wasn't ready to burn another bridge between them, considering the doctor had been instrumental in helping him through his own latest rough patch.

A lingering thought inside him warned he might need the doctor again.

CHAPTER 3

The main lodge of the resort reminded Tessa of those built during the Great Depression by the CCC camps. Her great grandfather had been a young man when he left home in 1933 to help build the Pere Marquette Lodge in Grafton, Illinois. She'd gone there as a tribute to him and loved the old-fashion ambiance of a bygone era. This resort was no different. It was both grand and humble, elegant and cozy, the dining room boasting expensive linens and crystal.

After dinner, Tessa and Chase explored the lodge, taking in the game room and bar that could have hosted a hundred people. Fortunately, being the early part of the week, only a few businessmen and older couples shared the space.

"Shouldn't we toast our new life together?" she asked, spotting a young couple who may have been newlyweds considering how many times the young woman gazed at her ring then at the man. "They appear to be celebrating, too."

"You don't drink. But you might enjoy a little champagne."

"No, not a drinker, but I have had it mixed with fruit juice. Loved it."

Chase called the waiter over to the outdoor seating area where they had decided to watch the sunset that fought with the black clouds trying to crowd it out. He explained what they wanted and the special occasion.

Once more, Tessa grew aware something was off with them. They had waited what felt like an eternity for this to happen. An element they were strangers crowded in on her. Silence had overtaken them riding into town earlier, and the situation had not really changed. Usually, she couldn't keep from asking questions or talking about their work, or her kids. It wasn't uncommon for them to interrupt each other with an idea, comment on a new book they'd read or a movie they wanted to watch. Today, silence. Was he having second thoughts about marrying her? Could he be thinking about her being with the Tribesman that one night a few weeks ago?

The thought of being naked in Chase's muscular arms for the first time left her second-guessing the sanity of her decision to jump into getting married so soon after finding out the Tribesman was alive. Chase continued to make her swoon at watching him walk through the door and fill a room with his overwhelming presence. How many times had she imagined what this day would reveal about both of them?

The man had a great deal more experience than her, not to mention he'd left many a shattered heart along the way. There had only been two men in her life: one was the father of her children and the other a wild tribesman from Afghanistan who saved her life. But Chase had always been the one she fantasized about in the middle of the night, found excuses to meet for lunch on the university mall, or work with on a project or mission. Having his approval meant everything.

Although she'd fought the attraction and never succumbed to the flirting or advances, part of her rejecting him had to do with being married. She now understood it was also that she wondered if after a one-night stand, he'd be satisfied he'd gotten what he'd tried hard to capture and then walk away. The man loved a challenge, and she'd given him plenty. But her heart loved him more than she thought possible. Right now, she was a jittery mess.

"On the house." The waiter set down the tray of colorful drinks in champagne glasses. "A new idea we are trying for our special guests, such as yourselves." He went on to explain the different samples: champagne cocktail with strawberries, blackberry, fruit punch, mimosa, and what turned out to be Tessa's favorite, champagne lemonade.

She gulped it down like she was at a Vacation Bible School picnic on a hot summer day.

"Delicious," she admitted, reaching for another sample.

Chase cautioned her, "Better go easy on that stuff. It might taste like fruit juice, but it will kick you in the butt if you aren't careful. You aren't used to alcohol."

Tessa laughed as she tried the blackberry champagne. "It's a special occasion. I can barely taste the"—she finished it off—"chamblame. I mean champagne. You only took a sip of yours. Let's toast for real."

He lifted his glass and offered one of those devilish smiles that gave her goose bumps. She was going to need a couple more of these if she was going to loosen up and drive him crazy.

"To a new life," he toasted as they touched glasses.

"A new life," she whispered. Once more, he took a sip of the champagne while she emptied her fluted glass. She wondered if he was going easy on the fruity drink because he still took medication for his injuries. Maybe later she could have a look at the leg and…

"Why are you smiling like a Cheshire cat, Tessa Hunter?"

She dropped her glass, but Chase reached out and snatched it from the air before it hit the floor. "I was remembering the first night we spent together. You walked out of the bathroom in nothing but a towel."

"You nearly had a stroke, Tessa. You tried to escape the room."

She waved him off and laughed a little louder than she intended. "I was just playing hard to get." In spite of the cool breezes blowing across the veranda, Tessa felt warm. She twisted her hair into a knot on the back of her neck and noticed Chase's gaze explore her body, taking in the provocative way she'd moved. Lowering her arms slowly, as if tempting him further, she carefully reached for another sample. This time, the liquid courage didn't taste as good, and she decided to set it down but missed the table, spilling the rest of the contents on her pale-blue dress. Jumping up, she caught the edge of the tablecloth in her bracelet, jerking it sideways. The remaining glasses tipped over, crashing against each other.

Horrified at the mess, she watched Chase rise and motion for the waiter who stood in the doorway. He apologized for the disturbance and asked to put the broken stemware on his bill. Then like an experienced 007 agent from a movie, he reached for her arm and slipped it through his.

"Time to go." He smiled, unfazed. "I think you've had enough."

"I'm fine. Really. Oh." She stopped and hugged his arm. "Did we just have an earthquake?"

"I was hoping to hear you say that later—under different circumstances—but no, we didn't have an earthquake." He maneuvered her to the car and gently helped her into the passenger seat.

Because she couldn't figure out the seat belt, he reached in and secured it for her.

"These foreign cars are tricky," she huffed in exasperation.

"It's a Cadillac."

"Thanks, Chase. You're my knight in shining…I forget." She laughed then laid her head back against the headrest. "Can we put the top down?"

"If it were a convertible, we could." He grinned at her. "Tessa, it's going to be all right."

"Damn straight it is." She gave him a thumbs-up. "Woohoo!" She powered down the window as he pulled out onto the narrow road to their cabin. "Let's do this."

"You know you're drunk, right?" He smiled wolfishly.

"No, I'm not. I've never been drunk. I don't drink, remember?" She powered the window up then down again. "Don't be silly."

Chase didn't comment again until he pulled up at their cabin. He came around to help her out, and she felt sluggish as she walked. "Careful," he cautioned as they took the few steps down to their cabin.

~ ~ ~ ~

The waiter headed toward the kitchen, rolling the pushcart of soiled linens, broken glasses, and pieces of fruit. He quickly returned to the game room then joined a gentleman who had observed the couple on the veranda the entire evening. During dinner, he had positioned himself in a dark corner of the giant dining hall with an older couple who were staying at the lodge. There was a lot of conversation, and laughter. It surprised the waiter when the well-dressed gentleman went to the game room alone before calling him aside.

The guest was considered a person of great importance and had asked for him to be his waiter in advance. Although he had often received large gratuities and gifts from hotel guests, this was a first for him.

"Yes, sir?"

"The couple on the terrace. I want to know who they are and how long they'll be here. I believe we're old friends, and I'd love to surprise them."

"Oh, that's Mr. and Mrs. Hunter. Newlyweds. Spending a few days with us. Just arrived today. I would be happy to ask them if it's okay to join them?"

"And ruin their first night of a honeymoon? No. I'll touch base with them tomorrow. But I could surprise them with something special."

"They asked for champagne, sir."

"Excellent. My treat, but there is a catch."

The gentleman had surprised everyone present with free champagne, but wished to remain anonymous. He insisted on arranging the glasses in a certain way. This felt odd to the waiter, but since he offered to pay 500 dollars, and he was a guest of honor, too, the waiter agreed.

"Sir, I believe the couple has retired for the evening. Mr. Hunter barely touched his drink."

"Yes. I noticed." He handed the waiter an envelope with five one hundred-dollar bills. Although it felt wrong to accept, he also needed the money. The man handed him another two hundred dollars and finally made eye contact with him. He shivered at the gray-blue eyes that almost appeared opaque. They reminded him of a wolf he'd seen on the National Geographic Channel. "I prefer the couple or anyone else never knew who offered the free drinks."

"Of course. But, sir, you've paid me enough. This isn't necessary."

"I understand your little brother requires a blood transfusion and other lifesaving medical treatment."

"Yes. But how did you—"

"I know everything, young man. Now because you have done your job well tonight, and I understand you are a hard worker, I've made arrangements for your brother and mother to be my guests at one of my facilities. We specialize in this kind of disease of the blood, and I believe we can help him. Insurance doesn't always cover the treatment of such things, and I'm sure your salary barely covers what is needed. I can only imagine how difficult it is to make ends meet."

"I don't know what to say, sir," the waiter stammered in shock. "Thank you."

"I require privacy and wish not to be disturbed. I will reach out to the other people here at my convenience."

"Thank you. Thank you so much. This means the world to me. I've been working extra shifts to try and—" He stopped when the man held up his hand.

"Take this," he ordered, handing the waiter a business card. "Everything will be explained when you contact them tonight. They're expecting your call."

The waiter smiled and held out his hand toward the gentleman who ignored it and stood.

"Good evening." The guest strode out of the room without another word.

The waiter stepped aside and stood at attention. He dared not speak again in case the generous offer was retracted. He watched him move nonchalantly toward the terrace to where the Hunters had been seated. Whatever the interest the man had in them, he thought it best not to be too curious. Nonetheless, he watched him run his fingers over the chair where the woman had sat and stared up into the sky. Clouds blocked the remaining light, and thunder echoed softly in the distance.

Soft laughter drew his attention to the billiards tables. It had only been a few seconds, but, when he glanced back at the terrace, the strange benefactor had disappeared.

CHAPTER 4

The lights were turned down low in their quaint cabin. In spite of the effort to layer the cottage décor right down to wood floors and gingham window coverings, modern amenities remained in place for comfort. Tessa found a radio jazz station and sighed as she turned to face Chase. When he caught sight of his expression and stance in the antique mirror hanging on the wall, he tried to relax and replace the intimidating demeanor. He resembled a drill sergeant eyeing a green recruit to measure what they might be capable of.

The dappled light highlighted Tessa's soft skin and curly hair that fought to free itself from the knot on her neck. Even at her current state of tipsy, she maintained the elegant beauty that had transfixed him for several years. She hummed with the music while staring at him. Leaning against the dresser, she wore a come-hither smile. He longed to help her out of the off-the-shoulder blue dress with a streak of strawberry champagne she'd spilled down her breast.

As he moved toward her, she stepped forward and wrapped her arms around his neck. "Let's dance."

He circled her waist, pulled her tight, and let her sway with the music. Having her in his arms, and knowing unethical behavior no longer existed, he let his imagination generate images of what he desired for way too long. Spinning her out then twirling her in a circle, he pulled her back into his arms. She tripped over her feet and tumbled like a rag doll as she grabbed his biceps.

"Whew. Guess I'm a little dizzy," she slurred, forehead creased. Pushing him back, Tessa blinked nervously. "Chase?"

"Tessa, you okay?"

Ghostly white, Tessa covered her mouth and gagged. She shook her head and stumbled toward the bathroom. He watched her clamp unsteady hands onto the doorframe.

Chase grabbed her arm to pull her toward the toilet, but not fast enough. Before he could position her on her knees before the toilet, she got sick on her dress. He gently pushed her onto her knees. He kneeled next to her and held her hair back until she stopped retching. Standing up, he grabbed a wash cloth and soaked it in cold water before filling a disposable cup for her.

"Rinse out your mouth, babe, and spit."

She nodded and obeyed.

After helping her stand, he gently washed her face. The sadness in her eyes spoke volumes. "It's okay," he assured her.

"I'm sorry," she sniffed. "I-I…"

"Down," he ordered, easing her back to her knees, and this time she hit the target. Once again, he held her hair with one hand and rubbed her back with the other. "Better?"

Several more times, he washed her face and hands, gave her water, and smoothed her hair back until he managed to find a clip to control the curls.

"Not. Very. Romantic." Her words were still a bit slurred, her forehead creased in pain. "Maybe we should go to bed."

"Let me help you out of these clothes." Before he could start the process, she closed her eyes and collapsed into his arms. Was he disappointed at the turn of events? Yes. Was he amused? Absolutely. It wasn't a surprise they would have a honeymoon bordering on comic relief. He carried her to their bed and laid her on top of the covers. Tonight, she tried hard to resemble a woman of the world and failed miserably. She was going to have a lulu of a headache in the morning.

The shopping bags she'd brought in still rested on the dresser. After he retrieved one to see if there was anything he could use to make her more comfortable, he pulled out a black, lacey teddy that forced him to turn and stare at the Grass Valley housewife.

"What exactly were you planning for me, Mrs. Hunter? I guess it can wait one more night." He chuckled and went to peel the soiled dress from her body before tucking her in for the night. He moved a curl from across one eye and leaned in to her kiss her forehead. "You're the best part of me," he whispered.

After lowering the lights, he entered the kitchenette to make coffee. He checked in with headquarters and updated them on a suspicious person he'd spotted, only to be informed they were being tracked by an unknown threat. Maybe it was a good thing, at least for tonight, his wife was incapacitated.

While he waited, he phoned one of the Enigma team.

"Why are you calling me on your wedding night? Do you need instructions?" grumbled Carter Johnson, one of his best friends. "Oh, and thanks for not inviting me to the wedding."

"Well, if I did need instructions, I'd call Samantha who could give them to me."

"Ouch. What's up?"

"We're being watched. I noticed a man on the trail when we arrived at check-in."

"Are you being paranoid?"

"Maybe at first. Then, in town, I couldn't shake the feeling after seeing the same car several times when we moved from place to place. Tonight, I noticed a man with a group of people who kept glancing our way."

"They were checking out Tessa," he groaned. "She's a looker, or have you forgotten? I'm beginning to think you took a bullet to the head in Syria."

Chase went on to retell how the waiter continuously left to visit with the man after they went to the game room terrace. Soon, free champagne samples showed up. Once more, the gut feeling of things not being quite right weighed on him. He'd managed to grab a piece of one of the glasses in a linen napkin and stuffed it in his sports jacket.

"I want to send it to the lab tonight."

"On your wedding night?" he gasped. "Man, you also must have taken a bump to the head. If you just can't perform your husbandly duties, I'll be there in a couple of hours."

Chase informed him of the debacle of the night and laughed

along with Carter.

"Are you kidding me? Tessa never drinks."

"Well, she did tonight, and it was a disaster. But I'm wondering if something wasn't in those samples."

"Why weren't you affected?"

"I had a sip or two. I'm still on medication, and I gave up drinking after Syria. I don't need any more crutches to impair my ability to think."

"Okay. I think we have a contact who owes Enigma a favor, so I'll have him come by. Text me the address and, if he needs a passcode to get past the guard at the gate, send it along. I'll meet him halfway back to Sacramento."

"Thanks, buddy. Who is the guy?"

"Agent Dennis Martin. Your favorite FBI jerk. I have a feeling you should expect being called a number of unflattering barnyard excrements. I'll play dumb if he wants to know who he's meeting."

"That shouldn't be difficult." Chase couldn't keep the amusement out of his voice. "I appreciate it."

"I expect all the details about the honeymoon. The triple-X version."

"Screw you." Chase clicked off then immediately sent the information Carter requested. Having Dennis show up was not ideal because he tended to ask too many questions, and not in a polite way. He was FBI through and through and often threw his threats around like a playground bully.

Chase contacted Vernon Kemp, the brain behind their technology department. Knowing he'd probably still be up gaming or snooping around the NSA or the Pentagon gave him hope he could help identify the stranger who had watched them. Hacking into the resort's security system was child's play for the genius kid. He described the man in the dining area and thought maybe they were watched in town. Giving the coordinates and street address would speed up the search.

"I'll call you back within the hour, boss."

He clicked off and waited for a short time then went in to check on Tessa. He couldn't resist smiling at his wife who had taken up most of the bed. A dull ache in his leg caused him to rub it vigorously, becoming conscious once again how Syria had nearly killed him. The rain was pounding now, and he returned to the porch to wonder why he was paranoid. Had Syria messed him up so badly he'd see ghosts where there were none, the rest of his life? The Enigma psychiatrist thought he'd be able to work through it and regain part of the old Chase. He hoped, for Tessa's sake, that was true. He didn't want to be one of those guys returning home from deployment a shell of what he once was.

The phone vibrated, and he recognized the FBI agent's number. He texted him the passcode and watched a car approach then flashed his headlights twice before continuing to the cabin. He opened the front door to let the agent inside.

He shook the rain from his jacket. "Hell of a night to have me out, Hunter. What's so damn important I had to be at your beck and call. I'm getting pretty sick of this. Why don't you have one of your maladjusted rejects do your bidding?"

"I didn't want them to get wet and maybe catch a cold." Chase poured two cups of coffee then retold his concerns, ending with the suspicious feeling of being followed.

"So, you're telling me you finally married Miss Cookie Monster of the PTA, and you're worried someone is going to hurt you? Aww. Poor baby."

The FBI and Enigma didn't always see eye to eye on how things should to be done. And Agent Dennis Martin didn't enjoy being obligated to them for anything—yet he had been for several years.

Chase's phone vibrated again. "What ya got? You're on speaker. Agent Martin is here with me."

"Did you need a chaperone tonight?" Vernon teased.

"Why does everyone keep thinking I need help? I got this," he growled.

"That's debatable." The agent lifted his cup toward the bedroom. "Seems to me that little she-devil you married has had Enigma pretty much under her thumb since day one."

Chase frowned. "Go on, Vernon. Agent Martin is here and trying to torment me."

"Found several things. Open your phone to the photos while I talk." Vernon waited a few seconds before continuing. "Okay. Picture number one is you at what looks like a sidewalk café. If you can widen the screen, there's a reflection in the window of people on the street. I'm making it go to motion. See the one guy in the ballcap? No big deal, right? Except, he appears to stop and watch from across the street. I thought maybe the reflection of the sun interfered with the observation. Next is picture two, where you're standing at the car being all touchy feely—"

"Oh, for crying out loud, Chase. You two are absolutely nauseating. Have you no shame? She has all but put you on a leash." Agent Martin chuckled. "Next thing you're going to be telling me you'll have to ask Tessa if you can go kill someone."

Chase took a deep breath then narrowed his eyes at the agent. The man cleared his throat and refocused on the pictures.

"Anyway," Vernon continued, "I managed to pick him up several other places after you left the town and headed back. Not any old schmuck, either. Had a fancy car with a driver. Lost track of him since there are no cameras on those mountain roads."

"So that's it? Just a creep in town?"

"No. Watched you guys pull through the gates at the resort. Tapped into the cameras all around to see if there might be anyone else snooping around."

"And?"

"Nothing. Except that car in town breezed right through the gates without having to stop and give his ID like you did. Here is another picture of him getting out at the main resort where he is staying. The fourth camera caught his face as he turned around. Although he has on sunglasses, I think I got a pretty good scan."

Agent Martin grabbed the phone out of Chase's hand to get a better look. "This is not good."

"Who is he?" Chase asked as the agent returned the device. "Looks familiar, but the glasses hide too much."

"Andre Lavelle Vion?" Agent Martin snarled in alarm. "What the hell is he doing here?"

Chase felt sucker punched. "No way." He took a closer look.

"You're on his hit list, from what I hear at the Bureau. Not sure why, but you're a marked man, Chase."

"I know why. But no way he knew I'd be here."

"There's more," Vernon butted in. "Here are a few pictures of earlier in the evening. He was definitely in the same dining room as you. He's registered under an assumed name, I guess, since there was no Andre Vion in the computer. I caught video feed of you and Tessa. Oh, since when does Tessa drink?"

"Great. You got her drunk. Big man, Chase. Afraid she'd dump you when you dropped your drawers?"

"Is there no limit to your crude, inappropriate stab at humor, Dennis?" He picked up the sample from the glass holding the champagne. "That's why I wanted you to take this to the lab. We got several samples on the house as a congratulatory gesture. That champagne is pretty pricey, like four-hundred-a-bottle pricey. And there were a number of different kinds."

"So, you did get her drunk," Agent Martin groaned. "Shame on you."

"This man doesn't resemble the Andre I knew years ago."

"We all age, Hunter, even you. But, in this case, the man had some serious plastic surgery and has been working out. The changes have been subtle but continuous. The FBI has had him on our radar for ten years. All legit and nothing to nail him with. He's extremely careful. Pays his taxes here and in France. Donates to charities and supports politicians on both sides of the aisle, here and abroad. He's made more friends than enemies, and those powerful friends are at his bidding."

"Why is he on your radar?"

"Because something stinks. He's aloof; anyone who interacts with him is tight-lipped and refuses to offer anything up about him. It's like they're scared out of the minds. Why is Enigma interested? And why, pray tell, is he interested in you?" When Chase didn't answer, the agent released a breath as if he'd been holding it. He shook his head. "You're a dead man."

After Agent Martin left, Chase made another pot of coffee. He didn't want any surprises. The screened-in side porch looking out over the stream was a perfect place to observe if anyone was prowling the area. Getting a sense of the sounds and movements helped him decipher natural from problematic confrontations. Having a Glock ready and loaded did a lot for his peace of mind. He of all people knew what Andre Lavelle Vion was capable of.

~ ~ ~ ~

Last night had been a disaster. If the other Enigma agents found about her behavior, she'd never live it down. There had always been a line neither would cross as to their attraction for each other.

No matter how many times they rushed up to that line, national security, ethical guidelines, and moral responsibility put the brakes on their unexplored desires. Then last night happened.

In spite of being newlyweds, and concentrating on the night ahead, Chase had spotted a man watching them from the shadows. He could never turn off being suspicious and overly observant.

Samples of champagne mixed with strawberries tempted Tessa to indulge herself with the delicious libation. Her nerves were on edge at the thought of spending the night with Captain Hunter. Between rubbing his thumb over the back of her hand in a slow suggestive motion and leaning in to whisper in her ear how her fragrance was a distraction, the one thing she hadn't expected was a possible target on their back. It appeared even their honeymoon was not immune to obstacles.

She wiggled beneath the silky sheets then became conscious of wearing only her lace panties. A stabbing pain shot through her head as she grabbed the sheet up around her neck and moaned like a wounded lion. In the next few seconds came another jolt to her system when Chase jerked back the curtains, flooding the room with light.

"You have to take me to the ER, Chase," she mumbled.

He came to the edge of the bed to tower over her. The military stance tipped her off to his mood. "Why do you want to go to the ER?"

"I think I have a brain tumor." She rubbed her forehead gently then sent him a pleading gaze.

His burst of laughter caused her to squint at his lack of concern. "Get up. You have a hangover. You'll live. I know it's our honeymoon, but we've got work to do."

"Well, I would, but I don't have any clothes. I suppose you can explain last night considering I'm naked?"

"I tried to clean you up before tucking you in last night. You got pretty sick. Sometime during the night, you removed your bra." He pointed to the ceiling fan overhead.

Tessa opened one eye against the bright light then sucked in her breath. The expensive bra she'd purchased in hopes he'd finally remove it in a moment of passion was attached to the fan, circling like a flag.

He walked over and switched off the fan then climbed up on the bed to remove the bra.

Tessa opened her mouth to thank him when he tossed it to her. Since she still clutched the sheet up to her neck like a Kevlar vest, it landed on her head, straps falling down around her ears.
Furious, she glared at him with every ounce of disdain she could muster. A boyish smirk toyed with his mouth.

"You know what's good for a hangover?" he asked, flopping down on the bed next to her. "Sex." He gently tugged the bra off her head and fingered the lacy edges before cutting his eyes back to her. "A beautiful Israeli agent once told me that."

"I bet," she snarled. "I think I prefer to be hungover, thank you very much." She dared hold the sheet with one hand while trying to snatch the bra away from him, only to have him clamp down tighter on the strap. Without thinking, she jerked it, which caused him to lean in so close his mouth was a breath away from her face. For a split second, she thought about how much she wanted him, desired the intimacies they'd both craved for too long. All she could do was drown in those dangerous dark eyes and feel the hardness of his shoulder pressed against her.

The stubborn streak inside her fought with the realization, that, once again, he had been an officer and a gentleman the night before, not taking advantage of her drunken state. Why couldn't she just tell him thank you and that he was her hero?

Chase released the bra then moved her tangled hair out of her eyes. "I know you're a little scared of me and where we were headed last night." She took a deep breath and nodded as she tried to look away, but he took her chin in his hand, forcing her to gaze at him.

"I won't hurt you, Tessa. If it makes you feel any better, I was a little nervous, too. I don't think you know how you get under my skin." Someone started knocking at the door, crashing the mood between them. He rolled off the bed and smiled down at her. Without another word, he left her alone to deal with the disappointment of a wasted opportunity.

After a shower, clean clothes and several aspirins, she padded into the kitchen barefoot. The smell of coffee did wonders for her mood and pounding headache. She did an internet search for remedies and was surprised that having sex really was a cure for a hangover. Another missed opportunity.

She found Chase on the screened-in porch, talking on the phone. A cup of steaming brew sat on the small table next to him. Once he clicked off, he made a few notes and handed them to her. "I have to leave for a while. I'm sorry. Could you run these sources down and see what they say about the guy we saw last night? Not sure why he's here, but he's important. Headquarters thinks we're being tracked. He's clean as a whistle, and a corporate hotshot, I think, so maybe not by him. Apparently, he's waiting for another guest to arrive. Could be he recognized me from another place and time. If so, he isn't an innocent."

"Anything else?" she asked, glancing over the list. The silence drew her attention. Wearing a scowl, he focused on the outside landscape in the woods. With his mouth puckered and eyes narrowed, he appeared to assess an unknown enemy. "Chase?"

"Did you bring your weapon?"

"In my purse."

"Keep it close. Got a bad feeling."

"Where are you going? Can't I come with you?"

"You are not in the best shape right now," he grinned. "I know this isn't what we planned, but I have to check this guy out. If it's an old enemy after me, then I want you at a safe distance."

"I want to help." She rubbed her forehead to make it stop throbbing. A clap of thunder, followed by a downpour, pounded on the tin roof of the cabin. The air was thick and the sky a grayish-green. She'd seen such skies way too often in the Midwest before a tornado. She checked the weather app on her phone. "We're under a severe weather alert, Chase. I don't like being this close to a stream. I'm going to pack a bag in case we have to leave in a hurry."

"I'll check back with you later. I don't know how long I'll be gone. The staff brought us breakfast if you're interested. Pastries, yogurt, and fruit mostly. Your kind of food."

He was a straight-up steak and potatoes kind of guy, even for breakfast. "Thanks for last night," she said, standing to block his exit. "This is why I don't drink."

Without batting an eye, he pulled her into his arms and kissed her until she surrendered to the passion rising up through her body. Releasing her, he ran his hands down her hair and to her shoulders. A hint of regret softened the usual look of steel in his eyes.

"I have to go, Tessa. Let me know if you find out anything. I'll be back later and we can talk about—us."

If her head hadn't felt like it might pop off any second, she would have screamed, "I'm done talking, Captain Hunter, make love to me like there's no tomorrow." But once again, courage failed her and he was gone.

CHAPTER 5

The day passed quickly with the work left for her. She even managed to take a power nap. The rain stopped around two and she decided to stroll to the main lodge for a late lunch. The river was now swollen to the top of its banks, no longer clear and meandering like the previous day. Once on the path, she was surprised when a man came alongside her, binoculars hanging from around his neck. "Mind if I join you? I noticed you were alone, too." His shy smile was infectious. "I mean if you don't mind."

The French accent caught her off guard and charmed her at the same time. Tessa stopped abruptly and stared at him then took a step back. "Excuse me?" It was the man from last night that Chase felt concern.

"I am Andre Lavelle Vion." He extended his hand. When Tessa didn't take it, he withdrew it and pointed to the stream. "That is starting to look ugly. I'm glad I chose to stay in the lodge. I came here to bird-watch, but I guess they have more sense than me since I've been standing out in the rain for three hours." His laugh was infectious. "I found plenty of wildflowers to study instead."

His light chuckle won her over. The old saying, keep your friends close, but your enemies closer, might be the rule of the day.

This time she extended her hand. "Oh sorry. You surprised me.

I'm Tessa."

They engaged in a slow, cautious walk of strangers and exchanged small talk as they neared the lodge.

"My friends are late. Apparently, their flight has been delayed because of weather. Chances are they won't be here for our meeting. Guess I'm stuck waiting."

"And studying wildflowers instead of bird-watching," Tessa added. "Are they bird enthusiasts as well?"

This caused him to laugh which Tessa decided she rather enjoyed. It was warm and inviting.

"Not even close. I suggested this place because my travel agent mentioned it was a bird-watcher's paradise. I have not found that to be true today. However, the flowers bloom with abandonment so not a total loss." They reached the front doors. "Would you join me for lunch? I hate eating alone."

Over a quick meal of soup and salad, Tessa began to wonder if Chase had the wrong guy. He spoke of hopes for a better world and the work that needed to be done for clean water in poor countries. Afterward, the hypnotic voice and Nordic good looks had lulled her into complacency. Her research wasn't usually wrong. He knew her soft spots, touching on topics close to her heart. What she found out through her searches, was this man was elusive, stern, and hard to work with. This was not that man. However, there remained Chase's warning eating at her common sense.

"I'm sorry. I really need to leave. My husband will be back any time now." She started to walk away when he captured her hand and kissed it. "Thank you for a lovely afternoon, madame."

What was she thinking? The man could be the devil incarnate and she'd fallen for every word he fed her. Maybe he was dangerous. Once outside and nearly to the end of the trail leading to her cabin, she turned back to see him standing on the veranda watching her as he smoked a cigarette. Once inside her cabin, she locked the door, checked her weapon on her hip, and went to the porch to watch the stream, now muddy and filled with debris. Backing away, she knocked over a fern, breaking the pot and spilling the soil. Since she couldn't find a broom, she ended up scooping it up by hand. Now covered with soil and pieces of fern, she decided to shower again. By the time she'd showered and slipped into a skimpy, thigh-length dress with a plunging neckline, the rain had started again. At least she and Chase could dine in unless their timeline had sped up. He was not going to be happy with her information or that she'd engaged the target. Perhaps it would be wise not to mention she found Andre interesting.

Sitting on the edge of the bed, she noticed Chase had left his handcuffs on the nightstand. She fingered them carefully. It amused her to think he might have wanted to use them on her. Clicking one end onto her wrist, she thought maybe a little escape practice would be a good idea.

It wasn't. When she went to grab the key, a sudden gust of wind came through the window tipping the lamp over as the electricity went out. Running her hand over the surface of the nightstand, she felt the key slide off onto the floor.

"Tessa," Chase called as she heard him come through the front door of the two-room cabin. "Power is out. Lightning hit a transformer nearby."

Frantic, she dropped to the floor and searched for the lost key.

Walking through the arch that separated the two rooms, he halted as if he were letting his eyes adjust. "It just turned dark. The sky looks yellow. I think we're under a flash flood watch along with a tornado warning. Tessa, are you in here?"

"Yeah, just dropped something."

Unfortunately, he turned on the flashlight app on his phone and pointed it at her as she tried to stand up. She slid onto the bed innocently and smiled. When he stepped closer, she noticed his eyebrows lifted as he tilted his head and smiled.

"Why are you staring at me?" she asked, trying to move her hair out of her face only to realize it was the hand with the handcuffs.

"Well, aren't you the perfect fantasy." He stepped closer with a deliberate stalking vibe.

His light traced her from head to toe before stopping in front of her and staring down, amusement continued to toy with the corners of his wide mouth.

"Oh please," she moaned in frustration. "Get me out of these." She held up her handcuffed wrist.

"I'm thinking if I did that, it would be another missed opportunity for us—at least for me."

His chuckle reminded her of the Big Bad Wolf and Little Red Riding Hood. "Beautiful woman in my bed, wet hair, scantily clad clothing, and wearing handcuffs, begging me to help her?" He quickly removed them. "I'm thinking—"

"Oh, shut up. I mean it." She jumped up. "We've got to get out of here." She pointed out the window. "Tornado."

"Closet. Now."

Both managed to squeeze into the small closet as the roar of a locomotive rumbled overhead with breaking glass and the world crashing around them. It lasted a couple of minutes, when they decided to push open the door. Squeezing through, they discovered another problem. The cabin was tilting toward the now rising waters of the stream. Floodwaters crashed into the cabin as they pulled their way toward the door, only to find it blocked.

A voice on the other side yelled, "I'm trying to get this open." The man yanked it open, reaching in and grabbing Tessa by the arm. "Hurry, the bank is about to collapse," a French voice shouted over the swirling waters.

Tessa recognized Andre Lavelle Vion's voice and was never so glad to hear from a dangerous man.

Chase pushed her through and tried to follow but was swept off his feet. "Get her to safety. I'll make it."

"No," she screamed.

"Madame Hunter, let me help you." Andre didn't wait for her to respond but forced her with shoves and encouragement to keep going.

The darkness swallowed Chase as the cabin slid into the darkness and disappeared into the now ferocious, black water.

A golf cart waited with one of the resort workers. "Take her to the best suite you have. I'll take care of everything." Tessa couldn't stop sobbing. "Don't worry, Madame Hunter. I will find your husband. I promise. Now go."

She wasn't given time to reject the offer and was whisked away to higher ground. Two hours later, there was a knock at the door. Swinging it open, she found Andre with Chase's arm around his shoulder. "You see. I deliver, madame." Tessa helped him into the room and turned to discover Andre Lavelle Vion staring at the man he saved with narrowed eyes like a hungry wolf. The scowl on his pale face was not one of relief but hatred. Chase coughed and raised his head to stare back at the man who had saved his life.

"Andre," she choked, grabbing his hand then hugged his neck.

His expression softened as he refocused on her. "How can I ever thank you?"

"I'm sure I will think of something, Tessa. But for now, your gratitude is enough. It has been my honor." He laid a hand over his heart. He nodded and gave a two-finger salute to Chase. "Captain Hunter, it has been my pleasure to assist you."

Before Chase could respond, the Frenchman slipped away, closing the door behind him. Tessa ran to Chase and helped him stand from the wooden chair. He continued to stare after the man who had saved his life.

"How did he know who you were?" It dawned on her, not once had she mentioned her last name, yet he spoke it with familiarity. Who was this guy? Clearly, the two knew each other. Although Chase was scratched and bloody, he was in one piece. Tessa started a hot shower and helped him discard the ripped clothing. Together, they stepped under the hot spray so she could help remove splinters and mud. Tears streamed down her face knowing she could have lost him forever. She kissed his wet back and slipped out to wait in the bedroom.

$$\sim \sim \sim \sim$$

Chase towel-dried his black hair and body, before wrapping another one around his torso.

The mirror revealed an exhausted and sore soldier, but he was grateful to be alive. The lights from search parties along the river bank lessened the darkness in the bedroom. Tessa sat on the foot of the bed in a white terry-cloth robe he'd noticed hanging on the door earlier. She stared toward the sliding glass doors as thunder and lightning continued to threaten violence. Whether she sensed his presence or he had cast a shadow, she turned toward him, longing mixed with fear on her face.

This time, he would possess her until she begged him to stop. Stepping between her legs that dangled over the side of the bed, he pushed the robe back with both hands and held it tight. Even though he knew she couldn't move, Tessa never tried to be free. Slowly he released the hold so he could explore her body as she jerked his towel away to touch him for the first time. She leaned back in ecstasy as he began to taste her sweetness until she moaned for more.

When his body could no longer restrain itself, he entered the softest part of her and felt the pulsating longing inside him meet her own desires as she pleaded for him to never stop. The years of waiting and longing could not be finished in one moment in time or if ever. His body rocked with the rhythm of her arching body as she pulled him toward complete euphoria. Quivering with heat and uncontrolled satisfaction, he lay inside her until their heartbeats had calmed. Somewhere between the kiss of exhaustion and the realization they were one, sleep engulfed them.

The morning light filled the suite as Chase and Tessa took their morning coffee on the balcony, both still clothed in robes. A black limousine caught their attention as it pulled up in front of the resort. Andre Lavelle Vion walked alongside another man who struck a familiar chord.

"Looks like Monsieur Vion has some important friends," Tessa observed.

Chase grabbed his phone and focused on the second man as he slipped into the limousine. He increased the size of the picture to show Tessa. Her eyes widened as she recognized the head of the FBI.

He lowered the phone and watched the Frenchman turn his eyes up toward where they stood.

Andre Lavelle Vion smiled and gave them another two-finger salute as he joined his guest in the back seat.

"What should we do?" Tessa whispered.

"We do nothing."

"Because he saved our lives?"

"Because there's a target on our back. We need a safe place. And that's at Enigma." He faced her and touched her cheek. "I can't lose you."

CHAPTER 6

Director Benjamin Clark watched from the security monitor as his agents filed into the conference room. His propensity to keep tabs on the team's movements wasn't a secret to any of them. Their behaviors rarely changed because of the intrusion. One example was when the head of technical support, Vernon Kemp, walked up to the camera mounted in the corner and grinned. Using his extended middle finger, he pushed his glasses in place. After shoving both hands into his pockets, he stepped out of view. The director turned away to retrieve files he'd left on the desk.

"I'm headed to the meeting, Glenda. How's our guest?" The director tapped her desk as he passed.

"Much better, sir. She'll be ready soon."

He nodded and entered the elevator from her office. The personal assistant had her finger on the mounted weapon beneath her desk in case an unauthorized intruder was waiting. Although a breach was unlikely, those things happened. The levels of protection ranked with other places of national security. He rarely thought of a problem here. Maybe that was the danger in itself.

Pushing the button would take him to the underground conference center. It gave him little time to formulate how he would tell the team what was about to go down. Most of all, he wanted assurance Chase wouldn't go off half-cocked. For years, he had been full of vengeance, and this could disable his calm-before-the-storm mentality. Since he'd been given a clean bill of health, this new threat could possibly undo his mental stability. The director required guarantees that Captain Hunter still possessed the calculating mindset that enabled him to bring down targets threatening the well-being of the country.

~ ~ ~ ~

"Are you ready for the bombardment of BS from our teammates?" Chase asked as he and Tessa approached the conference room.

They were late in spite of having spent the night in her apartment. The university where Enigma headquarters was located was less than a mile away. With ethical and moral obstacles erased, they couldn't get enough of each other. Only the director knew where they were. Unbeknownst to the tenants, the building had long been wired for security. He requested Vernon Kemp be in charge of making sure they were safe.

"Can I stick my tongue out at Samantha and say 'I got him and you didn't'?"

"There are times I believe you have a death wish. Other times, I think the two of you are just messing with our heads."

Tessa grinned and tilted her head toward the door. "Let's do this and get it over with."

Opening the door, they found the rest of the team in various areas of the large conference room, exchanging small talk and holding cups of coffee. Simultaneously, they turned toward Chase and Tessa, straight-faced and unconcerned. Chase started to speak, but several held up their hand for him to stop. They squinted as if bringing them into focus then pulled out dark sunglasses and placed them on their noses before giving a sigh of relief.

Carter Johnson stepped forward. "Oh, it's you guys. That glow off your bodies now twisted in X-rated passion, nearly blinded us."

"I think I need a second pair to wear over these. Mine aren't working." Zoric took his off and examined them, before offering Tessa one of his yellow smiles. "Congratulations."

Carter hurried to Tessa and pulled her into his arms. "Just know, if you change your mind, I'm there for you," he offered seriously before planting a kiss on her lips. She stepped away and had to laugh as the captain pushed him aside.

"Hope you enjoyed that since it's never happening again." He fist-bumped Carter's arm.

Several others came forward to shake Chase's hand or give Tessa a kiss on the cheek followed by a hug. Good-natured insults and jokes mixed with plenty of laughter filled the room, which normally was a place where a new problem had surfaced. Chase could never remember it being this full of joy.

His thoughts traveled back in time when Tessa had been dragged into a room very much like this. To say they gave her a hard time would be putting it mildly. She stood her ground, although a bit frightened and tearful, claiming she was innocent of their charge of terrorism. By the end of the day, she'd cooperated with them long enough to help catch a Libyan terrorist. When they parted ways a few days later, he'd fallen in love with her.

Now here she was, both darling and troublemaker at Enigma. She and his lead agent, Dr. Samantha Cordova, were like two she-devils who couldn't get along for more than ten minutes in the same room. Over the years, they'd become unlikely friends but would never admit to such a relationship. There had been a time when he was positive Tessa had stood in the crosshairs of Sam's weapon on many occasions.

He didn't know when it happened, but Tessa had earned the respect of her nemesis. Maybe it was trusting an enemy in Russia who actually saved them from certain death, or when Tessa saved the Saudi Arabian prince's life. Then, once more, when she fought side by side with her in Syria. Whatever it was, she was now probably the only female friend of the senior agent, Samantha Cordova.

"I'm assuming you'll name your first child after me?" Sam asked Tessa as she leveled a haughty glare her way.

"It's a toss-up between Vlad the Impaler and Samantha Cordova," Tessa cooed in her sweet singsong tone.

"Humph. Well, if you want the kid to be a wimp, then go for the Vlad name." She flipped her ponytail to her back as she cocked her head and leveled one of her cobra smiles.

Conversations like that were normal for those two. He'd watched them spar at the gym, and Tessa always suffered the worst of it. But, in the last year or so, Samantha had to work a great deal harder to claim the win. She sauntered over to him and planted a long, hard kiss on Chase's mouth before turning to Tessa and arched an eyebrow. As she stepped toward the others, Tessa stuck her foot out, tripping the senior agent and causing her to fall into the nearby table.

"A little early to be drinking, Sam. We've talked about this." Tessa frowned. When Sam turned slowly toward her, wearing her death stare, she covered her mouth. "Oops. Sorry. I forgot I wasn't supposed to talk about that."

The others offered cautious chuckles. Thankfully, Director Clark entered, and he focused on the two women. "Sit down," he ordered. Instantly, the bomb was defused, and the team returned to being ready for action.

The director waited for them to be seated before he nodded to Vernon to activate the smart screen at the end of the table. A video of a mountain village began its promotional sales pitch. *"Located in the Blue Ridge Mountains, Helen, Georgia is roughly 100 miles north of Atlanta and sits at an elevation of 1,400 feet."*

"Fast-forward, Vernon, to the resort," the director interrupted. "This will be the location of our next assignment." At the end of the promo, the director continued. "As you can see, it is a beautiful setting. Helen, Georgia is a small town with lots of Bavarian charm that, along with the Southern charm of the Blue Ridge Mountains, European guests will certainly enjoy. The resort was chosen for its isolated location outside of town as well as its proximity to a large international center such as Atlanta."

"Chosen for what, Director?" asked Carter Johnson.

"It will be the conference setting for this year's Universal Reckoning Initiative. We'll just call them the URI for our purposes here."

Carter let out a whistle and leaned back in his chair. "That's a lot of brain power coming to our shores."

"Exactly. I've been secretly working on this for a year at the request of President Austin. He understands the importance of this group. President Austin attended last year and Vice President Warren the year before that."

"I'll be honest, I didn't know anything about them until you asked me to do research several months ago," Tessa admitted as she passed out folders to the other Enigma members.

"That's the way we like it, Tessa," the director admitted sternly.

There was a certain amount of surprise in the team's expressions as they stared at Director Clark.

"How do you think Enigma is funded?" asked Chase. "Part of the Universal Reckoning Initiative—sorry, URI, have had us under their thumbs from the beginning."

"I don't appreciate your tone, Captain Hunter," the director growled. "Not once have they ever interfered with our work or tried to influence our creator, President Austin. All they've ever wanted was a safer, healthier world."

"It sounds like you think this is about to change," added Tessa.

"Yes, well, I fear that it might. There are dangerous people trying to influence the group. Perhaps if Vernon will roll the next few minutes about the group, it will save time."

Once more, Vernon started the information reel on the smart screen.

"The annual meeting of the Universal Reckoning Initiative is a three-day forum for informal discussions to foster dialogue between Europe and North America. The annual meeting grew out of an abundance of concern expressed by leaders of both the political and industrial realm on both sides of the Atlantic. The collective gathering of European and North American leaders embraces the idea to work closely together to solve common geopolitical, economic, and environmental objectives to obtain a more peaceful and stabilized future for mankind."

Agent Nicholas Zoric, a Serbian by birth, released a flippant snicker. "Where were they during the Bosnian War?"

"The Serbs gave as good as they got, Agent Zoric. Shut up and listen." The director leveled a dark glare that would have stopped a stampeding buffalo from charging as he lifted a hand for the video to stop.

The Serbian narrowed his squinty rat-shaped eyes and clamped his mouth into a hard straight line.

"And just so you know," the director went on, "a young man attended these meetings before becoming president of the United States. Care to guess who that was? No? President Bill Clinton. He initiated Operation Deliberate Force, a NATO military response. It would have been a lot worse if he hadn't stepped in and used force to bring things under control. Remember that, Agent Zoric." The director lowered his hand, and the video continued.

"Each year, over two hundred political leaders and experts in the fields of industry, finance, labor, and academia are enlisted to brainstorm new ideas and possible solutions to today's growing domestic and international problems. Some years, the media has been invited to participate with strict guidelines.Roughly two-thirds of the participants are from Europe, the rest from North America. Only one third of the participants are involved in politics and governments, leaving the rest to other fields as mentioned earlier."

Once more, Vernon turned off the video and hit a few other keys and watched for the director to give him a signal.

"Tessa has created a brief Q&A sheet for you to help close a few gaps. Tessa, did you also send them a zip file?"

"Yes, sir. It's time sensitive and can't be opened until Vernon unlocks it after our meeting."

"Thank you."

"So why the big concern now?" Samantha Cordova asked, glancing over the sheet Tessa had given her. "If this is every year and you've never mentioned it to us…"

The director raised his chin at Vernon, and a large photo of a man appeared on the screen. Tessa sucked in her breath, and Chase slowly rose from his seat.

"This, my friends, is the reason. Meet Andre Lavelle Vion. He is a citizen of both France and the US. I can't emphasize enough that he scares the hell of out of me."

CHAPTER 7

Although Tessa's shock failed to match Chase's anger, she managed to slip her hand around his fist, drawing attention back to her. She tapped his skin lightly before she withdrew her hand. It was enough to break his trance focused on the screen picture of Andre Lavelle Vion. From the way his jaw tightened and released, he was not only doing a slow burn but evaluating this latest news.

"This is the guy who had a hit put out on me at Christmas. How could he be invited to such a meeting, Director?" he asked.

"We couldn't tie him to that, Chase," the director reminded him. "Although we know it came from an outsourced group called Goliath, there was no evidence he was part of that organization."

Tessa remembered all too well how she'd left Chase in charge of her children while she got stuck in a snowstorm near Reno, Nevada. Although her children thought it was the most fun, they'd ever experienced, Chase had battled several encounters with a criminal element who tried to kill him that night.

"He's been invisible for years. I know. I've tried to find him," Chase reminded the director.

That was news to Tessa. By the creased brows and narrowed glances from the other agents' faces, they, too, were surprised. This was not a good time to quiz him about the quest to find the man on the screen.

46

Andre had saved both of them during the storm just a few days earlier. How smug the man had appeared when he delivered Chase to her waiting arms. The Frenchman also made it possible for her to escape the rising water in their cabin by forcing the door open to grab her.

There was a heightened awareness in Chase after he survived. The following morning, when the Frenchman had saluted them from his waiting car, Chase said nothing about knowing the stranger on a personal basis. Now it fit. At the time, she was still too caught up in the passion that had engulfed them the night before. Even now, remembering how his body entwined with hers clouded any rational thought she possessed.

Several others asked a few questions while Chase poured two mugs of coffee. He handed one to Tessa and sent her a weak smile. "Your hands were cold. Thought maybe you could use this."

She always held her coffee cup with both hands to let the heat seep through her fingers. He squeezed her shoulder, glaring straight-faced at the larger-than-life picture of the Frenchman.

"Director, if you've kept this such a secret from us, why are you telling us now?" Tessa asked.

"Because, this year, he's finally wormed his way into an invitation. There's always been mention of his name because of his contributions to science and global pandemic health. Although there is no formal application to attend or be a participant in this forum, the steering committee often submits names. If that name is suggested by at least three members, then the chairman more times than not sends an invitation."

"In spite of your concern, you still invited him?" Tessa turned to Chase, confused. "I don't understand. How has he been so elusive? Enigma could track a gnat across the Rub' Al-Khali Desert, blindfolded. And you'd be leading the charge."

The last comment drew a few chuckles. Director Clark lowered his head to hide a smirk but managed to speak as he folded his hands on the table. "It's complicated."

Chase went rigid, with arms crossed on his chest and the veins prominently displayed beneath his many tattoos. She hated being kept out of the loop like she was a security risk. Clearly, they were in possession of information she knew nothing about.

"We'll visit your concerns after the meeting in my office, Tessa.

But, for now, I want to continue if you're finished with your colorful descriptions of what we do here."

"Yes, sir. Thank you." No one could make you feel like you'd been taken to the woodshed like Director Benjamin Clark. Samantha dared to make eye contact with her, arched a perfect eyebrow, and let one corner of her generous red lips lift at one side.

She wanted to sulk, roll her eyes, and pretend she wasn't listening, but that would get her a few hours of one-on-one refresher training with Samantha in the gym. Considering how she'd been feeling the last few days, she decided to be the devoted agent who hung on to every word anyone had to say—especially the boss.

Note to self. Get a doctor's appointment.

The director continued as if he wanted to tread lightly going forward. "Andre Lavelle Vion, as many know, has made his life's work harvesting plasma into a big business. He is now either the largest shareholder or flat-out owner of nine out of ten of the largest plasma banks in the world. And the other smaller ones have his fingerprints all over them—either sits on the board, is a stockholder, or has created an endowment for research."

"And this makes him dangerous?" Tessa dared asked because no one else would.

Samantha leaned forward in her chair to enlighten her. "This is the liquid portion of blood. About 55 percent of our blood is plasma, and the rest is red blood cells, white blood cells, and platelets suspended in the extraction. Plasma contains vital proteins and gamma globulin. One of the important things is an antihemophilic factor. I know this because I have a cousin who is a hemophiliac. He needs a plasma-derived concentrate to help with blood clotting."

Tessa skimmed the information she'd prepared. "Sorry. I didn't have time to read all of this. The director made a list of things he wanted me to download for you. This graph indicates there are roughly 1.125 million cases of hemophilia worldwide."

"I think when my cousin was diagnosed, there were maybe less than thirty-three-thousand cases in the US."

"So, is he dangerous because he's withholding treatment or jacking up the price?" Tessa continued.

"Actually, he has made it free for those who need this specific treatment. The dangerous part is that he now monopolizes much of the plasma in the world." The director pointed to Vernon again who pulled up a slide with more facts. "Plasma is commonly given in trauma cases, burn and shock patients, as well as for severe liver disease and, of course, the multiple clotting factor deficiencies. It works to boost the patient's blood volume, which, in turn, can prevent shock. Pharmaceutical companies use it to make treatments for conditions such as immune deficiencies and bleeding disorders."

"Let me guess," Zoric groaned. "He also owns pharmaceutical companies."

The director nodded. "Not all of them. But enough to make a difference if he wanted to corner the market. The one in France is the largest in the world. Rumors are he's a silent partner. The one in India and Austria lists him on the board of directors and as top shareholder."

Carter Johnson, a man of science himself, rubbed the stubble on his chin. "Tessa included a list of last year's guest list at the URI meeting. Lots of rich nerds attended along with political darlings."

"And there lies another concern. It's also another reason he finally was admitted to this rather unique club. The old adage, 'Keep your friends close and your enemies closer,' is certainly appropriate here. In the inner circle of the White House, Downing Street and, believe it or not, the United Nations, there are rumors Andre Vion has plans to run for president in the near future."

"In spite of the fact he was born in Philadelphia, I don't think the American people would go for that, considering he also has French citizenship and lived most of his life there," Tessa put in.

"It might surprise you that several people have risen to powerful positions after attending the URI: President Buck Austin, Vice President Warren, Prime Minister Joseph Bishop, the now Secretary of State Bonnie Finley. Even I have been considered for several positions. There have been many others over the last fifty years. Theodore Roosevelt once said, 'Walk softly and carry a big stick; you will go far.' This is exactly what Andre Lavelle Vion is doing." He blinked at Vernon who cut the video feed. "So, this time around, you will be attending with me." He lifted a sheet of paper to read off names. "Agent Samantha Cordova, you'll be attending as a well-known economy expert on the Continuity and Disruption of Global Financial Markets. Agent Carter Johnson, you'll spearhead several symposiums on the future of space exploration and innovative solutions."

Carter yawned until the director leveled one of his I-can-melt-steel, looks. "Oh sorry." He gave a thumbs-up. "No problem. I'm on it."

According to the director, Agent Vernon Kemp and Agent Zoric would get their assignments by end of day.

"Did you save the best for last?" Captain Hunter asked in a stern voice. "I'm assuming you have something for Tessa and myself."

"Indeed. Chase, you will be our expert on concerns with Russia and China. Ukraine has also been added this year for obvious reasons. Several from NATO who plan to attend can assist and serve in anyway deemed necessary."

"Tessa, you will serve on the Geopolitical Realignment panel. You have a great deal of insight to this topic, and it felt like a good fit."

"I'd be happy to do that, Director. Who takes the lead on the committee?"

"The devil incarnate. Andre Lavelle Vion will be the chairperson. "

CHAPTER 8

"Absolutely not," Captain Hunter growled. "He's a sadistic psychopath, and I don't want Tessa near him."

"We both know this is a way to corner him, Chase," the director spoke calmly. "He'll make mistakes, unlike other times."

"Too dangerous." He leaned back in his chair.

"I'm sitting right here. Don't I get a say in this?" Tessa interjected. "I'm going to be surrounded by Enigma no matter where I go. I imagine our own security people will be there, too. Besides, he didn't seem that scary and he saved both our lives."

The team was quickly briefed on what had happened at the resort where they had spent their first night together.

"When we had lunch—"

Chase jerked his head around to stare at her. "You had lunch with him? You never told me that?"

"There was a lot going on, if you remember. We were never alone. There was a lot of activity at the resort. I knew he was a suspect. I'm not a rookie anymore, Chase. He was a gentleman and talked about wanting to make the world a better place. He wasn't the guy you and the director are describing."

Captain Hunter's heart skipped a beat. The two of them had spent time together while he was gone that day. He should never have left her there knowing what Vion was capable of and the kind of woman the man was attracted to. "I know you're not a rookie. But you are too trusting."

From the smirks on their faces, the rest of the team were enjoying watching the two argue. Their silence was deafening. He decided to not to pursue it further, knowing it was only a matter of time until they banded together to level an unbearable amount of good-natured harassment.

"I've already decided, Chase. We can discuss it further after the meeting." The director once again took on the sternness of a hungry bald eagle about to swoop in for lunch. "This report has been buried over the years to preserve Vion's stellar reputation. He gives generously to charities, political parties, and supports cutting-edge advancements in medicine. His biography covers the passion for curing diseases such as hemophilia and other blood disorders as well as traumatic injuries suffered in battle."

"Yet, his halo is a little tarnished?" Nicholas Zoric asked.

"Let me go back in time. In Vion's younger days, he fell in love with a music major with considerable talent when he was working on his PhD in chemistry. She was considerably younger than him, and they made a striking couple on campus. Problems started almost from the beginning. He was possessive, manipulative, wanted to control her time, and resented her practice sessions, which were required. Her grades suffered and, ultimately, she lost her scholarship. That gave Vion another opportunity to control her by offering to pay her tuition."

Chase's body went on alert. He wanted to interrupt but twisted his mouth to chew the inside of his bottom lip. It kept him from getting ahead of the director with what he already knew.

"What happened to her? I didn't see where he ever married," Tessa asked slowly.

The director sighed. "At first, she sank into a deep depression. Vion isolated her from friends, family, and her music, thinking he would be enough to break through her sickness. One night, when he was teaching a lab, she committed suicide."

A few of the team lowered their eyes or shook their heads, but Tessa gasped and covered her heart.

"He must have been devastated. This is what turned him into—what?" Tessa asked. "A devoted scientist and entrepreneur who has revolutionized many of the medicines and technologies we take for granted today? I'm telling you, the man I met is not the monster you suggest."

Chase wanted to tell her the truth. He'd planned to tell her since they first met, but couldn't. There was never any reason. In the back of his mind, he'd thought there would never be a time when she was exposed to the monster Andre Lavelle Vion had become. But here they were, getting ready to set her up as the ultimate sacrifice to keep the devil himself from trying to take over the free world.

The director took a deep breath. "Yes, Tessa, he can be very charming. Over the years, there have been other women in his life. They either disappear from family and friends after a while or refuse to talk about their experience. All of them have had physical characteristics of his first love, Abigail. He has a type for sure." He nodded to Vernon who again clicked his computer to open a picture on the smart board.

Tessa stared at the screen. "She looks like me," she whispered.

"She could be your double," Chase admitted.

Carter whistled at the same time Zoric frowned the director's way. "I don't like where this is headed."

"He disguised who he really is when he saw Tessa," Samantha added in a serious tone. "We all know how gullible she is. This is not going to end well. Don't forget how the Tribesman managed to worm his way into her life."

"Shut your mouth, Sam," Tessa snapped. "I don't need you to remind me my decisions haven't always been the best."

"Yeah, well, I'm still waiting for your best moment. And you are a rookie. Baking cookies for the school bazaar or even tagging along to distract the crown prince of Saudi Arabia doesn't put you in the same league as us."

"So, you keep telling me. It's not my fault you feel threatened by me. Maybe if you weren't such a—"

"That's enough, you two," the director barked.

"Why do you always stop them when it's getting good?" Carter smiled wolfishly at the two women.

"Excuse me, Director." Tessa scooted her chair away from the table. "I need some air."

Chase tried to touch her hand, but she jerked away and headed to the door. When the door slammed shut, the men flinched.

Samantha grinned victoriously. "A bit touchy," she said sweetly.

The director cut in, "This seems like a good time to take a break. Chase, I'd like to speak to you in my office. Find Tessa and get her in there now. The rest of you, get some coffee and go over the folder she prepared for you."

"Yes, sir," Chase replied.

~ ~ ~ ~

"You knew from the moment we met that someday you'd use me for your own warped style of revenge and justice." Tessa paced in the director's office, waving her hands as she spoke. "Is that why you kept me around, because, clearly, I'm not cut from the same cloth as all of you. Although I have to say, I've tried my best to fit in and be like all of you. So much for hero worship." Tessa halted in front of him as she crossed her arms across her chest.

Chase had never seen her so angry and hurt. She was pacing, pausing only to point a finger at him as if it were a loaded gun. Her voice was loud, her face red.

"Tessa"—he approached, but didn't touch her—" I fell in love with you the instant I laid eyes on you. And you're right. You aren't like us. That's why we need you. You see things with a pure heart and common sense. We literally shoot first and ask questions later." He reached for her arm.

She stepped back. "Did you know what Abigail looked like before today?"

"Yes. But that had no effect on me when I first saw you. I wanted nothing to do with you. You were trouble. After that first day, all I could think about was if you were safe. Then when we concluded the mission and returned you to your home, all I could think about was how could I see you again. I wanted to reassure myself I didn't need you. But every time I saw you, all I wanted was to hold you. I thought if I did that, it would be enough. It never was."

She unfolded her arms, and the red disappeared from her face. "You used me."

"Yes, but only for Enigma business, not for Andre Vion. I was grateful the president got hurt because you saved his life and no way he was going to let you slip back into the life of a PTA mom." They had been involved in an assassination attempt on the president shortly after they met. She unwittingly had protected him and given him her blood for a lifesaving transfusion. "I thought if I kept you close, I wouldn't have this ache in my chest or want to be a better person. You did that."

"Everyone at Enigma is such great liars."

"You know I'm telling the truth." He captured her hand, and she tried to escape. He forced her into his arms so tight she couldn't move. "You made all the ugliness in my life tolerable. The hate that was eating me alive disappeared over the next couple of years."

"Stop it," she sniffed. "I trusted you."

"I know. I'm sorry. I should have told you after you signed on, and especially when he put a contract on me that Christmas. We made it a point to track down anyone involved in that. And although I couldn't prove it, I was sure Andre Vion had a hand in it. Since then, he disappeared into whatever hole he hides in."

"Did the others know I looked like Abigail?"

"To my knowledge, they knew nothing of that part of my life. Director Clark, of course, knew. He knows everything. I swear the man has some kind of crystal ball that tells him these things." He tried to smile, but the hard dagger glare she leveled against him hurt more than he wanted to admit. "I don't want you to do this."

She shoved him away. "Well, it's my decision to make, not yours."

"No. It's our decision to make. I know you're angry and hurt, but we can work through this."

"Can we?"

"It's my job as your husband to make sure I keep you and our family safe. Let me do that. Do you think if after I pursued you the last couple of years, I'd cast fate to the wind and be okay with this? Tessa, I don't know if you're ready for someone like Vion. Your instincts are good, but your heart sometimes gets in the way. What if I can't protect you? Several years ago, I'd have gladly given you the benefit of the doubt. Not now. Things are different with us."

Tears pooled in the corners of her eyes, but she dabbed them away and shook her head. "Chase," she whispered then stepped into his arms. "I'm hurt."

Chase held her and kissed her forehead. "I love you, baby. There has never been anyone in my heart but you. The only thing that kept me alive in Syria was the thought you were waiting for me. You forgave me for a lot of things I did. Please. Just forgive me this time, too. Whatever you decide to do I'll try and accept it, but don't make this decision without me."

She gazed lovingly at him and kissed his mouth, lingering longer than he'd anticipated.

"I trust you, Chase. I don't know why you kept this from me, but in my heart, I believe you will always protect me."

He embraced her tighter as the director walked into the room. She smiled at the director and excused herself to splash water on her face.

When the door closed, the director turned to Chase. "Did you tell her the truth? The whole story?"

"No. But I will." He wanted to change the subject. "Did you find out why the director of the FBI was with Vion at the Hidden Waters Resort where we stayed? I mean, what the hell?"

"I reached out but got nothing. I even contacted your buddy Agent Dennis Martin. He isn't a fan of the director and says there are a lot of rumors about him not doing his job. I also contacted the Department of Justice. Said they'd look into it."

"Fat chance it's anytime soon. Did you run it by the president? He appointed the Attorney General. Some of these guys sound scared of Vion. What do you think is going on?"

"No idea. But it's big. I didn't talk to the president but I did reach out to the Secret Service to keep a closer eye on him. They actually took my warning seriously. I believe the president meets with the director of the FBI on an almost daily basis, along with the CIA. Maybe he'll bring it up."

"I hope it doesn't trigger some kind of action on Vion's part."

"I have someone at the White House looking into it."

"Good to know."

CHAPTER 9

Chase eyed Tessa for signs of another possible emotional meltdown. She returned self-assured and, other than making too much eye contact with him, it appeared all was perfect in his new normal. He and Tessa had been working together for several years. There was nothing like living with someone intimately to make you understand you had a lot to learn about them.

Touching her in the middle of the night, sharing plans for the future, laughing at things others would never understand, made him feel whole. His experience in Syria almost killed him. Tessa stuck by him in spite of how he betrayed her. Now, once again, he'd confessed to using her. How much longer would she believe in him? She'd chosen him over the Tribesman, but it most likely wouldn't take much, at this point, for her to regret her decision.

Deep in thought, he realized she was standing next to him. He gazed down at her in amazement, as if seeing her for the first time. She had become his world.

Slipping her hand in his, she smiled up at him. "I love you," she whispered as the director walked toward the door and opened it slowly.

Chase slipped his arm around her. "I'm sorry."

"No more secrets that involve us."

He'd started to comment when a young woman entered the

room. Maybe one more lie would keep for a little while longer.

Watching the director link the woman's arm gently through his, followed by a fatherly smile, took Tessa by surprise. He spoke quietly to her, and she nodded as she laid her free hand on top of the arm that held hers. Her dark-blonde hair was straight, hanging down over her breasts. With flawless skin, a perfect fit for a soap commercial, the twenty-something woman revealed a flash of blue eyes when she glanced their way. She halted and leaned into the director. The word timid came to mind as well as frightened. But the director immediately spoke to her in a hushed voice so that she lifted her eyes to him and took a deep breath.

"This is Nora." She attempted to make eye contact then stared down at the floor. Remembering her own first day at Enigma, Tessa understood how confusing and terrifying it could be. Of course, no one had treated her with the kind of gentleness she was seeing the director extend. She, on the other hand, was handcuffed to a desk, threatened within an inch of her life, and thrown in a cell next to a Libyan terrorist. The number of threats promised to rain down on her made Tessa do unspeakable things in order to get her life back. Which, of course, she never did.

"Hello. I'm Tessa. Nice to meet you, Nora. Can I get you a cup of coffee—hot tea?"

The woman hugged the director's arm tighter but spoke without making eye contact. "Hot tea would be nice."

Chase moved to fix her a cup of tea. "Tess, would you like coffee?"

"Thank you, yes. This is Captain Chase Hunter. He's my husband." She sent a questioning look to the director who raised his chin toward the sitting area. It created a feel that you'd entered a library with comfy seating. Tessa moved to one of the brown leather chairs and sat down. "Would you like to join me?"

The director led the woman to a leather chair near Tessa. It occurred to her this meeting was exactly why Chase was sent to get her. Maybe the others could stare down a terrorist and make them cry like a baby, but one thing they couldn't do was show empathy and kindness. They were all brawn with the kind of brains that anticipated three moves ahead of an intended target. If you wanted sympathy for an injury, when you didn't follow the plan or couldn't improvise a better solution, then expect a come-to-Jesus talk with the no-nonsense director. An ass kicking in the gym with some Neanderthal would follow. She knew this from firsthand experience. For her, the Neanderthal was always Agent Samantha Cordova.

But she could calm a savage beast like Captain Hunter, sweet-talk a sadist in charge of interrogation like Zoric, charm a playboy astronaut like Carter Johnson with her chocolate chip cookies then cook dinner for three hungry kids before she helped with homework. She had survived Afghanistan after being kidnapped by the Tribesman, and saved the life of the president. She'd escaped Russia by the skin of her teeth and become instrumental in preserving the friendship between the Crown Prince of Saudi Arabia and the United States. That didn't come with brute intimidation, fire power, or money. It came with having humanity.

Chase and the director sat across from them on the couch after bringing the coffee and tea. Nora reached for the porcelain cup on the coffee table. She appeared more relaxed after taking her first sip of tea. The director leaned back against the cushions.

"Nora has experienced a terrible ordeal recently. She was a guest of Andre Lavelle Vion. It did not go well." The director made eye contact with Tessa as if to say, "Time to do your thing."

"I'm sorry, Nora. Do you feel comfortable talking to us?" Tessa lowered her voice and leaned toward the young woman. When Nora didn't respond, she continued. "Would you be more comfortable if the men left?" Still no answer. Tessa tilted her head toward the door for the men. Quietly, they rose and left the room.

They sat drinking their beverages as Tessa began telling her about her family. She thought sharing how she came to be a part of Enigma would comfort her. But truth be told, that was a little terrifying even for her to remember. What about being kidnapped in Afghanistan by a handsome Kyrgyz tribesman and then falling in love with him? No. That, too, was not a good start.

"How many children do you have?" Nora asked timidly.

"Three. But, when I visited Afghanistan, I brought six orphan girls home with me. They were part of a State Department initiative to introduce them to school and a stable family for a year. All the Afghan-American families ended up adopting the girls. But those sweeties still call me Mom, and I love it. We keep in touch.

We live about forty-five minutes from here."

"Do you have siblings?" Now she made eye contact. That was a good sign.

"Yes. Two brothers. Two overprotective brothers, I might add." Tessa chuckled, thinking of them.

Nora almost smiled. "I have a friend who is like my brother." She went back to sipping tea.

"Brothers are the best."

"I'm alive today because of him." Nora stared into her tea cup.

"How is that?" Tessa asked cautiously. She nearly spilled her coffee when the girl answered.

"He is the personal assistant to Andre Lavelle Vion."

~ ~ ~ ~

Just as he did every morning, Franklin Andersen stared in the mirror at his clean-shaven face and decided he'd aged while working for Andre Lavelle Vion over the last two years. His high cheekbones had taken on a hollow, almost a derelict appearance. Crow's feet etched themselves prominently at the corners of his eyes. Once upon a time, people said he had happy eyes. Now, that impression would no longer be a part of his physical description. His once-tall muscular body, was a bit thin now, in spite of his efforts to stay in shape. Once talkative and full of life, he now felt like a ghoul who followed Dr. Frankenstein to make sure every whim, command, and request was fulfilled as quickly and efficiently as possible.

He'd worked hard at getting the man's respect and confidence, albeit, he wasn't sure respect was part of his psyche. It helped to be a quick study and extremely observant. At first, he felt he'd stepped into a once-in-a-lifetime job working for the famous and elusive Dr. Andre Lavelle Vion. Then things began to come into focus, similar to when you looked through binoculars and had to adjust the lens to clear up the blur. Except, unlike Vion, he had a conscience and began to see that the quiet-spoken doctor the world thought was a miracle worker had a very dark and self-absorbed nature.

The more responsibility he received, the closer Vion kept him at his side until Franklin realized the man had made him a partner in his business dealings, macabre tastes, and the ability to circumvent the law. Once more, he reflected on how he'd gotten to this point.

He'd read about him when he first burst onto the scientific scene years ago, still trying to figure out what he wanted to do with his life. With his own PhD in business management and scientific research, he was quickly noticed by a friend of a friend who introduced him to Vion.

Several months later, he went in a different direction, thinking his life needed a bit of a change—he didn't know what. He pursued several things, and each job proved to fit his craving for adventure while still making a difference. Then the day came when he received an invitation to attend a seminar given by Dr. Vion, along with a personal interview.

Two days later, he packed his bags and followed the man in and out of his business network. The money was astounding. He drove an Audi, stayed at the best hotels, and was given access to a plush apartment if they stayed longer than several weeks. The more responsibility he was given, the closer Vion kept him. He was encouraged on many occasions to participate in parties that compromised his self-worth and better judgment. After deciding enough was enough, and planning to resign, he found a computer file on his laptop that showed him all the questionable behaviors he had willingly participated in.

Nothing was ever said to him about the file, and it disappeared as quickly as it had appeared. The message was clear. No one left Andre Lavelle Vion unless he said so. There was no other way to survive but to do his job. When he'd first been taken to the lab in the Cascade Mountains, he realized the man was harvesting plasma without the victims' permission. The worst part was, if it were a beautiful woman, then he harvested more than plasma until his appetite had been satisfied. No one dared ask what became of these people or where they came from. Not even him. His shame weighed heavily on his soul.

He found courage the day Vion pulled the sheet back from the young woman in the icy room with purple lights.

It was Nora, the girl next door who had been like his little sister growing up. Later, it had become something more, but she was much more of a free spirit than him, and he never expressed how he felt. She idolized him and told people he was her big brother.

Running interference with boyfriends who weren't good enough for her or being her plus one when needed, Franklin never let her down.

Seeing her lying on the table, he knew the hell the next ten hours might be for her and how it would end. Deep inside him, he found the courage to sabotage the grid long enough to help her escape. He wrote down a phone number on the palm of her hand, afraid in her addled state of mind she might forget. Knowing his life was on the line, he reassured her, in spite of the tears, if she called the number, people would rescue her.

They were Enigma.

CHAPTER 10

Tessa watched Nora stand and move to the floor-to-ceiling windows looking out over the Sacramento University of Science and Technology.

Enigma was based in twelve universities across the country. It was an ever-evolving pool of bright minds who could ease into the world of national security after being observed for their four years of learning. Students went on to be teachers, engineers, entrepreneurs, entertainers, medical professionals, and studied other typical fields you would find at a university. Others melted into the shadows of national security in one form or another depending on their abilities and fortitude.

Of course, Tessa seriously doubted Nora knew any of that information. She watched her hug her arms as if she were cold. There was an oversized Sherpa throw folded neatly at the end of the couch. Many a meeting had ended up in this office where she'd been given instructions or most likely, a stern talking to, and she always got cold. The man kept the room at sixty-five degrees. His excuse was he didn't want anyone to get comfortable enough to make small talk while sitting in his office. Mission accomplished.

"Here. Wrap this around our shoulders. I got it for the director one Christmas. I think I'm the only one who ever uses it." Tessa handed her the throw.

"Thank you," she whispered. "I'm not sure I'll ever be warm again." She offered a shy smile. "You seem a little out of place here, Tessa."

"You have no idea," she chuckled. "I ended up here a few years ago by accident and never left. I have to say, it's been quite an adventure. Although the folks here act and look like they belong on the cover of a futuristic robot military magazine, they all have a heart for justice to make the world a better place. Maybe that's why I stayed. I believe in what they're doing. I don't know much about this Vion man, but the director and my husband appear to think he is a real dangerous character, not only to those who come in contact with him but our country as well."

"I agree. The man is a monster." She turned her attention back to the common area outside.

"If you want to talk about it, I'll listen. But I'm here either way. Those guys have a tendency to make people feel uncomfortable at times. My husband can be pretty intense when he's trying to get to the bottom of a problem. The director is our resident bully."

"Your director has been incredibly sweet. I can't imagine him being a bully."

"Sweet?" Tessa gasped. "Don't let him hear you say that," she chuckled. "Out of all of the words in the world, I would never have labeled him sweet. But clearly, he has treated you well."

"If I could get another cup of tea, I think I'd like to tell you a few things about why I'm here." Nora pulled the throw tighter around her shoulders.

Tessa laid her palm on the back of the woman's hand and smiled. "I could use another cup of coffee, too."

~ ~ ~ ~

Director Benjamin Clark and Captain Chase Hunter escorted Tessa back to the conference room where the others waited. Walking slowly, the director asked her if she had any questions or reservations before talking to the team. She shook her head and assured him she was good.

"Tessa, the director told me Nora's story. I'm glad you had a chance to talk to her." Chase caught her hand and squeezed.

She returned the gesture, letting the anger she'd dumped on him earlier evaporate. "I understand now why you were upset. The man is a monster."

Now she wanted to do this—for Nora.

"I know you want to make a difference here, but there are things that can't be fixed, Tessa. The thought of you being near that guy sickens me. I'll have to be working, too, and I can't have my eyes on you every minute."

"Seriously, Chase? How many times have you used me as bait?" she asked flatly. "I'm probably more protected this time than any other op we've done. We don't even know if he'll remember me or think I look enough like this Abigail, to trip him up."

"We have people who can fix the problem of appearance," the director offered, touching the doorknob of the conference room.

"No. I go in like I am. If I look too much like her, he'll suspect something." Then she stopped and stared up at Chase. "You never did share why you hate him so much or your history with the man." She caught a glance between Chase and the director and pulled free of his hand. "I'm always the last to know about Enigma's little powerplay because, deep down, you don't think I can do the job."

"We can't stand out here all day and listen to your pity-party antics in order to get your way, Tessa." The director now wore one of those hungry-eagle glares. "I don't have time for it. You'll be filled in on what you need to know in order to make this plan successful, just like always. And if I thought for one minute you couldn't do the job, I would have let Zoric have his fun with you like the very first day you stumbled into Enigma's hornet's nest."

Tessa clamped her mouth shut and dared to glare at her boss. She wanted to stomp her foot in protest, but he was right. She didn't need to know the whole story, just how to do her part in getting this guy.

"Yes, sir," she managed to say firmly.

A few on the team were on their laptops, most likely going over the information sent to them about the mission. Zoric read his paper files, since he avoided the computer at all costs. The modern world annoyed him, and he preferred old-school methods on most things.

They glanced up and one by one, closed their laptops. In that moment, Tessa realized how much she loved each of them, even Samantha. They had changed her life in ways she would have never imagined a few years ago. Their rhetoric could be harsh at times, especially concerning her. But it made her stronger and better at her job. She knew they held a special place in their hearts for her and would go through hell and high water to make sure no harm came to her. Maybe she was feeling sentimental after hearing Nora retell her story.

Without being told, Vernon retrieved a picture of Nora and placed it on the screen. One was of her a year ago and the side-by-side picture was of her now. There was a marked difference. The light had gone from her eyes, for sure.

"I just finished an interview with Nora Olsen." Tessa pulled her chair out and sat down. Chase chose to stand behind her, leaning against the wall with his arms folded across his chest. She knew from experience he was stewing about this mission and wasn't going to jeopardize her safety or well-being. The man loved her. That, she would never doubt.

"Why didn't she come to talk to us?" Carter Johnson inquired.

"She's still a little shell-shocked at her ordeal, I think," Tessa explained. "Nora had been hiking with friends in Norway about six months ago. She got separated when she decided to take a shortcut. She'd had recently had an ovarian cyst removed and was still not feeling one 100 percent. Thought she'd go back to camp and wait. Of course, we now know she never arrived. Search parties were called out, but there was no trace. The search included helicopters but to no avail. Bad weather moved in soon after, and search parties gave up."

"Called off so soon?" Vernon quizzed. "That's odd."

"Nora, although on the trail, ventured off to take a few pictures. That was the beginning of the end for her. She stumbled upon several men who offered to help her return to camp. Instead, they flew her to one of Andre Vion's laboratories in the US, somewhere in the Cascade Mountains. She isn't sure how she got there because she blacked out after they gave her some water."

"Next thing she knew, she was lying on a table in a room where men in white lab coats were taking vital signs of other patients. She felt weak but alert, unlike the others throughout the room. When they came around to check her out, she pretended to be in the same condition. They poked and prodded her, took skin and blood samples, and overall performed invasive procedures. At times, she was fully awake, and other times semiconscious." Tessa took a deep breath before moving on, giving them a moment to digest the scene she'd presented.

"Nora wasn't sure how long she'd been there. But, one day, Andre Vion showed up. He immediately took a liking to her and provided a warm blanket for her comfort. She tried to speak but couldn't. Something inside her prevented speech. Fear, drugs, whatever it was, she was powerless to ask for help. Then she saw the boyfriend she had growing up, staring at her in horror. She thought Vion, with his interest, planned to save her from more tests and exams. As the medications wore off, she began to understand what was planned for her. Soon, she was taken to a cabin that turned out to be the quarters of Vion."

Tessa paused long enough to glance at Director Clark, hoping he could now fill in the gaps. Speaking of the man's plans disturbed her too much to continue. Chase stepped forward and pulled out a chair next to her and stretched his arm across the back of her seat. She placed her hand on his thigh for strength, and he quickly laid his free hand on top of hers, giving her the instant comfort she craved.

The director didn't skip a beat. He knew she couldn't go on, so he finished the story.

~ ~ ~ ~

Franklin Andersen lay in his bed, staring at the ceiling. He kept wondering if Nora had escaped successfully. How long had it been since he helped her run away? Each night, he replayed the nightmare over and over in his head. What was done was done.

The first thing that always came to mind was her shock when he entered the cabin. She was standing near the fireplace, looking frail and helpless. But when she saw him, she ran into his arms. They clung to each other for several minutes before he pushed her away.

"You've got to get out of here. He means you harm and will abuse you until you can no longer stand it, Nora."

"Why? What have I done? Come with me. They were draining those people's blood when I was brought here. Why? Were they sick?"

"No, they were as healthy as you. Human guinea pigs."

"Were they dead. I thought I heard begging."

"Yes. They always beg. He has it filmed to watch later. But they all die. As you will, if you don't do exactly what I say. He has a type, and you're it. Trust me, you are better off dead than what you'll go through in the next few hours. I've taken down the sensors on the perimeter." Even as he talked, he forced her to wear clothes that would camouflage her as she escaped. The smell was horrific, but at least the dogs would not track her scent. Finally, he wrote the phone number of someone at Enigma on the palm of her hand. There was a small backpack with a map and a few supplies. She was so weak; he didn't know whether she'd get very far. The terrain was treacherous and unforgiving. There were no cameras the way he sent her because it was nearly impossible to trek. But she was an experienced hiker and an Olympic athlete in spite of her helpless appearance.

"Go! Now! I can't come with you. Tell Enigma you saw me."

"Who are they?"

"Friends." He shoved her out the back door and watched her stumble at first then pick up speed. He prayed to God she made it. His training had allowed him to sneak back without being detected. His conscience, however, was plagued with guilt, knowing his hand had released the dogs on Vion's orders. Those men who searched for Nora were as good as dead when the dogs found them.

Andre Lavelle Vion had never mentioned the woman again or acted disappointed at the missed opportunity. Several days later, there was another person to amuse him. This time, the person didn't escape. To prove himself, he worked longer hours and became meticulous at each assignment given. Once, he overheard Vion tell several of the lab-coat men, if they worked as hard as Andersen, they would already be years ahead of what he wanted.

What Vion really wanted was beyond his reasoning power. He was one of the richest men in the world and admired in many circles. The darkness within the man's heart had destroyed any kind of soul he might have. Hopefully, he could also escape this invisible prison. But, for now, he had to stay to make sure others would discover the darkness of his evil.

It would help if he knew if Nora survived. Maybe then, he could finish what he started. Guilt was an isolating and dangerous companion.

CHAPTER 11

Maybe it was dwelling on the fact Tessa had exactly five weeks to get her ducks in a row that made her feel anxious and, to be honest, a little cranky. Three weeks! Then off to Atlanta. In the meantime, there were arrangements to make for the children. Her parents were flying out and, along with the neighbors, the Ervins, planned to help out while she was gone. Although it would only be a few days, she didn't want the children's father to be totally in charge. He wasn't dependable.

And then there was Nora. Although getting stronger each day, her simple desire for friendship and security also weighed on her. At one point, she had her brought to her house in Grass Valley to witness what real chaos entailed. Surprisingly, she brightened and helped out with the cooking and laundry. Tessa guessed having normal things going ninety to nothing acted as an emotional block to thinking about her ordeal with Andre Lavelle Vion.

Add in a new husband who was handsome, ever dependable, and understanding in spite of this being a new way of life. When she thought of him at odd moments, a fire built up inside her only he could quench. He had given her the desire to belong to another human. They'd made their peace with each other over what her role would be during the Universal Reckoning Initiative. To add to the stress, they still hadn't told the children, her ex-husband, or her parents they had gotten married. Things had happened so fast. He stayed next door at the Ervins who were like family to her. When the children went to school, they had quality time to themselves.

Add all that up together, and it was no wonder she wasn't feeling well. Tired. Not hungry. Hungry. What was going on? Granted, the last couple of months, no, the last year had been one of those you never forgot. Without telling Chase, she made an appointment with the doctor. There wasn't any room for mistakes on this mission. Andre Lavelle Vion needed to be stopped. Whatever was going on with her body, she wanted it to be taken care of before she went into character.

On top of everything else, Chase planned to tell her parents they married without them being present. If that didn't put a person over the edge, she wasn't sure what would. Her dad—being a daddy's girl had its disadvantages, along with having two brothers. They believed their God-given right and job was to watch over her to insure she made good choices. The announcement of her elopement would likely land Chase in the hot seat.

The paper on the examining table always sounded louder when it moved in such a small space. It crinkled and stuck to her skin as Tessa slid off the surface until her bare feet touched the ice-cold floor. These yearly exams never got easier, and once more she thought of Eve in the Garden of Eden and how she'd screwed it up for women for eternity. She planned to confront her once she got to those pearly gates and give her a piece of her mind. If possible, she planned to shove an apple down her throat. She would refrain from yelling, "Take that, bitch." But the thought made her grin, nonetheless.

The appointment had been scheduled for a year, as was customary, but given she wasn't feeling well, Dr. Patel fit her in earlier than planned. She was one of the doctors Enigma used from time to time for their staff. She understood the importance of being healthy for the kinds of work they performed.

By the time she arrived, she was miserable. Going to Syria had beaten her up badly, both physically and mentally. Shouldn't she be over that by now? There was a chance she'd picked up a bug there, and that would explain why she felt lethargic and out of sorts. Besides the usual female invasive exam, the doctor had ordered blood work the day before at her request.

Slipping into her jeans and pullover, she grabbed up her purse and headed out into the hall.

One of the nurses smiled her way. "Hey, Tessa," the nurse called, coming around the high divider separating the work station from the patients. "Dr. Patel is waiting for you. You can go right in. Come on. I'll walk you there."

Tessa nodded and followed obediently as the nurse, whose name she couldn't remember, chatted about the weather. "Thanks." She tried to fake a smile as she stepped inside.

"Close the door, Tessa," the doctor mumbled without looking up from the stack of papers she imagined was her medical history.

Dr. Patel was a young OBGYN doctor of Asian-Indian heritage. She was short, cute, and, according to rumors, quite the dancer at the local cowboy watering hole in town. Her dark eyes sparkled, making Tessa grin at the impish expression on her round face. However, the woman was serious as a heart attack when it came to her job and the ladies she took care of.

"I don't expect any problems with the exam. Be sure to get your mammogram."

"Mammogram? I thought I had a few years until I had to start that."

The doctor glanced back over her chart and nodded. "Oh, you're right. Never mind. Considering your condition, I would have canceled it anyway."

"My condition? What's wrong with me? I feel like crap."

The doctor clicked her tongue. "I'm afraid you have the Egyptian flu." She smiled.

"Egyptian flu?" she moaned. "I've never heard of it. Hopefully that isn't the new pandemic."

"No. No. Been around since the beginning of time." She chuckled. "You don't know what I'm talking about, do you?"

Tessa frowned. "Egyptian flu?" She shrugged at the doctor.

"Tessa, you're going to be a mummy! Get it?"

Tessa swayed in the chair. The doctor rushed around to her and called for the nurse. Next thing she knew, the doctor had put a cold compress on her forehead and spoke softly to her.

"I'm pregnant?" she whispered.

The doctor handed her a cup of water. "Not far along. Maybe four to six weeks. When was your last period?"

Tessa tried to remember. She couldn't. "Pregnant?"

"You had no idea?"

"How—"

"You have three kids. Surely you know how." The doctor patted her on the shoulder. "I'm sure Mr. Scott will be excited."

"There is no Mr. Scott," she confessed. "We divorced. Sort of."

"Oh." The doctor sat on the edge of her desk. "So, who is the lucky daddy?"

Tessa got to her feet. "Thank you, Dr. Patel. I need to go now."

"Sit your butt back in that chair. You're not going anywhere until I know you're okay. Almost lunchtime, and I'm buying. It's been too long since we shared a meal. My next appointment isn't until two thirty. You're eating for two now, so no protests. Besides, I want to hear this juicy story." She wrinkled her nose and chuckled.

Tessa sighed and nodded. "Okay. But I'm not sure you're going to believe it."

The doctor shivered with delight. "Come on. Let's blow this joint. I'm starved."

~ ~ ~ ~

Agent Samantha Cordova watched Tessa walk out of Dr. Patel's office, arm in arm with the physician. The doctor was laughing and telling Tessa she needed to put more meat on her bones. They breezed past her sitting in the waiting room to go in for her own yearly physical with another Enigma doctor. She was well aware that Dr. Patel was Tessa's OBGYN.

"You have got to be kidding me," she mumbled to herself. She wanted to cackle like the evil witch from The Wizard of Oz, but decided to just enjoy the moment as she thought about the possibilities. "I wonder who is going to be the daddy? Our own Captain Hunter or Roman Darya Petrov, who would just love having his own little tribal terrorist."

~ ~ ~ ~

At midafternoon, Tessa stopped by her apartment to pick up a couple of things she wanted to take on this next trip. A light tap at the door surprised her enough she checked security to find Samantha grinning at the camera like a spoiled feline. She ran her hand through her long black ponytail as if it were a seductive toy. Tessa cracked open the door when Samantha pushed her way in without being invited. Staring out into the hall for a few seconds to keep from being drawn into their usual hostile banter, Tessa's mood grew dark as she closed the door carefully as opposed to pulling it off the hinges.

"How did you know I was here?" Tessa scooted a barstool out to sit down. It had been a tiring day.

Samantha drifted around the room in her usual snooping-for-a-suitcase-bomb mentality. "In the neighborhood."

"Not like you to go slumming," Tessa responded indignantly.

"Thought maybe we could have a little time in the gym, sparring before you head home."

"And how did you know I was in town? Seriously, Sam, you've got to get a life and stop following me like a lost puppy. People are beginning to talk. But, no thanks. I need to get home."

The slow evil smile that tantalized men and caused women to turn green with envy spread across her perfect lips. She sauntered up to the end of the bar and propped her hands on the surface then exhaled patiently. "And will you be telling the honorable Captain Hunter tonight that you're pregnant?"

Tessa felt unsteady on her feet as her stomach flip-flopped. She ran to the bathroom and vomited her lunch into the toilet. Next thing she knew, Samantha was handing her a glass of water then leading her into the living room. She got her a cold wet cloth for her head then rubbed both of her arms vigorously.

"Thanks, Sam," Tessa managed to squeak out. "I-I…"

Samantha arched an eyebrow and took a step back. "I saw you come out of Dr. Patel's office this morning. You didn't see me. How far along are you?"

Tessa felt a little wobbly from all the drama and reached a hand out toward Sam. A burst of tears broke the emotional dam she'd been holding back all day. She fell against Sam who awkwardly put an arm around her shoulders. The woman who usually wanted to beat the crap out of her stroked the back of her head gently. It was strange to have the one person, who on many occasions, threatened to kill her and vice versa, then offer comfort. But both women knew their animosity was mostly a show.

"Tessa, how far along?" She pushed her to arm's length.

"Maybe six weeks at most."

"So, I'm guessing you don't know if this baby is Darya's or Chase's."

"I mean, it was just one time with Darya, to say goodbye, and with Chase it's every—"

"Please. Spare me the details. You might embarrass me," Sam moaned.

This caused Tessa to choke on her tears and start laughing. When she first came to Enigma, it was well-known that Samantha had a thing for Captain Hunter. The more he avoided her, the more she pursued him. When Tessa came on the scene, there was an instant dislike. Somewhere along the way, things began to change between them.

"Ladies don't kiss and tell." Tessa dabbed at her eyes.

"Then you're not doing it right," she smirked. "And we both know you're no lady, no matter how you pass yourself off to the others. I swear they're dumber than a box of rocks. You should tell him tonight. We leave in two days."

"This whole thing is centered around me. I can't back out now. He's wanting Vion so bad. I can't bail. Besides it's only a few days and you guys are going into helicopter mode as to my safety, I'm sure. I'd prefer to tell him in a special way, and hopefully he'll be happy. Because honestly, I don't know how he'll react, and if it's negative, then I might not be on my game for the mission. Please, Sam. Don't say a word to him."

"What did the doctor say?"

"She said I was good to go. Just don't try any crazy stunts, get plenty of rest, and eat right. The usual do-this not-that, list. I've already been through this three times, so I know the drill. The last six weeks have been a whirlwind experience. I've never been so happy. I'm just a little—tired. Normal stuff."

In the end, Samantha agreed to keep silent about the unexpected pregnancy. Later, both women wished they'd not made such a promise to each other.

CHAPTER 12

Reno, Nevada was a ninety-minute drive from Grass Valley, unless it was winter. In that case, the weather dictated the length of the trip. Since it was fall, Chase crossed his fingers the rains wouldn't come until November. Several times, he'd crossed the roads around Halloween and had to put chains on his tires to cross the mountains. The drought pretty much promised he wouldn't need to worry about picking up Tessa's parents at the airport.

What did concern him was their reaction to the news their only daughter had married a guy with a questionable past and who would be co-parenting their grandchildren. Fighting the Taliban and Libyan terrorists was one thing. But outmaneuvering three rambunctious kids who were a mix of Darth Vadar and Disney princesses could shake any battle-hardened special-forces soldier.

The worst of the three was Heather, Tessa's youngest. He was convinced if the CIA had her cunning, pouty lips and ability to throw a tantrum while wearing a tiara and a boa, the world would be a safer place. More than once, the little minx had melted his heart and wrapped him ever so gently around her little finger. She was a miniature Tessa, which spoke volumes to his inability to resist her requests. Well, maybe they were demands, but he loved how she tried to circumvent him. His badass routine rarely worked on her. The boys, on the other hand, usually fell into line with one of his laser-beam glares.

When Tessa booted their father, Robert, to the curb, Chase had tried to show up and be a male influence in their lives. They grew use to him dropping by, but a few of the other Enigma agents also participated in this act of friendship. She was a valuable asset to the team, and having her 100 percent to do the work was important.

When it felt like things were returning to normal for her, Chase made the decision to travel to Tennessee to ask Tessa's father for her hand in marriage. There was a time when he would have considered the tradition old-fashioned and a waste of time. But, with Tessa, he wanted everything to be by the book. No missteps that would derail his intention to make her happy for the rest of their lives. The woman had gotten under his skin the day they met, and his life was never the same. After a man-to-man conversation of who he was and tidbits of the kind of life he'd lived, Tessa's father agreed. Rushing home, he finally told Tessa he loved her and proposed. Then Syria happened.

The experience led to him being addicted to pain meds. He was captured, tortured, and fell in with the worsts kind of people who had little value for human life. If it hadn't been for Roman Darya Petrov, a former enemy, he would have died. He saved his life several times during that operation. Tessa married the man Enigma called the Tribesman when they were in Russia, and he was thought to have died in her arms. Both he and Darya had loved her and had nearly killed each other over winning her heart, but near the end, he gave Chase permission to take care of her when he died. After he showed up in Syria, Chase had felt the world come crashing down around him.

To protect Tessa, the Tribesman forced Chase to promise not to tell her he was still alive. Keeping that promise was easy as he spent months healing and learning to walk again. But secrets have a way of bursting forth like a damn no longer able to hold back the flood. Once he had told her the truth, he took her to the man who was legally still her husband. But Tessa forgave the Tribesman for the deception. Whatever happened between the two of them the night Chase left her with him was never discussed, nor did he want to know. Now she was his wife, and he had to make it work, no matter what.

"It's good to see you, son." Mr. Wakefield slapped him on the back as Tessa's mother hugged him and gave him a kiss on the cheek. "Tessa didn't come with you, I see."

He loaded their luggage into the car as Mrs. Wakefield slipped into the back seat of the SUV. That meant, Dad, was going to interrogate him on the ride home. He could feel it.

"No, sir. Robert is in DC, and she needed to pick up the kids from soccer practice and dance classes. I volunteered to come get you."

"Well, that's good of you. Thanks." Another slap on the back before he turned to take his place in the passenger seat. After buckling the seat belt, he turned to Chase. "You seem to be your old self again. I'm happy about that."

"Yes, sir. I'm told I'll be able to tell when it's going to rain for the rest of my life."

"Just like us old folks. Right, Beth?"

"Speak for yourself," she snapped playfully.

Chase glanced in the rearview mirror and found her staring at him. She winked, followed by a wide grin that reminded him of her daughter. He winked back and decided he liked the woman more than he realized.

"Are you two living together?" her father asked out of the blue as he pulled out onto the highway.

"Jinx," she stormed. "Really?" That was her nickname for Tessa's father.

"No, sir."

"Good. Don't think I could abide by that."

"Oh. Dear. Lord!" Beth fumed. "That is none of your business, Jinx."

"Humph," he huffed as he turned in his seat and frowned at her.

"Sir, if we could discuss this later, maybe with Tessa in attendance, then we might be able to answer all your questions and concerns."

"I think that will be just fine, sweetheart." Beth reached up and patted his shoulder. "No worries. Jinx is just being a silly old man."

"Mr. Wakefield, sir, I can assure you I have not brought any disrespect to your daughter's reputation. She is, and will always be, the love of my life. And I'm pretty crazy about the kids, too."

He tried to keep his voice even and unperturbed, in spite of the older man laying down some kind of parental challenge right off the bat.

Chase glanced over at the man who had a silly grin on his face as he stared out the windshield. He had to remember, in the future, it was possible he'd be the same way over Heather when a good-for-nothing guy came calling. Taking a deep breath and holding it for a few seconds, he slowly exhaled only to feel a fist bump on the side of his arm.

"Relax, son. Just doing my job." Mr. Wakefield arched an eyebrow and continued to grin.

"Yes, sir. I know."

That Mr. Wakefield's brother, Jake, didn't tag along was a blessing. The man had tried to kill him once and broke his nose in the process. There was a good possibility he still planned to do him harm in the future. However, Tessa referred to him as an old sweetie. Taking revenge on a family member probably was out of the question. In the meantime, he'd just keep a watchful eye out for booby traps and small explosives.

~ ~ ~ ~

The three kids ran down the porch steps and into the arms of their grandparents when they exited the car. Chase thought of both his grandfathers who had been instrumental in his raising. One, a powerhouse in DC, took him and his little sister with him during travel excursions when he served as ambassador or State Department representative. Living in China with his parents most of the year gave him a warped sense of how the real world operated. The yearly diversion opened his eyes to what was possible.

Papa Hornbuckle lived on the Qualla Reservation in Cherokee, North Carolina. Valuable lessons and history were taught about his Cherokee heritage during each visit. Their adventures took him into the mountains to learn the old ways of the people and how to survive when all else failed. His extended family gave him love and a faith he struggled to embrace.

His parents, who were medical missionaries, gave everything to the poor. When they were killed by Chinese soldiers, his belief in

God hung by a thread. His Cherokee grandfather would tell him, "Just because you've turned loose of the Almighty's hand doesn't mean he has done the same to you." Although he still struggled with religion, he found goodness and faith in a woman who had to be an angel to tolerate him.

The joy Tessa's kids expressed in their rapid conversations and squeals from little Heather warmed his dark heart. How did he manage to fall into such a place with this woman and her life? Knowing she would soon be in the crosshairs of one of the most ruthless and narcissistic men in the world made him question his own judgment.

Andre Lavelle Vion had been part of the reason his life turned wrong-side out. He destroyed the humanity inside him with his own black soul. The man robbed him of the ability to trust his fellow man. If it hadn't been for Director Benjamin Clark and the military, no telling where he'd be today. Even now, it was a struggle to remember the lessons both grandfathers had instilled in him.

Then Tessa Scott stumbled into his life, batting those blue eyes as she told him lie after lie and smelling like chocolate chip cookies. She was the sweetest and most optimistic person he'd ever met. Love came so easily to her. Kindness was nothing short of a spiritual gift, and her faith in a higher power made him both angry and hopeful.

Chase gave a short whistle at the boys and pointed to the luggage he'd set on the driveway that curved in front of the house. That was when he noticed another car parked where the drive exited onto the street. It looked like a rental. Before he could question the boys about the Lexus, each grabbed a piece of luggage and hurried up the porch steps. Heather, of course, skipped along holding her grandpa's hand like she didn't have a care in the world. He followed the three onto the porch before he could ask Heather about the car.

"Does your mom have a visitor?" he asked as the boys pushed the door open and hurried inside.

"Guess so." Heather glanced back at him and leveled one of those sweet smiles. "He talks funny."

"Funny how?" Chase entered the foyer as he watched Tessa hurry out into the hall that led to the kitchen. She cast him a shadowy glance, sending a signal something was amiss. But like a good daughter, she went straight to her parents with hugs and kisses.

"Boys, take Grammy and Papa's luggage to the guest room." Tessa spoke softly to the children, another indication she was trying to hold it all together.

The boys weren't about to hesitate with their grandfather present. He knew for a fact the man made them work when they came to spend the better part of the summer with him.

"Do we have company?" Chase asked as he glanced back through the large dining room windows off the hall.

Tessa paled but gave a weak smile and looped her arm through her mother's. "Yes. Actually, he was just about to leave. He's in the kitchen having a piece of peach pie."

"Peach pie?" her father said enthusiastically. "Did you make me that? What a good girl."

"Yes, Daddy, I did. Hope you don't mind I shared the first piece."

They entered the open-concept kitchen that adjoined the family room. A man stood at the sink, rinsing his plate before sitting it on the bottom. He wore business casual pants and a long-sleeved shirt. Even from behind, he appeared particular about his appearance.

"I see you got my first piece of peach pie." Her father walked up to him with his hand extended. "I'm Jinx. Tessa's dad."

The man pivoted and grasped Mr. Wakefield's hand and smiled as his attention slid to Chase. "I'm Andre Lavelle Vion."

CHAPTER 13

"And you must be Tessa's mother. I know now from whom she inherited her beauty." Andre lifted her hand to his lips and kissed it gently before trading warm smiles.

"What a sweet thing to say, Mr. Vion," she teased.

Chase had the overpowering urge to plant his fist squarely on the man's nose then lecture Tessa's mom about flirting with serial killers.

The children ran into the kitchen, but Chase extended both hands to stop them from getting too close before swinging Heather up into his arms. She took one look at Andre then put her arm around Chase's neck and held him tightly.

"Aww. Another little beauty. Heather, is it?" he asked, taking a step toward Chase who instinctively backed up when Heather buried her face in his neck.

"I'll walk you out," Chase said sternly as he handed Heather off to her grandfather then frowned at Tessa. "I'll be right back."

She exhaled like she'd been holding her breath for a while. Was she afraid for her family or what he'd do to the man?

"Have a great time catching up. It was my pleasure meeting you." Vion brushed past Chase and grinned satanically as he headed toward the front door.

Once both men stepped off the porch, and started down the

driveway, Chase spotted Ken Montgomery next door polishing his pickup truck. An alarm must have gone off, warning about Vion being in Tessa's house. Ken had taken up a position at the Ervins' house. He glanced Chase's way and then raised his chin toward the sedan at the end of the drive. Two men opened the front seat doors and stepped out.

"I see you brought protection." Chase squinted at the two beefy guys waiting for their boss.

"Yes. In my line of work, it pays to be vigilant. So many intellectual thieves, jealous competitors, sore losers, and so on. Not to mention those who like to fling false accusations concerning what they think is true when, in reality, certain people just deserve to die."

Chase stepped around him to stop him from proceeding farther down the drive. Andre halted and peeked around the brick wall of a man before him and held up his hand toward the two who stepped away from the car. Chase noticed how Andre watched Ken reach into the truck for something and was postured in a rigid stance.

"Do you have more to say to me, Captain Hunter? It is still captain, am I correct? You never quite made it to a higher rank because of your obstinate attitude toward taking orders?"

"I think it was more my inability to tolerate people who had no respect for human life. And I often felt the world would be a better place without them. Kind of like you, Andre. I'm waiting for the right time to make my dream of watching the blowflies lay their eggs in your fluids come true."

Andre Vion sobered. The captain knew he wasn't used to being confronted. The idea a person would threaten or promise impending death would be a great deal for Vion to process.

"I'll be on my way, Captain Hunter."

Andre started to step around him, but Chase cut him off again. "Let me be clear, Andre. You stay away from my family. Don't ever speak to those kids again, or I'll make your death a long and painful one. And I'll film it so I can watch it over and over to watch you squeal like a pig caught in a meat grinder."

"Interesting you didn't mention Tessa." Andre's expression had turned dark, and his eyes filled with hatred.

"I know why you're interested in her. So, forget it."

"And I know why you chose her to marry. I wonder if she knows the truth."

"I should gut you right here and now."

Andre turned and looked over his shoulder at the house. "Perhaps, but since the children are watching us from the windows, you might reconsider." Taking in a deep breath then letting it out slowly, he shoved his hands into his pockets. "I'm glad we had this chat."

Chase stepped aside and let him continue down the driveway. Another of Chase's men, Tom Cooper, eased out from the end of the porch. Those two were as protective as they came when it involved anyone on the Enigma team. This was going to be a delicate operation, and Tessa was going to be the most vulnerable. He continued to watch Andre as he entered the back seat of the car then slowly drove away.

"Want us to stick around tonight, Captain?" asked Tom Cooper, a former Marine.

"Nah. I'm here now. He just wanted to rattle me a bit."

"Did he?" Tom asked.

"Yes." He pivoted to head back inside. "Made a pot of chili. I'm sure Tessa seeing you two here will give her more peace of mind. Might keep me from losing my cool as well. I'm not sure why she let him in."

"I could use a hot meal," Ken said, slapping Chase on the back. "Our little tech genius is tracking him even as we speak. If we need to come back, we'll be close by."

~ ~ ~ ~

Tessa was serving up the chili by the time Chase joined them. Her mother was helping Heather set the table, and the boys were listening to their grandfather talk about the new colt born last week. Seeing Ken and Tom behind Chase reassured her that help was not far away when Andre Lavelle Vion decided to make an appearance. She felt unnerved to have him in her home, but the thought of Chase walking in was terrifying. What would he do? Thanks to her parents' arrival, there had been a fifty-fifty chance he wouldn't pull out a semiautomatic and turn the uninvited guest into Swiss cheese.

After introductions for Ken and Tom, the adults sat at the nearby table and the kids at the island bar. They still managed to join in the conversation and, for all practical purposes, it appeared they had forgotten Andre. Tessa's parents dominated the conversation with news from Franklin, Tennessee where she grew up. The kids wanted to know what their cousins were doing and would they be there in the summer when they came to visit the farm in Tennessee.

It was obvious to her that Chase barely spoke during the meal. His two buddies did a lot of head bobbing and grinning at her father's stories. Occasionally, they would catch her attention and sober up then lift their chin in the manner that meant, "I got this. Don't worry." But she did worry. The man that they were trying to stop had been standing in her home. What if Nora had been present?

"Nora was taken to a safe house once your alarm activated. I think Carter and Sam are with her now." Ken spoke to Chase but then turned his focus on Tessa. They'd waited until her parents had turned in for the night and the kids were tucked in tight. "We were here within minutes of Vion arriving. This is why we put extra security in and around your house."

Chase opened the front door. "Appreciate it."

They nodded and disappeared into the night. Tessa had no idea how they got there so fast or where they had been waiting. But if there was a next time, she had little to be concerned about.

As the door closed then latched, Chase turned to her; his "in-control face" had evaporated. She thought for an instant steam might be seeping from his ears. "What happened? Why was he here?"

"I picked up the kids from their after-school activities then ran by the grocery store for a few things. When I got home, we unloaded the car, and the doorbell rang. The boys, like usual, raced to see who could get there first. They were thinking it was my folks. Before I could stop them, they swung the door open." She tried to defuse him by laying her hand on his chest, but she could feel his heart pounding as his jaw tightened and released. "A florist stood there with a bouquet of flowers."

"Flowers."

"Yes." She pointed to the dining room where a vase of iris with sprigs of Queen Anne's lace graced the center of the table. "I turned to get my purse off the foyer table so I could tip him. When I looked up, Andre was holding the flowers. I jumped like a scared toad. He apologized, and the kids laughed themselves silly."

"And you just said 'come on in'?"

"Don't take that tone with me, Chase Hunter. No, I did not. He laughed and stepped inside and immediately teased the boys, keeping the laughter going. Before I could say a word, he introduced himself to the kids and told him we were old friends."

"Tessa, that was a dangerous thing to let happen. You should have ordered him out or gotten your gun and shot him," he fumed.

"In front of my kids?" She jammed her hands on her hips. "Are you insane?"

"You're making me that way."

There was a pause where they simply glared at each other. Tessa hated when they fought; she always had, even before they became husband and wife. Each mission had triggered irritational confrontation that covered up the real issue between them. Rarely was there a solution because there was no such thing as makeup sex between them. Now they had to talk it out, and hopefully their love would spill over into the bedroom.

"Chase…"

He pulled her into his arms and rested his chin on the top of her head. "He scared the hell out of me. Not only because you and the kids were in danger, but because my reflexes kicked in and it was all I could do to keep from pulling my weapon." He huffed a disgruntled growl. "Damn. I hate that guy. We need to have a serious conversation with the kids about answering these kinds of things."

"Without actually telling them the truth of what we do."

"Exactly." He kissed her temple, an act that went a long way to calming herself down. "Say the word, and we'll bail on this one. As badly as I want Vion, I would rather the team and I go in to do this. Stay home and visit with your parents and make sure the kids are safe."

"Martha and Francis are already poised to help out here." They were the neighbors next door that also worked with Enigma. Although they were older agents, their cunning and expertise always lent a degree of comfort when it came to the safety of her children. "Will there be anyone else?"

"Yes. Ken and Tom will be here finishing that apartment over the garage as their cover story. The kids know them already and won't think anything of them being here. I'll show your dad the plans tomorrow and let him think he'll be in charge of the contracting duties."

Tessa gazed up at him and kissed his lips quickly. "Do the guys know this? He's going to be like General Patton on this responsibility."

The comment gave Chase a chance to chuckle at the humor in the situation. "Yeah. They're use to taking orders even when they don't want to. They have their own set of plans to follow for the project. I know they can be stern and more than a little off-putting at times, but I think they'll know how to manage your dad."

"Any tech support?"

"Since Vernon will be a part of our team, he will put his best guy on it. Name is Lazarus."

"I remember now. Lazarus as in raised-from-the-dead Lazarus in the Bible? A chick magnet as I remember. Still makes me nervous."

"Super goth, too."

"I feel better already," she said flippantly. When Chase chuckled softly, she stopped him with another kiss that lingered long enough, she felt his body stir with interest.

Chase finally stepped away and tilted his head toward the Ervin house next door. "As much as I'd like to stay tonight, I better go. Your dad is wanting to know what is going on between us now. Thinks we're living together in sin, I think. Your mom is cool with it though."

"Dads are just like that. And I'd live in sin with you any old day. Maybe I could go next door to tuck you in this time."

~ ~ ~ ~

Andre Lavelle Vion seated himself in the elephant-leather captain-style chair. No matter that the leather cost $10,000 a square foot and he had six chairs and a couch on board. Ethical was not something he generally checked on his must-have list. Without being asked, his steward brought him a sparkling water and a cup of Black Ivory coffee secured from an elephant farm in Thailand. Elephants were fed raw coffee cherries, and caregivers waited for their digestive systems to do their job before the droppings were processed into a rare brew that hinted of chocolate and spices without all the bitterness. Andre felt like he was supporting rural communities and therefore contributing to a greater service than the care of the elephants.

Staring out the window, he let the image of Tessa enter his mind. How could one person remind him of his one true love, Abigail? There were differences, of course, but not enough to separate them entirely. He didn't believe in reincarnation, but was it possible for a spirit of someone from your past to enter another person's soul or body? And Tessa's daughter, Heather, she could have been the very image of Abigail as a child. When those shy, beautiful eyes looked at him, it was as if she knew the connection as well.

Yet she clung to that barbarian of a man, Captain Hunter. If he was her stepfather now, he owed it to the child to save her. He glanced across the aisle to his assistant, Franklin Anderson, for a split second, but it was long enough for him to feel the vibe that his immediate attention was required.

"Yes, sir?" he asked as he seated himself across the small cocktail table. He activated his tablet and waited.

"Tessa Scott Hunter has a young female child named Heather. I expect the two of them will be coming to visit me for an extended stay at my villa in the south of France soon. Make arrangements for their comfort."

Franklin ran his fingers like lightning over the keyboard. "Security issues?"

"Get the usual people to tighten things up there. There will be exams, of course, but it is only routine to make sure there are no problems. Perhaps you can secure their current medical files to guarantee if there is anything we should be made aware of."

"Yes, sir." He typed in the last entry then dared look toward his boss. "Anything else?"

"Perhaps lots of toys, stuffed animals, like unicorns—I believe little girls like those, along with mermaids. Oh, yes, and get a puppy. We'll get a pony after she and I have established a relationship. It will be a comfort to her later on."

"Later on, sir?" Franklin asked carefully.

"Yes. I believe Tessa may be a problem down the road and will meet an unfortunate accident. A pony may be just the thing for my little daughter."

CHAPTER 14

Nothing said home like the bluish haze of the Blue Ridge Mountains. Although the location of this stretch of forest lay in North Georgia, it reminded her of the many vacations she spent as a child, to both the Smokey and Blue Ridge Mountains. As a child, her family often traveled to Gatlinburg then across the mountains into North Carolina and Georgia. It was a way to escape the heat. The mountain streams and thick vegetation made everything ten degrees cooler. Even as a young child, Tessa dreamed of living in the mountains.

Cherokee, North Carolina was about thirty-five miles from their first stop in Gatlinburg. To think she visited Chase's reservation as a child still remained a point of amazement to her. Tessa's family traveled to Georgia to visit family and would hike to places along the Appalachian Trail. Those same trails were roughly fifty miles from the Utugi Mountain Resort where the Enigma team would spend the next few days.

They arrived a day early to get the feel of the area, rehearse their programs or speeches, and examine the outcome expectations of the mission. Tessa understood her part involved playing to Andre's specific behavior, followed by a set of particular consequences that would ultimately impact the success of the mission. The idea she could convince an influential man of the world still baffled her. The intel said otherwise.

Then there was her pregnancy to consider. She remained tired and wondered about the twinge she felt in the lower left side of her abdomen. Since this particular mission involved speaking to leaders, businessmen, and dignitaries, perhaps she would have a little time to plan a special going-home surprise for Chase. In the quiet moments, she watched him on the plane. When he worked, she liked to imagine his response. Would he be instantly euphoric or terrified his past life might affect the unborn child? Maybe a candlelight dinner in their favorite restaurant in Grass Valley could be the staging ground. A quiet evening at home when the children went to stay with their father would also be special. The thoughts of a new baby snuggled to her breast gave her great joy. But then the image of Roman Darya Petrov began to cloud the joy, as she wondered if the baby might be his.

The two were both ethnically darker than most of the men she knew. Chase was half Cherokee, and Darya was half Kyrgyz tribesman. Both had the kind of looks that allowed them to blend into Asian and Middle Eastern cultures without difficulty. When her thoughts traveled down that slippery slope, she felt despondent. It would be the ultimate betrayal for both if she kept this a secret— the two men she loved more than anything, although in different ways. Somewhere between Sacramento and Atlanta, Tessa decided some things were better left a secret.

"I wish I had time to visit my grandfather." Chase came to stand next to her as she stared out the picture windows toward the mountains. "He would love you."

"My heart is here in these mountains, Chase." She leaned into him when he circled her waist.

"I promise, I'll get us here. I'm tired of the rat race of trying to stop threats against the US. It feels like we put out one fire and three more start. We nearly lost each other, and I can't risk that any longer."

"Will Enigma let us go?"

He didn't answer until she turned to him. "I'm sure they will make it difficult." He stepped away and grabbed the rolling cart with their luggage. "Let's get settled in before dinner and then we can meet the others. Our rooms are being debugged." He started toward the elevators.

"I thought that kind of thing was a huge no-no here at the conference."

"It is. But there is always someone who doesn't play by the rules." Chase pulled the cart onto the elevator.

"In this case, Andre Lavelle Vion. Maybe we can finally end whatever he's up to."

"Utugi," he spoke in Cherokee. "Means hope."

"Utugi," she repeated. "A good name for the resort that will give you peace."

~ ~ ~ ~

The pounding of hammers, the occasional shrill grind of a circular saw, and the scraping sound of moving building supplies drifted throughout Tessa's house. Ken Montgomery and Tom Cooper pretended to be carpenter friends of Chase's who had been contracted to finish out the room above her garage. The plumbing for the bathroom had been finished days earlier and, except for painting and installing a mirror, there was nothing left to do. The large combo bedroom and sitting area still required Sheetrock, tape, and mud before painting.

Normally, in a job like this, loud music would be playing to help with the rhythm of the work. But not here, and not this time. Although the mornings remained cool this time of year, the new windows were wide open to help with circulation but mostly to be acutely aware of any unusual noise indicating an intruder on the property or an out-of-place vehicle driving by the house once too often.

Ken stood at the open window and watched Tessa's dad lead the kids out to her SUV he'd pulled to the front a few minutes earlier. At a sharp whistle through his teeth, all three kids looked up at the windows and waved goodbye. He gave a thumbs-up sign and waited until they drove out of sight before touching the earwig.

"They just left." That was what he needed to say before disconnecting. The trackers in the car, their backpacks, and clothing were as thin as a piece of cellophane and smaller than a dime. He'd applied them earlier while they ate breakfast. Tom Cooper had assisted with the backpacks and car while he took care of the clothing and gentle touch to their skin. They would evaporate after five days before needing a second application. If the dots got wet or ripped off, the residue left behind could still give a weak signal in a pinch.

Tessa's parents were not spared trackers, they might end up being targets. Andre's obsessive-compulsive desire to be in control of all the players in any scheme he might be undertaking, especially now that he knew where Tessa lived, presented another layer of concern, not only for her welfare but peace of mind. They couldn't afford to have anyone screwing up her head on this one. Her family was a top priority from the time she came to Enigma. That had to be protected for things to run smoothly.

Tom stared at a piece of computer equipment in what looked like a toolbox. "Trackers are activated and working perfectly, Ken. Tech support is in charge of the kids now. It will probably be twenty minutes before Grandpa Jinx gets back. I think he was stopping at the grocery store for a few things."

"Just going to do a scan of the neighbors to make sure all is as it should be." Ken peered through what resembled binoculars, but had enough spyware on it he'd be able to spot a spider crawling on the moon. He handed them off to Tom in order to check the rear of the property with a fence separating them from some common ground, a service road and, beyond that, a couple of one-acre hobby farms. After they exited the house the night before, they'd secured the perimeter with more sensors. "Anything?"

"Nope." Tom lowered the binoculars. He was a man of few words and Ken's closest friend at Enigma. Built like a tank, he was teased about having the personality of a drunken sloth. But when it was time to fight your way out of trouble, Tom Cooper became the man you hoped had your back.

"Boys?" It was Tessa's mom, Beth. "I have something for you."

Tom carefully secured the binoculars and closed the toolbox for their computer as Ken waited to intercept the epitome of Southern charm. She came down the hall toward the addition holding a pie dish with potholders. Dressed in a denim outfit and a flowery apron on top of that, she grinned her way toward him. Her flip-flops smacked the wood floors softly.

"Here comes trouble," Ken commented sheepishly, enjoying the way she smiled like a ray of sunshine. He imagined Tessa would look like her later in life and knew once again, Captain Hunter was a lucky man.

"Well, that is so right, you rascal." She held up the plate as if it would be a tasty sacrifice to Zeus. "Now Tessa said I should take good care of you boys and make sure you had enough to eat. Here are my cinnamon rolls I just took out of the oven. I'm making my potato soup for lunch. Jinx went to get sourdough bread to go with it. Since y'all ate my daughter's peach pie, I'll make you an apple cobbler for supper."

Tom came to his side and pushed in front to take the cinnamon rolls from her, careful to grasp the potholders. He winked at her and thanked her.

"Mrs. Wakefield—"

"Now, Ken, you call me Beth. You hear me? Tessa told me you boys are family and the kids call you uncle, so don't you be standin' on ceremony." She tilted her head in a flirty kind of way that made him want to chuckle. "Jinx is gonna barbeque a few pork steaks, so you plan on stayin' for supper, too. Well now," she said, pushing into the room in spite of Ken trying to block the entrance. "Lookie here. This is right nice. I think this would be a wonderful place for Jinx and I to stay when we come for a visit."

"Yes, ma'am." Tom failed to stop the icing dripping from the corner of his mouth.

Beth patted him of the cheek. "Now that Captain Hunter and Tessa are…" She paused as if waiting for the men to finish her sentence.

"We better get back to work, Beth," Ken announced, snatching one of the cinnamon rolls. "Tessa gets home and finds out we've gained ten pounds instead of getting her room finished, we might not get paid."

She waved a hand in the air as she spoke. "Oh, that girl. Yes, of course. I'll just get to work on the laundry. Do you know if their washing machine has been broken? There seems to be an awfully lot of it?"

"No, ma'am. I think—"

"I might need one of you big strong fellas to move the couch. Looks like no one has dusted back there since Noah built the Ark. Don't you tell her I said that now."

Tom shifted his eyes to Ken who stood clenching his fist over and over. "I'll be down in a little while, Beth."

"Aren't you the sweetest thing? Thank you so much."

As she disappeared down the hall, Ken turned to his buddy. "She's a distraction. These cinnamon rolls make me want to take a nap. That's where Tessa gets her—whatever it is she does to control all of us. The problem is, Beth has had years of experience doing it. She's pumping us for information."

Tom turned to get back to work. "That apple cobbler might do it for me. I'll spill my guts."

"Just don't let any of those other yahoos at Enigma know she's baking, or they'll be over here to get a free meal."

They returned to work until they heard the garage door go up under the room they were working on, meaning Jinx had returned from the grocery store. They paused long enough to hear the rumble of a motorcycle pull into the circular drive and stop in front.

The man removed his helmet revealing dark hair with a streak of purple on one side. Even before he dismounted, the two men had pulled their weapons and started toward the downstairs. They watched Jinx carry groceries into the kitchen while giving an update to his wife on a funny story the children had told on the way to school.

Tom pulled open the door and rushed out, leveling his Glock at the man stepping up onto the porch. He raised his hands slowly without changing the blasé expression on his face.

CHAPTER 15

Chase met up with Zoric to do a once-over of the grounds while Carter took Vernon with him to survey the inside of the resort. Since both had an eidetic, often called photographic memory, neither man jotted down notes. This was a trait NASA loved in their ex-astronaut and the Pentagon hated with their former tech genius. Vernon knew where all the skeletons were buried, in a matter of speaking. As to Carter, he always knew the answer before they knew what the problem might be. Both men were full of themselves for various reasons and had tended to give their superiors the middle finger over the years.

Taking stock of the outside world around the resort was Chase and Zoric's expertise. They were always in tune with the environment around them. Where most people saw a beautiful landscape, they saw opportunities for a security breach. Trails, detached bungalows, and maintenance buildings were opportunities for escape options or staging grounds for insurgents bent on disrupting the conference. These observations helped them envision alternatives to an otherwise unacceptable outcome. Chase didn't enjoy surprises, and Zoric didn't like not having an escape route. The men had worked together for a number of years and could formulate a plan in a pinch. It had saved their lives more than once.

Samantha and Director Clark were going over the final schedule of events for the participants and making changes to presentation locations for security reasons. There were lots of checklists to give one last once-over and contacts with various personal assistants to make sure the schedule was in order and their specific requests had been met.

Studying the portfolio of Andre Lavelle Vion's accomplishments, corporations, and awards was left to Tessa since she was the designated bait. She couldn't help but be impressed and wondered once more why Enigma, and especially Chase, hated him on such a personal basis. Even though Vion's last target, Nora, had escaped to give them a glimpse of the man's dark side, there was no indication or proof he was a monster. He'd given millions to cancer and hemophilia research and opened numerous plasma collection centers, along with storage facilities across the world. He now owned 99 percent of them. World leaders might be concerned the man might use access as a bargaining chip to escalate his own agenda and influence support.

The afternoon turned sunny and unusually warm for this time of year. The temptation was too great not to escape to the award-winning gardens that riveled the Biltmore Gardens in Ashville, North Carolina. Gardening was a passion and a way to relax for Tessa. Anytime she had an opportunity to visit famous gardens, she jumped at the chance. She only intended to take a short walk to admire them.

~ ~ ~ ~

"Whoa," the guy from the motorcycle said calmly as he raised his hands in slow surrender to the two Enigma agents pointing a gun at his chest.

"Start talking," Ken ordered as Tom holstered his weapon and frisked the biker then nodded to his partner.

The biker lowered his hands and jammed thumbs in his front pockets. "A little intense, aren't you?"

"Intense is me ramming this gun in your mouth to find an exit hole," Ken snarled.

"Normally, I would have already disarmed you, but since Vernon sent me here, I'm guessing you two are security for

Tessa."

"Normally," Ken mocked, "I would have been mopping up your blood by now. Shut the hell up and tell me who you are." Ken eyed him from head to toe and smirked. "Clearly you're not here to make a fashion statement."

"I doubt you'd know, even if I were, considering you are the poster child for a Home Depot ad." His dark eyes blinked slowly as he shifted his weight to one leg. "I'm Lazarus." Before Ken could ask him, he recited his badge number, operating code, and the daily password. "Sorry. I don't know the secret handshake if you're waiting for that."

Ken holstered his weapon just as Jinx walked outside. "Lazarus." He extended his hand in friendship before turning to the other two men. "This guy came to my rescue when I had a flat tire. Followed me home to make sure that spare wouldn't give me trouble. Guess I'll call AAA in a bit. I was telling him about the upstairs project. He says he used to be an architectural engineer and would like to see what you've done."

Ken arched an eyebrow at Lazarus but never got so much as a flinch from him. "Sure," was all he managed to say after narrowing his eyes at the new guy. He remembered hearing rumors concerning Vernon's new protégé but had never met him. The two soldiers avoided headquarters like the plague, even though both had jobs on the university campus. He recalled a few things he had heard about him.

Lazarus was nearly six foot five and so lanky people joked that if he stood sideways and stuck out his tongue, he'd look like a zipper. He sported a goth persona with no apologies, and it seemed to work for him considering how the female students on campus watched his every move. In the bowels of Enigma, he was all business, in spite of the way he dressed. The older agents envied his ability to make dressing in black and gray cool. The leather boots he wore laced up to the middle of his calf, according to several female employees, and reminded them of Robin Hood. The shaggy dark hair parted in the middle and hung down to his chin. It often appeared to not have been combed for several days. The five-o'clock shadow outlined his face to make an already severe jawline more prominent. There was usually a gray-and-black T-shirt sporting a heavy metal band beneath an open leather jacket with silver clasps running down the outside of his arms.

When talking to another Enigma agent or employee, he stood with his weight shifted to one leg and his thumbs jammed in his jean pockets. An intense tightness creased his forehead, as if he might be writing your thoughts and words into code. Because his eyes were dark, it was discussed in the break room that he might be wearing eye shadow or liner. The wide mouth rarely showed amusement. When he did talk, although soft-spoken, it was in a deep voice that tended to cause people to listen carefully. There were rumors he had several black belts in karate and drove a 1947 Indian Chief Roadmaster classic motorcycle. It added to his badass reputation. There was a secret office pool on how long he'd be employed when the director found out he occasionally wore black lip gloss and matching nail polish.

Director Benjamin Clark commented once he overheard his secretary, a woman in her fifties, say, "That kid is a hottie. Wish I was a little younger." Rumors flew that the comment hadn't set well with the director and tainted an already apathetic opinion of the nonconformist attire and lifestyle. The director was a military man through and through and could be judgmental of agents who created their own dress code.

Lazarus was one more thorn in the director's side on that front. Vernon had bragged the man knew technology as well as himself, and he wasn't so sure he might not be a little better. Although this protégé failed to display any designs on being the top dog in the tech department, the gossip circulated he was like a black mamba: unnaturally silent, and people should step lightly around him. He might be waiting for a chance to seize the position of power. Unlike Vernon, he wasn't disrespectful to those who gave orders. To be truthful, the goth tech genius rarely displayed a reaction or opinion on an assignment, mission, or national threat. There was calm and acceptance, as if this was the way things were and he would deal with it.

After Jinx returned to the kitchen to talk to his wife, the other three went upstairs to have a look at the addition. Since Tom wasn't a big talker, he continued taping drywall while Ken showed the progress they'd made.

"Are you really an architectural engineer?" Ken asked.

"No," was the only answer he gave.

Ken raised his chin and glared down his nose at the goth-inspired agent and dropped the subject. "Thought you were watching the kids."

"I got people on it."

Another short answer Ken didn't like.

"I was on my way up here," Lazarus admitted calmly as he inspected their handiwork, "because I was close by and noticed one of the sensors was sending a signal that the front left tire had suddenly gone flat. Mr. Wakefield had a cart full of groceries he was putting in the back of the car when I pulled up. I saw the flat and noticed it had been punctured."

"So not a case of a slow leak or picked up a nail?"

"Definitely not. I helped him unload the groceries so I could change the tire, but it needs to be replaced. Thought it wise I follow him home since it clearly was deliberate."

"Notice anyone nearby watching you?"

"No."

Ken huffed in frustration. "You said you were on your way here. Why?"

"I didn't want to email this to you or print it out. Thought it better I tell you in person."

"Tell me what?"

"Got a message from an outside source, don't know who yet. But there is high confidence that Tessa's daughter, Heather, is going to be taken."

CHAPTER 16

Tessa entered the garden and examined the wooden sign with the layout of the paths that meandered through the seven acres of themed gardens. She wasn't sure she was up to exploring all seven today since her body was once again reacting to being pregnant. Being tired was part of the condition, though, and it gave her a spark of joy knowing she carried a child. Maybe she should have stayed in the suite and taken a nap, but the touch of mountain air on her skin and the smell of pine was too big a temptation.

The woodland garden grabbed her attention, mostly because it was the first and largest one. On the map, she located several resting spots in case she needed to stop. The entrance showed a gradual incline which shouldn't be much of a problem. Within minutes, Tessa felt rejuvenated and like her old self. The sweet smells of the trees and pops of colorful flowers and plants enticed her to stop often and read the marker explaining the importance of the species. Learning of the historical significance among the Native Americans and early settlers gave her enough lingering moments that she didn't exhaust her fragile energy levels.

She'd been on the trail for twenty minutes when she saw a person ahead, reading one of the signs next to a bridge going over a clear stream. The rushing water was the exact sound that could lull her to sleep. Hesitating to intrude, she saw the man refer to a brochure before looking up in the trees and back down into the water. He strolled across the bridge but stopped in the middle to lean against the railing with his back to her. Grasping the railing, he appeared to be engrossed in the beauty of the water spilling noisily toward him.

Once on the bridge, her steps echoed softly, drawing the man's attention. He glanced her way then turned in surprise.

"Tessa?"

"Andre. I'm sorry to intrude." Although her heart lurched a bit, his welcoming smile put her at ease. The casual attire of jeans, T-shirt, and an open denim shirt, revealed he was in better shape than she imagined. At her home, he'd dressed professionally, revealing nothing.

His smile widened. "Well, it's nice to escape to something I don't have to take care of. I love the outdoors but rarely have time to do any hiking or fishing these days. I did a lot of that as a boy." He moved toward her but didn't get too close.

She thought he'd shifted his eyes to see behind her, but maybe she imagined it. Did he check to see if she was alone?

"I know what you mean. My parents used to bring my brothers and me to the Smokies and Blue Ridge Mountains when I was growing up. I think it helped make me who I am today." Tessa peered over the railing. "I should bring my kids here."

"This is my favorite of the gardens. I always find something new. They've done a good job at both educating and providing diversity. Would you care if I joined you? If you're trying to do a brain drain for the conference," he chuckled good-naturedly, "I'll understand you wanting solitude."

What was there about the man that she wanted to trust in spite of the warnings? There was a chance everyone was wrong. But then there was Nora. She had no reason to lie, and she was most definitely traumatized.

"I'm thinking this might be a good place to take the wrong turn and end up on the Appalachian Trail if I'm not careful. Your company is welcome."

Before she could refuse, he stepped up to her and looped her arm through his. "Well, if we end up on that trail, we are 47.5 miles lost." He pulled her along patting her arm with his free hand. "However, I think I can get us back easy enough."

For the next hour, they stopped and read each marker, took pictures with their phones, and slowed a few times to listen to the birds and wind through the trees. He never touched her other than by taking her arm, or handing her a leaf off the trail with a gentle touch of his hand against hers.

They came to an overlook where the mountains were postcard perfect and a little blue.

"I don't think I've seen them this blue. It's amazing." Tessa hugged her arms, feeling the breeze begin to cool. Andre removed the heavy denim shirt and placed it around her shoulders before she could protest.

"Did you know these Blue Ridge Mountains got their name from the Cherokee who first coined the phrase, Shaconage or 'the land of the blue smoke'?"

"No, but I'm not surprised. This area was populated with many Cherokees several hundred years ago. Isn't it a kind of chemical reaction that causes the blue smoke?"

"The short answer is we know that plants take in carbon dioxide and give off oxygen. What we hear less about is how plants also exhale volatile organic compounds, or VOCs."

"Well, that doesn't sound good at all." She grinned with fake concern.

Andre's eyes creased as if he were amused and turned his back to rest on the rock wall of the overlook and smiled at her. "VOCs does sound ominous, but, when they are released from plants, they are completely natural. Have you ever enjoyed the piney smell that wafts from a Christmas tree? That scent comes from the tree giving off VOCs as it breathes."

"I'm glad my living room doesn't turn blue at Christmas. It wouldn't exactly match my décor," she teased.

"Here there is a high concentration of VOCs, which are basically chemicals and cause the fog we see in these mountains, especially the Smokies. Throw in high-vapor pressure from the millions of trees, bushes, and other plants that come together, and you get the smokey appearance. Sounds very boring, doesn't it?" He smirked and turned back toward the mountains.

"You're saying when the vapor is released from the area's vegetation, this gas scatters blue light from the sky?"

"Exactly. It is what the Cherokee called 'blue smoke.'"

"Guess God was a romantic." She laughed lightly as he made eye contact with her and lingered long enough to make her fidget.

"You may be right." He offered his arm again and, this time, she took it without doubting the situation or Andre. "The clouds are moving in. We better head back. I think rain is expected."

"And, as you know, rain did not go so well the first time we met," she reminded him as they started the last leg of the trail. "With all the excitement and danger, I neglected to thank you properly. That was to be our honeymoon, and it wasn't what we had hoped it would be. You saved our lives, and I will be forever grateful, Andre."

His wolflike eyes narrowed as his mouth stretched into a straight line. It felt a little disarming when he didn't respond, but perhaps he didn't want to have unnecessary praise for something any human would have done.

~ ~ ~ ~

Director Benjamin Clark watched Andre Lavelle Vion laugh as he ran inside the automatic doors holding a denim shirt over his and Tessa's heads. The sky had opened up a few minutes earlier with a downpour, followed by rolling thunder and an occasional flash of lightning. His heart jumped to his throat, seeing them together, but Tessa showed no signs of stress. Andre jerked the shirt free as she leaned in to say a few words that caused him to burst out laughing. It was enough that he put his hand on his heart. The director casually moved toward them and cleared his throat.

"Ben," Tessa laughed enthusiastically.

They had agreed early on that they would go by first names to help the Enigma organization remain a secret agency funded in part by wealthy businessmen and powerful allies of the United States. They fell under the Homeland Security umbrella, although their existence was whispered in disbelief. Enigma blended into many of the divisions of Homeland. The difference being, Enigma was given "a go" on missions the president couldn't hand off to the FBI, CIA, or a number of other national intelligence organizations.

Their offices and recruitment facilities were located in twelve universities across the US. Director Benjamin Clark was in charge of the entire organization. Known in political circles as a force to be reckoned with when it came to national security, Ben had the ear of the president, was the prime minister of Israel's brother, and had more medals for his military service than Audie Murphy.

"Tessa," Ben commented drily as his attention shifted to Andre. "I see you've been walking in the rain again."

Andre and Tessa glanced at each other and laughed again. "Ben thinks I'm crazy for being a pluviophile. I even have a rain garden in my yard."

"I would very much like to see that. Maybe you could show me how to make one." Andre smiled then turned his attention to Ben. "I look forward to the conference. I understand you are the perfect man for the organization position." He extended his hand, and Ben quickly grasped it. "I'm—"

"I know who you are, Monsieur Vion. I'm glad you were able to make it." He nodded toward Tessa. "You didn't answer your phone in your room or your cell phone. I was getting worried after the concierge told me you asked him about going on a walk. He mentioned there had been a black bear prowling around last week."

Tessa slipped her arm through Ben's and squeezed. "He always looks after me. We are on the same team at the university and work together in geo-political conflict studies. I tease him that I think he's grooming me for the State Department."

"From what I know of your State Department, you would be wasting your delightful personality." Keeping his penetrating gaze on her, Andre took her free hand and raised it to his lips. "Thank you for a lovely stroll through the garden, Madame Hunter. Perhaps, before you leave, we can visit one of the other ones on the property. I'm hoping to meet with the panel we both serve on at some point as well."

It did not escape Ben how taken Tessa appeared to be by Andre's charm. The coy smile she leveled at him and lack of a promise to take him up on his proposal was her idea of a tease. Whether it would work on a man like Andre was unknown. However, he'd seen her melt the steel coating that encased his team into a puddle of nonsense more than once. Each time she brought in homemade chocolate chip cookies, wearing one of those irritating sunny smiles, she managed to worm her way into their hearts—well, except for Samantha Cordova, who clearly hated her.

"Nice to meet you, Monsieur Vion, but we have dinner

reservations for our group." Ben pulled Tessa away. "I'm sure Tessa would like to change out of those wet clothes."

"Oh, Andre. Would you like to join us? I'm sure we can fit one more in," she asked anxiously.

"Ah. As much as I'd enjoy such an invitation, I have work to do before tomorrow. I look forward to seeing you during the conference." He gave a slight nod of dismissal then strode away. Two men joined Andre from the shadows and walked two steps behind him as they began a security scan of the area.

Ben bit his tongue to prevent a stern warning and rebuke against her breaking the rules by being alone with Andre. Pulling her onto the elevator, he remained on mute until he'd escorted her into her suite.

"What was that?" Ben asked as Tessa tried to unlock her door.

"Doing my job," she answered flippantly. "I didn't know he was out there. I went for a walk, and there he was. Random encounter."

"I doubt that. You were not to be alone with him."

"It was fine. A perfect gentleman. Enigma was a lot rougher on me the first few days than Andre."

"That's because we believed you were a terrorist."

"Which I've never understood. Seriously. Do I look like a terrorist?"

"Let me think about that. You had a Libyan terrorist in your kitchen, managed to lock Captain Hunter in a holding cell, put Marine Sergeant Tom Cooper in the hospital with a concussion, escaped being handcuffed to a desk, and knew a high-level target we were looking for. Sound familiar?"

"Oh that." She smiled. "But it worked out, and this will, too."

~ ~ ~ ~

Security opened the double doors of Andre's suite. He hadn't broken stride since exiting the elevators. The assistant jumped to attention as soon as he entered, taking the wet denim shirt and pouring him a cup of coffee from the French press. His security alerted his assistant that the boss was on his way up and wanted to make sure all was in order.

Andre took the mug of hot coffee and moved to the balcony

where he could observe the gardens below. The rain had slowed and dripped off the overhang. Recalling the last few hours gave him pleasure. Tessa was like this spring rain: fresh, clean, rejuvenating. The sound of her laughter charmed him, a sensation he wasn't at all used to—at least not since Abigail had died.

But what to do about Captain Hunter?

CHAPTER 17

A chill ran up Ken Montgomery's back and quickly turned to fire in the split second when Lazarus told him Heather could be in danger. The prancing, singsong, unicorn-loving little girl was so like her mother it was easy to be manipulated by the child. She spoke in exaggerated tones when she cocked her head to address you. The big smile with a missing tooth nearly made him laugh each time she tried to tickle him. Tessa's boys were great, too, but Heather, the smaller version of Tessa, gave the team one more reason to keep doing the job they were destined to do in spite of the loneliness that plagued such a job.

Tessa saved his life when she accidently got involved with Enigma. He was forever grateful and over the years had grown fond of the woman. On more than one occasion, Captain Hunter had jokingly accused him of carrying a torch for her. He wasn't sure that was true, but, just like the rest of the team, there was no doubt he loved much about her.

He had no family to speak of, and she provided that for him, with her kids, the missions, her joys mixed with occasional sorrows, and her friendship. Mostly, the attraction was her optimistic attitude toward mankind and the belief in something bigger than herself that ruled the universe. Her biggest fault was she gave people the benefit of the doubt, a trait no one else at

Enigma shared. Their motto was, literally, shoot first and ask questions later. He enjoyed when the bleeding-heart liberal with the heart of gold proved everyone wrong. Roman Darya Petrov, aka, the Tribesman, became an example of them misjudging an individual. They had all been wrong about that worthless scumbag of a drug dealer. It taught him a valuable lesson.

When she kicked her ex-husband to the curb and grieved over the loss of Roman Darya Petrov, he, like the others, tried to be there for her. He wanted to stand out in the crowd, but it was always Captain Hunter who reigned supreme. There had always been a touch of magic between the two of them. The kind of magic he envied and wanted with a woman. But after the Tribesman disappeared from her life, not even Captain Hunter could ease the pain in her heart.

Whatever happened before the captain left for Syria brought Tessa back to life. Standing on the perimeter of Tessa's life would be Ken's forever fate. Yet the little girl, Heather, remained happy to see him anytime he dropped by. Until recently, that had been often, and he'd still hoped she would see him with the same eyes she saw the captain. When word came that she and the captain had finally married, he accepted the verdict. If he had to watch her walk away into the sunset with anyone, he accepted the best outcome would be with Captain Hunter.

At least he thought that until the captain offered her up for bait to a ruthless opportunist. Now, Tessa's children could be in danger. Since he was in charge on the home front, in the absence of the director and the captain, he intended to attack the problem with extreme prejudice.

He noticed Tom Cooper had paused with his drywall tape in one hand and a utility knife in the other as he locked cold eyes with him. The "once a Marine, always a Marine," didn't talk much, but his expressions spoke volumes. There was a running joke at Enigma about how little Miss Grass Valley Commando, Tessa Scott Hunter, had put him in the hospital with nothing more than a broomstick on that first day she was dragged into Enigma. He'd never lived it down. Humorous references to that day plagued him. There had never been much conversation between her and the Marine. As his best friend, he knew the man respected her more than he let on. Not often did anyone get the best of him, especially with a broomstick.

"You better watch out, Tom," she teased with her head tilted and a finger pointed at him. "Witches use brooms for all kinds of things."

"You would know," he grunted and walked away, causing her to laugh. Ken had watched him stride away that day with a grin. Whether he let on or not, he liked her, too. There was just something about that babe-in-the-woods air she wore that tricked you into believing she was helpless.

Lazarus shifted his weight to one leg and let his gaze go between the two men when he put his thumbs in his jean pockets. "Right now, the boys are accounted for and safe. I replaced the resource officers with our own at their school immediately."

"What about Heather's school?" Ken asked.

"That's a problem I couldn't immediately address without coming here since you're in charge."

"How is that different from the boys?" he drilled.

"Today is field trip day, and she has permission to go. Getting a bus driver, a resource officer, and a substitute tour guide for the trip were going to take too long. I only was able to access the school calendar this morning. They leave at ten. I don't have eyes on those vehicles. The buses are not back in the holding area where I can sneak in and tag them. Fortunately, Heather has several tags on her body and clothing. All are working."

"What the hell?" Ken mumbled, running his hand through his hair in irritation. "Did you have something in mind?"

"I got Tom a temporary commercial license and have a bus driver's disguise for him ready to go. You can be mobile security. I've already sent Mr. Wakefield a calendar update to his phone that he is to accompany Heather on the trip today. When I was changing his tire, I dropped the suggestion I worked at the Kincade Mining Museum and would be giving tours to school kids today. The regular tour guide is home sick."

"Sick?" Ken asked as Tom came alongside him.

"Maybe he's tied up," he said offhandedly, "if you get my drift. What I need from you is to say it's a go. The clock is ticking."

Footsteps ran down the hall to where they were discussing the plan then Jinx Wakefield entered the room. "Guys, I totally forgot I'm supposed to be Heather's escort on her school trip today. Not sure how I missed that. I need a ride."

"No problem," Ken said, dusting himself off. "Tell your wife we're going to miss lunch. Tom has some errands to run, too." He stuck out his hand to Lazarus who met his hard gaze with one of his own as he took Ken's hand. "Good to meet you, man. Appreciate your suggestions. Come back and see the results in a few weeks."

"Will do." Lazarus nodded at Jinx. "Going to be late. Nice to meet of you."

~ ~ ~ ~

Ken didn't like mines, especially underground mines. He grew up in West Virginia where coal was the bread and butter of most households. That was why he ended up joining the Army, got an education, and eventually chose Enigma as his reckless danger of choice. Now, here he was at a gold mining museum, albeit mostly a fake environment.

He wasn't sure why a bunch of runny-nosed kindergarteners needed to learn gold mining at this age, but here they were. Lazarus had morphed into a cheerful guide who spoke in short sentences, gave simple explanations of why gold mining was important to California history, and provided a few fun activities involving a water hose that slammed water against a rock wall. His goth attire had been exchanged for the bland, khaki uniform worn by the museum personnel. Accessories were now a park badge and a funny hat Smokey the Bear would have worn.

There were lots of giggles and "let me try next, that was cool" comments. Surprisingly enough, the mothers in the group hung on Lazarus's every word, butting in over the kids to ask questions.

"Great. The moms are hitting on our new Enigma vampire," Ken mumbled into his mike. Instantly, Lazarus calmly turned and located him hiding in the shadows then leveled a look of contempt as one corner of his mouth lifted sarcastically. "That's all we need is another example of the undead like Zoric," he muttered, lifting his chin and adjusting his mirrored sunglasses.

He didn't care if Lazarus was offended or not. Matter of fact, in today's climate, he'd probably be filing a discrimination lawsuit against vampires by the time this was over. Better get used to it if he was going to be working with a bunch of military and national security people.

The outdoor trail circled around to where the kids could pan for gold. This section was another hands-on experience. Lazarus gave directions on how to proceed for the parents who were helping a child. To his credit, he never stopped checking things out. Several moms grinned his way, apparently thinking he might be trying to catch their attention. He didn't miss a beat and added a steady gaze, followed by a narrowing of his eyes. The female reaction, in each case Ken observed, was a shy glance away then back as she tossed her hair away from her face or neck.

"Oh, brother, Lazarus, you're killing me." He chuckled. The image of Tessa swam up to his thoughts. He doubted she would fall for a stupid stunt like that. He was also pretty sure Agent Samantha Cordova would laugh in his face. But the question arose whether Lazarus's response to both Enigma's female agents would unravel that suave bag of horse manure once he came in contact with them. That was one performance he wanted to witness.

CHAPTER 18

Chase called out to Tessa when he entered the suite. When she failed to answer, he did a quick search. As he picked up his phone to call her, she walked through the door with the director, who looked like he'd been sucking a lemon. He knew that meant either there was trouble, or someone screwed up. Since Tessa was at his side, he guessed it was both.

"I was just about to call you." Chase shot a bewildered glance at Ben who raised his chin in frustration before cutting his eyes to Tessa and arching an eyebrow. "See you at dinner, Ben."

The silent treatment spoke volumes. The director's quick exit and final frown at Tessa was enough to alert him to a problem. In her usual fashion, she distracted him by wrapping her arms around him and landing a quick kiss on his mouth, followed by a disarming smile. "Have I told you today that I love you?"

"That's a sneak attack if I ever saw one, Tessa Hunter." He removed her embrace and stared into her eyes, as if doing so would unravel her like in the old days. She would bat those baby blues in a rapid flutter of eyelashes, stutter, and use her hands as she tried to explain. Now she used other wiles, like physical contact. "No, you haven't told me. Thanks. So, what's up?"

"You're supposed to say you love me, too." She stroked his chest, something he quickly stopped.

"I love you, too."

"That wasn't very convincing. Maybe we could—"

"Why is Ben ticked at you?"

"Oh that." She waved him off and moved two steps back. Another sure sign she'd broken a rule. A chuckle followed, then her hands went to her hips. This wasn't good at all.

"Tessa," he said firmly.

"I went for a short walk and neglected to tell him. That's all."

"How long a walk?" He stepped toward her, and she continued to back up.

"Not long. Maybe a couple of hours. The gardens are lovely. Maybe we'll have time to go look at them. There is the prettiest little waterfall just beyond a bridge. Then it opens up at an overlook, and you can see forever."

Now her back was up against a rustic antique library table. The statue of an Indian feeding a bear rattled as she bumped into it. Chase looked around her at the large painting of the Blue Ridge Mountains hanging on the wall then at her. She turned slightly to follow his gaze then jerked around to stare at him.

"I'm a big girl, Chase," she hissed. "Just because we're married doesn't mean you have to know my whereabouts every second. Is this the way it's going to be?"

"There are bears out there. Probably mountain lions, too. Don't think because we're at a resort everything is safe. I would have felt better if you'd waited for me or one of the others in the group. Always safety in numbers."

"Well, for your information, I wasn't alone. Andre Vion was in the garden and said basically the same thing, or maybe he just thought it because he escorted me around to show me beautiful plants I'd never seen before." The stubborn chin came up, and her eyes turned the shade of periwinkle that always alerted him to her mood. Angry.

"Stay away from him. He's dangerous."

"So you say. But I don't see it. He was a perfect gentleman. Don't forget he saved both our lives a few short weeks ago. I thanked him for both of us. I'm sure you neglected to do that."

"Damn right, I did. He's up to no good. I have my reasons for hating him—"

"Let me guess. You've dealt with guys like him all over the

world. They're all terrorists, drug dealers, human traffickers, and on and on."

"No. He's worse. He has respectable written all over him, and no one will believe he is a corrupt, narcissistic madman who wants the world at his feet. Stay. Away. From. Him."

"You're just jealous, and it really isn't becoming." She pushed by him and stormed into the bedroom. Before she could slam the door in his face, he shoved it open and kicked it shut with his foot. He stood there as she whirled around and stared at him, her chest rising and falling. In two steps, she ran into his arms.

"Chase," she moaned as she laid her head on his chest. "Are we safe in here?" "Yes, babe. We are safe. The listening device is behind the painting and almost undetectable."

"I was scared when I ran into him." He could see her watery eyes and trembling lips when she tried to pull away. "He was disarming and perfect, which made things worse. I found myself falling for his mannerisms and hung on his every word. Then I would see Nora's face and how terrified she still is."

"Why didn't you tell someone where you were going?"

"I told the concierge. I only planned to be gone a few minutes. I wanted a little fresh air. I'm so sorry, Chase. Really."

He pulled her back into his arms and held on for dear life. "Ben is in a twist. That's for sure. But the good thing is, we know Andre is interested in you. With any luck, he'll make a mistake and we can figure out exactly what he's up to, and how to undo the chaos he's planning on creating to gain control of, essentially, the world."

Chase's phone vibrated, and he pulled it from his pocket with one hand while keeping the other on Tessa's back. He glanced down at the caller ID.

"Ken? What's going on?" He listened intently, his entire body on alert. "Update when possible."

He clicked off.

"Chase? What is it?"

~ ~ ~ ~

Ken spotted a couple of groundskeepers in the same park uniforms as Lazarus. With hats pulled down low over their foreheads, they moved stealthily, neglecting several pieces of litter wadded up on the side of the trail. They never looked down, only pretended to stop and sweep once in a while, making no progress.

"Lazarus, you need to get the kids moving. There are two—"

"I see them," he responded, smiling at one of the moms. "Okay, kids, time to move inside. Mr. Wakefield, would you and Heather be in charge today and lead us through the mine maze ahead. Everyone follow at a safe distance without triggering a mine collapse." He pointed to his eyes. "Keep your eyes open for trouble. I understand there are snacks waiting for you. Wouldn't want any delays. All that ice cream could melt. We might cause a slippery mess in the mine. Mr. Wakefield?"

"Yessiree Bob. Let's go! Watch your steps."

Heather's grandfather took her little hand as she waved the others forward.

"We got these two," Ken spoke quietly then nodded to his partner to move in quickly and detain the two suspicious men under surveillance.

Circling both men, they transformed into predator mode, ready to attack and neutralize the threat with a snap decision. Ken approached from the front. Tom took the rear.

"Excuse me," Ken said, pulling out a map of the grounds and approaching the two men. "I'm confused as to where the administration building is located. I had a meeting there ten minutes ago, and I'm still going in circles." He chuckled and pointed to the map.

Both men followed his finger as he traced the path on the map. Neither spoke but offered a shrug as they stole a glance around Ken to watch the crowd of children and mothers move toward the next stop. One spoke something in Spanish to the other and grinned.

"Where you guys from?" Ken asked in Spanish. They frowned and tried to push around him. He backed up and blocked them once more. They were shorter than him by a head and about forty pounds lighter. "No Habla English?" he asked through gritted teeth. Both men eyed him cautiously. "Papeles de identificacion, muchachos," he ordered. When they didn't respond, he repeated it in English as he pulled his weapon. "Get your damn papers out. Now. And I'm not asking again."

Their hands shook as they dropped their brooms and dustpans. Chances were good if they had papers, they wouldn't have them in their clothing. Considering the expression of terror that leaped to their eyes, they had seemingly forgotten about the children. Ken guessed these weren't their guys. Tom spooked them even more when he came up behind them and gave them a quick pat down as they airplaned their arms for him.

"Why are you following those kids?"

Both men pointed and smiled as they explained their children were with the group, and they didn't want them to know they were watching. They were so proud of them going to an American school but didn't want them to spot them.

"Did you see anyone suspicious hanging around, senor?" Ken asked in a friendly tone. "We thought someone didn't belong. It is important we find this person."

"No. No. Muchas madres." Many mothers.

Ken told them thank you, and it would be better if they got back to work. They wanted to know if they were in trouble, and he patted one on the shoulder to reassure him they were not. With a "gracias," they picked up their brooms and headed in the opposite direction.

"False alarm, Lazarus," Ken spoke in his mouthpiece. No response. "Lazarus? Lazarus, confirm."

Tom Cooper sprinted toward where the children had disappeared into the mine maze while Ken kept trying to raise Lazarus. Catching up with Tom, he heard squeals in the distance. Both men repulled their weapons and eased down the maze until they caught up with the group. They had entered the section of the maze that simulated a working mine, therefore dim light spilled across the surface that resembled wet stones. More screams hurried the men down the tunnel. Occasional cascading rocks fashioned from sponges, rumbled down the walls followed by sound effects. An almost invisible net caught them.

The two men slowed as they witnessed the children and mothers exiting the tunnel with the gift shop ahead. Mr. Wakefield was visible, but, with the entire group following, it was difficult to spot Heather. Since he didn't appear to be concerned and laughed at what one of the children must have shared, the two soldiers relaxed.

"Where's Lazarus?" Ken mumbled to his friend as they pushed through the school group.

Ken scanned the area as they approached Mr. Wakefield.

Heather was gone.

CHAPTER 19

"Lazarus, answer me now, damn it!" Ken struggled not to panic. Both men scanned the crowd to see if maybe Heather visited with a friend. As the group strolled in the picnic area outside the gift shop, Mr. Wakefield passed out ice cream cups. Ken determined he was unaffected by Heather's absence.

"Ma'am?" Ken asked a mom dressed in yoga pants and a denim tunic. She grinned at him like a piranha eyeing its next meal. "Where is Heather, Mr. Wakefield's granddaughter?"

"Not sure. She had to go to the bathroom, and two moms offered to take her. And what is your name?"

"Two moms?" He glanced at Tom, who was already headed to the restrooms. "Do you know their names?"

"No. I've never seen them before actually." She glanced toward a little boy shoving his ice cream into another child's face with gleeful laughter. "Gavin, stop that right now," she ordered.

"Which child were they with?"

"What? Oh, come to think of it, I don't remember them being with any child. Thought maybe they were extras, like that big fella who drove the bus. Isn't that him over there?" She squinted at Tom.

"Yes, ma'am. The substitute driver. But you didn't know these women?"

"No. Is there a problem? They seemed nice enough." She huffed irritation. "Gavin, get off the top of the table right this minute," she yelled. "Sorry. I need to take care of this."

Ken touched his earwig when he heard groans and glass breaking. Tom picked up speed as they came into sight of the girls' restroom. Ken made out the sound of Heather singing her favorite Disney song, as Lazarus fought two unknown assailants. One was on the ground, bloodied and crawling toward a knife with a six-inch blade.

Aiming his weapon at the disheveled suspect on the ground, Tom rushed up and kicked the knife aside then jerked the suspect up off the ground with one hand. Dazed, with blood dripping down his face into his mouth, the suspect made a flimsy attempt at swinging a fist at the big ex-Marine, only to get tossed into a tree face-first. That ended any resistance.

Ken turned to see Lazarus jump back as the woman did a roundhouse kick toward his head. She missed, allowing him to return the favor. She didn't take an evasive move and took the full brunt, the blow knocking her back toward Ken, who caught her in mid-fall. Lazarus rushed forward, grabbed her out of Ken's one-arm hold, and spun her around. Pulling a zip tie from his pocket, he secured her hands behind her back. She had a deep scratch on her face and a split lip.

"You always carry a zip tie in your pocket, Lazarus?" Ken dragged the woman to the bushes where Tom waited with the other suspect.

"I was a Boy Scout. Pays to be prepared. Oh, and the one over there is a man."

Ken glanced at the suspect that Tom had shoved down in the bushes where Heather wouldn't notice. "I heard glass breaking."

"Mirror inside the door. When I grabbed this one's collar, he tried to pull the mirror off the nail and smack me. I dodged, and it hit his partner." He smirked. "Neither were women."

"Pretty good female impersonator if you ask me. I mean, jeez."

Lazarus shrugged. "Not really. Noticed early on, the nail polish wasn't salon perfect and the lipstick didn't go with the makeup. Thought maybe some kind of gender thing going on. Not for me to judge. Simple but suspicious considering there was no child clinging to either of them."

"I'm not even going to ask how you knew all that. And Heather didn't hear any of this?"

"She started singing at the top of her lungs and flushed a couple of times, which echoed like the Grand Canyon in there." He cocked his head toward the door. "Here she comes. Get lost."

Ken backed away and gave a warning. "We'll need to talk about your tone when you give me orders, Sir Dracula."

The new agent's face turned dark but otherwise remained expressionless. He approached the restroom as the door swung open. "Miss Heather," he said happily. Ken thought for a second how out of character it sounded for the new agent to clap his hands together at the little girl who was all smiles.

"I lost the mommies who brought me here. And the mirror is broken in there. I didn't do it, I promise." She glanced around with a slight look of concern, her smile fading. "I don't know where I am. Where's my papa?"

"Well, he is in the picnic area waiting for you to have ice cream. And because you helped me out today, you won the gift shop coupon."

"I did?" She giggled, jumping up and down.

"You sure did. Your uncle Ken donated fifty dollars toward the best helper today. So be sure to thank him when you see him." He held up the money then glanced toward the brush where the men hid.

Ken listened in disbelief as he felt his pockets. "Damn. That guy picked my pocket," he growled.

Although Tom didn't laugh out loud, his body shook as he held it in. Lazarus took the little girl's hand and skipped with her as they headed back to the others.

"I don't like that guy," Ken snapped.

Tom jerked his suspect to their feet. "I dunno. He's growing on me."

"Like a wart, I'm sure."

At this final retort, Tom laughed deep and long. "You know you're irritating me, right?"

~ ~ ~ ~

"Chase? What's wrong?" Tessa repeated as he clicked off his

phone.

He led her to the bed and had her sit down on the edge then joined her. "Everything is fine now. That was Ken."

"And?"

Taking her hands in his, Chase retold the entire day's events as Ken had reported and tried not to sound anxious in the process. He could feel his own blood pressure spike and wanted to call the whole mission off, considering what had happened. She grabbed for his phone to call home but he pulled it away.

"I know you want to reassure yourself things are okay. They are. Your dad let his guard down, but—"

"He should've known better. How can I do this, Chase, with my babies in danger?"

"That's a topic to be debated at a later time. Lazarus is—do you know him?"

"Yes. I mean, not well. Vernon brought him in to Enigma. Extremely smart and interesting. Why?"

Chase continued with his part in saving Heather and getting things in place for her protection. "Ken and Tom were there, too, babe. Heather didn't know a thing, nor did your dad as far as that goes. However, Ken and Tom are going to have a talk with your folks tonight about what almost went down."

Tessa buried her face in her hands. He slipped an arm around her, pulling her in closer. "They're also going to tell them we're married. I know we didn't get a chance to do that and still keep it from the kids. Lazarus will be there soon for dinner. When the kids are off to bed, then they'll spell out the plan from now on. School is covered. Security is round the clock, and anything they need will be delivered by Enigma. The guys are staying there on the premise of finishing out the upstairs room." He wiped her tears and kissed her lightly on the forehead. "We can stop this right now if you want. No questions asked."

"Who tried to take her? Was it random?"

"All signs point to Andre, but no solid evidence of that. The two involved will be interrogated."

"I wish Zoric was there to do the interrogation. He'd get the information."

"I know. Chances are there will be no clear evidence he was involved."

"Why Heather? My baby," she moaned.

"I guessing to control you when the time comes. She looks enough like you—Tess, I don't know. I'm extremely concerned."

"What's the downside of calling it off?"

"Whatever Vion is up to concerning geopolitical politics goes forward. Hell, it could anyway. We don't have enough intel to know, except it's big. But the most serious thing, to me, is that he has seen you and that most likely has triggered those memories of Abigail. According to Dr. Wu, he's very dangerous, and you are like gasoline thrown on a fire."

"Is there an upside?"

Chase sighed and stood. "We'd be home to watch over things ourselves, but life for everyone would change. I can't believe I'm saying this, Tessa, but my first inclination would be to send you to Montana to the Tribesman to protect all of you."

"What? No. We can't do that. That's a small place for all of us and, besides, it would be awkward with the two of you there."

"Tessa"—he took a deep breath—"I wouldn't be there. Only you and the kids. Maybe your parents if I could get them to go. I would have to stop this monster before he totally wrecks our lives."

"And you don't think sending me to Darya would do that? Seriously?" she said incredulously.

"I know. I know. It would be a gamble. But it's a bigger gamble leaving you in Grass Valley, hunkered down with three kids who aren't going to understand any of this. At least, there, with Darya, they'd get the ranch experience, and I wouldn't worry about them. Darya would never let anything happen to them or to you. It's isolated, and the guy probably has booby traps everywhere. The damn animals would alert him to trouble." He grinned in spite of himself. Then he noted the way she was biting her lower lip, either toying with the idea or confused he'd have to make the decision.

Sending her back into the waiting arms of Roman Darya Petrov, aka the Tribesman, made him uneasy. The man had a mental hold on Tessa he'd never been able to sever and had decided to live with it as long as she chose to spend her life with him instead of the rogue warrior. He and the Tribesman had been enemy combatants and tried on several occasions to kill each other, but, in the end, had become unlikely friends of a sort. Respect and trust, although turbulent, had forged their friendship because of one woman, Tessa. All he had to do was pick up the phone and call him.

Tessa's head was spinning. Not only had her child nearly been kidnapped, but Andre was most likely behind it. From everything she'd read about him, there would be no way to trace it back to him. Now she had to decide on the next step. Chase's suggestion to send her back to Darya would be a disaster. No way Chase would ever believe the baby was his if she went back to Montana. And she knew Darya well enough to understand he would make it impossible for her to leave him one more time. But what if the baby was Darya's, and not Chase's? A wave of nausea swept over her.

"I think I'm going to throw up," she confessed as she ran to the bathroom. He'd started after her to help when she held her hand out. "No."

When she finished throwing up, she stripped and stepped into the shower, letting the hot water wash away doubts and trepidation lingering on her conscience. Wrapped in a white robe, she inhaled deeply then left the bathroom. Chase was on the phone again and quickly clicked off when he turned around to face her.

"More bad news?" she dared ask, dreading the answer.

He rushed over to her and embraced her then held her at arm's length. "No, babe. That was Ken again. Your family—our family is secure. Your dad is a little beside himself about what happened and blames himself. Your mom may be arrested by morning for attempted murder." He grinned. This caused her to laugh. "Anyway, they were briefed concerning our meetings without giving away too much. At some point, we are going to have to come clean on Enigma with them."

"That won't go well."

"It might also mean this is your last field operation, Tessa." He rubbed her arms and stooped a little to make eye contact. "We can talk about it later. But for now, we need to make another decision."

"I have to make a decision." Tessa fell against his muscled chest then wrapped her arms around him to reassure herself she was doing the right thing. "It's only a couple of days that could change the trajectory of geopolitics. Right?"

"Possibly."

"We know he's done unethical human experimentation, and who knows how many he's murdered in the name of science."

"That we know for a fact. Proving it has so far been elusive."

"His possible interest in me—"

"Also, a definite." Chase led her to the bed to sit down. "Abigail is his kryptonite, and you have made more contact with him than anyone else."

"And that's why I think we should move forward. I mean, as long as my family is safe."

"There's added security around your house with several of Vernon's toys."

"But he is here with us."

"Lazarus is on it. Remember how Vernon said he was every bit his equal?" He retold the story Ken gave him, or at least Tessa thought it probably was the version the soldier had shared with his captain.

Tessa couldn't help but chuckle in spite of the weight of responsibility the job held over her. "I'm sure another version will surface when we return home. But Lazarus saved my baby."

"Yes. He did. Because of his quick thinking, Heather has no idea the dangers she faced. The suspects will be interrogated by the best."

"I have to see this through. I want"—she took his hand, desperate to tell him she was pregnant—"I want our life to be free of fear. It's important to me I make you happy and start our lives over like we both deserve."

"You are the bravest woman I've ever known." He kissed her passionately causing her to pull him against her so he could feel the warmth surging through her body.

CHAPTER 20

Andre Lavelle Vion stared at himself in the full-length mirror hanging on the wall in his bedroom. He'd secured one of the best suites in the resort. The balcony boasted a view of the Blue Ridge Mountains. The bluish haze, even now, reflected in the mirror. Cocking his head side to side, he admired how the blue cast an aura around his head, resembling a halo. A slow smile widened his mouth as he touched his neck-length gray hair. At the age of twenty-five, it had begun to change. There remained a few strands of black hair underneath, which he believed added a touch of mystery and class. Touching his face, he ran a finger down his jawline to feel the two-day beard growth that also created a faint mustache. The piercing blue eyes were from being partially color blind, although he could easily see shades of blue and green.

Smoothing his dinner jacket with one hand, he moved toward the living room then opened the French doors to catch the breeze flowing out of the mountains. His hair fell in his eyes, but he didn't bother to move it as his gaze found the gardens where he'd strolled with Tessa Scott Hunter. The coolness of the air chilled his feverish craving to be with her.

She'd revitalized his desire to share, to speak, to communicate, which had vanished long ago. It felt refreshing to have someone who listened to his vast knowledge with eagerness and asked questions as if it mattered. It was invigorating to meet a woman who recognized his superior intellect. He would want a first lady. Perhaps, with a little persuasion, Tessa would recognize her place—at his side to recreate the new world order according to him.

Of course, he would expect children. The sooner the better. She had birthed three children, two of whom were boys who did not interest him. But the little girl would appear angelic and perfect to stand with him in the future. It wouldn't take long for her to forget the others if Tessa cooperated, and she would. What choice would she have? The idea he could make the same mistakes he did with Abigail years ago were preposterous. This would be a glorious new beginning. All it required now was removing Captain Hunter from the picture. Whatever that involved would be a pleasure.

A light tap at the double doors diverted his attention back to the present without glancing toward Franklin coming inside and waiting patiently for him to respond. Finally, he moved his index finger at his side. "You have news?" Andre sent a sideways glance to the assistant.

Franklin stepped closer, tablet in hand. "They failed to accomplish your objective, Mr. Vion. Unfortunately, they are now in custody."

Andre turned to fully face the assistant but revealed nothing about how he felt about the news. "Where would that be?"

The assistant glanced down at the tablet. "They were taken to a police precinct nearby but later moved to another facility. We are trying to pinpoint the location now."

"I see. Activate the serum."

"But, sir..."

Andre snatched the tablet from his hand, scrolled for a few seconds, lightly tapped a button then handed it back to him. "There. Done. Now find out how they knew we were coming. But first tell me what else you found out about Tessa and her connection to the president."

The assistant swallowed hard, knowing the two he'd sent to do Andre's dirty work were dead from a massive dose of poison that had emptied into their blood stream. The vessel had been implanted into their arms without their knowledge.

"I don't believe they did know, sir. According to our source at the White House, Captain Hunter has a habit of being overprotective of his wife. It started when they first met. She saved President Austin's life and he insisted she be brought into his closest group of confidants."

"Do we know exactly what—this group does?" He spoke with a cool, almost uninterested, tone as he poured himself a brandy.

"Our contact at Homeland Security says they are a hit squad or problem solvers for incidents that might require no accountability as to their methods. They are funded by some of the world's richest men and women, some of whom will be here at the conference."

"What would they gain by doing this?" He stared into his glass then lifted his piercing glare to Franklin.

"They didn't like how the world was spinning out of control with new, or, some would say, offbeat ideology and religious extremism. According to them, it affects world economies, and human and environmental interaction as well as movement of populations due to unresolved conflicts."

"As the Americans used to say, too many chiefs and not enough Indians, if you ask me." He released a bored sigh.

"I believe it is more than that, sir. The financial consortium for these actions has no say in how the money is spent or what situation should be resolved. It is unknown if the president makes the decisions after conferring with the various intelligence agencies or if it is a collaboration. These people are invisible for all practical purposes, with no restrictions. Captain Hunter leads one of those groups. It makes sense he left specific instructions and security measures in place for his family."

"If all goes well, we'll have that little problem under control in a few days." He returned to the balcony and let the misty breeze touch his face. "It will be a great day indeed. We are almost there."

Franklin quietly stepped back but watched his boss smile and lift his glass in a toast to the Blue Ridge Mountains now covered in clouds. "Soon, my lovely Tessa. Soon. Together, we will change the world."

~ ~ ~ ~

Dinner reservations were for seven o'clock in the award-winning steakhouse. Tessa thought it would be larger considering the size of the resort. Turned out to be more rustic and romantic with candlelight, white tablecloths, and various taxidermic animal heads on the walls. It was an odd combination and included the soft sounds of a fountain in one corner. She half expected paper plates with a side of barbeque sauce instead of serving their steak and lobster on fine china. The avant-garde of it all made Tessa happy. Her grandmothers had never matched a thing in their lives, and it was that part of the South she loved. Dessert was the best coconut cake she'd ever eaten.

"I could lie down and fall asleep right here." She sighed with pleasure. "You guys can't possibly still be hungry?"

"I'm not sure we'll get through all the items on the agenda to discuss tonight." The director pushed his plate away then held up his hand for more coffee. "Guests will be arriving tonight and tomorrow. Everything is ready to go."

"Ben, I don't know how you pulled all this together," Samantha commented as she passed her dessert to Carter, who took it eagerly. Tessa doubted any sugar had ever made it into her body. "I guess after all these years of doing this conference, there is a set of plans in place."

"Yes, and a lot of people working on it the entire year. We usually try to include a global initiative in collaboration with the World Health Organization to focus on throughout the following year. Last year, it was the World Food Program. With the ongoing conflict in Ukraine, we lost our top producer of sunflower meal, oil, and seed."

Tessa dabbed at her mouth with her cloth napkin. "It's shocking to see the list of countries that are living with food insecurity."

"Conflict, economic shocks, climate extremes, and soaring fertilizer prices," Samantha added, "have caused a food crisis of unprecedented proportions. I believe the last report I read estimated 828 million people are unsure of where their next meal will come from. Now we can add Sudan's sudden political climate to the mix. Food workers have been killed trying to serve the most vulnerable populations."

"Samantha, you actually sound concerned," Tessa quipped, hating instantly that she'd spoken out of spite.

"Well, I thought it would make a bleeding heart like yourself feel more comfortable, considering you have little knowledge of what the real world is like." Her feline smile and narrowed eyes gave Tessa the chills. She took the dessert away from Carter and handed it to Tessa. "Here. You probably need this more than him."

Carter frowned and tried to take it back. "Why would she need it? Give it back."

"Having worked out with her numerous times, I feel it's important she eat more coconut. After all, it's high in manganese, which is important for bone health. Just being a good friend. Eat." She slid it over to bump into her plate.

"I think your definition of a good friend needs a little work." Tessa grabbed her fork and sliced off a bite.

Chase rejoined the conversation after conversing with Zoric concerning security. "Ben, has this consortium ever sponsored things other than food insecurity? Maybe vaccinations or education?" He slipped his arm onto the back of Tessa's chair.

"Yes. We've done those things, but I'll be honest. Each year, whatever we choose seems to be a drop in the bucket as to solving the problem. Our real goal is to shore up the social and economic infrastructure with countries who succumb to antiquated tribal customs leading to corruption and eventually war, which, as you know, sets up a domino effect as to stability throughout the world." Crossing his arms, Ben leaned back in his chair. Slowly, he turned his focus toward Tessa.

She felt as if the glare had turned into a microscope. She cleared her throat and felt her eyelashes do a nervous flutter. It must be her cue to weigh in with her opinion. "Tribal societies, even today, in places like Somalia and other third world countries, often times have an obligation to their families and village when they hold a seat of power. That's when people get placed into important positions. Americans have no idea what the qualifications are for the Secretary of Health and Human Services, the State Department, or other cabinet post positions. We trust our leaders will make the right decisions and the process of approval is thorough to make sure we are served appropriately. In many countries, the ones put into powerful positions have little to no training or respect for the rule of law. There are no checks and balances. It's gone on for centuries."

"Well, aren't you a killjoy." Samantha faked a yawn and pushed away from the table. "Okay. You're smart. Happy?"

"Bite me," Tessa said as she stood up.

"Are we thinking about a knock-down, drag-out right before my eyes." Carter reached out and retrieved the rest of Tessa's coconut cake. He put his hands together as if ready to pray and lifted his eyes toward Heaven. "Thank you, Jesus! I knew this day would come."

Tessa glanced at Chase who grinned but didn't try to interfere. "Let's take it to the ladies' room."

"Fine," Samantha snapped. She snatched up the plate of cake and handed it to the waiter.

"No," Carter protested. "You can't—"

"Let's go." Tessa walked off toward the foyer of the restaurant.

Samantha caught up and chuckled under her breath. "One of these days we're going to have to put on a demonstration for him."

"Will you let me win?" Tessa could feel herself about to laugh out loud as they moved out of earshot. That's when she saw Andre Vion approaching through the glass doors of the restaurant, with two of his security detail and a third man carrying a tablet. That must be Nora's former boyfriend who helped her escape. Did he know she was safe? Tessa reached out and touched Sam's hand.

"I see him. Relax." Samantha had an excellent poker face in any situation.

"I have to pee," Tessa mumbled from the corner of her mouth.

"Lock your knees."

"Who told you that would work? Good grief. I've had three fat babies. Do you really think my bladder will listen to my knees?" she growled.

"Tessa," Andre gushed as he came through the doors. He immediately took her hand and kissed it then focused on Samantha. No big surprise there. That was the entire male species' reaction when they saw her. She could feel her own image turn into a dowdy wallflower as if by magic. "Oh, Andre Lavelle Vion, I'd like for you to meet my colleague Dr. Samantha Cordova. She is quite the big deal in the world of economics."

"Yes. Of course. I have heard of you. My pleasure." He took her hand and kissed it without much interest, except when he stepped back. That's when he locked eyes with her.

Did he see a mean machine capable of decapitating him with a fingernail file she carried in her purse? Or maybe that she bowed to no man and his nonsense?

"This is quite a coup to have you join so many men of science, industry, and government, Monsieur Vion. I'm sure you'll be an enormous asset to the future plans discussed in the next few days." Samantha's voice took on that haughty tone that could freeze a man or woman in place.

A slow smile materialized on his lips as he appeared to map her face to memory with his dangerous blue eyes. "Yes, I'm sure it will."

The assistant pushed opened the door and whispered to Andre while his interested gaze switched back to Tessa. "Show her in, Franklin." He glanced behind him as a woman appeared from a side alcove. She was speaking to a hotel personnel. She nodded then turned her attention to an earbud, as if listening with her head down. The assistant opened the door and waved her inside to join Andre.

"Ladies, I'd like for you to meet my new head of security. Ms. Honey Lynch."

She didn't offer a hand of friendship but raised an eyebrow of contempt as her nostrils flared.

Andre quickly introduced her to them and mentioned they were having dinner to go over a few security matters concerning plasma donations over the next few days. "Honey is pretty marvelous at what she does. I'm so impressed with her resume. Never let it be said I'm not an equal opportunity employer." With a slight chuckle, he slipped an arm around her. "Ladies, good to see you. I'm sure we'll be running into each other throughout the next few days."

CHAPTER 21

"Are you freakin' kidding me?" Tessa moaned and washed her hands as Samantha reapplied her lipstick. "Honey Lynch. Did you know about this?"

"Of course not. I bet the director is in there receiving CPR after seeing her. Just one more instance of why that little piece of Irish trash can't be trusted. I'm sure she'll put a holier-than-thou spin on it, like she always does. Truth be told, we're all in her crosshairs—well maybe, except you."

"I'm not so sure about that."

The restroom door pushed open, and Honey strolled in, smiling like the cat that swallowed the canary. She rushed up, high heels clicking on the tiles, and hugged Tessa. She waved for Sam to come into the embrace unsuccessfully.

"Look at you." She pushed Tessa at arm's length. "You've put on a little weight since the last time I saw you. Of course, we were in Syria, and you were a hot mess."

"Good to see you, too, Honey." Tessa liked the woman in spite of herself. They had been through a few tough times together, one being she'd once planned to kill her family. It wasn't that she trusted her now, just found her unorthodox approach to life rather refreshing at times. "How's your mum?"

"Oh, she's lovely. Thank you for askin'. Recently had some

surgery, so I'm a little tapped out in the money department." She pulled Tessa to her side and looped her arm around her shoulder then played with her strands of hair that had fallen from her messy bun on the nape of her neck. "And, Sam—how are you? You are lookin' fit as ever. Still sleepin' with the prime minister of Israel, or has he tired of your teasing?"

"His stamina hasn't waned, if that's what you're asking, Honey. And my love life isn't any of your business."

"A little touchy." She smirked then put her lips to Tessa's ear. "I hear the handsome Carter Johnson is on the market again since he gave her the boot to the tush. I always liked him. Can you put in a good word for me, Tessa, luv?"

Samantha sighed in disgust. "You're incorrigible, you know that, Honey?"

"Oh, bringing out the big words now, are we?"

"I'm sorry. I forgot you have the IQ of a rock. It means a person not able to be corrected or improved. In other words, you can't be reformed."

Honey narrowed her eyes and stepped threateningly toward the tall woman. "Well, why didn't you just say that in the first place?"

"It's so much more fun to see confusion in your eyes and realize you're nothing more than a thug who likes to kill people for a living."

"The only difference between me and you is that you have the president of the United States' permission to off his enemies. I, on the other hand, have to work very hard to accomplish peaceful conflict resolutions when differences occur between opposing factions." She looked back at Tessa. "That sounded really good, didn't it?"

Tessa grinned and lowered her eyes from Samantha who would surely make her pay for siding with Honey. "Maybe you should tell us what you're doing with Andre?"

"That wasn't a sexual question," Samantha said drily.

"In that case, you might get bored with my answers. Still Enigma's resident nymphomaniac, I hear."

Samantha straightened to her five-foot-eleven height and took a step toward the Irish assassin, causing her to move back next to Tessa.

"Honey, you are playing a dangerous game," Tessa blurted out and touched the assassin's shoulder, which relaxed under her fingertips. "I'm worried about you."

"Aww. Such a luv, you are." Honey slipped her arm back around Tessa's shoulder, pulled her in tight, and landed a kiss on her cheek. "I've missed my bestie. At least you're glad to see me."

"Let's not get ahead of ourselves," Samantha snorted in a half laugh. "Miss Goodie Two Shoes is a lot like you—she plays both sides against the middle to get whatever she wants. She just doesn't kill people to make it happen. So, just tell us why you're really here and let's go our separate ways."

"She's always been a little jealous of our friendship, Tessa," she cooed in a loud whisper into her ear. "You're a saint to put up with it."

"You're exhausting. Explain." Samantha's face morphed into a picture of impatience. "We've got to get back."

"I needed the money. Someone from your organization contacted me about a security gig for this conference. I applied and got it."

"Just like that?" Tessa asked.

"Not exactly. Had to bust a few heads first and demonstrate I could do the job. You don't want those particulars, trust me." She moved to the full-length mirror to examine her appearance. "I had no idea you guys would be here."

"Let's go." Samantha brushed past her. "I've heard enough of her malarky." As she opened the door for Tessa, she looked back at Honey and smirked. "Oh, and that means nonsense talk, in case you didn't understand."

Tessa glanced back to catch a reflection of Honey in the mirror. Her normally pale skin had turned red, and her eyes squinted to slits of fire. Both women had a short fuse and were filled with mistrust and loathing for each other. It still befuddled her as to why the assassin had taken to her since they were nothing alike. The woman, although cunning, was one step away from being a dumpster fire.

The men were coming out into the restaurant foyer as Tessa and Sam exited the restroom. Chase stood tall, doing a security scan like he was in downtown Kabul. New places gave him paranoia. It had become part of his DNA. Post-traumatic stress was his shadow, and he had to fight every day to keep a handle on it. Syria did more than injure him physically. It messed with his head; thanks to the drugs he took to stay alive.

Now that he had his body back in shape, he was working hard on the rest of it. Dr. Wu, the Enigma psychiatrist, along with doctors at Walter Reed, had made that much easier, too. Although he had crossed swords with Dr. Wu many times over the years, he had to admit the man was a genius at getting inside your head, especially when you wanted no part of it. If it hadn't been for his care, Tessa would have crashed and burned a long time ago. He was thankful for his help and because of that, he consented to giving him a piece of his soul.

Now the ghosts of his past were starting to crowd in on him again, with Andre Lavelle Vion strutting around like he was the antichrist. For all he knew, he might be. He certainly had the personality to fit one.

But the secret he carried about Abigail had begun to weigh heavily on his conscience. Tessa didn't know the whole story, and he should have told her long ago, maybe the first week they met. He had an opportunity and didn't take it. But, in his defense, there was no way he could know that Tessa would become such an integral part of his life.

By the time he'd fallen in love with her, the thought occurred to him there would never be a time when she needed to know the truth of the story that happened long ago. The truth would cast a deceptive light on the reason he kept her at Enigma. He told himself keeping her close would ensure that someday Andre would make a mistake and he'd have Tessa to get what he wanted. Revenge.

As time passed, all he really wanted was for her to be a part of his life, to make a family, and start a life without conflict and deception. Now, here he was, using the best part of him as bait to destroy the evilest man in the world. He underestimated the attraction between Andre and Tessa. Although she knew the facts about him and even had Nora to give a firsthand experience, he could see the interest in her eyes when they spoke of him.

Tessa was a collector of bad boys. It was him on that first day they met, sparking a chord inside her that yielded to his every demand. Less than a year later, he let her slip through his fingers in

Afghanistan, only to be found by the Tribesman, who, like himself, did not give her up willingly. There had been a few with Enigma and others who had not been on the right side of the law. Something about her attracted trouble, and she always embraced it, thinking good would come of it.

This time was different. Andre Lavelle Vion was an evil man with ambition, money, brilliance, connections, and power to get what he wanted. Wanting to be in charge of two powerful nations probably was not uncommon to such men, but Andre might pull it off. But how?

He reached out to take her hand as she approached. Slipping her hand in his, he felt the coolness of her touch and stared down into her eyes that smiled back at him. Every time he remembered she was now his to have and to hold, his heart skipped a beat. If anything should ever happen to her, he'd never forgive himself.

Glancing toward the interior of the restaurant, Tessa squeezed his hand. "Can we go? If there is more to be discussed, let's just go to our suite."

"Your room is still bugged, I'm told," Ben admitted. "My suite is clean." He followed Tessa's line of sight. "Did he introduce you to his head of security?"

Before Tessa could answer, Honey breezed by them, offering a snide grin, but didn't speak.

"Ben, did you know she would be here? She implied Enigma contacted her about getting the job with Vion," Samantha continued.

"Honey doesn't keep me informed of her whereabouts and for good reason. I don't like it," he added. "And no, I didn't contact her. She is not on my Christmas card list, either. However, she has her usefulness at times."

"I don't like it, either." Chase pulled Tessa after him as the group headed for the elevators. "But having her on the inside might be to our advantage, especially if Tessa were to need help and we couldn't get there."

"I'm not going to be alone with him unless you guys are close by. Don't worry about that. Besides, Honey and I are good friends. She wouldn't hurt me. I'm sure of it."

The elevator doors closed as Samantha snorted a response. "There are times you astound me with your gullibility, Tessa.

She'd sacrifice her own mother if it meant a few dollars in her pocket. She is much like Vion in that she's a sociopath. You're just a pet human to her."

"Ouch," Tessa snapped. "Guess you are a little jealous of our friendship after all."

"Ladies," Ben butted in, "if I have to listen to any more of your bickering tonight, I'll off you myself."

~ ~ ~ ~

Honey took her time locating the table since Andre watched her like she might be on the menu. Her pale-lavender cocktail dress that sparkled around the scoop neckline, enhanced the red in her hair and the green of her eyes. Most of the time, she was mistaken for a petite, rough-and-tumble tomboy. Tonight, she emulated an elegante lady with the charm of a pit viper.

Her boss stood and held the chair for her. "You know the two women."

She sat down and reached for the wine the waiter poured for her. "Of course. Dr. Cordova is a dangerous and sinister agent of a government organization called Enigma. One of the president's pet projects. Or so I hear."

"And Tessa?" he asked offhandedly.

"A smart woman when it comes to geographical conflict and cultures. She works for the university, as you already know. But when it comes to common sense, she doesn't have enough to come in out of the rain."

He remembered running in the rain with her and thought her laughter sounded magical.

She continued. "Too trusting and not a clue when it comes to reading people. Why else would she have befriended me? It won't be as difficult to isolate and influence her as you hoped. However, Captain Hunter is extremely protective and possessive when it comes to her. I've run into him before. He's a dangerous man."

"Can you handle him and what we've discussed?"

She reached over and laid a cool hand on the top of his, drawing his frosty gaze downward. "You'd be surprised at what I can do, Monsieur Vion." She smiled, withdrew her hand then took another sip of wine. "Shall we order?"

CHAPTER 22

Tessa called home before the kids went to school to reassure herself things were as they should be. The night before her father contacted her to apologize for nearly wrecking their lives. His voice cracked several times as if he might be choking back tears. Thankfully, her mother followed with reports on their well-being. She took the cell phone to their rooms and videoed them sleeping.

"We're going to have a long talk when you get home, Tessa Marie. We did not raise you to be some kind of James Bond."

"I'm not a spy, Mom. I gather intel and use culture awareness to solve problems. You give me too much credit."

"Don't lie to your momma. Things have finally fallen into place with all my questions. And you tell your captain I'm going to horsewhip him when he gets home."

Chase called out, "You're on speakerphone, Beth. You'll have to catch me first."

"Humph. Not if I'm carrying my twenty-two."

"Mom, I have to go. I'll call in the morning."

The following morning, the kids were anxious to talk to her. Hearing Heather's voice in its usual singsong tone of excitement gave her peace of mind. They hurried off to get ready for school. Chase came to her side when Ken got on the phone.

"Ken, thank you for staying the night. I felt so much better with you and Tom there." Her voice had softened, and she wished she could reach through the phone and hug them both. "Was my dad a pain in the butt?"

"No, but your mom sure was. Zoric needs to pick up a few of her tricks for his interrogation routine."

Tessa smiled at his irritation. "Sorry about that." She passed the phone to Chase and continued to get dressed, fully aware that her husband was watching her every move with great delight.

"Ken, I owe you and Tom big-time. What's the plan for today?"

"Both the kids' schools are taken care of. All three are wearing trackers. Video feed started several hours ago to make sure nothing unusual was going on at their school. So far, so good. Tessa's dad is still a bit shook up, and Beth has been giving the kids way too many hugs and kisses according to Sean Patrick."

"And the new guy? Lazarus?"

"He's a piece of work, but he came through with flying colors. Had everything under control by the time we found out there was a problem yesterday. Kind of a weirdo."

Tessa smiled at hearing Ken's evaluation and Chase's chuckle at the description that followed. She shouted out so Ken could hear her. "I think he's kinda hot."

"So, Tessa has met him?" Ken asked through a groan.

She hurried over and leaned into the phone as Chase zipped up her dress with his free hand. "Only briefly, but he's just so mysterious and, you know, handsome."

"Should I be worried?" Chase spoke loud enough that Ken could hear. "Ken, maybe if you'd worn a little black lipstick, you'd be zipping up Tessa's dress instead of me."

Tessa frowned and slapped away his hand that had slid down her backside. Taunting Ken about his crush did not amuse her. "Ken, you're perfect the way you are," she teased to make Chase's eyes grow darker.

"Chase, I gotta go. I'm getting a call from Lazarus. Must be time to interrogate our guests."

Chase shoved his phone into a pocket before pulling her into his arms. "I say we skip the first session. It's just Ben welcoming world leaders." He chuckled.

In these tender moments, she realized how happy her heart was now and how empty it had been all those years with Robert, her kids' father. Nothing compared to how she felt when Chase entered a room and cast a hard glance her way. The best part was watching it soften as he held her determined stare to not be intimidated. The love he showered on her body and soul filled the deep crevices that had long been empty. Such emptiness prevented her from reaching her full potential. The moment Chase crashed into her life, those crevices began to close. Now, with no barriers to the love they both wanted for so long, finally materialized to this moment in time.

Yet one secret still existed that could possibly damage, maybe destroy, this fairy-tale love story. The baby. She had to tell him soon. But not now. A few more days wouldn't make a difference.

The phone hummed in Chase's pocket. Tessa kissed his neck and worked her way up to his mouth as he looked at the caller ID. He smiled at her and kissed her firmly before pulling away.

"Ben. Yes. Sorry. We're on our way." He clicked off.

"It's uncanny how he knows when any of us are trying to outmaneuver him." She walked over to grab her briefcase. "So much for skipping out."

~ ~ ~ ~

Ken Montgomery paced and gave his brain freedom to race through the day's events that brought him to this place in time. What had gone wrong? Why were the two suspects from the kidnapping attempt dead? They had been secured in the bowels of Enigma at the university headquarters. Tom Cooper, his partner, had continued as bus driver for the return trip back to the school and waited for security to take his place. Meanwhile, he and Lazarus took charge of the prisoners.

Each had their own cell with more comfort than they deserved, in Ken's opinion, but nothing had been left behind to commit suicide. So, how did they die? After dinner at Tessa's house the night before, Lazarus kept his tablet at his fingertips. He monitored their transition and recorded their conversations until they settled down. Vitals remained stable. Lighting and temperature created an environment for comfort to instill a sense of calm.

They weren't going to rattle their sensibilities until the morning when their guard was down. However, their ability to communicate with each other ended when the soundproof barrier activated. Previous guests often commented that the quiet was deafening. Although the basics of food and water had been provided on a tray before they arrived, there would be no contact until morning. Only Lazarus and several gatekeepers would be able to hear and see if a problem arose. None had.

"What the hell happened, Lazarus?" Ken got in Lazarus's face and, for the first time, the man appeared shaken. "Don't tell me you don't know. Give me answers. Now!"

"Right." He motioned for Ken to follow him to the computer sitting on a metal table outside the guest enclosure. "I put this feed on a fast track for you to see. I've been through it twice. I've broken it down in two-hour increments and had my people each take a section to reevaluate in case I missed something. Like me, they saw nothing unusual."

"What time did they die?"

"Our medical examiner took the bodies an hour ago."

"I know," he growled. "I was here when they were being transferred to the medical unit. I sent our forensics team in, remember? Do you need coffee or something?" Lazarus rolled his shoulders then leveled a dangerous, narrowed look at the man in charge. "Because not only do you look like a zombie this morning, you're acting like one. If I find out you were out hobnobbing with the undead and dancing naked under the moon instead of doing your job, I'll not only scrape that black lipstick off with my rusty pocket knife, but I'll turn you over to Captain Hunter who has the sense of humor of a rattlesnake." Once more, he was in the new agent's face.

This time, Lazarus leveled an icy glare back at the lieutenant. His nostrils flared, and he straightened to his full height, which made him tower over Ken. When he lowered his chin, Lazarus took on the expression of a demon. "No disrespect, Lieutenant Montgomery, but I find your breath rancid in my face and your tone offensive. Keep it up, and I won't be the only one hobnobbing with the undead—if you get my drift."

Ken couldn't help but be impressed as he felt his mouth twist into a half grin as his bottom lip jutted out. Having spent most of his life in the military and now Enigma, most men were easily intimidated by his macho bravado. Apparently, Lazarus hadn't gotten the memo concerning chain of command. He squinted a visual appraisal that raked over the agent's face.

"I don't like you, Lazarus," Ken admitted through clenched teeth.

"You're not exactly my cup of tea, either," he offered in a deep voice as one eyebrow arched. His face returned to a solemn, expressionless façade. "Now that we have got that out of the way, can I tell you what I do know until we hear from the autopsy results?"

"That's what I asked for ten minutes ago."

Lazarus hooked his thumbs into his black leather pants pockets and stood with his weight shifted to one hip. "The two fell into a deep sleep around ten. Vitals were good, and we stopped monitoring those when they entered into REM sleep. Visuals continued throughout the night. Nothing out of the ordinary. Environmental impacts were optimal for a nonthreatening experience."

"Just what the hell does that mean?"

"Means it was cool and the lighting perfect."

"Why didn't you just say that?"

Now it was Lazarus's turn to smirk. "Just messing with you, Lieutenant Montgomery." When Ken didn't take the bait to be taunted into another show of intimidation, the agent continued. "There were no visible signs of trauma when the first on scene arrived this morning. When they hadn't awakened by eight thirty, breakfast was delivered and the attendant recognized something was wrong."

"Could they have been poisoned? The food they were given? The water? The pumped-in air?" Ken cocked his head to insult the new guy. "That means the environmental impacts for an optimal nonthreatening experience."

The comment brought a wide thin smile to Lazarus's mouth. "I doubt it was poison. The ME will know for sure, but there were no visible signs of redness around the mouth, smell of chemicals, vomiting. The only symptom was the deep REM sleep you'd experience with being exposed to gas. All systems were perfect. As to the food, I asked the forensic team to check for any foreign substances that could be the problem. Again, there were no indications of food allergies, etc. They ate almost as soon as they arrived. Any toxin would have taken effect quickly and they would have gone into a number of medical alerts our program would have automatically detected then alerted us."

"Those CIA guys sometimes have a tooth capsule embedded where they can bite down and die within minutes." Ken knew he was just speculating on this one.

"I don't think that is the case. There would have been signs as I mentioned earlier." He activated the computer screen again showing the forensic team moving in the room in hazmat suits. "There were no power surges or time stamp deviations recorded from the time they entered the building." He glanced at the screen then to Ken, as if anticipating questions about the reliability of the computer. "Before you ask, our systems would pick up a cockroach walking across the floor. This is as good as it gets. Maybe better than NORAD."

"And how would you know that?"

"I worked as General Prescott's assistant. He was the commander there when I served in the Air Force. I helped him navigate the particulars."

"Somehow, I can't see you in a uniform." Ken gave a sideways glance when he spoke. Lazarus merely blinked and waited for him to continue. Ken cleared his throat. "I guess you can't imagine me in black lipstick, either."

"Actually, I can."

Ken frowned and got back to business. "We've got a few hours before we know any results of the autopsy. Any ideas as to what happened?"

"It's a long shot, but I wondered if there wasn't a kind of implant attached to their heart with a remote-control device that could stop their heartbeat. If that were true, then someone on the outside was watching when we took them in. Did you ever think you might have a mole?"

Ken could feel an inner shiver at the thought. "A mole? At Enigma? I was thinking more of a pacemaker."

"Exactly. That will be easy to find pretty quickly. As to the mole..."

"I'll get someone on that as soon as I leave here." He glanced at his watch. "Now I need to call the director with the bad news."

~ ~ ~ ~

Andre Lavelle Vion listened to Franklin without making eye contact. The cup of coffee he held in one hand while standing in the open French doors cooled quickly with the morning breeze caressing the room. Without speaking, he held out the cup, and the assistant strode across the room to retrieve it. In seconds, he'd returned with a fresh cup almost too hot to hold.

"Continue," was all Andre said as Franklin cleared his throat and began to speak once more.

"The two men didn't die immediately." When Andre didn't ask why, Franklin continued. "Something went wrong."

"Obviously," he whispered.

"They didn't appear to suffer."

"Pity." Andre took a sip of coffee and let the hot brew trickle down his throat to help chase the chill away. His eyes cut to the floor of suites below him, curving away from his section of the resort. The group with Captain Hunter and Tessa were spread out on that level.

"The bodies have been taken by the medical examiner. They may find the implants."

"Yes. That is likely. But they won't know what they are. We still have time." He took a deep breath. "Have we any information from our lab on the matter?"

"Not yet." The assistant flinched when Andre cocked his head and narrowed his eyes. "I'm told within the hour; they'll have a completed report. However, our phlebotomy technicians have arrived to take samples from everyone at the conference. We'll begin after your presentation."

"Do you have more intel on the group with Mrs. Hunter?"

"All work at the University of Science and Technology in Sacramento, California. It is one of twelve universities specializing in medical, artificial intelligence, engineering, and climate change. However, the usual fields of study you'd find in liberal arts colleges are also highly sought after. Interesting that they have an extensive political science department."

"How so?" Andre now turned his whole body to glare at the assistant.

"A number of those students have gone on to obtain jobs at the

State Department then on to government posts throughout the world. Many are now placed at the Defense and Justice Departments as well. There's talk of them being problem solvers for the president."

"That's what political science majors do, Franklin."

"True. But there appears to be a kind of connection between these twelve universities and the White House."

Andre eyed Franklin and waited for him to continue. "And?"

"It appears that Mrs. Hunter has been involved in several off-books clandestine ventures at the president's request. She saved his life several years ago, and he likes to keep her close."

This brought a slight smile to his lips. "And how did this fragile flower manage to do that?"

"The president was injured in an assassination attempt. Mrs. Hunter has type O negative blood."

"Making her a universal donor," he expressed with an almost cheerful tone to his voice. "So, her blood also runs through the big Texas president's veins. This is the start of a life-changing day, it seems."

"Mrs. Hunter—"

"Stop calling her that," Andre snapped then stormed across the room to pour himself a glass of fresh papaya juice. "Tessa will be enough. Having that troglodyte's name attached to hers is temporary."

"Yes, sir." Franklin ran finger in his collar as if he required more room to breathe. "What about the child, sir?"

"Plan B should be enough to encourage my future wife if she doesn't fall into line. Make the appropriate arrangements." He lowered his chin as he looked toward the assistant. "You're sure about her blood type?"

"Yes, sir."

"In that case, this time next year, we'll welcome our first child into the world." He took another deep breath and released it slowly as he gazed upward. "Definitely a good day, Franklin."

"Yes, sir."

CHAPTER 23

Three hundred invited guests mingled in the grand hall that resembled a hunting lodge with touches of Native American history mingled through the sparkle of crystal, fine table linens, and early morning pastries served beside the Arabian coffee on each table. The guest list consisted of heads of state, business giants, technology gurus, scientists, economists, and several university presidents who had been instrumental in the development of pathways toward a more peaceful world. Several nations were represented by their security forces, which included intelligent agencies.

Beyond the three hundred guests, an assistant for each was allowed to join the meetings as long as they didn't speak, take notes, or have a listening device. Their role was to be the eyes and ears of their boss in case they were asked later concerning a point or fact expressed.

Because security was tight, bodyguards and other protection entities stood their ground on the outside of any meeting room. They moved like shadows, quiet and almost invisible to the guests. At times, even the rich and famous liked to pretend they could live a normal life, free of threats and sacrifice.

This particular resort had been chosen because of its size, isolation, and comfort. Access to overseas flight in Atlanta then another eighty-seven miles to the resort felt ideal. A nearby airport could handle small jets to make the final leg of the trip. A few chose to do that, and others had their security drive them. It really depended on the financial circumstances of the guest.

Tessa loved the ambiance of the resort, including how spacious and old it felt. The warmth of the décor spoke of class and a bygone era mixed with a contemporary vibe that might appeal to the rich and famous. She had no idea if tourists visited or if it primarily served as a proper place for functions such as this.

She loved how the foyers circled the outside of the conference rooms and the great hall had its windows open with mountain breezes lifting gossamer-like curtains in a carefree dance. The smell of the outdoors and the recent rain refreshed her.

Standing here alone, Tessa felt achy and tired. Heather was almost six now, and remembering how it felt to be pregnant had faded with the years. The cool breeze made her feel better and reminded her she should eat, although nothing sounded appetizing. Focusing on the sweet lemony scent of the trillium flowers growing in abundance outside the windows settled her upset stomach.

"Good morning, Tessa," came a masculine voice, causing her to flinch. "I apologize. I didn't mean to break your reverie or frighten you," Andre Vion offered warmly. He took a step back.

"Good morning." She forced herself to smile. "I was just enjoying these trillium flowers. It's been a long time since I've seen them grow so profusely."

"Yes," he admitted, inhaling deeply. "They are quite refreshing. Be sure to visit the wildflower gardens here. The rhododendrons and azaleas should be blooming any day now. I'm told the mountain laurel is early this year because of the rains. Nice that Mother Nature decided to put on a show for us."

"It was very kind of her." Tessa noticed his comment was a show of good humor. She momentarily slipped and let herself think maybe he probably wasn't as bad as everyone kept telling her. Powerful men rubbed people the wrong way. But they were still just people. No way this man was a monster if he gave so much to charity. "Do you have a garden?"

"Not the kind I want—wild, unorganized, and beautiful."

"My father always said my gardens were willy-nilly. I would

tell him they were spontaneous growth patterns of delight."

This caused Andre to laugh good-naturedly. "And what did he say to that?"

"He said I had too much education and was too big for my britches."

This, too, made him laugh. Tessa had joined in the light moment when two people approaching them caught her eye. She turned her head to see Honey and Samantha glaring straight at her. In that moment, she felt as if she'd been caught with her hand in the cookie jar.

"Morning, ladies." Andre forced a simple stretch of his lips to mimic a smile. "I hope you rested last night in this beautiful place." His eyes raked over Samantha then met her glare with one of his own. His attention switched to Honey. "Ms. Lynch was telling me late last night"— his mouth turned up at one corner with a devilish insinuation— "the three of you are old friends. I would very much like to know more about how you came to—tangle, as they say."

Tessa could feel the hair rise on the nape of her neck looking at Samantha who might just kill the woman if the opportunity arose. There was no love lost between them. And being caught in the middle was no place she wanted to be. Before she knew what was happening, Andre lifted her hand to his lips then raised his eyes to hers, leaving a sense of breathlessness inside her.

"Unfortunately, my assistant is paging me from inside the grand hall." He kissed her hand and smiled. "Perhaps we can stroll the gardens again later today."

Before Tessa could protest, he nodded to the other two women and was gone. When she refocused on her on-again, off-again friends, she noticed they were giving her the if-looks-could-kill expression. To shift the focus off her, Tessa moved closer to Honey.

"Oh my gosh, are you sleeping with him, Honey?" Tessa growled.

"I can categorially say there was no sleeping involved." She smiled. "I suggested maybe Samantha would like to join us tonight, since she enjoys such things." Her smile thinned as she eyed the much taller, and stronger woman.

"Be that as it may, I'm a little more discriminating on who I—"

Samantha's voice had turned icy, when Tessa butted in.

"Stop it," she said, rolling her eyes upward. "Do you guys think about anything but sex? I mean, seriously." Tessa leveled her disappointed-mom look at them both. It froze her kids in their tracks, but it didn't appear to be working on these two.

"What's he up to?" Samantha scanned the area around them to spot nosey guests.

"I'm just here to offer protection. He's aloof and as engaging as a wet paper towel—until he wants something."

"You mean like last night when you went into Vion's suite and didn't leave until early this morning?"

"Aww. You've been keeping tabs on me, Sam. I'm touched. Were you worried?"

"Damn right I'm keeping tabs on you, you sick psycho."

"Careful, Sam," she whispered. "You don't want to hurt my feelings."

"Feelings?"

Tessa once more interfered. "That's enough, you two. Honey, honestly, I'm concerned about you being his security. I know you're capable of protection, but, according to Enigma, Andre Vion is dangerous. I've experienced firsthand how suave and interesting he is, but he has a ruthless reputation. Whether it's true or not, there's no way any of us knows for sure."

"Chase knows," Honey smirked. "Or hasn't he told you?"

"Told me what?" Tessa said flippantly. She knew the woman enjoyed toying with her like a killer whale would a baby seal before it was eaten. "Never mind. You're just trying to rattle me." She'd started to walk away when Honey snaked out a hand and grabbed her arm in a vise grip. Tessa stared down at the hold then up into the dead eyes of an assassin.

"Look, luv, me and you are friends. Everybody has something to hide, even you, and most certainly your captain. As to Andre, be careful. He wants you to think he's a gentleman, but, in truth, he is a cunning pooka." Tessa shot her a bewildered expression. "A pooka. A goblin. He will trick you into believing he's one thing, and that will not be the truth. Even your handsome captain is being a pooka."

"We're done here," Samantha fumed, pushing Honey's hand off Tessa. "If there's anyone who is a pooka, it's you. Stay away from us. You're a menace to anyone you come in contact with. If any of us come to harm because of your actions, I will slowly gut you with my car keys then drag you up and down a dirt road, tied to my bumper."

"Then you'd better bring help."

"This time, Andre Lavelle Vion will be your undoing. I almost look forward to that part." Samantha took a step away then turned back to get in Honey's face. "And I don't need any help where you're concerned." She pivoted toward Tessa. "Let's go. Now."

~ ~ ~ ~

Honey Lynch could feel her body tighten and release over and over until she took a deep breath to discharge the unfamiliar sensation of anxiety surging through her veins. Rolling her shoulders in a slow, careful motion revealed nothing as to her discomfort. Slipping her hand into her jacket, the Sig Saucer in her shoulder holster reassured her. The movement of her long fingers then moved to the side of her belt, where she kept a knife. She reminded herself of several other weapons fastened on various parts of her body, slim enough to feel weightless.

Samantha Cordova was the one person she'd never been able to intimidate or frighten. Sometimes she enjoyed such banter, and other times a rage deep inside her flared up so fast it nearly overwhelmed her. This was one of those times. Being threatened, nine times out of ten, ended up with a person unable to walk back a threat of pain. One of these days, she would deal with the woman.

Then there was Tessa. What to do about that awful, little thick? In Ireland, the term "thick" was used to describe someone who was stupid. It felt right in this case. Honey stood statue still, chin down, staring out through her lashes as people buzzed around her. Tessa. Tessa. Tessa. Even her name irritated her. Didn't she know the danger surrounding her future?

What was it about the Grass Valley housewife that men just fell over themselves for her? She wasn't that pretty and was a clumsy clown at times. Yet men like Captain Hunter and the Tribesman desired her to the point of becoming more dangerous than they already were to protect her from people like—her. A good description of Tessa on most occasions would be something like a ball of sunshine and a basket full of puppies.

Then there was Andre Lavelle Vion, a man wired not so differently than herself. She'd recognized the sadistic thirst for control and obedience the moment they met. Keeping him protected was only part of what he wanted from her. Although sex the previous evening was unplanned, it was pleasant enough until it wasn't. The man satisfied himself then asked her to tell him about Tessa. Talk about a buzzkill. But what did she care? She'd done the same thing dozens of times in order to get close to a target. But not once had she ever become invisible to the man in her bed—until last night. Tessa had more to worry about than Vion.

"Let's not make this more than it was, Honey." Andre slipped into a satin robe.

"Don't flatter yourself," Honey cooed. "Just testing the waters on my part." She swung her legs to the floor and pulled on her clothes. "Now that we have those questions answered, I can concentrate on what you hired me for." When he didn't respond, she turned her head to see him watching her like a hungry raptor.

"I hired you to do my bidding when it comes time to take a kill shot. Then you can disappear into whatever hole you live until the next time I require your services."

Honey stood and smoothed her clothing slowly, pausing on different parts of her body as she faced him. "Exactly who do you want me to kill?"

"Captain Hunter for sure." He walked around the bed and smiled wickedly before jerking her into his arms and slowly undressing her. "But I suspect you'll need to deal with Samantha Cordova first. Will that be a problem?" He kissed her neck and shoulders.

"Not at all. I'll even do it for free." She pushed away from him and ran her hands down her body. "But this is not free," she said tilting her head. "And Tessa?"

He took a deep breath and stepped away to study her. "I'll keep you posted concerning her. But no harm should come to her."

"She's fragile," Honey warned.

"I like that. Makes things easier."

"What kind of things?"

"Why, Honey, do I detect concern in that cold, dark heart of yours?"

"Absolutely. I don't want things to blow back on me. I plan for every possibility. Captain Hunter is in charge of a whole squad of people just like me, and none of them would think twice at putting me in their crosshairs if I don't do this right. Tessa flits around like a freakin' butterfly without a care in the world. They find that endearing. I suspect it's because they're all a bunch of animals and she is their token get-out-of-hell-free card."

"Sounds to me like Tessa possesses a great deal of influence."

"At one point, she considered me one of her closest friends."

"I find that hard to believe." He glared down his nose at her. "You are an acquired taste."

He reached out and toyed with the red hair that fell into her eyes.

"Evidently, we both have a taste for roughness."

"Yes." He smiled slowly as he eyed her from head to toe. "Something I rather admire about you."

"Stick to business, and pay me well," she said pushing his hand away, "and I might show you other things I have a taste for. No charge."

Andre's lips pressed together hard enough they puckered as his gaze grew dark and penetrating. "And do you think Tessa is of the same mind?"

"Tessa is a babe in the woods."

"Perfect. I like breaking in…" He smiled. "Maybe we could pretend how I might do said 'babe in the woods.' You've given me much to think about." He tugged her into a tight hold and inhaled her scent. "Show me those things you have a taste for. Maybe I'll keep the two of you to have some diversity."

CHAPTER 24

Chase watched Tessa enter the grand hall, only to stop and speak to several people. One was a famous writer who wrote geopolitical thrillers and often spoke at national security functions in DC. The two women kept in touch after meeting at their university. There was also Bonnie Finley, the current Secretary of State, who had lied, clawed, and blackmailed her way into one of the most powerful positions in the US government. She and Tessa had a history together in Afghanistan. He wasn't sure what the Secretary of State held over Tessa's head, but they always played nice in public and pretended to be friends. They were both tight-lipped concerning Afghanistan, and he could guess why. The Tribesman.

"Madam Secretary, it's good to see you again," Chase lied, slipping his arm around Tessa's waist.

"Captain Hunter. You're looking fit after such an ordeal in Syria in the last year." Her gaze went from him to Tessa then back to him. "I see the two of you finally are together. Congratulations." Her eyes bored into Tessa. "I hope everyone is as thrilled as I am over this newest development."

Chase leaned in and whispered, "Now's your chance to hoodwink the Tribesman like you do everyone else. Just be careful. He's not as nice as me."

"Yes. I remember," she sniped with a quick glance at Tessa who had paled. "I suppose that's part of his charm, don't you think, Tessa?"

"Ben wants us to be seated." He didn't want the woman to rattle Tessa. "Nice seeing you, Madam Secretary. Fingers crossed you'll be able to rule a third world country in my lifetime."

Tessa waited until they had reached their table near the front of the stage to giggle. "That was mean."

"But funny. The woman is a cutthroat politician and will do anything for power. I don't know what she is holding over your head concerning Afghanistan, but whatever it is, I'm on your side. Remember that."

She hugged his arm. "I know you are. It's mostly that I…"

She'd killed a Taliban soldier to protect a young girl and the secretary from being assaulted. "I know, Tessa. I'm proud of you for whatever you had to do to stay alive there." She looked up at him, vulnerable and a little sad. "Heaven only knows the things I had to do to survive in Syria. I love you no matter what you've done. Understand?"

"Yes. I understand." She nodded. "That goes both ways, Chase. I just want this to be over with and to start our life together."

"That's what I want, too."

"Is there anything you haven't told me about your connection with Andre besides his reputation? How well did you know this Abigail I'm supposed to look like? Were the two of you involved? Is that why the two of you hate each other so much?"

He didn't really want to have this conversation right now. "I knew her only as a friend of my sister's. We never really got to know each other. When I went to visit Christine, she took my undivided attention. They weren't roommates. Both were majoring in music. I met Andre one night when he came to pick her up. I went to one of her performances, much to my displeasure. All classical oboe stuff. Have you ever had to sit through one of those kinds of concerts?" He frowned and rolled his eyes upward in frustration. Making Tessa smile at his deceit shamed him only a little. "What makes you think there's something else?"

"I saw Honey in the hall, and she—"

"Honey," he snapped, "is a half bubble off most of the time. I swear the woman enjoys stirring things up. The mere fact she's with Andre now should demonstrate she's a lost cause."

Occasionally he'd dreamed of wrapping his fingers around her neck and giving it a good snap. "Avoid her at all cost. Pay her no mind, Tessa." He nodded toward the podium. "Ben is about to start the meeting."

The Enigma Team did not sit together as did other groups who may have either traveled together or represented a geographic region. Instead, they positioned themselves throughout the room, mingling with men and women known to have political or economic agendas. Although there was no open animosity among these attendees, Enigma never underestimated the importance of self-preservation or the ability to avoid total transparency with each guest's wish list for the upcoming year.

From now on, at any large gathering, such as this, they would never be seated with the same group of people twice. The endgame was to form friendships and alliances. Attendees were encouraged to explore the possibilities required to obtain the world peace initiative. Enigma people were used to dealing with chaos. Peace initiatives were not really their thing.

For years, these meetings had provided economic recovery for sick and devastated nations around the globe. In spite of Asia and Africa being, once again, snubbed, it was thought that would no longer be possible after this year.

Applause rippled across the room as Ben took his seat. Chase hadn't heard a word he said. The thought that Honey Lynch had been playing mind games with Tessa disturbed him. Honey had worked with him several times over the years, and they had been intimate a few times. It would be just her style to bring up ancient history to plant a seed of distrust. Hopefully, Tessa could outmaneuver the woman's mind games. He had told her all things related to Honey Lynch soon after they met. The idea they might be friends continued to disturb him.

Unfortunately, there were a couple of other things he'd failed to disclose, thinking there would never be a reason to tell her. Now, here he was, married to the woman he'd desired for way too long, and she had no idea why he hated Andre. When would be a good time to confess?

"Chase?" Tessa touched his arm lightly. "Ben asked you a question."

"Oh sorry." He blinked back to reality then turned to Ben. "I'm a little wiped out. Didn't sleep much last night."

Ben glanced at Tessa and grinned, before shifting his eyes back to Chase who chuckled seeing her blush. He nodded at the director as he spoke. "I had to go over my notes for today. The whole kidnapping attempt kept pressing on me."

"Yes. It concerned all of us. My question was if you'd heard from Ken this morning." Ben sounded cool as his attention scanned the area.

"Before I came down here." Chase stretched a stiff leg then rubbed the area as if in pain. "He had an incoming call and cut me off. I should hear back in an hour or so. I suspect they'll be doing interrogations soon enough."

The program chairperson finished giving last-minute instructions and dismissed the guests. A few mingled, making their way to the exits. Others checked their phones or the schedule. Several of the Enigma Team joined them as they rose from their table. Vernon was doing his technology updates and checks from his room. They wouldn't be seeing much of him, given he was keeping tabs on various persons of interest.

"Zoric, you're on the panel for global arts." Ben glanced at his phone as it buzzed. "I understand the other members are a little intimidated by you. Try not to—excuse me. I need to take this." Ben moved a few steps away with the phone to his ear.

Chase watched Ben's forehead crease as he lowered his head. His lips pooched out in irritation like it often did when things went wrong. Ben jerked his chin up then pivoted toward the group. His eyes locked with Chase as the others followed his line of sight to the director. Their faces became solemn as if they sensed trouble. They waited patiently for him to click off and return.

"Please tell me my kids are safe." Tessa folded her arms across her chest.

"Yes. They're safe, but we have upped the security." Ben patted her shoulder as if a concerned father. The man rarely showed compassion to anyone. Although he favored Tessa, it was odd for him to openly show unease. "Ken has informed me our two suspects were found dead this morning in their cells."

Between the intake of breath and a couple of colorful words, it was easy to determine the level of shock.

"What happened?" Chase pulled out his phone to check for

messages from his lieutenant. There were none.

"Our medical examiner is in the process of answering those questions. There was no hint of distress, poison, intrusion, or suicide. Sleeping peacefully, until they weren't. Lazarus is in the process of sending a report. Nothing out of the way. Hopefully, we'll have more information soon."

"Someone didn't want them interrogated." Carter Johnson, former astronaut, knew a thing or two about tight spots since he'd spent a great deal of time on the International Space Station. "Might check the ventilation systems. Were there signs of nightmares or snoring? Those are two of the things NASA watches out for because astronauts can wake up oxygen-deprived and gasping for air. A bubble of their own exhaled carbon dioxide could form around their heads. I doubt those jokers were in as good a shape as astronauts. Could have been subtle and no one caught they were in distress."

"I'll pass that along, Carter. Thanks." Ben nodded and exhaled slowly. "Those cells are nearly a hotel room, with fresh air pumped in round the clock, beds rather than a hard cot and even a piece of carpet on the floor. Doesn't mean things didn't go wrong, though, or maybe got sabotaged."

"Who was in charge?"

"Lazarus."

~ ~ ~ ~

Ken Montgomery didn't pace outside the ME's lab. Instead, he stared at the door as if by doing so he'd be able to open it and digest the information he needed to keep one step ahead of whatever was happening. His heart didn't race, and his blood pressure was normal according to his smartwatch. Although he hadn't glanced at it, he knew. This was one of many dangerous situations he'd survived to fight another day or at least knock some heads together to make sense of chaos.

His breathing was slow and even. Focus was channeled in the right direction. That direction was cause and effect. Deviation endangered him from putting the pieces together. One piece that didn't fit was why no one knew there was trouble. With state-of-the-art systems, all kinds of bells should have been going off.

Staring at the door continued. Questions kept rising.

One of the tech guys brought him a file folder he'd asked for concerning the late-night schedule. He scrolled down until he found a name.

"Lazarus," he growled through clenched teeth. "You'd better hope that name gets you back from the grave a second time."

CHAPTER 25

"And in conclusion," Andre addressed the packed room, "finding cures for blood diseases such as those you see listed on the screen means all of us must step up to do our part. The impact and benefits that collected plasma offers not only affects your citizens but other countries who are desperate to save future generations." He stepped closer to the audience and pointed to the twenty recliners with a lab technician at each station, posed as if ready for action. "Therefore, I have set up these stations for the next two days to begin that process of making a difference."

The screen then showed before-and-after pictures of people, mostly children, who had benefited from Andre's work. The music was gripping, and the narration pulled at heartstrings and would have made National Geographic proud if they'd been involved. When the screen went dark, Andre placed a hand on his heart and slowly appraised the audience.

"Today, I ask you. Will you step up and donate plasma for research, for someone who needs saving, for a new beginning? I'm so sincere and passionate about this project, I will give each person two thousand dollars for donating on this first day." There were surprised murmurs across the room. "All participants will be entered to win a million dollars for a charity of their choice. The drawing for that prize will be on our last night of this conference. If you have questions, my assistants in the yellow blazers can help. Please. Don't hesitate to change the world."

Although the room was crowded and a certain amount of movement toward the donation stations blocked his view, Andre spotted Tessa standing in the back, near the double doors. She watched him with an aloofness his bioengineers often wore. They were often cold and unaffected by the outcome of their progress. In many ways, they were very much like him.

Tessa, on the other hand was a ray of light with the enthusiasm and energy of an unspoiled child. The joy in her blue eyes and the laughter in her voice gave him a kind of reprieve from the drab, unemotional world he lived in. What was it about her that made him feel—normal. It was intoxicating.

His entire life he'd been different from others. Then he met Abigail. Even when she committed suicide, he felt nothing but frustration that his plan had not been fulfilled. Remembering she had that same glow as Tessa gave him pause. Unfortunately, with time, the glow began to fade. Confidence was high that this time, things would work out.

Whatever mistakes he'd made then would not be repeated. As he slowly approached her, others stopped him to offer congratulations, but he never took his gaze off her. Her attention bore into what was left of his soul. She stood rigid with her head tilted slightly, as if she saw him in a new light. Unforeseen events in her life must have made her both hurt and angry. Others were feeding her segments of a story he hadn't finished writing. He'd seen the same look on Abigail long ago.

"Tessa, I'm glad you stopped by. Were you here for the whole presentation?" It took effort on his part, but he managed a thin smile. He noticed her eyes turned from blue to violet. Interesting. It must be a temperament thing. How did she do that and how could he manipulate it?

"Only the last ten minutes or so. The session I presented ended earlier than expected. Most wanted to rush over and catch all or part of yours." Her face remained without expression, giving Andre the desire to make her stop.

"I won't apologize only because it also brought you here." He watched her eyebrow arch in skepticism.

"Are you flirting with me, or are you always so coy with women?" She narrowed her eyes and surveyed the room, appearing interested in the various heads of state and scientists that were standing in line to make a donation. It occurred to him that seeing her interested in other people made him a little jealous. Another surge of feeling normal.

"I'm definitely flirting with you." He grinned in amusement, causing her to turn her attention back to him. Now those eyes were blue again. This time, one corner of her delicate lips turned up. "And yes, I try to be coy with women. Meeting people, especially women, does not come easy for me. Probably because I work all the time and get out of practice."

"Just so you know, you're doing a good job, Andre Lavelle Vion."

He wanted to ask how the color-changing technique in her eyes worked but decided to experiment on his own. "Would you like for me to tell you about the work we do?" He fanned his hand out toward the stations.

She nodded and took a step in that direction as Andre locked his fingers behind his back and walked slowly to prolong the encounter.

"My field is cultural and geopolitical geography, so I'm afraid I don't have much of an understanding of biochemistry or molecular biology unless it relates to the movement of populations or affects cultural nuisances. I thought, since I'm serving on a panel with you later today, I should see what all the excitement is about. I warn you, you may be talking over my head."

He hoped his smile was contagious enough to see one of hers. It wasn't. "Ahh. Well then, I can show off a bit in hopes of winning you over."

"Winning me over?" she uttered as she halted and stared at him, the violet color seeping back into the blue of her eyes.

"Yes. I want you to discover that my work is important and can affect threatened populations around the globe."

She blinked, and the curves of her face softened. It was like a switch had turned on to reveal the light in her skin and eyes. Was this what falling in love felt like?

"Please, tell me what you're doing here today." She stepped toward a station.

"Stop me if you feel a yawn coming on. I get carried away with all of the advancements we've made. The next couple of days, we're concentrating on the collection of plasma."

"I had a couple of friends in college who would donate plasma for extra money. But honestly, I never bothered to find out exactly what plasma is used for. Blood transfusions are so common, along with blood drives, that I never stopped to consider plasma was so important."

"Plasma is used to produce therapies that treat people with rare, chronic diseases and disorders such as hemophilia and a genetic lung disease, as well as in the treatment of trauma, burns, and shock." He cocked his head toward her and was pleased to see that he had her undivided attention. She really was interested. "It helps boost the patient's blood volume, which can prevent shock and helps with clotting."

"I had no idea." She nodded to the person being readied for plasma extraction. "Is it painful?"

"Not at all," he chuckled. "It's a technical process, but simple in nature as well. Basically, the liquid portion of the donor's blood is separated from the cells. Blood is drawn from one arm and sent through a high-tech machine that collects the plasma. Once that is done, the donor's red blood cells and platelets are returned to the donor mixed with saline. Takes only a few minutes longer than donating whole blood. As a matter of fact, my process has greatly accelerated the process."

"So, then what? I mean the plasma here, I'm sure you can't just pack it in a suitcase." The smile he had been waiting for appeared and he waited a few seconds to respond as he drank in her expression. Soft blonde curls kept teasing her forehead. Watching her push the unruly curls behind her ears gave him the urge to do it for her.

With a measured smile he responded. "If I could figure out a way to do that, I might be able to save a lot of money on shipping and storage. However, donated plasma must be frozen within twenty-four hours of being donated in order to preserve its valuable clotting factors. We store it up to one year and can thaw it for transfusion when needed for a patient." He pointed to what appeared to be stainless steel freezers. "We have hired transport at the end of each day while we're here to avoid any delays. The mountain weather is temperamental this time of year so it seemed prudent to be proactive."

"You don't strike me as someone who leaves anything to chance." Her voice became cool as she tilted her head slightly to glare at him. Again, the eyes shaded to violet.

"I don't," he said in a way that matched her tone.

"Thank you for sharing. I should go. I have a luncheon with some Biblical archeologists to discuss ongoing problems in the West Bank. The prime minister requested I attend." She turned to leave, but Andre reached out and took her arm firmly. She flinched and jerked free.

"I sense I've done something to harm our budding relationship." When he took a step closer, she didn't budge, but her eyes narrowed. "Whatever it is, I apologize."

"I have to go."

"Could I show you the wildflower garden later?"

"I don't think so. My husband…" Her voice faded. "Thank you again, Andre—for everything." She pivoted and disappeared out the double doors.

Andre stared after her, disappointment bordering on rage at her audacity to leave so abruptly. At least she had spunk. He could work with that. Images flashed in his mind of the woman he intended to train to be the perfect mate. The way his heart was racing, he wondered if he wanted to sacrifice or keep that side of her. All this emotional nonsense was a temporary side effect of not acquiring immediate gratification. He would tire of it soon enough.

He heard his assistant stop several steps away. "Yes, Franklin?"

You have a meeting with the World Health Organization in the Azalea Room. You are part of the panel discussion. They wanted to go over a few things before guests arrived."

"What kind of things?"

"Who would be moderator. It's assumed Director-General Javier Gonzalez will be in charge."

Andre jerked his head around and stared at the assistant. "Did you correct the mistake, Franklin?"

"I'm sorry, sir. They brushed me off and said I had no authority at these meetings. However, they expect a packed house since you will be there." He pulled his shoulders back and waited patiently.

"Contact the Chinese equivalent to Secretary of State and tell him the problem. After all, he's the one who made sure Gonzalez got the job after a great deal of money changed hands. He has no scientific experience other than climatology."

"And if he refuses?"

"Remind him of what is implanted in his neck and that I have the app to make such decisions easier. I'll be there when I get there. Can you get this done by the time I arrive?"

"Yes, sir. I've also made sure you are seated next to Tessa on the panel."

Andre Lavelle Vion raised his chin in approval. "Excellent."

CHAPTER 26

Ken Montgomery wrinkled his nose from the smell of autopsies as he stared at the Enigma medical examiner. A box of donuts with a clear cellophane top rested on the desk. He noticed several were missing and wondered how anyone could possibly eat in here. Pulling up his mask, he recognized after seeing death most of his military life and causing a number of those, this place, this job, made him queasy. Poking around in a dead body just wasn't normal. Necessary, yes. Normal, no.

Dr. Gifford washed his hands while humming, of all things, a Christmas song. Gritting his teeth kept him from telling him to shut the hell up and give him the information he needed to know. The director and the others were waiting on him.

He'd checked on Tessa's children and her parents a few minutes earlier. All was well, but he was seriously thinking he needed to move them to a more secure location. To think how close they'd come to losing Heather yesterday still unnerved him. Chase had called and left a message that if needed, call the Tribesman. That was code for he was concerned about their safety, too.

Dr. Gifford turned and exhaled a long sigh as he locked eyes with Ken. The man's head resembled a peeled onion, and his mouth was too big for his face. The lips were thick like he'd had them enhanced. The beady, close-set eyes gave him a Mr. Potato

166

Head appearance. At the moment, although he had no reason to despise him, he could barely keep from shifting into his badass-soldier mode and giving him a shake before crashing his head into the box of donuts.

"You seem a little tense, Lieutenant Montgomery. First time in a morgue?" A condescending grin toyed with the clownish lips. When Ken pulled his mask down and lowered his chin slowly then glared at the ME with the darkness deep inside him, the man's grin faded. He cleared his throat and motioned for him to approach.

"What happened to these men?" Ken took a couple of stealthy steps in Dr. Gifford's direction. "Poison?"

He pushed his glasses up on his wide, narrow nose and shook his head. "Yes and no." He turned to a silver-colored tray and lifted an object the size of a flat pencil eraser. "There was one of these in each man's arm. I only noticed it because this one"—he pointed to the older of the two— "had a rash. When I examined it closer, I noticed a slightly harder object. I extracted it. Whatever was in it, he had a physical reaction. I noticed some skin eczema in several places. Could be why I found it. Nothing obvious on the other man."

"Any idea what it is?" Ken asked, amazed at the small size.

"Come." Dr. Gifford moved to a microscope and placed the object on a slide. He focused it then stepped back for Ken to take a look. "You'll see there is a slight opening, shaped like a slit. I'm guessing since both men died, they both had a kind of program to have it rip open and spill a toxin or maybe a time-sensitive bot that has a job to do and was released into their system."

"Could this have been done remotely, or were they doomed from the beginning?"

Dr. Gifford shrugged. "I need more information. I'm sending this to the lab to let them have a crack at the thing. But whatever it was leaked out, causing both of them to have a heart aneurysm. The usual symptom is severe pain in the middle or side of the abdomen in men. The pain can radiate intos the scrotum then—"

Ken held up his hand as he struggled to keep a straight face. "Geez, Doc. Spare me the particulars. There was no sign of them in pain or discomfort of any kind on the video feed."

"Yes. Well, in the early stages, an aortic aneurysm doesn't show symptoms. But this came on quickly. Bloodwork indicates there were several substances in their systems that may have calmed them down when the thing in their arms opened. Acted as a sedative so they may have continued to sleep and breathe normally. The killing ingredient is what I want to find."

"Any idea how long that's been in their arms?"

"No. There was no scab and only a pinpoint scar that looked like a freckle. Interesting it was in the exact same place on both men."

"How long would it have taken to happen?"

"Probably depends on the health of the individual. Both these guys appear fit."

"Could it be placed anywhere in the body?"

"Again, I just don't know. I would say yes, but I haven't seen anything like this before. You hear about CIA and other spy craft doing crazy things, but this is new. If it can be done safely, I don't see why it couldn't be done in the brain, for instance. Talk about mind control, especially if the subject knew it was there."

"Get that to the lab ASAP. I'll let the director know what you've found out." On his way out, he stopped to look down at the box of donuts in disgust. He then glanced over his shoulder at the doctor who continued to watch him, covering his mouth to smother a chuckle. "Write it up. You know the drill. Then I want results by day's end." He grabbed the box of donuts and dropped it in the trash. "That stuff will kill you." And he left.

~ ~ ~ ~

"Where's Tessa?" Ben asked as Chase sat down across the table from him.

"Taking a nap, I think. Said she was a bit worn out. The close call with Heather did a number on her. She finished her panel discussion. Get this—someone made Andre the chairperson of the panel. How did that happen? Guess he pulled some strings. Anyway, Vernon is watching our room with his tech toys. Monitoring Andre's whereabouts as well. By the way, your fatherly concern is touching."

"I'm thinking of pulling out, Chase."

His heart began to pound. "Why? Has something else happened? Are the kids okay?"

"Yes. The family is safe and secure, although you may have to take Ken down a notch or two when we return. He's being a bully and well—acting like you when things aren't going right. He scared the hell out of the medical examiner, locked horns with Lazarus—he doesn't really have horns, does he? I mean Lazarus."

"I don't know. Maybe. Might be a fad I don't know about. He's a bit different. Tessa says the ladies love him, but he doesn't seem to let it distract him."

"I don't give a damn about his love life. I think there's trouble between Ken and him."

Chase grinned. "If Lazarus is a screwup, there's no one better to straighten him out than Ken. Also, I trust the man being in charge while I'm gone. He did a hell of a job while I was recovering from Syria."

For an instant, he reflected on that time, knowing Ken took extra care to make sure Tessa wanted for nothing. He also knew the man had a bit of a crush on her, even though she was oblivious to his attention while she prayed Chase would return home to her. How many times over the years had he noticed how he stole glances at her, grinned like a teenage boy when she laughed. Before he proposed, Ken was about to make a move on her, but then Syria happened. One thing he could count on was Ken putting the team first. He rescued him in Syria and made sure Tessa was protected.

"Why are you upset and want to pull out, Ben?" The director informed Chase of the new information Ken delivered. "What the hell?" he growled. "Let's just pop the bastard now and be done with it."

"We don't operate like that."

"Since when?" Chase fumed.

"We don't have enough evidence to know what really is going on and whether the monster has infiltrated other bio-systems, or heaven knows what. Take him out and those problems could be activated without us knowing how to stop it." Ben emphasized by jamming his finger into the tabletop.

"Then why pull out if you're so concerned?"

"Tessa." He leaned back in his chair. "Vernon pulled up a couple of video feeds to spy on him, and discovered Vion was tracking her movements. One actually picked up Andre watching her in real time. If anything should happen to her, I'd never forgive myself. This was my idea, and I talked you into it, knowing full well you could be manipulated because of your sister's death."

Chase felt the weight of regret. He should have come clean with her a long time ago. Now it might be too late. Tessa would think he groomed her for this one moment in time to take revenge on the man who killed his sister. The most important thing right now was to keep her safe. Whatever Vion was planning certainly involved Tessa. The risk was too high, especially since he now knew she was being stalked.

He glanced at his watch then stood as he pulled out his phone and punched in her number. "I'm going to check on Tessa. She should be getting up by now." No answer. "The woman sleeps like a bear in hibernation. I've never been able to sleep like that." He chuckled. "The first time we forced her onto a plane with us, she snoozed like she didn't have a care in the world. I'd better go get her up."

Several sessions ended causing the corridors to be crowded. A line formed at several elevators, so he took the stairs. Opening the door to their suite, he called out to Tessa. With no response, he expected to find her in a fetal position on her right side. He loved to watch her sleep and memorize every move she would make to fall deeply into slumber.

"Tessa?" he called when he found her gone. The bathroom door was ajar, and it, too, was empty. He walked to the windows in the living room as he lifted his phone to try and reach her.

There in the courtyard stood Andre Lavelle Vion holding a bouquet of white lilies. He extended them to Tessa. Even from here, he could see her beam her approval with that radiant smile she could be so generous with. The two of them moved to a cushioned glider swing and sat down. Vion slipped his arm on the back of the glider as he spoke. Tessa turned her head toward him, and now the man had a captive audience.

CHAPTER 27

Tessa slept thirty minutes and felt refreshed. Being pregnant had initiated wanting to take naps at the weirdest times. They could be long or, like today, just a catnap. Too many things were weighing on her mind. She called home to reassure herself her world was safe and secure. Marine Sergeant Tom Cooper caught her up on safety protocols in place for the family. His monotone voice, with "just the facts, ma'am," attitude, gave her comfort.

"I got this, Tessa."

"Thank you, Tom. You have my utmost confidence. You're the best."

There was no reason not to return to the conference and enjoy a session then maybe grab a sandwich before she had to participate in a panel discussion on movement of populations due to climate change. Even the title made her yawn, but she hoped enough people would show up to understand how important the topic was for national security around the world.

She purchased a boxed lunch and headed outside to the gardens on the north side of the resort. It would be cool there and filled with shade-loving plants. Just as she finished and disposed of her box and water bottle, movement near the entrance of the garden caught her eye. A man walked slowly toward her carrying a large bouquet of fragrant Casablanca lilies, some of her favorite. Her first thought was Chase had sent them to her. As he lowered the bouquet, she saw, instead, it was Andre Lavelle Vion.

"Andre?" She could smell the heady aroma of the lilies. They were magnificent.

"I saw these in the garden shop and thought of you. I also wanted to apologize if I somehow annoyed you earlier. It was not my intent to go on and on about myself and my work. Then, after the panel discussion we were on, you left quickly. Another reason why I've managed to stay a bachelor, no doubt. Please accept these as a gesture toward friendship."

Tessa smiled in spite of herself but stepped back in a show of stubbornness. "I need to know something first."

"Of course. Anything."

"Did you try and kidnap my daughter yesterday?"

Shock filled Andre's expression as he nearly dropped the flowers.

"Because if you did—"

"Madame, I do not know what you're talking about and am insulted you would think me a monster."

"Did you?"

"No." He frowned. "Why would you think such a thing?"

"My husband thought you tried to take her to hurt him, to drive a wedge between us. Then you could ride in on a white horse and save the day."

"Your husband would turn God Almighty against me if he could. He has never forgiven me for…"

He paused and pointed to the cushioned swing. She dared follow him and sat down as he offered the flowers to her once more. This time she took them. Slipping his hand on the back of the swing behind her, she felt a chill run up her spine. The man was hypnotic even though she knew him to be evil. She wanted to believe he wasn't behind all this.

"First, tell me your daughter is safe," Vion said anxiously.

"Yes. Safe. Happy."

Vion sighed with what sounded like relief. Was he for real? He wasn't a monster. His concern was sincere.

"Why would he want to punish you for something? I don't understand."

"Because he believes I killed his sister." He spoke slowly and placed his hand on hers that held the flowers. He motioned for a man at the gate to come forward. "Please take the flowers and have them delivered to Mrs. Hunter's suite." The man nodded and left with the Casablanca lilies.

Tessa felt shock at hearing his words. That couldn't be true. Why wouldn't he have told her it was Andre? The story he'd told her right after they met was that her lover had killed her with drugs. There was never a mention of who it was and, for the most part, he didn't want to talk about it. She figured it was still too painful since he felt responsible for not being able to protect her all those years ago.

"You?" she choked, holding a hand to her throat. "That can't be. Were you lovers?"

"Absolutely not. I was certainly under suspicion because I was dating her friend. But I had an alibi. I was miles away at a conference, receiving my first humanitarian award. I was still reeling from Abigail's death. I could barely function after she committed suicide. I wasn't even allowed to attend the funeral. Christine, your husband's younger sister, was her roommate and…" He pulled his arm back and stared into the distance.

"And what?" she begged. This was all new to her. Didn't Chase say they weren't roommates? Was it a lie? Who was actually manipulating her emotions?

"Christine was jealous of me."

"Why? I thought they were best friends."

"So did I. But as time went on, I began to see that Christine's affection was more than just—college best friends."

"They were lovers?" she whispered in bewilderment.

He shook his head vehemently. "No," he insisted. "Definitely not. But Christine was pushing her in that direction, laying guilt trips on her, saying she was leading her on and trying to manipulate her. Christine had a breakdown. She was very needy. I tried to help, but my Abigail wanted me to step back in hopes of helping Christine. Now I regret doing that because Abigail gave in to Christine's demands."

"What demands?" Tessa could see tears forming in the corners of his eyes as he turned back to her.

"I had no idea Christine was using drugs. Things being the way they were, Abigail began pulling away from me. But it was too late. Mentally, she was always too fragile and gentle. Eventually, Christine took over her life. All these years I've wondered if I had rescued her from the clutches of that horrible woman, or told her parents or maybe school authorities, I could have prevented the night she took her life. To this day, I believe Christine pushed her to commit suicide. She belittled and tormented her, literally, to death."

Stunned, Tessa stared wide-eyed at Andre, not wanting to believe what this could possibly mean. "And Christine's death?"

"She left a note of how alone she was with no one to love her now. A few weeks after Abigail died, she also committed suicide. Not being able to attend Abigail's funeral was a blow for me. It was telling the world I had something to do with it, that I didn't care."

"And why were you a suspect in Christine's death?"

"There had been many times people saw Christine and I arguing over her interfering with my relationship with Abigail. She even got Abigail to get a restraining order. By that time, I hardly ever saw her. She called to apologize and said it wasn't her idea. By then, she'd stopped going to class. I was frustrated and wounded."

Tessa laid a hand on his forearm and he touched her hand with his long fingers. They felt cold. "Oh, Andre."

"I heard from one of her professors, wanting to know why she dropped out of school." He sighed. "I was a PhDs student, so I had to teach two classes the evening Abigail died. Next thing I knew, I received a phone call...I was prohibited from seeing her even then."

"And Christine? What of her?"

"I don't really know. I saw her once a couple of weeks after the funeral I was forbidden to attend. I wanted answers. Because the conversation was heated, I became a suspect after she took her life. But I had nothing to do with her death, Tessa. You must believe me. It has haunted me all these years. And your husband has stalked, threatened, and sabotaged every good deed I've ever tried to do until the last few years. After seeing you together at Hidden Waters Resort, I realized he had made a discovery to finally get even with me. It was you."

"Me? I don't see how. Chase and I were friends before we ever considered taking our relationship to the next level."

His wolflike eyes searched her face recklessly. "Don't you see? He knew I'd see Abigail in you. Thought he could use you to trip me up into admitting I had something to do with his sister's death." His expression softened as he tried to smile. "At first, I did see her in you. But now I see someone much stronger, more intelligent. Like her, you are soft spoken and kind, but ready to defend what is yours—like the scare with your child. Abigail was fragile and easily manipulated by others—like Christine."

"It sounds like you still love Abigail."

"I love the thought of her, the missed opportunities I made with my own work and shortsightedness. I should have paid more attention to what was going on. Something hardened in me."

"Maybe to protect yourself."

"Yes. I think so." Once more, his gaze explored her face as if mapping a memory. "I know we have met only a few times, but I feel a little more relaxed and interested in the world around me with each of our visits."

Tessa felt like he was reeling her in. It wasn't unpleasant as his voice became deep, and a sexiness warmed and chilled her at the same time. She found herself staring into his hypnotic essence that paralyzed her ability to think straight. It was only when she heard another male voice that she snapped out of her reverie.

"Tessa," Chase shouted as he came through the garden gate.

She jerked back away from Andre and scratched her hand on a jagged piece of wood sticking out from the swing. As she rose, Andre pulled out a handkerchief and wrapped it around the cut. He tilted his head toward Chase, revealing a dark, sinister stare that frightened her.

"Chase. What are you doing here?" she asked, removing the handkerchief and returning it to Andre.

"It's almost time for your panel discussion. I thought I'd attend since I'm free this hour." Although he was talking to her, he was leveling a deadly glare at Andre. "Better go. I'll catch up."

She nodded and hurried away, wishing she'd never accepted the flowers or sat down with Andre Lavelle Vion.

CHAPTER 28

Both men watched Tessa leave the garden before returning their focus to each other.

"Stay away from my wife," Chase ordered in a deep, threatening tone.

"I'm afraid that is impossible, Captain Hunter." A slow, thin smile spread across his mouth.

Chase noticed several of the man's security enter the garden, aware there might be a problem.

"I see you're still unable to fight your own battles, Vion." He raised his chin at the muscle approaching cautiously.

"Yes, well, you can't be too careful in this day and age. The riffraff is abundant in this country, as you well know. As to your wife, I am only seeking out a friendship that appears to suit both of us. I understand she knows nothing of your stalking of me all these years or that your pitiful sister took her own life."

Chase eyed the three men approaching and decided not to engage them since he was outnumbered and in full view of other guests coming and going. He took a step back and narrowed his eyes. "My wife knows everything she needs to know."

"Tell me, Captain Hunter, are you using her as bait to catch me in some kind of sinister plan?"

"You bet I am, but mostly it's about bringing you to justice for

176

my sister's murder."

"Excellent. Then I won't mind taking her from you as well. Your interference with Abigail ended badly. Hopefully, you'll not make the same mistake twice. In any case, I anticipate a more permanent and fulfilling relationship with Tessa in the future."

Chase's demeaner snapped as he lunged toward Andre, only to be intercepted by a brute who shoved him back. He took a deep breath and pointed a finger at Vion's chest like it were a loaded gun. "Look all you want, but don't touch and don't seek her out. I have ways of taking you out, Vion."

"I'm well aware of your neanderthal strength and legendary kills over the years. While you have kept an eye on me, I've also been tracking you. Soon, I will make you pay for ruining my life."

"Go to hell," he growled as he turned toward the gate.

"I plan to make you wait there for me."

~ ~ ~ ~

Andre finished the last session of the day and returned to his suite to see if his assistant, Franklin, had the information he required. A table had been prepared on the balcony, set with china and crystal. A warming center nearby held a late-afternoon meal.

Just as he was finishing, Franklin returned and handed him the iPad with the results of the Tessa's blood test. He'd taken the bloody handkerchief and handed it off to one of his lab technicians who was in charge of the plasma harvest. He slowly stood and reread the information before staring at Franklin and returning the iPad.

"Well. Well. Well. Looks like Madame Hunter is pregnant." He tapped his jaw thoughtfully. "What to do about that little inconvenience."

~ ~ ~ ~

Chase sat in the audience, oblivious of the topic the panel discussion in which Tessa participated. All he could do was stare at her. When he caught up with her before going on stage, he'd tried to touch her elbow. She immediately jerked away and frowned at him.

"You don't need to stay and listen. I know you'll be bored out of your mind," she offered coolly.

"Not true. Anything you're a part of interests me, Tessa. Why would you say such a thing? I've always listened with new appreciation for what you do."

"Suit yourself." She pivoted and took her place on stage.

No doubt Vion had done a number on her. How could she gloss over the attempt to kidnap Heather and still be in his court, believing he was misunderstood. He could envision her justification; he'd done many amazing things in the medical realm to make a better life for the sick. What kind of black magic was he pouring into her anyway?

She'd become moody in the last week, and tired. They had been working hard on this mission. Dealing with the home front and the worry over their family may have emotionally drained her. Handling Vion on top of all that had probably made him edgy as well. Maybe he was losing sight of the mission to bring the man down before he did too much damage to geopolitics around the world.

There were no hints of alliances yet, and American intelligence had detected nothing in our government. President Buck Austin had warned his cabinet to have no connections with Vion or any of his business enterprises, no matter what benefits it appeared to have, both here and abroad. To do so would mean immediate dismissal, even if it were one of their subordinates. Anyone under their direction who broke the rule would be an indication of not managing the department adequately. The president wasn't a man to cross and let down. That was one thing Chase appreciated about the man.

He would have been a great sheriff back in the 1800s in an old Western town overrun with shady characters. It was well-known among the Secret Service that they had to keep a close eye on him and his guns. To abate any chance he'd shoot someone after a tempestuous meeting with a bunch of congressmen, they kept the weapons locked up. Each week, they took him out to target shoot, unless he was on his ranch in Texas. There, they had to spend a few days in the wild, hunting. Chase thought he did it just to show them he was a tough old bird and enjoyed a good laugh when they couldn't keep up.

"You did a great job, Tessa," Chase said as she came his way. It appeared a little of the steam had evaporated from her attitude.

"Thanks." She adjusted her purse and briefcase.

"Why don't we put our stuff away and go for a walk. The azaleas are blooming, and I know how you love them. The temperature has dropped, too."

"Okay. Fine."

"We could skip dinner tonight. Want to eat in?" he asked, taking her briefcase.

"Fine."

"I can put in an order before we go on our walk."

"Sounds good."

Okay, maybe her attitude had turned frosty. He didn't try to interact again until they reached their suite. As the door opened, a maid arrived with the bouquet of Casablanca flowers. Chase wasn't about to take them. "I'm going to let her have these. Okay?"

"Fine." Tessa brushed past him and into the suite.

The maid gave Chase a sympathetic eye roll and disappeared with the flowers. He slammed the door shut and dropped her things on a nearby chair. "That was three fines, two goods, and I'm pretty much convinced you said 'screw you' a minute ago under your breath."

"If I had been so crude to say that, you would have heard me loud and clear."

"I don't want you talking to Vion, understand? I warned you he was trouble. Think about the kids."

"He said he had nothing to do with that," she said, putting her hands on her hips. "I believe him. And how dare you suggest I don't care about my kids."

"You always were so gullible, Tessa. Vion could sell sand to an Arab, and you are walking a thin line to trouble."

She grunted her displeasure and threw up her hands. "All this time I thought it was me you loved. Andre said your sister died of an overdose, not because he stuck the needle in her arm but because she was in love with Abigail and couldn't handle her death. You never told me that part. Why? Was it because the truth is you saw me that first day and realized I resembled Abigail and might someday help you seek revenge?" she fumed.

"I do love you. I didn't tell you the other part because I never thought it would come to this. That's why I want you to go home."

"It's a little late for that, Chase." She headed for the bedroom with him hot on her heels.

"Don't walk away from me," he ordered, slamming the door behind them.

Tessa flinched and whirled around as he held his finger to his lips then took out his phone. He waved it throughout the room. When a light flashed green, he laid it on the nightstand. She covered her mouth and ran into his waiting arms.

"Chase," she sighed as he kissed the side of her head then ran his hands up and down her back. "You sounded so angry just now."

She trembled in his arms. "I know, babe. This act is getting out of hand. I never thought he'd be so open in coming for you. I'm not sure I can protect you if you slip off like that again. Apparently, he's watching your every move."

Tessa sought out his mouth and let him devour her with his kiss before she laid her head against his chest. "He scares me, but, at the same time, he's so convincing." She told him what she'd asked concerning the kidnapping and everything else he'd dropped on her. "Is any of that true?"

"Sadly, it is."

"Which part, Chase?" She stepped back.

"The part when I first saw you. If I remember right, I compared you to her that first night we were together at the motel in the mountains. I could see her standing with Abigail, laughing and pulling pranks on me. At the time, I wondered if Vion would see the same thing in you."

Her eyes blinked in disbelief and betrayal. "So, all this time—"

"No," he said vehemently. "I had fallen in love with you by the end of that mission and knew it was an impossible situation. I tried to put as much distance between us as possible, but then our paths crossed again in DC months later. At that point, I knew I wanted you, and the only way to do that was to make you a part of Enigma. I played on your thirst for adventure and worked at being your best friend with no strings attached."

"But slowly, you drew me in. It got really difficult to deny my feelings for you," Tessa admitted.

"The idea of using you to get revenge evaporated because it was you I loved—not Abigail. She and Christine were best friends, not lovers. They were like sisters. Her family took Christine in when I went to West Point so she could finish high school." He ran a finger through his hair. "They were just nineteen when they died, Tessa. It nearly killed me, too. Both girls were good and beautiful. Abigail got involved with Vion after being in one of his classes. She did poorly, and he waived a failing grade in exchange to have one dinner with her. That's when his obsession started. Christine tried to intervene, but eventually I stepped in. It only made it worse."

"His take was somewhat different." She spoke softly when she sat down on the edge of the bed and repeated the twisted version.

Chase sat down beside her. "Babe, I'm sorry you have to go through this. Don't go anywhere alone with him."

"What if Honey is along?"

"I can't trust her, either. She's as much of a sociopath as he is. I don't care if she tells the world, you are best friends. Friendship is just another tool to her." He pushed her hair from her forehead. "I love you," he whispered. "Say the word, and we're done here. You are the one who saved me from myself. I was eaten up with revenge, hatred, and little conscience when you came into my life." He grinned. "Boy, that was a day I'll never forget."

"Me, either." She chuckled then sighed. "Let's just stick together and wait it out. It's two more days." Taking his hand, she leaned over to him. "Then, let's go home to our family. We have a lot to talk about."

"I agree," he admitted, wondering if they were thinking the same thing. He wanted her out of Enigma. Was she going to tell him her days there would soon end and afraid he'd be distracted from this mission? "The reason I came looking for you was because Ken called with an update on the two men found dead this morning. It appears they had a kind of implant in their arms that may have released a toxin into their system. Preliminary findings are still underway. Probably found a weakness in their blood or DNA to release a deadly dose. Designed-to-die kind of thing."

Tessa held up her hand where she'd scratched it.

"How did you do that?" Chase asked, examining her hand.

"I sliced it on the swing. Andre used his handkerchief to stop the bleeding."

"Where is that handkerchief now?" He wasn't prepared for the answer.

Her eyes widened in fear. "He took it with him."

CHAPTER 29

"Mr. President, you don't look well. "Can I get you anything?" His secretary laid a few papers down in front of him, even though his eyes were a little glazed over. "Mr. President?" She waved her hand in front of his face. "Mr. President!"

In seconds, the Oval Office was swarming with medical personnel, lots of anxious voices, and a tearful First Lady. A helicopter waited to rush the president along with his personal physician to Walter Reed Hospital. There was no time to keep the press from spotting the anxious White House staff as he was rushed on board and disappeared into the sky.

~ ~ ~ ~

"It's all over the news about the president," Ben announced to the Enigma Team when they gathered in his suite. Vernon was nearby, monitoring the situation, and the others stood in shock.

"Do you have any idea what is wrong?"

"Nothing definitive. One minute, he was okay, and the next, he wasn't. Even the sensors that constantly monitor his vitals had not kicked in. It's a miracle his secretary became concerned and came in when she did. He's stable, and tests are being run even as we speak. Right now, they are baffled. Thankfully, his physician was at the White House at the time. All agencies are on alert, as is the Pentagon, along with NORAD and NATO. You can imagine what this is doing to the stock market."

"Has the vice president been sworn in as temporary man in charge?" Chase asked.

"They're being tight-lipped right now. To say yes would cause more panic, but I assume so. I've tried to call, but, as you can imagine, everything is chaotic, and I'm probably not on the list, since technically we don't exist."

Carter Johnson shook his head. "We're just a bunch of brainiacs from a university who are part of a DC think tank."

"Exactly." Ben nodded. "And we're going to keep it that way."

"There will be a press conference with various officials including medical staff later tonight. Right now, most Americans have no idea how serious the situation is." Ben leaned against the arm of the couch. "They never do. In this case, it is probably a good thing."

"Our military is on high alert throughout the world, I'm guessing," Chase added as Tessa came to stand next to him.

Ben nodded. "We're going to go about our business. Nothing else we can do. However,"—he paused as he surveyed the group— "I'm suspicious of the timing. We have two dead assassins back home who targeted Tessa's family. The ME says something is not right there. They had a tiny disc, the size of a freckle, implanted in their arms. It contained a kind of toxin, yet to be identified."

"I'm getting a call from Dr. Kelley, the president's physician." Chase stared at his phone. The two had a history from serving in the military together. He had been a medic and brought a number of wounded to her and was instrumental in saving their lives.

"Mary Pat, what the hell is going on there?" he said quickly. "Better yet, why are you calling me?"

"I don't have to fill you in, Captain Hunter. I've been trying to reach Lazarus, your new guy at Enigma. He isn't picking up. I have to speak to him. ASAP. Let me talk to Ben. Is he there?"

"Yes, ma'am. He's here. I can have Vernon patch Lazarus through to you when you are finished with Ben."

"Excellent. Ben? Dr. Kelley wants to speak to you. I've got to hunt Lazarus down." He pointed to Vernon who switched the call to Ben's phone so he could try and reach Lazarus.

"What do you need me to do?" Sam asked in her no-nonsense tone.

Chase glanced to Carter, who, by all accounts, was involved with Sam then back at his agent. "Call Prime Minister Levi to see if they've heard anything. Don't let on anything is wrong. Mossad has an uncanny way of knowing things before anyone else."

She turned her back to Carter and the rest then walked to another room to make the call. Chase figured the call would start out X-rated since the Israeli leader was her last lover. He was also Ben's brother.

"Zoric, can you find Honey Lynch for me and have her meet me someplace private?"

"And if she refuses?"

Chase narrowed his eyes at the man.

"Don't worry. She won't. I'll guarantee that. At last, a bright spot in my day." He disappeared from the room in a matter of seconds.

"Carter, could you go with Zoric to make sure there isn't a problem? She might warm up to you a little better than him. Go." Getting Carter away from Sam might be the best means of keeping the team on task.

~ ~ ~ ~

Honey felt like a fish out of water with so many high-profile and wealthy people walking around as if they owned the world. Maybe they did on some level. A few had ties to unscrupulous crime syndicates at one time or another, and she'd been given a lucrative contract to take out the competition. For all she knew, they had prospered because of the lack of diversity. Obviously, they ran with a higher class of friends now and had left the old ways behind.

Then there were the leaders, scientists, and industry leaders who hoped for a new world order. It wasn't hard to pick the military brass connected to national security from various countries. They were the watchers, intel gatherers, and interpreters of hotspots to keep in their crosshairs of concern.

And, finally, there was Enigma; the brilliant yet suspicious group of university elites who had the ear of the president, and, often times, the disdain of the FBI. She called them the Supermen of Deception, a bunch of Clark Kents. One minute, they were teaching economics or French literature, and the next, they were escaping Russia with a bunch of American scientists to save technology from getting into the wrong hands. Strange how there was always a trail of blood when they came home. Stranger still was no one appeared to care.

She often pictured Enigma members with feathery wings and tarnished halos carrying machine guns or Molotov cocktails. If that were true, then they were death angels, except for Tessa, of course. She was the epitome of the word enigma. Unlike the others, she was a soccer mom, sang in the church choir, took an interest in her students, friends, and neighbors, and baked cookies like she was the star on a PBS cooking show. Next thing you knew, the domestic commando was lying like a dog. She made friends with unscrupulous men who believed they were misunderstood and she could fix them.

A Christmas misadventure had cemented their friendship in spite of creating a mix of oil and lighter fluid that nearly killed both of them. Now here she was on the other side of the law again and had Tessa in the crosshairs of a new kind of conspiracy. Andre Vion, for some reason, was fascinated with her. What would a self-absorbed, evil man want with Tessa?

She wasn't pretty, in her opinion. There was no denying she was clumsy, along with the fashion sense of a homeless person who shopped at the Goodwill Store. She had the profiling skills of a child who had been offered a puppy from a stranger in a black van. Was it because she had book smarts? Come to think about it, everything turned into an educational experience with her. Nerd. Or could it be because she'd once saved President Buck Austin's life? Even though the woman created chaos on a regular basis, if the most powerful man in the world said take care of Tessa, you took care of Tessa.

Honey spotted Nicholas Zoric headed her way with a locked-and-loaded glare boring a hole through her head. The man was dangerous, and the two of them had locked horns a time or two, but nothing serious. He enjoyed his gift of interrogation a little too much for her liking. Every time he stared at her, she imagined he was thinking of creative ways to make her scream.

"I'm going to get something to eat," she told the guards who were watching the entrance to where Andre would speak in a couple of hours. "Andre went for a walk in the wildflower garden across the driveway entrance to the resort. I just went inside to check things out. The lab techs are still taking plasma from the conference guests. Hotel security is in there, along with the refrigeration company to keep the vials safe and secure. Monsieur Vion did not want me to tag along, so someone needs to be out there in case of a problem."

"Yes, ma'am." They reminded her of two well-dressed polar bears as they lumbered off. She guessed they were there for their brute strength. It certainly wasn't for their clever interpretation of possible danger. That was her job.

"Captain Hunter wants to talk to you," Nicholas Zoric grumbled when he came alongside her. The guards moved away from the room used as a plasma collection area.

"Hope they don't get lost on their way to protect the boss. Dumb as a box of rocks," she said in a monotone to the Serbian, pretending she didn't hear what sounded like an order.

"Follow me."

"I don't work for Enigma, and I'm certainly not taking orders from the walk-on-water Captain Hunter. If he wants to see me, he should ask me himself." That was when she saw Carter Johnson trying to catch up to them.

Now, there was a good-looking man with a lot of charm. The idea he could charm the volatile Samantha Cordova into being his sometime partner was cause for a great deal of curiosity. However, for whatever reason, she could feel herself smile as he approached. Maybe it was the cowboy persona or the idea he'd been an astronaut that had her picturing a close encounter of the one-night-stand kind. Nothing would make her happier than to share how she'd hooked up with her partner.

"Hey, Honey," Carter greeted her in his Texas drawl then added a grin. "You're still prettier than a field of Texas bluebonnets."

"You see, Zoric? That's the way to invite a lady to meet with your boss." She continued to gaze at the ex-astronaut. "Good to see you, Carter. I've missed our little secret chats."

Zoric leveled a disapproving gaze at Carter. "I wasn't aware you two knew each other that well."

Carter used his disarming grin as Honey winked at him. "I wouldn't say we know each other as well as I'd like. Maybe we could get a drink tonight, Carter. I mean, if the old ball and chain doesn't have you all locked up." She tilted her head. "An interesting thought however."

"Ahh. I don't see the harm in one little drink." He offered her his arm, and she quickly took advantage of the gesture.

"You clearly have no idea what I'm capable of." She hugged his arm.

"I'd say the same is true of me, my wild Irish rose."

"I just love all these flower metaphors."

Zoric fell in behind them as they walked down the corridor. "I think I'm going to be sick."

~ ~ ~ ~

This was definitely one of those times Tessa felt useless in an emergency meeting. After all she'd been through and supplying vital intel, they still thought of her as a soccer mom with a great deal of luck on her side. She stood there watching each person, wanting to interject a profound suggestion, but she was clueless as to what to do to help. A wave of nausea came over her, and she could only excuse herself to the bathroom. There appeared to be a spot of dried blood in her panties.

She did a quick Google search for information and was relieved to see it was harmless. Most likely spotting from a developing embryo when it plants itself in the wall of the womb. Not uncommon to have it happen when she would normally have her period, or so her internet search suggested. A follow-up with her doctor was recommended, sooner rather than later.

Tessa quickly made an internet appointment with Dr. Patel for the following week. She wanted everything to be perfect when she told Chase. No worries. No problems. No surprises. Just a sweet baby in their future. Before she walked out to join the others, she tried to imagine how he would react. The best version was he lifted her up and swung her around as he laughed. The not-so-good version was his surprise and concern in his eyes that he might not be the father.

Why did everything always have to be so complicated?

"You're as pale as a ghost, Tessa," Sam declared as she clicked off her phone. "Everything okay?"

"Yes. Just concerned over the president. One more worry."

"You never were very good at departmentalizing your personal life with Enigma work."

"And you were never good at hiding your insane jealousy of me or your envy that I can wiggle my way into people's good graces without—you know, wiggling my backside to get there." Tessa smirked and was moving past her when Sam reached out and pulled her back.

"The day I'm jealous of you is as likely to arrive as a snowball surviving in Hell."

Tessa jerked free. "Miracles do happen," she said sweetly, batting her eyes. "Don't ever grab me like that again."

"Or what?" she snapped. "You going to smack me with your fly swatter?"

"Yes. And her name is Honey Lynch."

"Figures you'd get someone else to do it. Still can't do anything on your own."

Tessa sighed. "Yes. You're so right. Isn't it great I have all of Enigma at my beck and call? Sorry you have to see that all the time. It must make you crazy."

Before Sam could respond, Tessa left the room. Each time these kinds of conversations ensued; they left her a little shaken. Time was, she was terrified of the woman. Now it was more annoying than anything that she still couldn't completely win her over.

Stepping out into the foyer of the suite, she felt her phone vibrate. When she pulled it out of her pocket, a picture of Lazarus appeared.

"Lazarus? Dr. Kelley has been trying to reach you," she said anxiously. "Chase is trying even as we speak."

"Listen carefully, Tessa."

"Okay." She waved at Chase to come over as she put him on speakerphone. The deep tone of his voice gave him a creepy vibe. "You know I'd never hurt your family, right?"

"I appreciate what you did for Heather. I owe you."

Chase moved closer as she held her finger up to her lips.

"The president."

"Yes. You know he is in trouble."

"Yes. It's imperative you tell Dr. Kelley to check his left forearm. There will be a slight irritation. It needs to be sliced open immediately."

"Lazarus, what are you talking about?"

"Just do it, Tessa. There is a microchip with poison that can be released slowly or all at once with a remote. He's got only a little time. I thought I removed it so he would be safe." He choked on his words. "Please. Please tell Dr. Kelley I'm sorry. I tried my best to save him."

"Lazarus!" she said as he clicked off.

Chase's face grew more solemn than usual as he continued to hold the phone to his ear. "How long ago did he disappear?" he asked a person on the other end. "I want him found. Did you hear any of the conversation just now with Tessa? Then you know what to do when you find him." He clicked off.

"That was Ken. Says Lazarus is nowhere to be found."

~ ~ ~ ~

The door to Ben's suite where the team had been meeting and comparing notes swung open. Carter ushered Honey in with his arm linked through hers. Zoric wore a mask of disgust as he pushed past them toward the bar. He was thankful both Sam and Tessa had left for their panel discussion sessions on their topics of expertise. Having three moody women together who claimed to hate each other was a recipe for madness. Nothing would be accomplished with them in the room while he talked to Honey.

She strolled around the room, studying details as if it might be for sale. He knew she was biding her time or checking for traps. The woman was always wanting to know her escape route if she deemed one necessary. That's why she was still alive today.

"Hello, Ben."

Ben raised his eyes momentarily when she spoke to him and lifted his chin in a kind of greeting. "Honey," was all he said.

"I need to talk to you." Chase nodded toward a love seat. "Sit down."

She didn't comply but instead crossed her arms across her chest and shifted her weight to one hip. No one could wear leather better or sexier than her. She smirked as he surveyed the complete package.

"You're looking—incredible as usual."

"Hmm. As are you, luv. Syria actually made you more appealing than I could ever imagine. As a matter of fact, the last time I saw you, you resembled a corpse more than a soldier of fortune. I guess married life agrees with you."

"Thanks. I guess." The two of them had shared a physical and professional history. "I'm going to get to it. Why are you with Vion?"

"I'm not with him," she said with pouty lips. "I work for him. He pays me very well. More than Enigma ever did."

From across the room, Ben interjected, "I don't believe we ever hired you."

She smiled at Ben then focused on Chase. "Oh, that's right. But thanks for the gratuity after the fact. It was a nice bonus. Will you be paying me for information?"

"No." Chase stepped within two feet of her, causing her to go on the defense and drop her hands to her side. He knew very well she could take him down if he wasn't careful. "Just a little professional courtesy would be nice. Everything doesn't have to have a dollar sign."

"I pretty much think it does. In my line of work, I don't have social security or a 401K plan. A girl has to start saving along the way. So, what's in it for me?"

Ben's voice boomed from across the room. "A get-out-of-jail-free card if this goes sideways, like I think it's going to."

"I already have that kind of security with Andre," she sighed. "I want more. You don't think I just signed on with someone like Vion without reassurances in writing?" She stuck out her bottom lip. "And I thought we knew each other so well, Chase."

"Carter, and Zoric, we're out of here." Ben stood. "We're going to leave you to it, Chase. We have places to be."

In seconds, they were gone.

"Alone at last," she cooed as Chase closed the gap between them. "Hopefully the little woman won't be walking in on us."

In the time it took to exhale, Chase grabbed her around the throat with his large hand and slammed her up against the nearest wall. He then released her to grab her deadly hands and forced them behind her as he pressed his legs firmly against hers so she couldn't budge.

She licked her bottom lip before speaking. "You always did like things a little rough."

Pushing his face into hers made her smile with delight.

"Shut up and listen. This is what you're going to do for me."

"I'm liking this already."

CHAPTER 30

Lieutenant Ken Montgomery went into a form of combat mode as did Marine Sargent Tom Cooper. They pulled people off other projects and put Willy Robbins, a former Secret Service Agent, now with Enigma, in charge of Tessa's family. She was top-notch at what she did and it would be one less thing he had to worry about.

Today was one time he wished Vernon Kemp had stayed behind instead of leaving the new guy, Lazarus, in charge of tech support. If anyone could find a needle in a haystack, it was Vernon. Ken was unsure if it was storming into the tech headquarters like the country had gone to DEFCON 1 or the grizzly expression on his face, but two people volunteered to pass their duties off to others and follow him into the fray.

"You know the job better than me." He spoke matter-of-factly as he brought them to a section of Enigma neither had ever seen, judging by their surprised faces. "I'm hoping you've had a chance to get to know Lazarus, too."

Their bewildered expressions said otherwise.

"Not really. Stayed to himself mostly. When Vernon left with your team, he was put in charge. Vernon made sure everything was in place for our various operations so Lazarus would realize we didn't need or want a babysitter." The young tech guy pulled out a chair at a terminal when the older of the two did the same.

"Weird thing was he watched us to the point of creeping us out. It was like he was hoping we'd fail," said number two.

"He made a few adjustments for angles of the cameras around campus. That was expected. We do it all the time, but he did it every day. Left instructions that if we saw a couple of guys to let him know. We were given descriptions and face recognition data."

"A couple of guys? What guys?" Ken barked.

"Actually, they showed up two days ago. The time stamp is 6:30 p.m. He must have been waiting for them to show up." He clicked through security photos then pulled up a video. "Here. Backs to the camera. Let me circle around."

"Yeah. That's the guys I was looking for. Can you circle back so I can watch Lazarus?" Ken asked calmly.

"Is he in some kind of trouble?" Number one asked.

Ken didn't answer him but leaned in to watch the video. Lazarus kept looking up at the camera he must have positioned earlier. Why wasn't he trying to hide from being watched?

"Did you report this to anyone?" Ken asked.

"No. It was like he already knew. Lazarus called in everyone who wasn't already here that same night. He'd set up early schedules for all of us with no time off. He was making arrangements for the Scott children by that night, which also wasn't unusual, given the mission Captain Hunter was on. Just seemed like extra security. School calls. The whole nine yards. Pretty frantic around here for a few hours. Once in place, he watched those monitors like the world depended on it. We just figured he didn't trust us. Or maybe was testing us. Next thing I knew, he said he was going to see you."

"By then, we knew there was a problem with the children, so they were under constant surveillance. Since he was going to be on the field trip and you guys would be there, too, we thought things were tight," number two tech guy said, turning his chair toward him. "We have the whole takedown on video. Agent Willy Robbins was in here making sure nothing more was needed to be done. Smooth."

"So where is Lazarus now?" Ken asked. "You've got enough equipment here to spot a cockroach on the moon. So do it." He growled as he stormed toward the exit then pointed to both of them like he was holding a loaded gun. "I'll be back within the hour.

Have what I want."

Number one opened his mouth to speak as doubt filled his eyes.

"Make that forty-five minute."

"Yes, sir." Number one gave a thumbs-up sign.

Ken leveled the if-looks-could-kill gaze, causing them to turn toward their monitors. He had exited into the corridor when an unidentified call lit up his phone.

"Lazarus, this had better be you," he snapped.

"I need your help," Lazarus confessed with an unemotional voice.

"Then, come in. Or I'll meet you wherever you want."

"I can't do that. You'll only arrest me—or worse. I didn't kill those men or hurt the president."

"Fine. Come in and we'll talk about it. But you need to do it now. Enigma is looking for you, and it's only a matter of time before they find you."

"I was protecting the integrity of the mission. That's all."

"What mission? Are we talking about the same thing here? It looks like you poisoned those guys last night and maybe the president."

"That's a miscalculation on your part."

"Now listen to me, and let me be perfectly clear—"

"No. You listen to me, Lieutenant. You're wasting time trying to find me. I need your help, and this is how."

"Why should I?"

"Because if you don't, every leader at that Universal Reckoning Initiative will either be dead by this time tomorrow or securely under the control of Andre Lavelle Vion. Are you ready to listen?"

~ ~ ~ ~

"Let's go on that walk," Chase said, taking Tessa's hand and leading her outside. "I promised you a visit to the wildflower sanctuary."

"Are you sure about this?" she asked in a whisper then glanced over her shoulder. "You know nothing about flowers." She slipped her arm through his as they entered the garden across from the major entrance of the resort.

"I know that you do and that they make you happy. It's part of the reason I fell in love with you." He lifted her hand to his lips and added a kiss. "This may not work, Tessa," he spoke out of the corner of his mouth and continued to scan the area. "Besides, getting away from the craziness upstairs will do us both some good. Are you sure you're okay? You're a little pale."

"It's so much to take in. The president falling ill, Lazarus missing, my family—"

"They're my family, too, now, Tessa. I care what happens to them. Sometimes you act like I'm a bystander on the outside looking in."

They entered the garden section labeled Butterflies and Bees. She took a deep breath then glanced around at the different species before responding.

"I don't mean to do that. I know you care. I'm used to being the one who looks out for everyone."

"And you don't have to do that anymore. I'm here to lighten the load," he insisted.

"I know," she retorted. "You don't have to be so defensive. I don't need an alpha male lording over me as if I can't take care of myself."

He pulled her around to face him.

"Alpha male? Is that what you think of me? My job is to watch after my family whether you like the thought of that or not. I consider you my partner, not a competitor. And maybe you shouldn't be reading all those shapeshifter romance novels if you've started thinking of me as a kind of wolf mate."

"So, now you're going to tell me what I can and can't read?"

"That isn't what I meant. It was just a metaphor."

"A very inappropriate one."

"What has gotten into you? Ever since Andre Vion has been hanging around you, it's like he has turned you against me."

"Don't be ridiculous." She pointed to the entrance. "Can I just go through the garden on my own? I need to think things out."

"I can't leave you here alone."

"But you will, right? Because we both know romancing me in a garden might bring out that touchy-feely part of you that might make you appear weak. Go. Please." She turned her back on him and walked away.

~ ~ ~ ~

Their voices were out of range, so Andre circled closer like a hungry wolf waiting for the weaker of the two to move away. Chase and Tessa had been arguing. Was it because of him? The thought made his mouth stretch into an unfamiliar smile. He even touched his lips to make sure of the feeling without taking his narrowed sight off the captain as he stormed away.

He thought he heard a sob escape her throat as she stared after him. Had the captain made them turn violet like when she was angry with him? It would be an enjoyable activity to make them do that at his leisure. He closed his eyes for a few seconds to imagine the scene. It was—pleasant.

Opening his eyes, he watched her pivot toward the grapevine arbor to the wildflower garden. The quick info file brought to him of her likes and dislikes held pictures of the gardens around her home. This would be his way in, to grab her attention instead of appearing like a stalker. Close enough to hear her sigh, he wondered why she was moving away from where Chase had left her and toward the unkempt area along the bank of the manicured garden.

The breeze caught the stems of the lacy flowers growing wild as she stared at them. He knew what they were even from here. Fascinated with her dance toward danger, he continued to watch. Transfixed with the possibility of either losing her or the baby growing inside her that would be unable to survive if she touched such a plant, Andre noticed a path that meandered through thick patches of wildflowers. She took one step onto the path and stared at the white lacy towers of flowers bobbing with the breeze as she outstretched one hand.

"Tessa, stop!" he yelled then withdrew from his place of cover and ran toward her.

She whirled around and took a step back as if she'd bolt. Her ankle twisted, she toppled toward the white flowers, Andre reached her in time to yank her into his arms. Although he lost his breath in the sudden rush to save her, he felt invigorated that now he held her in his arms. The full press of her body sparked an explosive longing inside him. Those startled eyes stared at him in fright.

Carefully, he released her, only to feel her wobble. He took her arm to steady her.

"Those flowers. They're deadly. I saw you reaching for them."

"Nonsense. It's Queen Anne's lace. It grows everywhere." She stared down at his hand, which he slowly removed.

"It looks like Queen Anne's lace, but it's actually hemlock. The deadly kind. You didn't touch it, did you?"

Tessa stared down at the plant in horror then rubbed her hands against her slacks. "No. No, I didn't. Are you sure?"

"Yes. Look." He picked up a stick and pushed at the stalk of the plant. "Although it resembles Queen Anne's lace, the white flowers grow in an umbrella-shaped cluster. The hollow stem has purple splotches, unlike the Queen Anne plant. See?" He found the plant he was looking for. "No splotches, and the flower head is flatter than the hemlock. The delicate leaves resemble parsley, and you'd be surprised at how many people get poisoned every year trying to live off Mother Nature. Most of those people have no clue as to what they're doing in the first place." He threw the stick into the flowers.

Tessa's eyes were still wide with fear or maybe it was gratitude. "Andre, what would have happened to me?"

"Most of the time, just touching it won't hurt you unless you have an open scratch. Then it could get into your bloodstream and cause a lot of problems. Most of the time it causes harm when it is ingested. You touch the plant on a hike. As time goes on, you touch your mouth, and then you have poisoned yourself."

How pale she'd become. She was a fragile flower.

"I bet I have this growing in my yard," she groaned. "My children run into it chasing a baseball or playing hide-and-seek."

"Then it's probably Queen Anne's lace, or they would have gotten sick by now. Besides, you know what to look for now. Get rid of it if you're worried."

"I don't even know what to expect if they were to get poisoned."

"Sweating, vomiting, rapid heartbeat, and," Andre said slowly then paused as he noticed Tessa shiver in spite of a few beads of sweat on her brow. "Tessa, are you sure you didn't touch the hemlock?" She didn't protest when he took her wrist and felt for a pulse.

"I don't feel so well, Andre. Could you take me inside, please."

"Of course." Andre could never remember feeling concern over a person's well-being, except for Abigail. "Tessa, I'm going to slip my arm around you since you seem unsteady. Is that okay with you?"

She nodded as his arm went around her waist. Then he watched her eyes roll back in her head and collapsed in his arms.

~ ~ ~ ~

Chase entered the security observation suite where Vernon Kemp observed Tessa on the monitor. He pulled a chair next to him and leaned in to watch.

"Was that an act, or were you really fighting?" Vernon shifted his attention to the boss.

"A little of both, I guess. It kind of escalated. This doesn't have audio?"

"No. But Tessa knows the hand signal for help. And we're literally twenty seconds from the garden. That's why we chose there to draw Vion out again." He stole a glance toward Chase. "About Lazarus, boss," he said shaking his head. "I don't believe he did anything wrong. Do you?"

"No. But the man has secrets."

"Don't we all?"

"Yes. The one I'm carrying around right now is dangerous and a ticking bomb that could blow up in my face."

"Want to share?" Vernon zoomed in on the monitor to pull up the images of Tessa and Vion. "Boss, you'd better look at this."

CHAPTER 31

Lazarus watched Lieutenant Ken Montgomery speed walk across the campus trail students used to burn off calories or relax from the university grind. It meandered through tall trees that were said to be at least one hundred years old. One giant redwood tree, the only one this far inland, which kept visitors at a steady stream, making this a perfect spot for meeting the lieutenant. The trail circled back along a creek that was dry until winter rains fell. Then it had the feel of a mountain getaway. Early spring ferns dared appear as did other lichens and mosses, only to dry up by mid-July when the ground was parched.

He closed his laptop and returned it to the satchel he carried over his shoulder before falling in behind Ken. He did so without drawing attention to himself. The soldier walked like a man on a mission with those muscled legs. The thought occurred to him that, even though the lieutenant was in the reserves, he probably worked out every day as if he were headed to war. Fortunately, his own strides were capable of keeping up since he was six five. However, when the trail turned to head back, he lost sight of his contact and halted to listen.

A stick cracked as the hard cold press of a gun pressed against the back of his head.

"Looking for me, pretty boy?" Ken asked matter-of-factly.

Lazarus held up both hands, slowly turning to face his tormentor. He stared at the soldier for a few seconds then took action. In one fluid motion, he sidestepped the soldier as he clamped his left hand over the top of the barrel of the gun and jerked it upward. Before Ken could pull the trigger, he took his right hand and clamped onto the back of the gun. By doing so, Lazarus was able to rotate away from himself and twist it around in a downward motion, causing Ken to lose balance and control of the gun. He straightened up and stared in surprise as the gun was now pointed at him.

"Nice trick," he said through gritted teeth as he took a step back only to have Lazarus step forward. "You better be prepared to use that because in about ten seconds, I'm going to ram it down your throat."

Without taking his eyes off the soldier, he ejected the magazine then handed both back to Ken. "And if you point that at me, I'll just embarrass you again. You're like a playground bully, and I've had enough of your bravado."

"Bravado," Ken said with a sinister smirk. "That's a pretty dangerous threat coming from a guy who probably has lace on his drawers."

"Don't knock it until you've tried it."

"You're in a lot of trouble. Start talking."

"Put the gun away."

Ken holstered the weapon after replacing the magazine cartridge. "Happy?"

"Let's keep moving to make sure I'm not followed." He nodded toward a side trail that split off toward Old Town Park. The security scan the soldier began gave Lazarus a sense of safety. Once they came to several benches that overlooked a pond full of noisy ducks, he pointed to suggest they sit. The soldier remained vigilant as he scanned the surrounding area before joining him on the bench.

Lazarus reached into his leather jacket, and Ken's hand went to his weapon, causing him to pause. "I'm getting paper and a pencil out."

"Slowly, pretty boy."

"If I'm being followed, they'll have long-range listening devices," he wrote on the paper. "I've already written down what I know and even what I don't—yet. But, trust me, I'm not the villain in this."

Ken nodded then took one more security scan before Lazarus handed him an eight-by-ten sheet of typed paper. At the top, in bold letters read, TO SAVE THE PRESIDENT. There was a list of items pertaining to his encounter with the president.

"This paper is in case we are interrupted and I need to leave or you need to take cover. Scan it into your phone now." He waited a minute as Ken did as he asked. "My replacement for Dr. Kelley's new assistant worked for Andre Vion. I was tipped off by someone in Vion's network. I don't know who. It was meant for Dr. Kelley but came to me since I took her messages as part of my job."

"So, you knew the president was a possible target?"

"I found out a few minutes before arriving at the White House to assist with making sure he followed protocol. He'd already started when I arrived. You need to understand, the president gets threats every day. I doubted the authenticity of the threat but wasn't going to take any chances. My hope was that I could report it when I arrived, but the president required me to remove my replacement."

"Why didn't you alert his protection detail then?" Ken snapped.

"The president was miffed at the attendant's bumbling, and I took over immediately. It was then I realized the threat was most likely real. I focused all my attention on the president. However, I noticed the new guy had inserted a needle. It had been botched. I cleared it out with saline. No blood appeared, so I believed no damage had been done."

Ken cocked his head at Lazarus and frowned before checking the area with a security scan. When there weren't any visible signs of being observed, he continued. "Go on. Why didn't you alert the Secret Service, then?"

"I did, but didn't relay my concern because I hoped to take the guy by surprise and deal with it once I'd secured the president and called Dr. Kelley."

"Weren't you afraid there was still a possibility of the president being poisoned?"

"Yes. I knew there was a potential of poisoning, but thought I'd interceded in time. I'm still sure of that. However, if even a drop of the hemlock had gotten into his system, there would be a chance of a deadly reaction. I'm sure it's hemlock."

"Stop right there. Didn't you report this to Dr. Kelley, Chief of Staff—somebody in position of power?"

"I didn't report it then because I wanted to catch the guy, but he gave the Secret Service the slip with some excuse he needed to get to Walter Reed Hospital for Dr. Kelley. Since I hadn't tipped them off, he left the White House in a bit of a hurry. I tracked him down. He'd been T-boned by a hit-and-run vehicle. Killed outright because his airbag didn't deploy and he wasn't wearing a seat belt. He was driving at a high rate of speed as well. I left the scene without reporting what I suspected. It had become messy, and I had no proof of anything. The tip I received was untraceable."

"That's no excuse. You were derelict of duty."

"On the chance I'd sound like a dangerous lunatic, I contacted the director of the FBI. Since the guy got past the Secret Service, I thought it prudent not to contact them. After all, the FBI is part of the executive branch."

Ken remembered hearing a concern of Captain Hunter when he first saw Andre Vion at the Hidden Waters Resort. He shared the information with Lazarus. "So, did you hear from the director of the FBI?"

"Almost immediately and admitted I assisted the president. I would have been thrown in jail or worse for withholding that information. The FBI reassured me it would be a high priority and would make sure Dr. Kelley was informed. It came with a warning not to speak of this to anyone. They would take care of everything. They thanked me for my service and said they'd be in touch. It wasn't until the two men died of poisoning this morning that I realized how big this was. Another tip concerning Heather came from the same computer-generated voice a few hours before I met up with those two."

"Is that the reason you didn't mention this to Enigma?"

"Exactly. I figured the FBI would take care of everything. I was in the clear." Ken folded the paper and shoved it inside his vest then stared straight ahead. "I've heard enough. You need to stop stalling and come back with me. We can protect you."

Lazarus pulled out a second piece of paper and handed it off to Ken. It brought Ken to his feet. It read: You should arrest me now and take me to a safe, undisclosed place so I can do my work and get everyone through this." Lazarus stood and extended his hands, as Ken used his earwig to call for backup, which arrived within a few seconds.

Lazarus realized in that moment, the soldier had been watching for other agents to swoop in and assist all along.

"Okay, pretty boy. Got anything else you want to say to me before I rub that black crap off your mouth and eyes?"

"Just this," he whispered. "Abigail is alive and well."

~ ~ ~ ~

Chase jumped out of his desk chair so fast it flipped over as he barreled toward the door. In seconds, he was at the front door where Andre Vion was carrying Tessa across the threshold in his arms. Two of his guards were close behind, talking into their wrists, commanding action. He stared down periodically at Tessa and barked orders for people to get out of the way. A paramedic and nurse hired to be on staff for the conference arrived with a gurney.

"What happened?" Chase helped him place her on the gurney.

"I'm not sure. She was looking at wildflowers when I noticed she was about to touch wild hemlock."

"Hemlock," Chase said in disbelief. His whole body felt like it was shutting down as his heartbeat increased. Tessa was pale as a ghost, and perspiration beads dotted her forehead. He grasped her clammy hand in his and spoke softly to her.

"Chase?" Her eyelids fluttered open. "What happened?"

"We're taking her to our infirmary," a paramedic announced calmly. They pushed the gurney toward a nearby room where Andre stood with the doors open.

"I've called my personal physician who is also attending the conference." He waved to a man rushing toward them. "There he is now."

Chase was encouraged to stay at Tessa's side since she clung to his hand for dear life. "I won't leave, babe. Promise."

She tried to sit up, but he asked her to be patient and let the doctor check her over.

Andre frowned and stood back watching things unfold. Finally, he approached and leaned in to speak to Tessa as Chase helped her sit up. The doctor patted her on the back and asked a few questions and then declared her well enough to leave.

"This is my fault, Tessa. I'm so sorry." Andre handed her a bottle of cold water. "It was hot in the sun, and I rattled on about that damn plant to you. I remembered you cut your hand earlier and I—"

"How could that have made her faint?" Chase snapped in a suspicious tone.

"Oh, Andre, I don't think you're to blame." Tessa tilted her head to look at him and smiled sympathetically.

"You were so concerned about your children getting into the hemlock back home that your brain went into overload. I told you what to look for in case of an accident, and you immediately got sick. I'm so sorry. The power of suggestion. You're sure you didn't touch the plants?"

"Yes. Thanks to you. I was going to because I love Queen Anne's lace. If you hadn't been nearby, I would be in serious trouble." She cast a dubious glance at Chase. "He literally saved my life. Again." She added, "I haven't eaten much today."

The doctor patted her shoulder then turned to Chase. "She's dehydrated. Standing in the hot sun, no food, and her blood pressure is a bit low." He shook his finger at her. "You need to eat, drink, and get some rest."

Chase shook the doctor's hand. "Thank you. I'll make sure she follows your orders."

Helping her to her feet, Chase turned to Andre and raised his chin in a stubborn show of resentment. "Thank you, Andre. Once again, you have come to the rescue. Perhaps I've misjudged you."

Andre arched an eyebrow, and a sly-fox grin toyed with his lips. His eyes shifted to Tessa then back to him. The nonverbal message meant the man was far from finished with the manipulation of Tessa's opinion of him.

Could she resist another lost puppy who required a little love and understanding? How many of those would she collect before one of them attacked?

Andre reached for Tessa's hand and kissed it. "Madame, again, I must apologize, and I'm pleased you are going to be okay."

His smile appeared genuine, but Chase wasn't buying it for one second.

Tessa leaned in and kissed him on each cheek. "Thank you, Andre." She linked her arm through Chase's, and he quickly laid a hand on her forearm before connecting his glare with Andre's.

"I think we're staying in tonight. I've got work to do, and Tessa probably does, too, for tomorrow's presentations and panel discussions."

"Yes. Well, until then. I hope you're planning on attending the final dinner. I believe there will be an awards ceremony and project recognition."

"I understand you are one of those who will be speaking." Chase led Tessa toward the exit door. "I'm sure it will be enlightening."

Andre sobered. "I'm planning on it. Until then."

CHAPTER 32

The idea Captain Hunter could still push her buttons remained a point of irritation to Honey Lynch. They'd been through a few tight spots over the years and, through it all, had remained friends, even lovers for a while. But a man like Captain Hunter had ethical issues she couldn't live with and, besides, his idea of a long-lasting relationship involved commitment, family, and living on the scraps the United States government handed their heroes. Not that he wanted that kind of life with her. He'd once slurred his future dreams to her when he was drunk at a bar in the country of Georgia. Those were the days.

Now for some ungodly reason, she agreed to helping Enigma once more. She'd already decided her current employer was going to be a little difficult to manipulate. The truth was she had no qualms working for disreputable clients. It never took long to figure out their weakness in case she had to escape or needed a little leverage down the road.

The last few years, she'd strayed away from those kinds of people. They were unpredictable and often wanted her to hurry up, cut corners, or lower her fee after she'd done the job. Such things always ended up being messy for them, and a bit painful if her contract wasn't fully restored. Scaring the hell out of them was often the best part of the whole experience.

Ah, but the little family of Tessa had given her a new perspective on life. Honey could work for the good guys and still do what she excelled at. Having Tessa around almost gave her a conscience. Almost. She enjoyed the thought of having her as a friend. The bonus was when she defended her in front of that Amazon Samantha Cordova with the fancy degrees and designer clothes. The way she treated Tessa as if she was an imbecile annoyed her.

Then there were her children: sweet, rambunctious monsters who tugged at her black heartstrings. The little girl, Heather, had once told her she wanted to be just like her when she grew up. No one had ever told her such a thing, especially a little innocent child who thought she was what she pretended to be.

Honey had befriended the father and the three kids. She'd been hired to kill them and even the score with Enigma and Captain Hunter. Unbeknownst to her, he had Tessa with him. From that moment on, she decided maybe her life could use a bit of transforming to what little Heather imagined her to be. It had proved easier said than done.

Now, here she stood in the spacious suite of world-renowned Andre Lavelle Vion. A man full of himself, who just might have the Biblical mark of the beast somewhere on his body. She'd been chosen for this job, thanks to several references from people not so different from Andre.

"Do you have a conscience, Ms. Lynch?" Andre had asked her upon their first meeting.

"No. And I don't work for people who do. So, if that wasn't the answer you were wanted, then I'm out of here. I don't like crybabies, wimps, or squeamish bosses who, after they hire me think twice about their decision. It's best not to try and renegotiate the contract with me." Andre arched an eyebrow and let his gaze run over her body. "And I don't give out samples unless I want to. Do we understand each other?"

"I think you are exactly what I'm looking for, Madams. My assistant will pay you in full, now, to the account of your choosing if we are in agreement to your fee. If it isn't enough—be sure to let Franklin know." He invaded her space and lifted her hand to kiss but never took his gaze away from hers. "I look forward to"—he smiled, kissed her hand, and continued—"working with you."

"I was going to say the same thing, Monsieur Vion." She cringed as his cold lips touched her hand.

Three months had come and gone. She had helped shore up his personal security requests and watched the replay of the missing guest at one of his labs. Although she didn't know the particulars of why the guest left unexpectedly, Honey pieced together enough information to know the guest was female and wanted desperately to leave. She was given limited access to computer files and security footage, but, with her obsessive-compulsive diligence, realized the woman who escaped wasn't the first to be taken to the cottage in the woods for Vion's pleasure. She was, however, the first to escape. The video footage was meant only for Vion's pleasure. His treatment of guests at the cottage sickened even her.

Now the Enigma Team was involved. The combination of Vion and Enigma was bad for her. If Vion found out she'd worked for them in the past, the golden goose could suddenly become a threat. And Tessa was involved: unassuming, naïve, and the fair-haired girl of Enigma. Everyone's little darling, well, except for Sam's, of course. The woman clearly had the housewife in her crosshairs. However, Honey knew without a doubt Samantha wouldn't take to harming one of their own. This growing interest Vion possessed concerning Tessa, put Honey on edge.

One of the things she did for him each day was check out his living quarters for listening devices, cameras, or dangerous toxins that could derail his life. Honey thought he was being overly paranoid, but she had found things on several occasions. They were easily traced, fortunately, and those people were no longer employed. As a matter of fact, they were nowhere to be found. He apparently had people who dealt with those kinds of glitches. Her primary job was to take care of him on any up-close-and-personal matters. The money was outstanding, and no way did she want to blow this job.

Well, until the day she found a drawer full of recent pictures of Tessa. A few were of her doing normal everyday things like jogging in her neighborhood, grocery shopping, or cheering on the kids at soccer games. Others involved previous missions with Chase, including the last one in Syria.

"What the hell were you doing in Syria, Vion?" she mumbled to herself.

Syria had been a nightmare for the team. If he had pictures of them being there, he knew she was part of that operation. But, once again, all of the pictures either involved Chase or the rock star he was guarding. Had he funded that disaster? After a great deal of investigation and good old-fashioned snooping, there were no links to her. He was definitely going after Chase during those days of conflict and almost killed him.

When she was informed of this conference, alarm bells went off. The man had given her strict guidelines for the event and wanted to make sure she kept track of Chase and his misfit bunch of associates. The other peculiar order was to run interference with any security types of important guests who appeared angry and threatening. She'd been around enough important people in a number of industries to know a show of aggression rarely arose in public with high-dollar targets. He hinted everyone at the conference was a potential target. A target for what had not been revealed to her. How was that even possible? A bomb? A pathogen like Covid to isolate them from the world? An EMP to shut down the power grid?

As the inside of her arm began to itch again, she glanced at the redness and a tiny mark. She wondered what she'd done to irritate the area and applied a dab of lotion from a basket in the bathroom. It quickly took care of the problem.

She recognized an iPad on the desk as Franklin's. In the three months she'd been with her employer, not once had she seen him without it. She had memorized the password, one of the many things she'd discovered, spying over his shoulder one day. She could have sworn he let her see it on purpose. There had been a few instances where she caught him watching her carefully, as if he wanted her to react. A dangerous game to flirt with a person like her. Or was he pointing her in a particular direction. Today was a prime example; he'd walked out of the suite without the iPad when she entered.

"Forgot your second brain, Franklin," she meowed coyly as he'd started out the door.

He glanced her way then at the iPad. "I'll be right back. Do whatever you planned to do before I get back."

"So, let's have a snoop around your iPad house, Franklin," she mumbled under her breath. The first surprise that popped out at her was a blood test on Tessa. "What the hell?" she thought, picking up the iPad and reading the information carefully. "My girl's pregnant?" Being engrossed in reading the lab report on Tessa kept her from hearing Andre enter the suite.

"Your girl?" Andre Vion's cold voice spoke from the doorway. "Put it down."

She slowly closed the iPad and returned it to its original position. "If you don't want me to check things out, Andre, then don't leave them lying around where I can see them." She tilted her head and nonchalantly fluffed her hair. "That's what you pay me for. I'm a curious sort, you know."

He stormed across the room and jerked up the tablet. "You'll be punished if that information goes beyond here. Do you understand?" His voice was frosty.

"I understand you are slightly obsessed with Mrs. Tessa Hunter." She slid her fingers down Vion's lapel. "I'm thinking, by now, the handsome-and-mighty Captain Hunter has put you in your place when it comes to Miss Perfect."

He grabbed her hand and squeezed. "Do. Not. Make. Fun. Of. Her." When she jerked her hand free, he continued, "Captain Hunter is a mere speed bump in my plans. And as to the baby—accidents happen."

It was all Honey could do to keep from killing him on the spot. Too many witnesses knew she'd come here, and even Franklin had left her to find the information. Was she being set up?

"How well do you know Tessa and Captain Hunter's menagerie of half-baked assassins?" he asked.

"I tried to kill her husband and children once. The FBI and Chase got wind of it since I was working for a Libyan terrorist group. When things blew up, I got out of Dodge, as they say. Tessa never forgave me. One Christmas, she saw me in an airport and tracked me down. It wasn't pleasant, but I didn't kill her. Aren't you glad I resisted?" she cooed. "I follow the money. The pie-in-the-sky housewife believes I've changed."

Vion glared at her as if he was a robotic scanner, evaluating each word and idea she spewed. His chin was lowered, and those wolf eyes narrowed like they might transform into laser beams. "Then perhaps you can get her to come to your quarters tomorrow evening, and I'll have plenty of time to make an impression. I'm sure with her misplaced devotion to the captain, she'd feel coming here would be inappropriate. In your quarters I can…" He sighed. "Just do it."

The voice, cold and calculating, caused her to shiver.

"I'm not a matchmaker, Andre."

"You'll do it or the little spot on your arm just might be the death of you."

She lifted her forearm and glanced down at the red spot then at Andre. "What have you done to me?"

He stepped closer and whispered in her ear. "You belong to me, said the spider to the fly."

CHAPTER 33

"What do you think you're doing flirting with Andre Vion?" Honey quizzed Tessa as she ran her hand across her back while she sat at a secluded table near the windows overlooking the Blue Ridge Mountains.

Before Tessa could answer, she pulled a chair out to join her and Samantha Cordova whose face appeared to have turned to stone.

"Nobody asked you to sit down, Honey," Samantha spoke low and threatening.

Tessa shot the two women an exhausted-mom look then rubbed her temples with both hands. "If you two are going to spat, then take it outside. I'm in no mood for the way you flex your muscles."

Both women appeared to bite their tongues when the waiter came to get her order. Honey ordered a cup of tea then thought better of it and changed the order to a latte. "I do miss my mum's tea. You Americans are always wanting to cut corners and take the joy out of it. Why, once, when I was in Saudi Arabia, I stayed in the American compound. This one family actually put a pitcher of water on their patio to make a drink called sun tea. Disgusting. And they ate on paper plates. What's the use of having china if you aren't going to use it? So wasteful."

"No way they let a Catholic into Saudi Arabia unless you were working with one of the oil companies," Samantha snapped. "And I doubt that you were."

Honey turned her green eyes to Tessa and smiled mischievously. "Your Prince Mohammed invited me. Guess I made an impression in Syria. Thought I might help him with a little problem and, given I was a woman… Well, I'm sure you can fill in the blanks, ladies."

"She's lying," Samantha chimed in. "What do you want?"

Honey's expression of amusement faded as the waiter set her latte before her. After one sip, her good nature morphed into a low warning. "I repeat, Tessa. What do you think you're doing flirting with Vion? He's not your type."

"Type?" Samantha interjected. "She doesn't have a type. Men just get stupid around her with that whole domestic-diva-I'm-so-precious act. And, most of the time, she smells like cookies."

"I'm right here, Sam," Tessa moaned. "As usual, you make me think I'm invisible."

Honey ignored Samantha. "I watched the two of you talking after his presentation. And let me tell you, he's following you everywhere you go. That isn't a good thing."

"Your concern is touching," Samantha continued. "I'm with her. We all are. Butt out and stay clear, or so help me, I'll—"

"What? Have me arrested? We both know I have too many people indebted to me for that to happen."

"I was thinking of something more permanent."

"Would you do this yourself?" Honey retorted quickly then refocused on Tessa. "Look, my friend—"

"She's not your friend, Honey," Samantha continued. "Unless you're going to tell us what Satan's spawn is up to, then stop trying to pretend you care about her well-being, when, in reality, you can't stand that Vion may find her company better than yours. I'm guessing he's already sampled your merchandise and found he could definitely do better."

"Oh, for heaven's sake. I feel like I'm in high school when I'm with you guys." Tessa pushed her salad around with her fork.

Samantha had hit a nerve from the way the Irish assassin leveled a dark glare of revenge at the Enigma agent. "The only reason I haven't killed you before now, Sam, is that I expect you to watch after her when I'm not around."

"Ha. Fat chance."

"Then I don't need you after all."

Tessa reached over and patted Honey's hand. "Never mind. I'm all ears. What do you want from me, Honey?"

Honey enjoyed the touch of the Grass Valley commando. Whether Samantha ever understood how Tessa's soft touch calmed her, probably was a secret well keeping for now. The Grass Valley mom was both her muse and kryptonite.

Leaning in, she dropped the bombshell. "He knows you're pregnant," she whispered. "He also knows your blood type."

Tessa jerked her hand free and leveled a betrayed gaze toward Samantha. "You promised," she fumed.

"I never told her." She leaned back in her chair. "You should know that."

Honey pooched out her lips in a pout. "The idea this nymphomaniac is in your confidence and I'm not hurts me, Tessa. I thought we were BFFs." One slow sip of the latte led to a slight smile after licking the cream off her upper lip before she sighed. "This is so good. I should try your ways more often. It's just—"

Tessa spoke through gritted teeth. "How does Andre know I'm pregnant? I haven't told Chase. And why would he want to know my blood type?"

"I understand from Franklin that you scratched yourself when you were in the garden," Honey said, grabbing her hand and flipping it over. "He used his handkerchief to stop the bleeding."

"Why would he check my blood type?"

"He doesn't have access to your files here, or maybe Franklin just didn't have enough information to find them. But I'm guessing anything to do with you is locked up nice and tight since you work for Enigma. Once Andre had a few tests run, he discovered your secret." Tessa tried to pull away, but Honey pinned her hand down with a slam, rattling the cups and causing people to glance their way. "He knows you're a universal donor with your blood type. That makes you gold to him."

"What does that mean?" Samantha hissed. "I don't know what you're up to, but stay out of the way. Tessa has a job to do here, and it's important." She rolled her eyes. "I can't believe I just admitted that," she growled as her glare shifted to Tessa. "Don't misunderstand that comment if it sounds like I care or anything."

"No worries there." Tessa grimaced. "Do you have proof he tried to take my daughter?"

"No. I would have warned you if I'd known." Honey pressed harder on her hand. "You listen to me. For whatever reason, Andre wants you for more than just a roll in the hay."

"Why is he being kind to me?"

"He's a sociopath."

"Humph," Samantha grunted. "You would know."

This was one of those moments when Honey cringed at the forces tugging at her ability to think straight. She withdrew her hands and started to pull them under the table when Samantha snaked one hand out and grabbed Honey's gun hand and pointed her own weapon against her thigh under the table.

"Get to the point before I lose my patience."

Honey glared at the only woman who wasn't one bit afraid of her. She wasn't quite sure why unless they were cut from the same piece of cloth. Deciding to reach for her latte, Honey took a long sip and watched the Enigma agent. Honey knew the woman might strike like a rattlesnake at any moment if she didn't stop provoking her.

"Get that gun off my leg before I come across the table and rip your head off." Honey smiled. "Call in your dog, Tessa."

"Please, Sam. Let's hear what she has to say."

The gun withdrew from her thigh. "Ah, that's better." She held her cup in hand as if warming her fingers then sniffed the brew deeply. Waving the waiter over, she pointed to the cup. "Bring me another one of these. Be a love and more whipped topping this time. And I want it to go, please."

He nodded and left.

"Well?" Tessa asked.

"Not sure what is going on with Franklin—"

"Andre's assistant?" Samantha asked.

"Yes. But he looked right at me and left his iPad on a table where I would look at it. Made an excuse he was going to check on something. The man never leaves his tablet. I swear he sleeps with it."

"And?" Tessa asked as the waiter returned with a latte.

"Andre is taking the blood, extracting the plasma, and using it to create a kind of power switch. I did a quick search and, as near as I can figure, besides using it in trauma patients or things like liver disease, it can boost blood volume, which can prevent shock, and helps with blood clotting."

Samantha faked a yawn. "Common knowledge."

"Did you know he's just secured 75 percent of the world market of plasma? And he's on the board of 15 percent of the rest? These companies are all over the world. Because he's been a pioneer in treating blood diseases with his methods, these companies welcome him into their confidences and are more than willing to give him whatever he wants."

"You're right about that." Sam leaned in and spoke quietly. "There are a number of blood disorders, and he has cornered the market for treatment methods and supplies for conditions such as blood clots and blood cancers. It has been a growing concern the cost will soon be beyond most medical institutions' ability to serve the needs of people."

"That must be where he thinks he will be able to manipulate people of power. Get them to sign on for his intrusion until he is in control of more than blood and plasma banks." Tessa shook her head.

"There's more. He's developed a kind of switch that goes in the body. When activated, it sets into motion a slow death. He came in before I could read the notes I found. He was pretty miffed when he saw me snooping."

"Geeze, Honey." Tessa reached over once more to lay her hand gently on hers. "You need to be careful. Why are you even working for him?"

"Money was really good and I understood it to be more of a protection job with some security improvements. Didn't let me know until after I accepted there would be another opportunity for me to serve him with my special talents, if you get my drift."

Tessa frowned. "What was that?"

"Kill Captain Hunter and kidnap you."

CHAPTER 34

Andre Lavelle Vion lifted his head then slowly closed his laptop as Honey walked into his suite. He didn't trust the woman, or was it he found her offensive? Up until now, she had been everything he'd hoped for in a security chief. Occasionally, he had used her as way to get rid of those urges that often slowed him down. It fascinated him to no end that she energized him in both a positive and negative way.

Several times, while she slept, he stood by the bed and stared down at her, wondering if this would be a good time to finish her. The implant was already in her arm. No one would trace it back to him. The truth was, he'd decided to destroy her while she was awake so he could watch. He hated how she treated him as an equal. It fueled an appetite for a painful consequence. The implant was a mere backup in case he ran out of time.

"I'm waiting," he said calmly.

"Captain Hunter sent his goon to fetch me. When that didn't work, the astronaut stepped in. I couldn't resist that one." She smiled at him, but he didn't see the humor. "Anyway, I did as you asked. Told him I snooped around, but all I found was benign things like new research I didn't understand."

"Was that true?"

"Understanding the research? The part I understood was that it would save lives. The rest didn't matter. My expertise is not in chemistry and nuclear medicine. If it were, you wouldn't have hired me."

"Did he believe you?"

"I doubt it. Hard to say. We have trust issues that go way back. He at least pretended to be satisfied." She shrugged. "Besides, he was more interested in you and Tessa than anything."

He cocked his head. "How so?"

"Thinks you have more than a passing interest in her." Honey rolled her eyes. "Seriously, I can't imagine why. She's a nerdy data operator for the geographical section of the university she works at. My bet is she works for the CIA or NSA."

He stared at her without blinking.

"Do you?" Honey ran her finger along his desk without breaking her eye contact with him.

"Do I what?"

"Have other plans for her?"

"I find her charming, educated, and quite lovely. Nothing more." He stood slowly then smoothed his gray suit. "But knowing I'm getting under Captain Hunter's skin is worth my attention."

"You don't want to cross him. He's bad news."

"Oh, I think that is exactly what I want to do. Men like him will jump the gun on what they perceive to be true or if their family is threatened. That insures mistakes. Besides, I don't believe he and Tessa are enjoying marital bliss."

Honey cooed. "Considering how he came on to me when the room emptied out, I'd say that was correct. The man knows how to make a woman like me,s happy. Tessa, on the other hand, probably—"

"That's enough. I'm well aware of what a woman like Tessa needs to be happy."

"Somebody like you?" she teased.

"I understand you had lunch with her and that other woman…"

"Samantha Cordova. Has the personality of a wolverine that has been locked up in a suitcase for a couple of days. Always thinks she's in charge."

"I'm not interested in your opinion of her. What did you discuss?"

"You."

"And?"

"Tessa kept saying how kind you'd been to her, and Chase was a little obsessed with her liking you. But good ole Betty Crocker thinks the sun rises and sets in you for all the humanitarian work you've done throughout the world. Of course, saving her from the hemlock went a long way with her. I'm sure there have been heated arguments between her and Chase. He isn't one to be second fiddle. I learned that the hard way." She gave a short chuckle. "But she is true blue and will drool all over the floor for Chase when he walks into a room. He enjoys that kind of attention. Might not be so happy if she knew about his interest in a little extracurricular activity with me."

"Either you're a liar or a whore," he said in an edgy voice.

"Aren't you lucky I'm a little bit of both? Chase has never complained."

"He is a troglodyte with few manners or insights to what would make the world a better place."

"I'm not so sure I even know that. I'm supposed to be protecting you, and I would hate to have to shoot such a fine specimen of a man."

He walked over to her and smiled. "But you would for me."

"In a heartbeat." She reached out and slid her fingers down his lapel. "Money is my love language."

~ ~ ~ ~

Chase had to be at several panel discussions on increased security risks from third world countries that may pose economic risks to Western nations. This would finish up the day for him. Everyone except Zoric had a place that required their attention. He took over being Tessa's bodyguard. When she referred to the Serbian as her arm candy, he tried unsuccessfully to hide a pleased grin. With his chiseled Serbian face and dark circles under his eyes, he resembled a vampire instead of a famous artist who painted angels.

Having Zoric with her would mean one less thing she had to worry about. The man was sour faced and unapproachable. If anyone wanted to talk to Tessa, he agreed to step back a few paces and pretend to check his phone. He'd listen to her presentations and escort her to her next scheduled appearance. That might be a casual conversation at the coffee shop or getting better acquainted for a future project connected to the university. Zoric wouldn't care if he intimidated the interested party and would make sure Tessa didn't try to encourage any unwarranted attention. Several times, she suggested she would be fine if he left her alone in such a public place.

His response would be, "No."

Then she'd try sweet-talking him, saying he was a softy or how handsome he was dressed up, but the answer would still be, "No."

Chase was comforted knowing the man could not be swayed. At least here, she wouldn't dig in her heels and pout how she was being treated differently than the other agents. There would be a litany of not-being-trusted comments, when would they believe in her to do the right thing, or, the best one, this was just bogus. No. Here she would be her sweet self and act professional. The thought caused him to pull up a picture of her on his phone. Even looking at her picture made his chests ache. To think Vion might spoil how happy she'd made him drove him a little crazy.

The picture of her faded to a call from Ben. He listened for a few seconds before he clicked off and hurried to meet the director on the balcony overlooking a mountain stream. When Chase arrived, the director was staring down at the water.

"Ben?" he asked as he came up alongside him. "You, okay?"

He nodded then released a deep breath. "It's the president."

Chase stiffened for bad news.

"He's going to make it, thanks to Lazarus."

"So, he wasn't behind this?"

"Not exactly." He retold the new agent's story of how he tried to intercede on the president's behalf and what followed. "He managed to pull that dot out with a suction device. Unfortunately, a tiny dot of poison remained. It was no bigger than a pinpoint, Dr. Kelley guesses. That's why it took so long to work its way through his body maybe. The doctor is pretty tight-lipped right now."

"Honey mentioned Andre may have created a power switch."

"Ken and the ME from Sacramento called again and verified there was a small mechanism. It couldn't be seen with the naked eye or any equipment in that lab. Fortunately, the medical school at the university has a transmission electron microscope that can pick up tissue sections and molecules. That's how they found it. Even though it was a minute sample, the poison had the chemical makeup of hemlock."

"Hemlock?" Tessa stood frozen behind them, Zoric at her side.

Chase hadn't noticed her approach. He glanced at the Serbian, but, as usual, couldn't read his expression.

"That's what the test indicated on one of the men who tried to take Heather." Ben reached out and touched her shoulder then withdrew his hand as if he thought better of it.

"Looks like the video watching them would have indicated distress. I read a little about it after yesterday's mishap. Tremors, muscle aches. Something." Tessa sounded bewildered.

"You would think so," Ben continued, "but it is also true they could have developed a slow heartbeat along with low blood pressure. Muscle paralysis may have prevented them from calling out for help if they were conscious. The ME told me there's a real possibility their central nervous system was also depressed. They most likely died in their sleep."

"And the president?"

"Whatever Lazarus did to him, it saved his life," Chase said, surveying the area, hoping Vion's spies were not close. "He's a good man. I never doubted him."

"Nor did I," Ben admitted sadly. "But he's in trouble, nonetheless. He may even face prison time. If only he had come forward—"

"I'm sure he had a good reason," Chase said in the man's defense.

Ben shifted his attention to the peaceful sound of water tumbling over the rocks below. "It may not be enough to save him."

"What does that even mean?" Tessa asked. "Isn't it possible that if Andre did this to the president—"

"We don't know that for sure yet. Lazarus didn't know the aide he relieved. He hadn't been there long, and now we've learned his information was created by AI, so we are having trouble tracing it to anyone." Ben continued to stare at the water.

"Then couldn't all the people lining up inside to give their plasma be at risk?" Tessa added slowly.

Ben whirled around. "How so? What are you talking about?"

"Andre told me after his speech the other day, the liquid portion of the donor's blood is separated from the cells. It basically is drawn from one arm then sends it through a high-tech machine to capture the plasma." She swallowed hard and had a hard time breathing, now gripped with fear. Chase reached out and rubbed her arm. "Then—then the machine returns the blood cells and platelets to the donor. I think he said with saline." She leaned against Chase and stared up at him in horror. "It's always been a safe technique. Andre claims he cut the time in half for the process. That's why so many have signed up to donate. Well, and he promised some of them money. They didn't want to waste any time and miss a program they'd signed up for."

Even Zoric took on a grimace of panic. "How many have donated? Think of the many powerbrokers of the world here. In one fraction of a second, he could control the world as we know it."

"How are we to know who he has implanted without searching medical records and, just like anywhere else, those are kept private with the HIPPAA Privacy Rule. We couldn't get them in time," Chase admitted.

Ben's eyes widened. "Yes. There might be a way. Ken said both men had a small red mark on their forearm as if they'd been scratching an itch. That's the place where they found the chip."

"No!" Tessa was turning to leave, when Chase jerked her back.

"What? Where are you going?" he snapped.

"Honey. She had that mark today at lunch. She kept scratching at it. I thought it was a mosquito bite. Andre has put the poison inside her. I can't let her die." Tears welled up in her eyes. "Please. Help her," she begged Chase.

CHAPTER 35

The four agents hustled their way to Hunter and Tessa's suite. Ben completed a quick call to one of his medical agents in the building posing as part of the security detail. He entered the suite calmly; being told he should appear unconcerned. His conference badge indicated he would periodically check on attendees or any questionable concerns. Since he bore the same-colored badge as the Enigma Team, it was like having a get-out-of-jail-free card as to his movements.

"What's up?" he asked when he spotted four agents. "Tessa, are you okay? After your scare yesterday, I went out to check on the hemlock you told me about when Vion's physician left. There wasn't any. It was all Queen Anne's lace. Hemlock is purple stemmed and can get six to ten feet tall. Did you actually see any of that?"

"No. He intervened so quickly that I backed off because—well, it scared me." Her forehead creased when Chase came to stand next to her. "So, he lied?"

"Not sure. The landscape team I interviewed indicated they had been through there the week before and cut a lot of things back. You weren't looking for hemlock, so you didn't see it. If Vion is acquainted with that kind of danger, he may very well have spotted it. Either way, it's best you know about it now. If I'm not here for

224

you, why am I here?"

Since the doctor had clearance, it would be expected he might go to check on Tessa. After being read in on the possibility of danger for the hundreds of guests who had given plasma and may have been injected with a timed poison switch, Chase felt it imperative to bring Honey into the fold before it was too late.

"I made a call to Honey that I want to see her. Ben is taking Tessa next door as if they're working on statistics for tonight's awards ceremonies. We have a connecting door so if Vion is watching, he'll not know they are here. We've already been debugged, so, no worries there. I think they've given up on that front, but we'll remain vigilant."

The doctor sent for his medical bag and a few things he might need.

Ben moved toward the door. "Let's go, Tessa, so it looks like we've got things to do. Bring your briefcase. Can you keep a conversation going as we move to my room?"

"Of course. What makes you think Honey will come? You know how she hates taking orders from any of us." A little confusion was in her question.

"She'll come. Vion has certain ideas of how to come between us, and she is one of them."

"How do you know that?" Alarm was in her voice. "Did she tell you that, or has she…" She faced him, a look of insecurity in her eyes.

"She told him as much, I'm sure. He knows our history, if you get my drift. She shared with me that he was up to something but wasn't sure of what. At this point, it's hard to say whose side the woman is on but—"

"Tessa," Ben snapped, "can you interrogate your husband later? Let's go," he ordered with the door standing open. "Now."

She moved quickly to the door but pivoted. Walking backward, she added, "Honey wouldn't betray me."

Ben took her elbow and pulled her around. "Let's not count on that just yet."

The door closed behind them just as Chase touched his earwig to hear Zoric announce he'd found Honey talking to Andre before he went into a meeting where she wasn't allowed. "That Franklin guy went in with him. There's security outside the door because a number of world leaders are inside." He snickered. "Once the doors closed, she started bossing security around, and they aren't thrilled. Oh, here she comes."

"Tell her it's imperative she come to see me."

"Will do. You know how much she enjoys my company," Zoric moaned. Chase could picture him approaching her like a wounded animal in need of food.

In spite of expectations of her rebelling again to go with Zoric, he managed to persuade her to quickly get on the elevator. Tessa tapped at the connecting door. Chase glanced over his shoulder as Dr. Rory let her and Ben into the suite. She hurried to Chase's side and laid a hand on his back.

She was safe here with him, away from Andre. What if the monster had done something to her as well, to manipulate her alliance. Without warning, he pulled her into his arms and kissed her then whispered, "I love you." She laid her head against his chest and slipped her arms around him with a firm embrace. "You're done being near him. Anything we planned to trip him up is over. I don't want you caught in the crossfire of whatever he's planning."

"I'm thinking we're too late." Tessa released a deep sigh.

The door felt like it opened in slow motion as Zoric and Honey entered.

Honey stared down at the floor before lifting her eyes to examine the room full of her intermittent enemies. She jutted out her bottom lip in a deep frown. Her sharpest gaze went to Chase, who had demanded she appear. "Well, what is it?" she said as her nostrils flared and her stubborn chin lifted. "I have a job to do that doesn't involve Enigma."

Tessa hurried to gather the assassin in her arms.

Confused, Honey pushed her away. "Don't be touching me like that," she fumed. "I only let your husband do that." A smirk lifted one corner of her mouth as she tilted her head toward Tessa.

"Honey..." he started when Tessa tried hugging her again.

This time, the assassin peeked over Tessa's shoulder at Chase in bewilderment. Her hands went to her friend's back and stroked it slowly. "Are you cryin'?" She pushed her to arm's length.

Tessa sniffed. "I was afraid you were going to die."

"That has been a concern of mine as well, from time to time. Now what is going on?"

Chase walked over and grabbed her arms then shoved her sleeve up on each. "There. Dr. Rory? Take a look."

Honey tried to pull free, but Chase continued with his vise grip. "Tessa indicated you were scratching your arm. Did Andre do anything to you to cause this rash?"

She managed to jerk away. "I'm not sure. He said if I didn't get Tessa to come to my suite tonight, he'd make me pay because he now owned me." Honey surveyed each face before her, including the grim-faced director of Enigma. "I thought he was just trying to intimidate me. I played along." She rubbed the area.

"Stop rubbing it," Dr. Rory demanded. "You're going to make it worse."

"You're not my mum. And I thought you were security. Who are you to tell me what to do? Did they put you up to playing the part of a doctor?"

"We think Andre put a hemlock switch in your arm, Honey," Tessa said, laying a hand on her shoulder. "And yes, he is security, but that part is an act. He's really a doctor. He is going to remove the switch in your arm if it is there."

"A hemlock switch? Well, the dirty bugger," Honey growled. "I'm going to kill him." She turned to leave, but Chase easily reached out and pulled her back. Once again, she squirmed free. "For all I know, this is just another one of your elaborate schemes to save the world or undo whatever you started in the first place. Andre is a pill; I'll give you that. But he has done a lot of good."

"You said yourself, he is a sociopath," Tessa reminded her. "He just happens to be one who can blend in to normal society when he chooses to."

Chase calmly retold how the two men in Sacramento had tried to kidnap Tessa's daughter then died under suspicious circumstances. He recited the medical examiner's report as if he might be reading a business report of quarterly earnings. He knew she'd listen to him if he spoke slowly and with a calculating voice. Her evil eyes landed on him as she gave him her complete attention.

"Why do you care if I die?" she snapped at him.

"I don't," he admitted. "I need your help here. I owe you for what you did for me in Syria. We may not always work on the same side, but you have talents I need from time to time."

Tessa huffed and pushed in front of him. "I care, Honey. I'm serious," she said softly. "I care more than I realized when I thought you'd die before we got you up here. Please. Let Dr. Rory check you over."

The glare of a deadly dragon about to blow fire toward them came over Honey's face. Chase knew she was weighing her options. One of those was whether to trust them. Finally, she let her hard gaze land on Tessa. "Why should I trust you?"

Tessa gave her one of those sweet-mom smiles she usually saved for her kids. "Because we're best friends. Remember?"

"Even though you now know I was going to have you come to my room tonight for Andre's pleasure?"

"Would you really have done that?" Chase asked through clenched teeth.

Honey's glare went from him to Tessa standing like a scared rabbit. "You bet I would," she admitted. "It's a job. It's what I do."

"Oh," Tessa said in disappointment and lowered her focus to the floor.

Honey grabbed Tessa's chin and jerked it up. "But I would never have let him hurt you."

With tears streaming down her face, Tessa pulled Honey into her arms and hugged her. The assassin rested her chin on Tessa's shoulder then glared at Chase with the expression of a pissed-off dragon. He couldn't help but wonder, even now, whose side the woman was on. Did she actually have a soft spot for Tessa, or was it just a convenient event to worm her way into Enigma when she wanted a favor. It was obvious to everyone who knew his wife, she'd believe the devil himself if he swore to be good.

Maybe he should let Andre take care of Honey once and for all. It would save him a lot of time and worry in the long run. She was never going to be anything but dangerous, and he didn't want her around his family.

A chill crawled up his back as Honey studied his reaction when she slipped her arms around Tessa and stroked her back lovingly, letting a sly grin play across her mouth.

He narrowed his eyes at her and decided the Andre option was a much safer idea.

CHAPTER 36

Tessa checked her appearance one last time in the mirror. Her mind skittered back to her family in California. They were having a great time with her parents being available for every whim, board game, snack, and thirty more minutes until bedtime until she returned. Ken kept her updated or sent the information to Vernon who relayed it to her by way of email.

Agent Willy Robbins had, for all practical purposes, moved in to assist her mother with the household chores and meals, shopping and laundry. The woman was new to Enigma and had fit in from day one. Currently, she was Ben's new assistant since the other one had retired. Tessa had met the woman before their Syria mission and had appreciated her attention to detail and no-nonsense manner. It was her hope they could become friends. It would be nice to have a female friend who wasn't crazy or self-absorbed. Apparently, she attracted those kinds of friends like a heat-seeking missile. The possibility of a new friendship, of course, would have to wait.

She laid her hands on her stomach and wondered about the baby. Would it be a boy or a girl? She was pretty confident it wouldn't be blond-haired and blue-eyed since the father... Once more she gazed into the mirror and thought about Roman Darya Petrov, the Tribesman. His skin was tan but not as dark as Chase who was a Cherokee. Roman's hair was dark brown, and Chase's was the color of a raven's wing. Both men were built like warriors.

Would Chase suspect he might not be the father? The major difference between the men, and it was subtle, was their eyes. Chase had the almond-shaped eyes of his people, and Darya had inherited a slightly Asian shape from his Kyrgyz mother. Would her own eyes be enough to soften that characteristic, or would it be the trait that told the truth?

Another sharp twinge hit her lower abdomen. This time it felt like Braxton Hicks, which she usually experienced during her last month of pregnancy. But it was gone as quickly as it began. There had been no more spotting since yesterday. Stop worrying, she told herself. She was healthy as a horse and in the best shape of her life.

The only thing gnawing at her was how to tell Chase she was pregnant. There was no way he wouldn't do the math of the timing. The baby would be a great joy to her, but how would he react? He wanted children, but would he want the child of a man who had been his enemy until the last couple of years?

Tears threatened to spill down her cheeks, another side effect of being pregnant. She was so emotional, tired, and stressed. Pull it together, Tessa, she told herself sternly.

"What did you say?" Chase joined her in front of the mirror. He circled her waist and kissed the back of her exposed neck. "You look beautiful."

She turned in his arms and planted a kiss on his firm, warm lips. "Have I told you I love you today?"

"No. Get with the program." He frowned.

"I love you. I love you." She added a short kiss each time she chuckled through the admission.

"Ahh. That's better. I'm pretty fond of you, too, Agent Tessa Hunter." He grinned.

"Agent Tessa Hunter. Hmm. That sounds pretty good to me."

"If all goes well tonight, then we can head home tomorrow. Hopefully, we'll find out what Andre is up to during his speech. He won't want to miss being the center of attention in front of world leaders and influencers."

"Any word on the president?"

"Going to be okay. How they managed to keep it out of the press other than a mention he had a slight case of walking pneumonia and required rest is beyond me."

She yawned. "Guess it's too late for a nap," she chuckled. "Hope this isn't a late-night event."

"Me, too, but considering who we're dealing with, it might be more than any of us bargained for." He ran his hands across her shoulders. "You'll be careful tonight."

"I will."

"Don't trust Honey further than you can throw her."

"I can't believe she didn't want us to remove the hemlock switch from her arm."

"She has trust issues." He toyed with a curl that fell across her forehead. "I think she believes Andre is going to make his move tonight at the general assembly then come after you, so watch your step. Make sure one of us is always with you."

"I don't think Honey will hurt me or let anyone else."

"I wish I believed that. Sam will go to Honey's room during dinner and wait. I know Honey didn't like the idea and thought I didn't trust her, which I don't, but I'm a believer in leaving nothing to chance. At least, with Sam, I know you'll be protected if things go sideways."

Normally, Tessa would have bristled at the suggestion she couldn't take care of herself. She'd fought her way out of several dangerous situations over the last few years. But the truth was she didn't feel like she could fight her way out of a paper bag lately. This pregnancy was catching up with her in a hurry.

The one person who could make her feel better, and to be happy about the pregnancy had no idea about the turmoil going on inside her. Three people did know. One was an assassin and the other was a self-absorbed nymphomaniac who would make a great dictator for a third world country. Finally, there was Andre Lavelle Vion, who was a mixed bag of Mother Teresa and Darth Vader with a god complex.

"Earth to Tessa." Chase kissed her quickly before he turned to check his phone. "Worried about tonight? You got awfully quiet. I'm going to be right there and, when I'm not, someone else will be." His phone buzzed. Lifting it to his ear, Chase listened as he cut his focus back to Tessa. "How far out are you?" Without another word, he clicked off and sighed.

"Are you sure about this?" she asked, picking up her evening bag.

"Lazarus insisted on being here if there is a takedown. He's done a hell of a job at Enigma the last few days. If it hadn't been for him, Heather might be in the hands of a monster. I know he made mistakes, and he's going to have to answer for the way he dealt with the president. Ken has another trick up his sleeve if there's a glitch. Hopefully, it won't be necessary."

She cocked her head. "Trick? He won't hurt Lazarus, will he?"

"I think he's calmed down now, but he was pretty fired up yesterday. Lazarus is pretty sure he has a way out of all this."

"I think I like him. I hope he isn't facing jail time."

"He most likely will. But there is a deal to be made if he pulls this off tonight and you remain safe. Ken backs him, so that is something at least."

Tessa took his hand. "Okay. No more questions. The less I know, the more convincing I'll be." She stepped up against him, knowing his guard would let down at her touch. "Is this one of those secrets you should have told me long ago?"

"Yes." His lips went to a straight line, and his jaw flexed several times. "I love you, Mrs. Hunter. Just remember that. No matter what."

She lifted her hand to touch his face and they took a moment to gaze at each other. "I believe you."

"And trust me?"

"I do," she whispered.

~ ~ ~ ~

The general assembly of guests finally took their seats after an announcement. The quiet chatter and tinkling of wineglasses continued. The master of ceremonies smiled at the 300 men and women who had contributed much to the success of the Universal Reckoning Initiative before he glanced at his cue cards.

The large screen behind him came to life with an abstract design that continually reconfigured to emulate ongoing change. The obvious absence of the name of the group was evident. Although there were to be no pictures, recorders, and reporters, collecting evidence of the meetings was strictly forbidden. Not even the date appeared on the screen.

There were no expensive suits or glittery evening dresses to strut. Over the years, it had become more of a business-as-usual dress code. The dining arrangements could have been prepared for a state teachers' association or a chamber of commerce awards banquet. Everything was nondescript and unassuming for people who were used to the best or at least being catered to. Here, there was no difference between a prince or a scientist, business giant or Pulitzer Prize winner in this arena. The only thing that mattered was a person's ability to make or embrace change. To be invited was enough for most.

Andre tapped his finger slowly against the white tablecloth as waiters moved quickly to serve salads, iced tea, and hot rolls. Plates of steaming entrees and mixed vegetables were delivered by the time the salads had been consumed. The idea he had to eat before being the keynote speaker irked him enough, he merely picked at his food. Dessert, already on the table, appeared unimaginative and loaded with fat, another thing he wasn't interested in consuming. Coffee was decent and he instructed the waiter to keep it coming.

"Is your steak not to your satisfaction, Monsieur Vion?" A waiter stopped beside him. "I can have the chef prepare another one."

"No. Thank you," he answered calmly. "I'm just not hungry. My compliments to the chef. I'd love to have his name in case I need an event catered."

"Of course. I'm sure he has a card. I'll get one for you."

Andre nodded and focused on Tessa three tables over. She was surrounded, not by the university or Enigma people she'd arrived with but the head of the president's Chief of Staff and Secretary of State Bonnie Finley. He met both of them at the end of one of the sessions earlier. The Chief of Staff barely had time to acknowledge him because of the constant text messages, until he finally handed his phone off to his assistant. The fact he remained calm, knowing the president probably was dying, impressed him. Why he didn't rush back to Washington was still a mystery he wanted answered. The only news of the president's condition was that he had pneumonia. He dismissed it as a cover-up, like most things in Washington. That was one more thing he intended to change.

Bonnie Finley, although mildly attractive, was a flirt and

annoying as she tried to worm her way into his good graces. Tessa had saved him from further conversation by inviting him to coffee. Clearly, they were friends. He'd seen them together several times, but he'd noticed a twinge of friction in the Secretary of State and impatience in the way Tessa stood. Maybe she would tell him about their relationship in the future. Now, he wondered how to return the favor, watching her eyes glaze over with fake interest.

He couldn't help but admire how lovely she looked wearing a simple burgundy dress with a scoop neck and pearls. He wondered once more what it would be like to taste that skin and finger the rebellious curls that had been pushed behind her ear. He held his breath when the Chief of Staff leaned in to whisper a few words to her. Whatever it was, she laughed as Bonnie Finley laid a hand on her hand.

They had the rest of their lives to explore the past. He didn't want to push too hard, or stoo fast. At least in that department. After tonight, life would be different in many ways. Tessa might be confused as to her role in the future, but he was confident she would mold to his wishes. Even if she didn't, he had ways to bring her under control. Abigail was weak, emotional, and fragile. She had no vision of how glorious the future could be with him. Tessa had demonstrated he deserved better. Yes. Soon, she would be at his side, helping to forge the way.

Unexpectedly, she gazed his way and smiled causing him to return the gesture. In that second, he knew he had to take her tonight, even if it were against her will. Captain Hunter had strutted around the last couple of days as if he were a Greek god in charge of anything he came in contact with. Why did she choose such a clumsy brute with the IQ of a cockroach? He leaned toward Franklin to whisper, "Remind Honey of her obligation later tonight. Don't send a text or email. Go. Now. I don't want any possibility of it leading back to me."

Franklin nodded, rose from his seat, and exited.

Andre continued to stare at Tessa, who kept stealing glances his way. Temptation was not an emotion he had experienced. Watching her make small talk to people he would own by the end of the evening gave him a desire to rescue her from their tedious chitchat. He'd noticed how people were drawn to her and how she always listened.

Powerful men and women required people like Tessa to listen. From what little time he'd been around her, she had a way of making him feel—special. Not just important or someone to be admired for all his work, but unique. The way she focused on him as if no one else was in the room flooded him with longing to have her. Own whatever it was that caused men like Captain Hunter to abandon the beast inside him and try to change. Her DNA might have clues he could use to recreate such traits.

Music began to play from a small ensemble offstage. The master of ceremonies introduced them and encouraged the crowd to enjoy the presentation and maybe dance to lighten how hard they had worked the last few days. Since there were more men than women, only the women could choose partners.

The ladies stood and moved about the room, teasing their male equals by snubbing them or making comments that generated a great deal of laughter. But Andre's focus was glued to Tessa who locked with his admiring gaze. She rose like a beautiful swan from the water and moved past her husband toward his table. Several men tried to flatter her into stopping, but she continued toward him. When she stopped next to him, he stared up at those beautiful eyes and couldn't help but smile. She reached down and took his hand then whispered in his ear, "I have one dance for you, Monsieur Vion. It would be my honor for you to escort me."

The elusive Andre Lavelle Vion stood then lifted her hand to his lips. The smile she tried to suppress was beguiling, exhibiting a sexy, come-hither expression he'd never observed before. He realized she desired him. His heart didn't pound with anticipation, only lust of things to come.

They passed Captain Hunter who had been chosen by Bonnie Finley, the Secretary of State. The irritation and warning in the soldier's eyes sent a powerful message to Andre. One he would ignore as he pulled Tessa into his arms. She slid her hands up his arms then around his back. The music was soothing yet playful so that they could sway back and forth without releasing each other.

"Meet me later, Tessa. I may never see you again after tonight," he lied. There was no possible way he'd leave without her. "We need each other. I can feel it," he whispered in her ear as he held her tighter.

She stepped back so he could twirl her then he brought her back so that he dipped her body and lowered his face to inches from hers.

"You take my breath away, Andre. I'm a married woman. This is impossible. I'm sorry." She spoke softly as he pulled her up and smiled wolfishly at her. "However..." Her voice faded when she gazed up into his eyes, as if searching for a decision.

"Honey Lynch will take you to meet me," he said. "I'll join you when I'm finished here. When I take the podium, slip out quietly."

"Tessa, it's time to take your seat," Captain Hunter said as Tessa pushed back from Andre. "I'll take you back to your table." He nodded toward Andre. "Monsieur Vion."

He watched the captain lean down to speak in her ear as she sat down. When he laid his hand on her shoulder, Andre thought he detected a shrug to pull away. Others were coming back to the table, so the captain left, a snarl on his lips as he sent a warning glare toward Andre.

It was too much to resist letting a smile spread across his lips. Captain Hunter thought he had it figured out. Thanks to Honey Lynch's loyalty, he did not.

CHAPTER 37

The master of ceremonies thanked the musicians as they slipped away. Their presence would not be acceptable at the conclusion of these ceremonies. These meetings were secret each year and formed decisions for the world no one would ever be aware that was their doing. Chase surveyed the room for his team. Each member had been placed at different tables, thanks to the director. Ben wanted to make sure he had eyes and ears on whatever was about to go down tonight.

Due to his science and celebrity status, Carter Johnson sat with a few scientists and NASA executives. He knew the language of brilliant men and women. They were laughing at whatever the ex-astronaut was telling them. Chase guessed it might involve the aliens walking among us or perhaps the rule he broke on the International Space Station that caused him to get fired.

Zoric found a spot with the creative crowd and remained morose. The dark circles under his eyes and the smell of cigarette smoke clinging to his skin and garments always sent a vibe to leave him alone. He was a good listener, though, and pretended to be interested in what he would later call drivel.

Samantha Cordova had planted herself with a few royals and a prime minister. As usual, they were eager to get her attention. Even dressed in a black pantsuit, she was the most stunning creature in the room. Whatever question she asked would be a trigger for each person at the table to outdo the other. The woman was an information magnet.

Tessa sat with the US Secretary of State and other high-ranking government officials she knew from working as an intel analyst. Strangely enough, they usually talked freely around her and often asked for an opinion on a geographical concern. His little Grass Valley commando who had been shy, scared of her own shadow, and would stutter a nervous answer to interrogation a few years earlier, could now swap lies with the best of them and not bat an eye.

Vernon was up in his little technology cave keeping an eye on everything to make sure the event was recorded in case it was crucial to go back through for answers. He was also keeping an eye on the spaces outside the banquet room in case Tessa made an unscheduled exit. He spoke to Ben and Chase through their earwigs and often left an off-colored evaluation of one of the members.

Chase and the director shared a table with national security people from several nations, including the US. Vernon often referred to them as the grim reapers and noted their sour expressions and suspicious natures. Chase chose the table primarily because he could watch Andre Vion. He sat with several pharmaceutical industry giants, along with a representative from the World Health Organization, and a key player in the World Bank.

"Boss," Vernon said, "I just got the list of how many donated plasma the last few days. I'd say at least two hundred of the three hundred guests are noted. There are other names on here, likely personal assistants or security. That group was given money incentives to donate. Won't take long for them to switch loyalty if Andre pulls the trigger tonight."

Chase remained silent, afraid of being overheard. His concern spiked when he noticed several of his tablemates scratching at a place on their forearm through their jackets or uniform. He scanned the crowd and noticed several others doing the same thing. It wasn't overly obvious, but he understood the danger that lurked in their skin.

"Boss, I know you can't say anything, but I have another list of people who…”

Chase touched his earwig and tapped. Nothing. His eyes went to Ben who was staring at him and shook his head in confusion and concern.

“Excuse me. I have to step outside for a minute.” Chase stood and moved toward the double doors. Once outside he tried again “Are you there? Vernon?”

“Whoa. Yep. Here I am. Not sure what happened there. Power surge maybe.”

“I thought you were set up not to be bothered with a power surge.”

“Mostly. But it’s not perfect. A thunderstorm is moving in over the mountains. I’m good now.”

“What were you going to say earlier before you cut out?”

“I know since you can’t have your phones in the meeting, there’s no point in sending you the list of people we tried to talk to about their plasma donation. And besides, it got erased when the surge happened. Trying to get back to it now. I think maybe a third of the list volunteered to get checked out.”

“Were they told about the problem?”

“Not that I’m aware of. A panic could have gotten them prematurely killed. We have doctors from DC on the way, Dr. Kelley being one of them. No way we could neutralize all those people in short order.”

“I get that. We will have to intercede when the time comes.”

“How’s Tessa?” Vernon asked sheepishly.

Chase understood the tech genius had always thought of her as a big sister or even a mother figure. She was one of the few women he could actually talk to without freezing up.

“Nervous.” Chase scanned the area. “I’m counting on you to follow her.”

“No problem.”

“I have to go,” he grunted.

Awards were being given out by several people depending on the topic. Applause floated across the spacious dining hall like a slow wave of thunder. The upper windows periodically flashed with lightning. Normally, he would have enjoyed a good thunderstorm, especially with Tessa who loved them. They could have gone out on the covered balcony and enjoyed the show.

He glanced her way. Like a trooper, she was focused on the awards and clapped with her delicate hands as if she was a princess. For the millionth time, he recognized how lovely she was and how much his life had been enriched with just breathing the same air as the woman. Whatever it was that drew unsavory men to her, he understood because he had been one of those men not so long ago. And yet, not even he could explain why she touched his soul.

Was it her faith, her belief in the good of mankind, or maybe those damn chocolate chip cookies she constantly made? Whatever it was, he wanted more of it—a lifetime of her undaunting love of life. One thing he would never doubt; even with all his faults, she loved him unconditionally. When this was over, he wanted a serious conversation about having a baby. He didn't want to wait for the kids to accept him.

"Thank you one and all for your service to the world and to this institution. Your efforts over recent years have made the planet a better place." The master of ceremonies went on to thank their director, Benjamin Clark, for the hard work at making this year's conference a success.

Finally, he introduced Dr. Andre Lavelle Vion and expressed his gratitude for agreeing to be their keynote speaker for the evening and offering incentives for his work in blood plasma research. The praise for his accolades were lengthy.

"Dr. Vion, if you'd make your way to the front, please."

The man rose like a god overlooking his subjects. He stood still for a few seconds, listening to the applause and shouts of praise. Impressed with their adoration, he laid a hand on his heart, bowed his head in a humble fashion, and mouthed, "Thank you" several times. Slowly, he approached the stage then turned toward his captive audience who now stood on their feet, cheering and clapping their approval.

He and Ben remained seated and took a sip of their water.

Chase checked to see Tessa standing then applauding with much enthusiasm. That troubled him silently. In spite of the possibility Andre had been involved in the kidnapping attempt on her daughter, she smiled and encouraged his pompous self-love.

Had she forgotten the escaped girl, Nora, and how she'd gone into great detail about his laboratory experiments? Then there were his peculiar tastes with the women he planned to use for research. The man was nothing short of hypnotic, not only to this crowd but to his wife. You'd think they were smart enough to know that if it sounded too good to be true, it probably was. He prayed Tessa was just acting as part of the ruse to catch Vion in whatever he planned.

As people took their seats again, Sam excused herself from the banquet hall. She would be going to Honey's room to wait for Tessa to arrive with the assassin. That was one agent he could always count on to follow orders. The two women had their issues, but Sam would not let anything happen to Tessa. She was just wired to protect and serve.

~ ~ ~ ~

Sam punched in the key code to Honey's room, double-checked both ways down the corridor, and slipped inside to darkness. Fumbling for the light switch, she felt another presence nearby as her fingers touched the button that flooded the room with light. Pulling her weapon from the holster on her hip, a foot rose up and kicked it from her hand.

"Hello, luv," came the sinister voice of Honey Lynch as she bent down and picked up the gun then started backing up as Sam followed.

"What the hell do you think you're doing?"

"What I always do—looking out for number one. Now be cooperative and I won't have to hurt you."

Just as she lunged at Honey, a muscled arm went around her neck and squeezed. She was then spun around and met a fist upside her head. Although she gave him a punch to the throat knocking him to the floor, Honey blindsided her by tripping her to slam against the marble coffee table with her jaw then on top of the beast struggling to get up. The last words Sam heard as she began to drown in darkness were in an Irish accent.

"That's a good lass. Can't say I didn't warn ya."

~ ~ ~ ~

The flash of lightning was followed by a roll of thunder that shook the building for only a second, but there were a few gasps.

Guests from other countries were not always prepared for a good old American thunderstorm. Several could be heard saying even American weather was violent and temperamental. It was easy to spot the Americans who grinned at their tablemates' startled expressions. But when the lights flickered, Chase became uneasy. He tapped his earwig.

"I'm here, boss. The storm should be out of here in about thirty minutes."

Chase turned to see Honey come through the entrance doors and weave through the tables to reach Tessa. She bent down and whispered in her ear, like they planned. Tessa nodded as she stood. Together, they exited.

This was the beginning of the end for Andre Lavelle Vion. Between Honey and Sam, surely his plans would be foiled. If not, they'd go to plan B.

"Thank you, ladies and gentlemen, for your warm welcome. It has been an astonishing few days to be able to move among such noteworthy men of science, geo-politics, economics, and the arts. My brain is on overload with the opportunities presented here and the possibility of a better world."

More applause.

"First order of business is to remind those who participated in donating your plasma, your two thousand dollars has been deposited in the account you indicated when filling out your information."

Money could be an enticement, no matter the amount. Now that Vion had personal information on those who'd donated plasma, his power had increased.

"The three recipients of the million-dollar prize for the charity of your choice as indicated on your information has already been donated. The winners did not want their names mentioned, so I'll only name the charity. Open Doors, a school opportunity for children of war-torn countries, Emerging Markets for Women in Africa, which promotes their skills to sustain their families during drought and conflict. Finally, Carmichael Research Hospital for Children in Edinburgh, Scotland. I expect great things from these people."

Chase had never heard of any of those charities and doubted they even existed. The possibility they were connected to Vion's shady business dealings was an idea worth investigating after the conference. But the audience bought it hook, line, and sinker.

Applause followed with another standing ovation.

Lights were dimmed leaving candlelight flickering like a yellow orb on the tables. The speech began with the big screen lighting up with reels about the work that was being done through his blood and plasma research. Video of children surviving the worse days of their lives, along with adults who lived to fight another day and make a difference. Even Chase was inspired—to a point. Then the speech took on a darker tone. The video became more of a military thriller at that point, demonstrating the turmoil in the world. It emphasized the lack of leadership in many of these countries.

"A few of those countries have attended here over the years." Vion lowered his voice to sound as if he were warning the audience of something.

A sudden chill filled the air, and guests glanced at each other in confusion mixed with outrage at the insinuations. He continued the speech in a calm, authoritative voice that put the room on edge.

Chase turned around to survey the room and spotted two men dressed in the yellow lab coats at all six double doors. They stood with their feet apart and their hands locked behind their backs, military style.

Vernon's voice broke into his earwig. "The plane is forty-five minutes out, Chase. And Vion's plane is gassed and ready to go. He has already filed a flight plan for Paris. There's something else you should know." A moment of silence followed then, "Hey, who are you?" The sound of a scuffle before Chase was disconnected.

Since Ben touched his earwig and squinted at Chase, he assumed he heard the same confusing transmission. Chase tilted his head toward the double doors as he stood. The two Enigma men moved toward the back and were joined by Carter and Zoric only to be stopped at the door.

"Return to your seat, sir. No one in or out until the speech is over."

"Personally, I'm over the speech. Now let me pass," Chase demanded.

Zoric nudged him in the back, causing him to pivot. "I think we'd better listen to the speech, Captain."

A waiter had shoved a gun in the Serbian's back, and a second waiter had done the same to Carter.

Ben scowled at the men and motioned for them to sit down at a nearby empty table.

Chase leaned in and whispered to the man blocking the door, "If I were you, I'd not stand too close when that door comes flying off the hinges. My people are on their way, and they enjoy messy. Just warning you."

Pulling his shoulders back, he moved to the table and sat down before smiling at the guards who watched him with a new kind of interest, along with an abundance of caution.

CHAPTER 38

"Aren't we going to your room, Honey?" Tessa asked as they headed out a side door that flanked a walking path for guests with dogs. It was a short walk through a grassy area with trees and held a strong smell of urine. The stench caused Tessa to stop and vomit her dinner.

"Holy Mother of God, Tessa. What did you eat? A side of beef?" Honey pushed Tessa's hair back then dug in her backpack for a bottle of water. "Rinse your mouth out and splash some on your face."

She did as Honey suggested and felt better. "I don't want to do this."

"A little late for that," Honey fumed, shoving a breath mint into Tessa's mouth. "You don't want to smell like a dead pooka lying on the side of the road."

"Pooka?"

"Irish goblin. Stinky. I've told you this before."

"Oh my gosh," Tessa said, having an attack of the dry heaves. She held out her hand toward Honey. "I'm good. I'm good. Do I stink?"

Honey took a sniff and shrugged. The sky suddenly opened up, and a heavy downpour drenched both women. She grabbed Tessa's elbow and pulled her toward a driveway. "Not anymore, luv. Now you'll have an excuse to get out of those wet clothes. Maybe Monsieur will let us help each other."

"Oh my gosh," she moaned. "Are you serious?" She tried to pull free of Honey's grasp but felt too weak to make it happen.

"Sometimes, Tessa, you are just a prude." She sighed in exasperation.

"I'm not undressing for anyone except Chase."

"Now there's an idea I bet Monsieur Vion hasn't considered. Force him to undress you and then—"

"Stop. I thought you were here to help me be safe."

A black SUV came to a screeching halt beside them, and two men jumped out. "Sorry, luv, there's been a change of plans." Honey pointed to the inside of the SUV. The man on the passenger side manhandled Tessa into the back seat, and Honey slipped in beside her.

The darkness covered the person on the other side of her. "Get over," Tessa demanded. Then the lighting flashed and Tessa gasped. "Sam," she cried out, pushing her tangled hair away from the agent's face, finding blood coming from a cut on the edge of her eye.

"She's alive," the assassin said, pulling Tessa's hands away. "I don't want blood on you. I promised your latest fan you wouldn't be upset when he came for you."

The SUV jerked into full speed, screeching tires throwing up puddles of water that were running off the upper embankment. They swerved several times, which did nothing for her upset stomach. The road was narrow and dark, only visible from the beams of headlights and lightning that forced the driver to brake too fast then start up again.

Tessa stole several hard looks at Honey who had focused on the driver and the front passenger. She'd never seen her like this before: a steely glare that could have sliced a diamond with one swing of her Irish sense of justice. Her bottom lip protruded, and those cat-green eyes were narrow and unflinching. The hollow cheekbones flexed constantly as her determined chin lowered. The woman was terrifying.

The road opened up revealing a stretch of flat land with bright lights in the distance; the private airport guests had used to fly in from their first stop in Atlanta.

"Honey, where are we going? Is that the airport?"

She turned her cold dead eyes on her and blinked then concentrated on the men in the front. The car picked up speed before the vehicle water planed for a few feet, but the driver managed to correct his mistake.

Honey reached up and tapped the man in the front passenger seat on the shoulder. "Do that again and I'll make sure Vion drains your blood in a most unpleasant way."

The man poked the driver in the arm and nodded back toward Honey.

Tessa tried to find the seat belt with no success as Sam came to with a groan. She lifted her handcuffed hands to her head then turned to Tessa.

"Tessa?" She sounded bewildered. "Where are we?" With a great more strength than Tessa expected from a woman who was bleeding, Sam displayed a determination to straighten in her seat before leaning forward to see who was sitting on the other side of Tessa. "I should have known."

Honey leaned across Tessa and winked at the agent. "Yes, you should have. No worries," she whispered. "Be a good Enigma agent and I might save you, too."

"Lucky me," Sam groaned through clenched teeth. "If you harm this woman in any way, you'll have the full force of Enigma hunt your sorry ass down and—"

"Threats will do you no good, Sam. Besides, I would never let anything happen to my BFF," she said, planting a wet kiss on Tessa's cheek before giving it a rough pat.

Tessa pushed the assassin away and leaned into Sam. "I think I'm going to be sick," she admitted, pressing a palm to her chest.

"Hold that thought for a wee bit longer," Honey said almost in a whisper.

~ ~ ~ ~

The audience mumbled a sense of outrage as Andre proceeded with his speech. Pictures on the big screen faded in and out with chaos and a dying planet. He turned and pretended to see the screen for the first time. Then a picture of a laboratory showed several men in prison uniforms.

"These men volunteered for experiments as a chance to reduce their sentences. I thought I'd do a demonstration in a minute. But first, let me explain why I am here. It is my hope that with my leadership throughout the world, it will become a much safer and healthier place to live. No more unwillingness to share the wealth and resources of a nation with those less fortunate. No more conflict because of petty tribal demands or even threats of nuclear devastation due to power mongering by corrupt tyrannical leaders. I am the person who must lead the world into a new age of peace and harmony."

"No such thing," a person in the back shouted. "Not everyone will comply."

"Exactly," Andre answered. "That is why I have you to lead the way to help me attain my goals of operating as a leader of your countries, companies, and creative endeavors to get the word out."

The grumbling became deafening.

"Enough," Andre shouted. "Let me demonstrate how this is going to work."

He stepped aside so not to block the video screen. The two men extended their arms while the lab technician explained they were donating their plasma. They were the same machines brought to the conference.

"This is where it gets interesting," the lab technician explained. "Both of these men are leaders of rival gangs inside this prison." The technician held a small tablet device. He removed the silencing headphones from each man's head and asked, "Will you give up your leadership roles as of this minute for a more peaceful experience for everyone at the prison?"

Both prisoners frowned and then laughed at the idea.

"Very well," the technician responded calmly. He touched a spot on the handheld device and, in seconds, the men were dead.

People rose to stand on shaky feet in the banquet hall.

The screen went dark as Andre continued, "When the men agreed to volunteer for this experiment, they had no idea that as the blood circulated back into their arms, it carried a small device. When we remove the tubing then attach a magnetic catch, it pulls the device to the bend of your arm."

"This is outrageous," a man in the front row shouted. "And unethical."

"Yet many of you," Andre said, pulling up pictures of different people in the crowd doing the very procedure they witnessed at the prison, "have this same device planted in your arm. It has a small amount of hemlock. For most of you, it will cause you a little discomfort if I press the button." He held up a tablet. "Others, depending on your position, have a larger amount to make sure you understand the severity of the outcome—which is sudden death." He smiled. "I wonder who is who?"

People were jumping to their feet and pulling up their sleeves. Panic spread like a wildfire.

"Sit down, everyone, and stay calm."

Chase noticed how quickly everyone obeyed. He watched Andre step off the stage and move among the people. Guests stared at him in disbelief and fear. When he neared the center double doors, a United States general stood again.

"I don't believe any of this. You're a madman."

"Believe it. Observe the waiters." He touched a button on the tablet, and they immediately collapsed. "I'll be in touch, ladies and gentleman. Remember, I can access the switch in your arm no matter where I might be. I look forward to leading you into a better tomorrow."

The Enigma group got to their feet and tried to reach out to the closest waiter, but he was already gone. Men in yellow lab suits blocked any chance to escape as Chase tried to reach someone on the outside.

"Sam!" he demanded. "Sam!"

Carter stepped up. "I already tried her. Nothing."

Zoric arched an eyebrow and pulled a small device that appeared to be a cigarette lighter. He took a pack from his pocket and passed it around. "You got fifteen seconds after I light these. Powerful enough to blow those doors open and a hole in Vion's henchmen."

"Stand back," Ben ordered the guest seated at the nearest tables to the door. "We're going to try and get you out of here. Everyone else, protect yourselves and be prepared to leave."

The guards had suddenly come to life as the Enigma team rushed them with the explosive burning like a cigarette. It happened so quickly, the security could barely retrieve their weapons when a cigarette was shoved in a pocket, down the front of their suit. In Zoric's case, he rammed it under the hood of one yellow-clad guard.

The explosions started a shock wave of panic plus cries of despair. The crash of doors falling and bloody men now lying in various positions drove the guests to rush through the carnage to safety.

Once out in the foyer, several US generals, the president's Chief of Staff, and Secretary of State Bonnie Finley joined the Enigma team. They were stunned but able to function.

"Good thing you checked us out this afternoon, Ben," General Goodin admitted. "Of all times not to have my weapon."

"I need you to organize this mayhem right now. We've lined up ten doctors who now know what is going on," Ben admitted as people continued to stumble through the corridor. "They are set up in the ballroom on the mezzanine level. Can you take charge and get the ones we couldn't reset this afternoon?"

"Done," he said and walked off.

"Bonnie, are you okay?" Chase asked when she stumbled over and fell into his arms. "I need your help. Can you hold it together a little while longer? You have no worries. The switch was deactivated in your arm."

"Yes. I think so. Just tell me what you need."

"Take care of the political ramifications that are about to hit the fan. You and the Chief of Staff have your work cut out for you." Chase pushed her to arm's length. "Use that bossy attitude to get things done and secure. Make sure our embassies around the world are on high alert."

"You got it. Thanks for saving my life." She patted his arm then pulled her shoulders back. "I'll check with you later."

"No side effects from the extraction this afternoon?" He started backing away, anxious to find Tessa.

"I'm good. Where's Tessa?" Her brow wrinkled, and she glanced around the area for her.

"With Agent Cordova. I'm going to check on them now." He hoped he sounded more confident than he felt.

She gave a weak smile and nodded before going off to the job ahead of her. She was a wrecking ball when it came to getting her way and making people listen to reason. She just never gave them a choice other than acceptance of her will. In a way, the woman was a lot like Andre. At this point, he was satisfied with that characteristic.

Ben came alongside him. "I'm going to go check on Vernon. He's still not answering."

"We're headed upstairs to Honey's. Andre should be there by now. I don't want him to get away."

"Just so you know, the elevators are down on the west side. Try the east side."

Chase took Zoric and Carter with him, knowing the chances were good Andre had more security waiting. Considering his wounded leg had not returned to its pre-Syria condition, he prayed the elevators were working there. When Carter punched the Up button and the doors opened, he breathed a sigh of relief.

Fortunately, they had secured their weapons in the lobby safe before racing to the elevator. They were uncomfortable the entire conference without them and had placed a few on the floors they thought might require lethal resolution if things went sideways with Andre.

The men cautiously approached Honey's room, and Chase was shocked to find security removed. The hall lights flickered after a bolt of lightning shook the building and rain pounded against the window panes at the end of the hall.

The door was ajar and the lights out. All three men took defensive positions then burst into the room, only to find it empty. Zoric flipped on the overhead light, halting the men at the sight of the room in disarray. "Tessa?" Carter asked, turning to see Chase search the room then pick up a scarf Sam had been wearing. "Sam?"

Chase shook his head. "Both are gone."

"By the looks of this place I'm thinking she put up a fight. I'm betting Sam is in the thick of it." Carter stared at the mess around the room.

"What has Honey done with my wife and where in the hell is Andre Vion?"

CHAPTER 39

"You need to pull over," Honey ordered.

"We're not supposed to stop for anything, Madame Lynch. Boss's orders." The driver turned slightly to speak over his shoulder then slowed to take a curve.

"Fine. You can explain to him that even though I tried to make his latest fascination comfortable, you kept driving and let her puke all over the car and on herself. Pull over, man," she fumed. "She's carsick." Honey turned those cold dead eyes back to Tessa then Sam and let a narrow smile stretch across her mouth as her eyebrow arched.

It wasn't exactly a fake, but Tessa made a gagging noise that sounded like a sick dog. She leaned forward and put her hand on the driver. "Ahh."

Another gag had him pulling over on the shoulder of the road. "Make it snappy."

The man in the passenger seat jumped out and quickly opened the back door for Honey to scoot out.

"She needs help," Honey ordered, pointing to the interior of the car.

"Ugh," he groaned impatiently. "Come on."

He reached in and took Tessa's hand as she scooted out. She ran a few steps away when the dry heaves started again. An unfamiliar sound caught her attention. She spun around in time to watch Honey pull her weapon and shoot the man in the chest. Her scream was lost in the night.

She ran forward, fearful the driver would take revenge immediately.

Honey shoved the man aside like he was a pesky lightning bug then held out her hand to catch Tessa by the front of her dress. "Better not look in there, luv."

But she did look. Sam had sprung into action by putting her handcuffed hands over the driver's neck and jerked herself back in the seat, pulling as hard as humanly possible. The man fought to be released, and Tessa thought for sure he was winning. With one last yank against his neck, he fell silent. Sam collapsed against the seat and stared out at Honey then Tessa.

"Can you drive, Sam?" Honey helped Tessa inside and buckled her up then reached over her and unlocked Sam's cuffs.

"Yes." She opened the door and swung her long legs out to the ground. In minutes, the two women had dragged the driver to the ditch along the shoulder of the road with the other dead security guard.

"I'm going to Hell," Tessa shouted in frustration.

Honey buckled her seat belt and smiled back at her. "Nah. You're goin' to Heaven, and we all expect you to keep your foot in the door so we can sneak in, too."

"I think St. Peter will have something to say about that," Tessa said, rubbing the image out of her head.

"I'll take care of him." Sam glanced in the rearview mirror at her. She let one corner of her mouth lift.

Honey passed back a bottle of water. "Be a good girl. We're almost there. Dig in my backpack and clean yourself up. I also put in a pair of slacks and a top. You're supposed to look amazing for Andre."

Tessa did as she was told. "I can't imagine why."

"It's called temptation," Sam cooed. "You've been doing it to Chase and the Tribesman for years. Toughen up and do what you're told. Trust us." She glanced at Honey. "Well, trust me."

~ ~ ~ ~

Chase and the other two agents joined Ben in the lobby. There was still chaos among the guests and a lot of loud arguing and fear. Since the US delegation had their Hemlock Switch removed earlier in the day, they were now in charge of helping get things back on track. Cell towers were down from the storm, but other means of communication had been dismantled by Andre's people.

"Where's Vernon?" Chase asked.

"I found him unconscious. He's being looked after now. When he came to, he managed to tell me Andre's people had burst into his control center and wrecked everything, along with erasing video on the computers he used to keep track of security and Tessa. All the evidence of Andre's deception disappeared.

"So, we have no evidence now," Chase huffed.

"Fortunately, our young agent of conspiracy backed everything up to an offshore server."

"He needs a raise," Chase said drily.

"I'm inclined to agree," Ben said, looking around at the chaos. "But, first, we have to find our people. Since Andre has his plane ready to go at the nearby airport, I'm betting that's where he's headed."

"Sam has a tracker embedded in her clothing, but, with internet down here at the resort, I can't find her." At Carter Johnson's anxious comment, Chase put his hand on his shoulder.

"We'll find her." Chase stopped a CEO of an electronics company he remembered working with Vernon to upgrade their equipment a few years back. He told him the problem and that he needed help ASAP. "Have you had your arm checked out?"

"I didn't volunteer for that. I hate needles, and it basically creeped me out." He waved off the idea. "I'm good to go. Here's what I have." He motioned for him to follow. "I brought this as a demo for the military and intelligence crowd. I figured if they liked it, I would have a better chance at the Pentagon going for it."

"You get my people back and I'll speak to the president on your behalf," Ben said forcefully. "Let's do this."

"Better yet, take my car. I have a CB radio installed. Also, there are a lot of Ham radio operators in the area. These people around here have them like you wouldn't believe. Always thinking like preppers in case of a EMP attack. You can reach out, and they'll give you information you might need. I'll go on first and introduce you. Got to love 'em," he chuckled. "In the meantime, I have a drone in my trunk and—"

"Wait," Chase interrupted. "You take a drone with you when you travel?"

"Doesn't everyone?" A bewildered expression creased his forehead. "Anyway, there's a good chance if you're wanting to track your agent, then it will put off a frequency that the drone can pick up. All I need is to know the frequency. Do you have that?"

"I'll get it," Zoric said, walking backward toward the elevator. "Vernon will know."

They started toward an exit door leading to the parking lot. Chase followed the CEO as he continued to explain. "Don't worry. I won't give away what is going on here. I just have to mention government overreach and they're in. Ham radio operators have volunteers that track down illegal transmitters. They practice doing this in what is called a fox hunt. Someone hides a small transmitter, and they have to find it. They do this by using a receiver set to the broadcast frequency connected to a directional antenna called a Yagi-Unda. It's the same principle as finding animals that have a tracking collar. Two, maybe three people with Yagi antennas could find it, providing they know the frequency. Won't take long to fix you up once I have that. In the meantime, I'll alert these guys, along with the CB crowd."

Chase nodded. "You must be one of Tessa's angels."

~ ~ ~ ~

Andre Lavelle Vion's driver pulled into the hangar where Tessa would be waiting for him. His plane was parked inside, gassed and ready to go after he took care of unfinished details. An incoming plane landed and turned into the gigantic hangar system. Another plane was being guided into the far end of the hangar.

The inside was bright as day, revealing an almost serene environment. Ground crews were unloading boxes and stacking them on pallets. The plane didn't appear to have passengers, but his people were going to go down and check it out while he went into the VIP reception area he'd reserved until Tessa was ready to leave.

His sources from the evening's event sent him a few messages that the resort remained in panic mode. Nearly one hundred men and women were pleading with his assistant, Franklin, to speak on their behalf in joining him in the new revolution. As Andre exited the facilities, he heard an explosion, and he spotted three attendees who had not been present for his speech. It infuriated him enough; he pointed his controller at them.

"What's going on?" one industry giant inquired. "Sorry I missed your speech, Vion."

"Not as sorry as you're going to be," he answered in a condescending tone.

He pushed the button and, in ten seconds, they dropped to the floor. Instead of hurrying out the door with one of his guards, he watched them wither away as they stared up at him in shock. Taking a deep breath, he raised his sights to the hotel staff who had brought the men to the hangar. They watched in horror. He couldn't resist pointing his device at one or two. A venomous smile toying with his lips, he pressed the button. The guard's eyes widened as Andre targeted people.

"Don't worry. They are replaceable. You are not. Let's go."

None of that mattered now. Tessa need not know the scope of what happened at the resort. He'd placed most of the attendees on a timer, the Americans being the first to feel the effects of the Hemlock Switch. When they started dropping like flies, the other countries would fall into line. According to Franklin, support was signing up. Now to make the night a complete success was to bring the woman he wanted at his side. Tessa.

The door to the VIP lounge opened slowly. There she stood, his beautiful Tessa. A delicate flower who would join him in his quest to control parts of the world with their misguided agendas and attempts at correcting global warming. Bringing the world into compliance with his effective method of submission would solve today's problems in a revolutionizing way. Thanks to him, insecure world markets and geo-political conflict could be controlled by simply pointing out to what they had to lose if not compliant. With Tessa's background and experience in cultural geography, she would be able to assist him in evaluating the movement and environmental impacts of his decisions. It was a glorious moment for him. He couldn't wait to share his vision with the future Mrs. Vion.

He strode toward her with outstretched arms. Why didn't she run to him and fall into his arms? The reasonable answer was shyness, or perhaps she was unsure of how Captain Hunter would react to finding her gone, his agent dead in Honey's room and his technology wizard battered. His usefulness was over for this Enigma group, and he guessed he would be collecting unemployment soon enough.

"Tessa." He smiled, taking her hands in his and staring into her eyes. "I'm so glad you decided to join me." Her hands were shaking. He dared push her damp curls away from her face as Honey moved up beside her.

"I know you had other clothes for her to wear, Monsieur Vion, but we were soaked before ever getting into the car. I didn't want her to catch cold, so I loaned her things I had packed."

Without taking his eyes off Tessa in her pale-blue shirt and white slacks, he marveled at how stunning she looked in whatever she wore. "Still as lovely as ever," he whispered. He kissed each hand then looped one arm through his. "I know you are frightened at coming here. I fly to Paris tonight, and I want you to come. I have packed for you. Everything you need. And if there is something else, I have a fashion stylist on standby. She knows what I like."

"What about the things I like, Andre?" Tessa sounded perturbed as she pulled her arm free and faced him. "I came with Honey to tell you I won't be going with you. I love my husband and won't be unfaithful."

He smiled as if listening to a stubborn child. "Nonsense. You're worried he'll do something irrational and try to stop or hurt us. I guarantee you that is not the case."

She jumped back from him. "No, Andre. It isn't that. I could never be with anyone who physically hurts women like you have for your own self-indulgence."

His expression turned dark. "Who told you such a thing?"

"I did," came a voice from behind him.

Andre jerked around to see the woman who escaped his lab several months earlier. He thought the wolves or perhaps hyperthermia had finished the job he planned to do himself.

"I don't know you," he lied, motioning Honey to step forward.

"You recognize my face, my body, but never bothered to find

out who I was. I mean who I really was."

Andre frowned and sighed. "Pay no attention to her, Tessa. I have this problem all the time. People enjoy getting my attention for money, a favor—many things." Grabbing Tessa's arm, he jerked her alongside him. "So, who are you, mademoiselle?"

"She is Nora, my best friend since we were children and, later, my girlfriend." Franklin walked out from a stack of boxes. "I helped her escape. You're a monster, and I have enough evidence to put you away for a very long time."

Andre tilted his head, his usually narrow eyes wide with astonishment. "Traitor," he said calmly. "I take no pleasure in killing you, Franklin. Remember, you were at my bidding and did a great number of the things you claim were repulsive. I think you rather enjoyed it."

"Shut up, Vion," Franklin barked.

"Honey, kill him."

Honey pulled out her 9mm and shot him in the chest. She strolled over to his crumpled body on the floor and pried the tablet from his hand as his girlfriend burst into tears. With casual disregard for the woman who now fell across her true friend and lover, Honey chuckled and joined Andre.

"Done." She handed the tablet back to him.

CHAPTER 40

Tessa covered her mouth in horror to prevent herself from screaming at the callous disregard for life. She stared at Honey and wondered if there were no limits to her ability to shock her.

A long sigh of impatience came from Andre as he turned to Tessa and offered a patient smile. "My dear Tessa, I'm sorry you had to witness such an act of disloyalty. I don't like betrayal. Franklin left me no choice. I realize now I entrusted him with too much about my work. That will no longer be the case since I'll have you at my side. Together"—he pulled her into his arms and kissed each cheek—"we will forge a dynasty."

She pushed away. "I'm leaving now. I will have nothing to do with ruling the world or being a part of your life."

Andre lowered his chin in stubbornness. "I've frightened you and I beg your forgiveness. But every great man must make decisions to further the work that lies before him. I had hoped you'd come on your own, but I see now there is a willfulness in you that will help you survive the life I lay before you."

"I'm. Not. Getting. On. That. Plane," Tessa said forcefully.

"Yes, you will. And later, we will get to know each other better." He turned to Honey. "Drag that pitiful woman off Franklin and put her in the cargo area. We can dispose of her when we are out over the ocean." Tapping his cheek, he smiled. "Better yet, I did not get a chance to visit with her before she escaped. I think maybe I will do that before we take off."

"No," Honey said coolly. "And I won't be putting Tessa on the plane, either. This is too much even for me."

He held up the tablet. "Remember, you belong to me now. Do it."

Honey shifted her eyes to Tessa and mouthed, "Sorry." Her nostrils flared as she hurried to Nora's side and jerked her up. "Stop your sniveling, woman. It won't bring him back." She pulled her toward the plane and shoved Nora onto the steps so violently, the woman fell face-first. "Oh, for the love of Mary and Joseph." She reached down and yanked her up again before dragging her onto the plane.

Honey exited the plane with the strut of a runway model. Once off the step, Tessa glanced toward some new rough-looking characters who had come from the far end of the hangar. She didn't know who they were, except she'd heard Andre order them to check out the unknown plane. These reminded her of beefy soldiers and appeared to be on high alert, their eyes constantly on scan mode and moving about as if checking out their surroundings.

Would Chase make it here in time to save them? What did Andre plan to do to Nora? And to her? Her heart pounded. In tough times on each mission, she had a way out or at least the means to protect herself. Although she stopped those goons from driving them to the airport, there was a good possibility Honey still hadn't decided which way the winds were blowing to save her own neck. And what of Sam? Where did she go after arriving? Had she been discovered?

"Who are those guys?" Honey nodded toward the men.

"Part of my new army."

"And what did you promise them?"

"Same thing Enigma offered you, a get-out-of-jail-free card I think they call it." Andre's lips stretched into a sneer. He lifted the tablet. "But then again—accidents happen." He grabbed Tessa by the arm and tugged her after him, although she tried to dig in her heels.

Stopping once and yanking her up into his face, he growled, "Your unwillingness to participate is beginning to annoy me, Tessa. It's time to leave, and you are getting on that plane." He pulled her after him but stopped when Honey stepped in front of him. "Get out of my way."

Honey shifted her gaze from him to Tessa and twisted her mouth a bit to the side. "Ahh, luv, I tried. Sorry. Whatta ya say I be your personal bodyguard?"

"I say that doesn't work for me," Andre quipped. "I say I don't want her purity exposed to the likes of you."

"Excuse me? Who do you think you are, Vion? You're a killer. No matter how hard you say you are saving the world, you get off on killing people, especially if you don't get your way."

"I've heard quite enough from you," he snarled at Honey then released Tessa for just an instant so he could push the Hemlock Switch. "You're done."

Tessa screamed, "No," as Honey fell at Vion's feet. "No," she cried again. "Please."

"Begging is a nice touch. Get used to it," he said offhandedly.

"I never got used to it," came a feminine voice from a woman walking through the hangar doors.

A woman stood between Lieutenant Ken Montgomery and Agent Lazarus.

Andre's eyes widened. "Abigail? Abigail is that really you?" he gasped in unbelief.

"Yes. All these years you thought I was dead, I was actually living a new life and identity away from the family you managed to destroy."

"You died."

"No. It was all a ruse created by Captain Hunter." She glanced toward the men stationed around the room like soldiers.

In an instant, Ken pulled up the automatic weapon he held across his chest.

Lazarus came to slip an arm around Abigail's shoulders and began to speak. "I was just a little kid when you nearly destroyed my sister. Captain Hunter and his sister Christina made it possible for her to go into hiding. But we could never be a real family again."

Samantha appeared from behind stacked storage containers with her weapon drawn. "Tessa, I want you to move over here next to me."

At her first step, Vion grabbed her, pulled a gun from inside his jacket, and pointed it back and forth between her and Abigail. "She's going with me."

"Turn my wife loose, Vion," Chase demanded, pulling the hood down on the yellow cover-up he'd gotten from the grounds crew. The other men did the same and exposed their weapons. "We disarmed your people at the other end of the hangar.

It gave her great comfort to see Zoric and Carter were also present and prepared to do battle.

"Ah, the great Captain Hunter. Yes, I did kill your most annoying sister. I didn't know how she managed to convince my Abigail to take her life, but I was sure she did."

Abigail sniffed in disgust. "She talked me out of dying. I wanted nothing to do with you. You're a monster. Thanks to Captain Hunter, I have been able to wait until this moment when I could tell you I was alive, living free, and loving my life—thankfully without you in it. When I heard about the work you were doing, I reached out to Benjamin Clark and Captain Hunter. It was time to stop you."

"Tessa, go to Sam," Chase ordered.

It felt like minutes, but it took only seconds for the world to spin out of control.

Vion tightened his hold on her neck. She sidestepped him and brought her fist down with all her might, slamming it into his crotch. The arm released enough to run to Sam who raced forward at top speed and weapon drawn. When Tessa reached her, and was jerked to the side, she lifted her weapon toward Vion.

Tessa spun around as the man put his finger on the trigger, aiming at Samantha.

"No," she said, slamming Sam into a pile of boxes. An explosion from his gun grazed Sam's arm.

At that same moment, Honey grabbed Vion's leg and sank her teeth into his lower leg hard enough, he lost his hold on the gun. Honey tried to snatch it but only managed to send it flying to Abigail's feet.

She picked it up and stepped slowly toward Vion who backed away.

"Abigail, it's all over. Don't do this," Chase called. "He can never hurt you again. I'll see to it."

Abigail lowered the weapon to her side and nodded acceptance.

"Gutless coward." Vion straightened and narrowed his devilish eyes.

Abigail raised the gun and emptied it into the chest of Andre Lavelle Vion. "You're right, Andre. I should have done this a long time ago."

Lazarus rushed to relieve her of the gun and placed his arm around her. "Come on. It's over now." He kissed her temple when she leaned into him.

Carter ran to assist Samantha, extending a hand as he complained. "Can you ever play nice?"

Samantha chuckled and let him fuss over her as she pointed to Honey. "Tessa, you better go take care of that hot mess."

Chase ran to Tessa and scooped her up in his arms. "Are you okay?"

"I knew you'd make it in time." Tessa kissed him on his mouth then hugged him tightly. "And what about the guests at the conference?"

Something moved on the floor as Nora ran from the plane to Franklin. He rolled over cringing before he opened his shirt and exposed the bulletproof vest. Honey joined Nora and extended a hand to help him up.

"Damn, Honey. That hurt."

"It would've hurt worse had you not had that on. Told you to be ready."

"Thanks. Oh, and I put a block on all outgoing commands for the timed switch. There shouldn't be any problem getting everyone taken care of before the switch is able to activate. It takes about seventy-two hours to be effective."

"Who are those guys Zoric and Ken are talking to, Chase?" Tessa asked as she watched them shaking hands. "I've never seen them before."

"That's Johnny. He's one of the members of a local amateur radio club. They provide emergency communications in disasters. They are pretty good at helping with search and rescue, too. They tracked you down and decided they'd come give us a hand in case we ran into more trouble than we could handle." He chuckled as the sound of sirens neared.

Ken made his way over to hug Tessa gently. "Glad you're okay. The family is just fine. No worries."

"Thanks, Ken."

Chase shook his hand. "I owe you, buddy."

"Tessa," Honey said anxiously, "were you hit?"

"No," she said weakly. "Why?"

"Your legs are covered in blood."

Tessa looked down, pain ricocheting through her abdomen. Why did Chase's voice sound like an echo as she tried to say, "I'm sorry?"

"Tessa! Tessa!" His voice was the last thing she heard as he lifted her into his arms.

CHAPTER 41

The whoosh sound of ER doors and the rattle of a gurney being pushed down the corridor felt like a nightmare. Paramedics were talking to a doctor running alongside with a nurse saying words that weren't registering to Chase. He held Tessa's hand and watched her go in and out of consciousness, but the paramedics reassured him it was the sedative they gave her.

Although the storm had knocked a few systems out, their generators had kicked in immediately and resulted in business as usual.

"Has she been shot?" he asked for the tenth time.

"No, sir. Not that we could find. Please let us do our job," the biggest guy said as he threw out his arm to stop Chase from following them through the doors where decisions would be made. "I want to go in there."

A nurse came barreling into him and rammed a finger into his chest. "This has been a hell of a night, whoever you are, and your wife isn't the only one who has come through here needing immediate help. Go sit your butt in that chair over there, and I'll be out in a few minutes to let you know where to go. Got it?"

Chase straightened. "Yes, ma'am. I apologize."

She nodded and displayed a frown that could have easily dragged her bottom lip to the floor.

But he didn't sit. He paced. Ten minutes. Twenty.

When the rest of the team showed up, Sam's arm was bandaged and her forehead butterflied. She waved off his concern, as did Honey who appeared a little ragged after the evening's ordeal. Other than being more concerned than usual, she appeared unscathed. Vernon had taken a pretty good bump on the head and was told to take it easy for a few days but had insisted on coming to the hospital.

The director put his hand on Chase's back. "Do you know anything yet?"

"No. They don't think she got hit by a stray bullet." He ran his fingers through his hair. "I don't know. I should have been with her."

"Chase?" It was Sam. She looked at Honey who quickly diverted her eyes to the floor. "I think it best you call Dr. Patel in Sacramento."

"Who? Why should I do that?" he asked, staring at both women.

"Because that's her doctor," Sam spoke in a hushed voice.

His forehead creased in confusion.

Honey raised her eyes to meet his and swallowed hard. "Tessa is pregnant. I think that is the problem—the blood…"

"What?" he boomed. "Tessa is pregnant, and she didn't tell me? No way. Is this one of your sick jokes?"

Sam tried to touch his arm, but he jerked away. "It's true, Chase. She found out just before we left."

"No. Why would she keep that from me? I would never have let her come if I'd known."

"Exactly," Sam said as Carter came to stand next to Chase. "It meant so much to you and to the team. We made it sound like everything hinged on her being the bait to take this guy down. She had three kids to get squared away, and this would only be a few days. Nothing physical involved."

"You should have told me," he yelled loud enough that other people were starting to stare.

"I promised to keep her secret, but she assured me she'd tell you."

His eyes cut to Honey.

"Don't blame me. I didn't find out until Vion ran that blood test."

"You mean to tell me even that sociopath knew about her pregnancy before me?" he choked.

"Yes. I was also sworn to secrecy," Honey admitted softly.

"And since when did you ever keep a secret that didn't have a price tag on it? If you really cared for Tessa, like you claim, you would have come to me or talked her out of this mission." He got in her face, but she never budged.

The director put his hand on Chase's chest and pushed him away from Honey. "We are all guilty in this, Chase. All. Of. Us. We put too much pressure on her, and she did great. Let's wait and see what the doctor has to say. In the meantime, I'll contact Dr. Patel." He turned to the other three men of the team. "Keep an eye on him and—"

Zoric spoke out of the corner of his mouth. "We know, sir. He can't whip all of us."

Chase frowned at the comment. "Are you sure about that?"

"Tessa wouldn't want you getting into trouble because of her. Respect that, son," Ben said, patting him on the back as he turned away.

The same stern nurse returned to talk to Chase, eying everyone around him. "Your wife is on her way to surgery."

"Surgery!" he groaned. "Can I see her?"

"Nope. She's already upstairs. You and your loud, obnoxious friends can go up to the second floor and wait like good little boys and girls. If I hear of any bullying, threats, or bad language, I will send security and have all of you thrown out. Do you understand me?"

"She doesn't know who she's talking to," Honey hissed.

"You listen to me, missy. That is one strike against you already. Now, get out of my ER, get some coffee, and wait."

Honey opened her mouth to spew venom, but Chase held his hand up to her. "Yes, ma'am. Thank you. We won't cause any trouble."

The nurse's nostrils flared then pursed her lips. She pivoted like a drill sergeant and disappeared into the office.

A midnight moon broke through the clouds as Chase stared out the windows in the waiting room. He told the others they should go get some food, but they refused until they heard about Tessa. How could something so beautiful as a moon over the Blue Ridge

Mountains happen while his world fell apart. He and Tessa had taken turns to deceive each other over this mission, and now she was in trouble.

The doctor pushed through the swinging doors and approached the crowd in the waiting room. They jumped to their feet and stood behind Chase.

"Are you Captain Hunter?"

"Yes, sir."

"Could we speak privately?" Chase nodded, and he took him aside. "I'm very sorry to tell you this, but the fetus did not survive."

Chase choked back tears and put his fist to his mouth as if he might cough. "Did…was she injured in some way to cause this?"

In spite of having walked away from the others, they remained standing near enough to listen as the doctor continued.

"Let me be clear. This was going to happen no matter if she were home lying on the couch or jumping out of an airplane."

"I don't understand, Doctor. She seemed so healthy."

"Yes, I'm sure she did. Tessa had an ectopic pregnancy, which occurs in a fallopian tube. Usually referred to as a tubal pregnancy. It can't proceed normally. The fertilized egg can't survive. The growing tissue may cause life-threatening bleeding if left untreated, as in your wife's case."

"Is she going to be okay?" Chase said, shifting his weight from one leg to another.

"Yes. She is sleeping now, and I'll have someone take you back in a few minutes. You're welcome to stay with her as long as you wish."

Chase nodded and stared up at the ceiling.

"Captain Hunter, your wife is young and strong. She can still conceive. But I will warn you. There is still a chance it will happen again. Be sure to keep your medical professional up on any plans to have another child, and, if you detect another positive home pregnancy test, get advice and checked out immediately."

Chase extended a hand to shake the doctor's. "Thank you."

"I'm very sorry. These conversations are difficult to initiate and even harder to hear."

Chase turned to see his team struck with a sadness he'd never seen before. His buddies gathered around him and were at a loss for words but managed to lay their hands on his shoulder or back. Honey and Sam stood alone by the windows, eyes puffy but no signs of tears. Their arms were crossed across their chests. He walked up to them.

"I apologize for the way I spoke to you earlier. This was not your fault, except for the part you should have told me."

They nodded but remained silent.

"Come here," he said, opening his arms. Both women stepped into his embrace and laid their head on a shoulder. He thought he heard a sniffle. "Thank you for protecting her this evening when I failed to. Thank you for being one step ahead of that monster."

They remained quiet and refused to step out of his embrace. He held them until they made an excuse to leave. He hugged and patted each of them on the cheek. "I owe you."

EPILOGUE

Tessa felt her eyelids flutter open and tried to figure out her location. She was hooked up to a machine of some kind, but it didn't look serious. Hospital. She was in the hospital. Dropping her fingers from her chest to the bed, she touched warmth, drawing her attention to Chase. He'd laid his head down on the covers and was hunched over in the chair he'd pulled up next to the bed. Several times, she'd awakened during the night and thought he was bending over her, encouraging her and telling her how much he loved her.

She let her fingers run through his thick black hair. Stirring, he rose up and smiled.

"You're awake." He stood. "I wish I could sleep like you always do."

"Just need the right kind of drugs. This place has good stuff." She chuckled.

He pushed her hair away from her face and sobered before taking her hand. "How are you feeling? You lost a lot of blood."

"A little weak, but I'll be fine in a few days. I want to get home."

"Tessa, I don't know how to say this"—he choked again—" but…" He waited as her bottom lip trembled, and tears streamed down her face. He gathered her in his arms, making her feel safe like he always did. "The baby…"

"I know. I know. I'm so sorry, Chase. I should have told you," she muttered through sobs. "I wanted it to be a happy time for us. Not this horrible man and what he'd done to you so many years ago hanging over us. What you did for Abigail was an act of pure heroism. I'm glad I could help bring Vion down. I thought if I told you afterward, we could truly start over with a joyful surprise."

"I love you, Tessa Hunter. We've got lots of time to make a family together, and I plan to enjoy the kids I already have whether they like it or not."

She smiled as he wiped away the tears. "Sounds like a plan." She motioned for other team members who stood at the door to come in. "Come in, but you'd better have coffee or chocolate for me."

Zoric and Vernon were timid about expressing their feelings but wished her well. Carter gave her a kiss on the mouth then grinned at Chase. "Oops. I missed her cheek. Sorry, buddy."

"Get out," Chased chuckled. "This isn't a place for you. There aren't any mirrors to admire yourself."

"I'm out of here. Oh, the director said he'd swing by later. Ken sends his love and is taking Lazarus and Abigail back to California." He then leaned in. "There are two really hot women outside the door wanting to talk to you. They tried their best to get me to stay with them last night, but I remained vigilant and stayed right here in the waiting room in case you needed me."

"He snored so loud the nursing station complained as did a few of the other patients," Chase reminded him.

"I need my beauty sleep."

"Then you haven't had enough." Chase walked toward the door. "Come on. Let the ladies in for a while. I'll have Carter get coffee, Tessa."

Tessa watched as Chase stood outside the glass windows. He spoke to the two women outside looking in, appearing to be giving them orders. Although they leveled hard glares at him, they didn't backtalk. She wondered if he was telling them what they could and could not say to avoid upsetting her again.

"Morning," Tessa said, straightening up in her bed. "You guys look pretty good for getting smacked around last night."

"Carter is driving me crazy with his 'are you okay, do you hurt anywhere,' blah, blah, blah. He wants me to be a wimp like you, Tessa." Sam moaned. "I'm about ready to drop a little hemlock in his hair gel."

This caused Tessa to burst out laughing. "Maybe just crack a few of his mirrors."

"I don't have enough time to do that. Besides, where would I start?"

"I understand." Tessa focused on Honey who was extra quiet but watched her intently. "I'm glad you're okay, Honey. Thank you for not dying."

Honey moved forward and sat on the edge of the bed. "Thanks for making me get that thing out of my arm when you did."

"You certainly resisted at first," Tessa reminded her.

"True. I'm a little afraid of doctors."

This brought more laughter between the women.

"Anyway—" Tessa started then stopped when Sam sat down on the opposite side of the bed.

"I'm sorry about the baby, Tessa. Really," Sam confessed. "I should have told Chase. I should have been more understanding."

"Stop." Tessa shook her head. "This was not your fault."

"You saved me from a bullet." Sam swallowed hard and lifted her chin. "I'm not sure why you did that, considering I've been—a little hard on you. But thank you."

"A little hard? Seriously?" Tessa rolled her eyes.

"It could always be worse," she said flippantly.

Honey took Tessa's hand in hers. "I would never let anything happen to you, luv."

"I know that, Honey. Thank you."

"I mean, I might hurt Sam and let her rough you up a bit so I could swoop in to save the day."

Sam stiffened. "As if that was possible."

Tessa laughed again and opened her arms. "It pains me to admit it, but I do so love you two."

The two women leaned in and allowed her to hug them for the longest time. They didn't try to squirm away and let her cry softly into their faces and shoulders.

Carter and Chase stared through the window at the women talking then hugging. "What just happened? Are they hugging? I don't want hugging. I want a knock-down drag-out fight in a mud pit. Throw in a lot of cussing, threats, and a rack of barbequed ribs and I'll be a happy man. Good lord, did Sam just give Tessa a kiss on the cheek?"

"Maybe. Probably an accident." Chase grinned. "Of course, Honey didn't want to be undone and also landed a pretty big wet one on the edge of her mouth."

"What? I'm going to demand a replay. What do you think they're talking about in there for so long?"

Chase folded his arms across his chest. "I think maybe they are planning when the women rise up and move the men underground, they'll use us only for breeding purposes."

Carter started into the room with a tray of coffee. "You say that like it's a bad thing."

Chase continued to watch as Carter entered the room and made his wife laugh. The unlikely friends who continued to cause havoc in Tessa's life brought joy to her face. Things were going to get better from here on out. He did the math on Tessa's pregnancy. Maybe it was his baby and maybe it was the Tribesman's. It didn't matter and never would have. They'd talk about that later, when she felt better. He loved her more this minute than he ever had. Nothing would change that.

THE END

Author's Note

Where in the world did you come up with that story?

People ask me that all the time. Other times they comment it must be weird living inside my head to come up with such crazy ideas. Do I sleep at night? Well let me take you into my research to show you a little about how I created this work of fiction.

Universal Reckoning Initiative – This doesn't exist. I know of no group called this. However, there is a group I've been following for about ten years and fascinates the heck out of me. It is the Bilderberg Group. Conspiracy theorists claim that the members are plotting the New World Order and are planning on global domination. Considering they are a collection of elite North American and European politicians, business leaders, financiers and academics, it stands to reason they attract a certain amount of negative attention from the public. Security is extremely tight at this yearly function.

Each year the Bilderberg Group meets in a different city in late May or early June. In May 2023 they gathered in Lisbon, Portugal. (Washington DC was the host in 2022.) The group publishes its guest list the day before its annual meeting which is attended by 120-150 guests. Also included is a list of subjects concerning issues to discuss. Economic concerns, terrorism and cyber-security are only a few of those topics covered. No minutes are taken or shared with the public or press. This adds to the mystery of the group and that there has to be something sinister underfoot by the rich and famous attendees. In my book I tried to match a few of these topics.

Who are some of the famous attendees that have been invited to the Bilderberg Group? Do a Google search for this year's attendees and be amazed. Look back over the years and see others who have made a difference in today's world. No surprise you'll find royalty and presidents in attendance.

I have concerns about the meetings every year because of how important the members are to our global well-being and security. In my book, I put that at risk to demonstrate how such gatherings could go horribly wrong.

Hemlock vs. Queen Anne's Lace – This is a true one. Remember Socrates? He was poisoned with hemlock. Hemlock trees are not dangerous—unless one falls on you. It's the Hemlock plant that can cause the problem. It looks a great deal like the roadside plant that is irresistible to touch, Queen Anne's lace. I have picked it for wildflower bouquets. Until I researched this book, I had no idea how much the two plants resembled each other. So, here is how you can distinguish the two.

Poison hemlock stems are smooth, while Queen Anne's Lace stems are solid green and covered with tiny hairs. Hemlock will have dark purplish splotches on its stem, and can grow six to ten feet tall. Queen Anne's lace has a small purple flower in the center of the cluster of blooms. Hemlock has an umbrella of blooms that are entirely white.

It is important to remember that all parts of the hemlock plant are poisonous, including the flowers, leaves, stems, roots, and seeds. You won't get a rash from touching it. Typically, hemlock is poisonous when ingested. Always be careful when handling poison hemlock if you have sensitive skin or dermatitis, and especially if you have an open cut. Don't touch your face or mouth.

There is no antidote for hemlock poisoning. If you suspect that you have come in contact with the plant, go to your healthcare professional immediately. Here are symptoms to alert you there may be a problem. In some cases, there can be delayed complications.

sweating, vomiting, dilated pupils, excess salivation, dry mouth, rapid heartbeat,

high blood pressure, restlessness or confusion, muscle weakness and twitches,

tremors and seizures

Plasma Collection

Here is a reminder right off the bat. Plasma collection is a safe process that will benefit sick and injured people everywhere. There are plasma collection centers in many cities across this country and the world. Safeguards are in place to make this an uneventful experience for your generous donation. Do not be concerned that Andre is standing in the wings watching you.

The system of collection mentioned in this book is authentic. It is a painless process and a much-needed element for saving lives and staying healthy. Used to maintain blood pressure and volume, it also provides critical proteins for blood clotting and immunity. Electrolytes such as sodium and potassium are elements of plasma that are used in muscles. Cell function is aided by plasma by maintaining a proper pH balance in the body. It is used to treat more than 80 autoimmune diseases.

CSL Behring operates one of the world's largest plasma collection networks, and is headquartered in Melbourne, Australia. It employs over 30,000 people, and claims to deliver lifesaving therapies to people in over 100 countries. They are proud of the work they're doing to improve health of individuals and their website has a lot more information than I have room to share here.

In this book, Tessa has O negative blood and Andre Lavelle Vion is quite excited about this information. In reality O negative blood is valuable because it can be transfused to anyone, regardless of their blood type. The universal plasma donor has Type AB blood.

It was my idea that if you controlled the blood and plasma banks of the world, you might just be able to put yourself in control of geopolitics as well. If you implant a toxin in people of power through their generous donation of plasma or blood, then someone like Andre Lavelle Vion could easily begin to take over the world by manipulating those people.

Do I sleep at night?
Honestly, not much.

ABOUT THE AUTHOR

Besides serving as a Solar System Ambassador for NASA's Jet Propulsion Lab, and attending Space Camp for Educators, Tierney served as a Geo-teacher for National Geographic. Her love of travel and cultures took her on adventures throughout Africa, Asia and Europe. From the Great Wall of China to floating the Okavango Delta of Botswana, Tierney weaves her unique experiences into the adventures she loves to write. Living on a Native American reservation and in a mining town, helped fuel the characters in the Enigma and Dark Side series.

With 21 books, and four audiobooks under her belt, Tierney now enjoys working with writers in their quest to become a published author. Her new love is speaking at conferences and writer groups to help others avoid the potholes of being a writer.

OTHER PUBLICATIONS BY TIERNEY JAMES

Enigma Series
An Unlikely Hero
Winds of Deception
Rooftop Angels
Kifaru
Black Mamba
Knight Before Chaos
Invisible Goodbye
Martyrs Never Die
Education
How to Market a Book
African Safari – Thematic Lessons
Children's Books
There's a Superhero in the Library
Zombie Meatloaf
Mission K-9 Rescue
Education
How to Market a Book
African Safari – Thematic Lessons

Dark Side Series
Dark Side of Morning
Dark Side of Noon
Lipstick & Danger Series
House of Miracles
The Rescued Heart
Stand Alone Books
Turnback Creek
Dance with the Devil's Trill
Lipstick & Danger –Short Stories
Novella
Secrets, Lie and Chocolate Chip Cookies

Audio Books
The Rescued Heart

Dark Side of Morning
Dark Side of Noon
An Unlikely Hero